MISS DETERMINED

MISCHIEF IN MAYFAIR—BOOK SEVEN

GRACE BURROWES

GRACE BURROWES PUBLISHING

Miss Determined

DEDICATION

To all the determined ladies and lords.
May your persistence be rewarded!

CHAPTER ONE

"I am a looming scandal." Trevor, Marquess of Tavistock, had learned in recent years how to decipher the arcane dialect of the solicitor, and yet, he was confounded—and not a little angered—by the figures on the page.

"My lord overstates the situation." Across the gleaming mahogany table, Giles Purvis tidied a half-dozen documents into a stack. "By the current standards of the peerage, you're in fine fettle. You own an enviable number of assets, but are plagued by a temporary shortage of revenue, which you are ideally situated to address. Had you tarried in France another few years, one might not be as sanguine."

How could Purvis be anything but sanguine when his office boasted walls hung in burgundy silk, Aubusson carpets chosen to complement that staid hue, and furniture as well upholstered and substantial as the solicitor himself?

"Let's have another look at the list of properties," Trevor said, shifting on a chair built to accommodate shorter frames. "Most are familiar to me, but some of the smaller ones have escaped my notice in recent years." As had, apparently, the state of their finances.

Purvis sorted through his papers and passed over a single page. "That's in order of size, though not necessarily in order of value. Larger properties can require more maintenance or have less land under cultivation. The bigger the dwelling, the smaller the market for potential leaseholds, and mortgage terms varied with the fortunes of war."

Trevor's finger stopped halfway down a list of about a dozen properties. "Mortgage terms?" He had a healthy dread of mortgages and the people who offered them. If his father had had one redeeming feature—*if* being the operative word—Papa had at least bequeathed to his heir a solvent marquessate.

"Why, yes, my lord." Purvis beamed at him patiently. "A mortgage is when a bank or other lender provides money, a sort of loan, and takes a security interest in a real property as a guarantee of repayment. Your father arranged for mortgages on the Yorkshire land and nearly paid them off. We've renegotiated the terms since his death. The Tavistock seat and the other entailed assets are not mortgaged, because those would be harder to sell. Your heir would have to agree to break the entail, and in the present circumstance..."

Purvis trailed off delicately and reshuffled his stack.

"I comprehend the concept of a mortgage, Purvis." And the *present circumstances* referred to Trevor's bachelor status, though a cousin of sorts racketing about on the Continent served as the Tavistock heir presumptive.

"What of this Twidboro Hall?" Trevor asked as a clerk brought in a tea tray. Jones was sandy-haired, soft-spoken, and good with figures. "I can't think of any reason I'd need to bide in Berkshire when I own a monstrosity in Surrey. Why not sell Twidboro Hall?"

"One could," Purvis replied, steepling his fingers and tapping his thumbs together, "but Twidboro Hall is a self-sustaining little jewel barely a day's ride from Town. The DeWitts have been good tenants, insofar as they pay their rent timely and haven't burned the place down. Twidboro will hold its value and might make a perfect dower property twenty years hence, while some of the others..."

Financial discussions were necessary when one had wealth, but part of the joy of biding in France had been distance from the solicitors, bankers, tenants, and other plagues intent on blighting a fellow's freedom.

Trevor nonetheless grasped his duty and further grasped that he'd ignored that duty for too long. Step-mama never chided him, but her letters always included passing references to time flying and this or that splendid match getting off to a *fine start.*

He thus endured the item-by-item review of his holdings, something he should have insisted on when he'd made his annual gallops through London. He'd instead contented himself for most of the past decade with glancing at reports and tossing them into a drawer.

The clerk—Jones—returned to remove the tea tray after some hour and a half of manor houses, mangel-wurzels, and hay meadows, by which time Trevor's head spun and his belly roiled. No wonder Papa had had such a sour nature, if regular lectures from the solicitors had figured prominently on his schedule.

Though they likely had not. Papa had indulged himself liberally with blood stock and blood sport, neither of which interested Trevor in the slightest. Wine and winemaking, by contrast, fascinated him. He was also fond of the ladies, competent at the pianoforte, and something of an amateur artist.

"I'd best go on an inspection tour," he said. "I've never laid eyes on some of these properties. I should look them over before I decide which to sell, which to rent out, and which to keep."

Or he could—novel thought—actually live on one of the country estates. Grow some grapes, paint a few vistas dotted with sheep and cows. The notion appealed far more strongly than spending the rest of his days in Town to the accompaniment of droning solicitors.

Purvis jerked his chin toward the hearth, and Jones obligingly moved the screen aside and added more coal to the flames.

"My lord must do as he wishes, of course," Purvis said, "but Town will soon be filing up, and your return has been much remarked. The hostesses would be disappointed if inspecting hog wallows in Berkshire held more appeal for you than turning down the ballrooms with the young ladies."

Purvis wiggled his bushy eyebrows while Jones found it expedient to sweep the spotless hearthstones.

"The ladies have other bachelors to stand up with them," Trevor said, setting the list of properties aside. "The marquessate has only me. Please send along a copy of this list with the names and directions of the relevant stewards and tenants. I'll start with the holdings closest to London and work my way north as the weather moderates. You are not to alert anybody to my plans, Purvis, and I mean that. Not the tenants, not the stewards, and certainly not Mayfair's hostesses."

Step-mama would know of Trevor's plans because he would tell her himself. If he tried to keep his intentions from dear Jeanette, she'd drop a question or three before her husband's vast and nosy family. Within a sennight, Trevor's arrangements, right down to what vintage filled his traveling flask, would be common knowledge among the Dornings.

"My lord, if I might speak frankly." Purvis grasped his lapels like a barrister preparing to harangue a jury. "You have all but absented yourself from London for better than five years. In that short space of time, England has changed. Tens of thousands of former soldiers have come home to drive wages into the dirt. The weather has disobliged us with failed harvests. The destruction of the French blockade and the ceaseless enterprise of everybody from the damned Americans to the Swedes has upended commerce and decimated our trade. Fewer and fewer heiresses come to Town each spring, but this year they will all be setting their caps for you."

In other words, Trevor was to take his place in the long and miserable line of Vincent menfolk who'd married for money. He'd suspected as much, but to have that suspicion confirmed blighted an already dismal mood.

An answering lecture begged to be delivered: *I am no longer sixteen, new to my title, and tolerant of presuming, self-appointed honorary uncles whose fingers always seem to be in my pockets. You have overstepped for the last time.*

Papa had excelled at delivering such lectures.

Trevor stood, his back stiff from sitting too long. "One appreciates the benefit of your thinking, Purvis. I will want to see income and expense statements for each of these properties. I also need to know how they were acquired and for how long the Vincent family has held them."

Purvis rose and came around the end of the table. His coat brushed the stack of papers nearest the edge and sent them cascading to the carpet.

"Jones," he said, snapping his fingers at the papers on the floor, "make yourself useful."

Jones scurried over to clean up the mess, a much easier task than cleaning up the marquessate.

"From now on," Trevor said, "I'd also like for Smithers and Purvis to send me an itemized quarterly invoice rather than the usual lump-sum request. I want to see who is working for me and how many hours they spend on what tasks." Colonel Sir Orion Goddard—Stepmama's brother—had suggested that measure, which among the shop-owning classes was standard practice.

Purvis rubbed his brow with pale, manicured fingers. "But, my lord, assembling such detail will take additional effort that will only increase what we must charge you."

Nice try. "Oh, perhaps," Trevor replied, "but without that detail, you cannot possibly *know* how to accurately bill me for your services. To make one more copy of what must already be in your files wouldn't take Jones but half an hour. Isn't that right, Jones?"

Jones rose, a stack of papers in his hands. "My lord is correct, of course." He set the documents on the table and began organizing the cups, saucers, plates, and napkins on the tea tray.

"Another half hour's effort will be well worth the additional expense," Trevor said, lest Purvis trot out more sermonizing and prevarication. "Let's start with this quarter's billing and, as Jones has the time, work backward for a year. I'm at the town house for the nonce and will expect that list of properties and names by... tomorrow afternoon, shall we say?"

Purvis offered up a martyred sigh. "A week from today would be more reasonable, my lord. With everybody returning to Town, the clerks are kept quite busy. Leases to be signed for fashionable rentals, first-quarter reports assembled, marriage settlements discussed in anticipation of happy news later in the Season... We are at springtide, my lord."

Bollocks to that. "Purvis, you have my deepest sympathies on the surfeit of business your firm is enjoying. Nonetheless, if the request of a client of long standing for the simplest information takes you a week to prepare, then perhaps that surfeit has become a mixed blessing."

Purvis stared at him oddly for a moment, and Trevor thought perhaps he'd spoken in French. He still did that, when tired or vexed or taken by surprise.

"I'll have the list to you by sundown, my lord. Jones, fetch the marquess's coat."

"I'll see myself out." Trevor bowed politely and accompanied Jones from Purvis's office. The other clerks were all bent over their desks, scribbling away, suggesting Purvis had spoken honestly.

"Is the firm truly deluged with work this time of year?" Trevor asked as he accepted his coat from Jones.

Jones sent a glance back in the direction of his fellows. "Smithers and Purvis needs more staff, my lord. You work a fellow too long and hard, and he makes mistakes, and then the work has to be done over, and apologies have to be offered all around. Mr. Purvis the Younger tries to reason with his pa, but Old Purvis won't hear of it. Says clerks with time to linger over their nooning are clerks who get up to mischief."

"Are the wages adequate?" Maintaining a vineyard required skilled labor. A slip of the shears, negligent watering, haphazard harvesting... all very costly. Working exhausted was a recipe for regret. One paid well for a job done properly, according to any self-respecting vintner. Anything else was a false economy.

"Oh, aye, the wages are decent." Jones passed over Trevor's hat. "That's how Young Purvis gets us to sign on. Offers good pay. What he doesn't say is that we'll never see the sun once Old Purvis gets hold of us. We have the information you've requested, my lord. I collect it up myself and do the figuring, but we've been on forced march since the new year, and the errors have started. Somebody forgot to list one of your properties, for example."

Trevor tapped his hat onto his head. "Thank you for keeping a sharp eye out, Jones." Better another hog wallow to inspect than another grand ball to attend. "Add it to the list, and I'll get around to calling there. Where is it?"

"Right next to Twidboro, my lord, which is why leaving it off the list was such a glaring mistake. The two were one property a couple of centuries ago, then the fourth marquess divided the parcel and put a new manor house on the prettier half. If you want to see the marquessate's little jewel, drop in at Lark's Nest."

Trevor pulled on riding gloves. "You've seen it?"

"Gone past. I'm Berkshire-born and bred, and my granny dwells out that way. She was on staff at Lark's Nest years and years ago. You've plenty of good lumber in the Lark's Nest home wood too."

The rain had let up, which meant it would come down in torrents before Trevor reached his own doorstep. The weather was much better behaved in Paris.

"When was the last time you saw your granny, Jones?"

"Not since I started work here, sir. I do write, but Gran isn't much for trusting the post. You haven't a coach, sir?"

"I prefer to stretch my legs rather than make a coachman and team loiter about. Please say nothing to Purvis about the omission of Lark's Nest from my list of holdings. I wouldn't want to see anybody castigated for a harmless oversight."

"Of course, my lord."

Trevor ducked lest his hat hit the top of the doorway and moved off up the street. The list had been prepared in Purvis's hand, and the oversight had to have been his. Trevor had thus set a trap for Purvis, which was bad of him.

Nonetheless, when the list of properties and stewards and whatnot arrived, Lark's Nest had once again been omitted.

~

"I'll go to Town in your place," Diana said, striking her favorite pose by the hearth, a hand resting at her throat, her adoring gaze on Papa's portrait. "We still have time to hem your new dresses to fit me, and I know all the dances. My French is good, and I've been rehearsing my sonatina for the musicales."

Amaryllis DeWitt continued knitting and sent up a prayer for patience—*another* prayer for patience. Sixteen was so very much younger than twenty-five. "That's a noble offer, Di, but you'll have to convince Mama to approve your sacrifice."

Diana flounced off to the sideboard, a hint of coltishness about her stride. "Mama's determination makes Wellington look like a ditherer in comparison. You have to ask her for me. Mama listens to you. We need a fresh pot."

The DeWitt ladies needed a miracle. "Why don't you ring for one? I could use a sandwich or two."

"I must rehearse my Clementi." Diana tipped her chin up in what she clearly believed was the essence of feminine self-possession and sashayed from the room.

"One ought not to hate," Grandmama said from the depths of her favorite chair, "but that sonatina has worn out its welcome with me. Diana's plan is worth considering."

Amaryllis reached the end of a row and stashed her knitting into her workbasket. "I agree, but Mama cannot be swayed. She's very loyal to Papa's memory." Then too, convention declared that the oldest sister married first, and Lissa was, by a pathetically wide margin, the oldest.

"You are a diplomat," Grandmama said, her embroidery needle moving in a slow, graceful rhythm. "You get that from your father, along with your considerable settlements."

"I wish I could keep the diplomacy and give the money back." Along with Papa's nose, another difficult legacy. His stubbornness made the list, too, as did his loyalty to family. How much easier life would be if Lissa could simply take Grandmama to Paris and knit shawls by the dozen.

"I had three Seasons," Grandmama said, a point she raised frequently. "Many girls would envy you those settlements, Lissa. It could be worse."

"You're right, of course. I could be five years older, five inches taller, or have five thousand pounds more a year. My hair could be flaming orange instead of dark red, and I could be inclined to tittering."

Grandmama smiled at her embroidery. "You're testy when you're peckish."

"I am peckish. I'm also plain, common, and tall. Dangling after heirs and Honorables is beyond me." Lissa knew that now, after last year's disastrous, interminable Season at an age considered ante-diluvian by Mayfair standards. Her initial foray into fashionable Society at eighteen, equally disastrous, had been cut short by Papa's death.

One still had to try, though, in the circumstances. Mama was right about that.

"Your grandfather was nine years older than I." Grandmama smoothed her fingers over a butterfly rendered in imperial blue thread. "We weren't a love match, but we had a grand time together. You must be willing to compromise and see the best in a fellow. Then the babies come along, and you are a family, not merely husband and wife."

Diana's sonatina blasted forth from the music room, filling the air with adolescent pique in the key of C major. Di had her party pieces, and Grandmama had her familiar refrains too.

But I am not yet immured in Mayfair. "Do you need anything, Grandmama? A fresh pot, a tray?"

"Not a thing, dear. You want some sunshine, methinks, and if you don't escape now, your mother will soon be here making her lists and schedules and budgets. That child's pounding would wake the dead."

Beyond the parlor windows, the afternoon looked warmer than it was—bright, early-spring sunshine poured down on trees that had yet to leaf out. Crocuses had given way to daffodils, and a time of year that ought to be full of hope and promise instead bore a weight of dread.

Lissa added a log to the fire—they burned wood out here in Berkshire. "Grandmama, did you ever think of running away?"

Grandmama's needle halted above the fabric. "Your dear brother ran away. That strategy has little to recommend it for those left to deal with the consequences."

"Agreed." Though any day, Gavin might come toddling up the lane, proffering an explanation for his extended absence. Corsairs, a blow to the head, illness, *something*... "I'm away for a ramble before Diana's sonatina parts me from my wits."

"If only she were as devoted to the andante as she is to the spiritoso, and God spare us from the day she tackles the vivace. Give my regards to our Mr. Heyward."

"If I see him, I will."

Grandmama held up her hoop. "You could marry him, Lissa. He's a sweet fellow and of age."

That plan was even more farfetched than Diana's. "We're friends, nothing more, and I would not take advantage of Phillip by marrying him." Assuming the solicitors, trustees, and other meddlers didn't object first.

"Go see your friend, then, and I will look for you at supper."

Supper, with Mama's prattling, Diana's sulking, and poor Caroline's trying to make sense of the spatting between her elders. Grandmama generally kept her peace at meals, unless somebody disrespected Papa's memory.

"Don't let them wait supper for me. Phillip and I will pay a call on the brood mares' pasture."

Grandmama resumed her stitching. "Gather ye rosebuds while ye may. Old Time is still a-flying."

The rest of the verse popped into Lissa's head. *And this same flower that smiles today, Tomorrow will be dying.*

"You're sure you don't need anything, Grandmama?"

"Be off with you."

Lissa made her escape into cold, sunny air and five minutes later was on the path that connected Twidboro Hall with Lark's Nest.

~

"Why now?" Sycamore Dorning poured Trevor a portion of excellent claret. "Why come back to England this year? You've threatened to abandon France before, but here you are in the handsome flesh. What's changed?"

Trevor had called on Dorning—Step-mama's husband—not at his home, but at the club in which Sycamore was the senior partner. The Coventry blended elegance with daring—gambling was illegal at least in name—and good supper fare with better gossip and honest tables.

"It's time," Trevor said. "At my age, my father was already married and raising me. I love France, love the whole business of winemaking and champagne in particular, but one has obligations."

Dorning, who was as tall as Trevor, dark-haired, and not that much older, poured a drink for himself. "To your prospects."

An odd toast. "To your health." The wine savored more of Merlot than Cabernet, with a pleasantly smooth texture and decorous hints of red cherries and raspberries. A polite wine, from a man who could be polite when he pleased to be.

"Is this one of Fournier's?"

"He considers this vintage suitable for every day and prices it accordingly. The man is daft. He could charge twice what he does for this and sell three times as much."

Xavier Fournier was French and had happily returned to his homeland for most of the year. He made fine clarets and adored his wife at the ancestral home in Bordeaux. He knew more about making clarets than Sycamore Dorning knew about all of his siblings combined.

Trevor settled on a sofa that looked about the right length for napping. Dorning's office was tidy, masculine, and comfortable. He had opted for neither ostentation nor a cluttered hub of commerce.

Or perhaps Jeanette's hand was evident in these surrounds. She spent a fair amount of time at the club as well.

"I might well return to France," Trevor said. "The solicitors are trying to marry me off to an heiress."

Dorning perched on a corner of his desk. "Any particular heiress?"

"Any heiress will do, provided her papa is reasonable about the settlements."

"Change solicitors."

The advice was welcome, though unexpected. "The Dornings are notoriously impecunious, or they were, while the Vincents have traditionally married money and prospered accordingly. Do you object to that approach?" Trevor did, for reasons he could not quite articulate.

Dorning dipped a finger into his drink and dabbed brandy on the back of his hand, waved it about, then sniffed the results, an old vintner's test for assessing a wine's subtleties.

"If you had a daughter or a sister," Dorning said, "would you want some impecunious lordling pretending to care for her when what he truly wanted was her money?"

If Trevor had a daughter or sister... He had five female cousins—each one well dowered—but that was apparently of no moment. "The lady would become my marchioness and enjoy both standing and material security."

Dorning ceased sniffing his hand. "Don't be a dunderhead. A title will not comfort a woman in the agony of childbed. A title will not understand when the megrims are upon her, or hold her when memories make her wistful. A title cannot learn how she likes to be kissed, or what her favorite novel is. For that matter, a fortune can't rub a fellow's back when he's feeling old and creaky, be he ever so robust in truth. A fortune can't make him laugh in the midst of a bad day. A fortune can't climb into bed beside him and cuddle up for a long chat."

Sycamore was shrewd, bold, and increasingly wealthy, but he was lamentably prone to intuitive leaps rather than sound logic.

"My father never brought my mother flowers, that I know of," Trevor said. "He might have sent a bouquet to a mistress when he was a young man, but as for the other..." All quite sentimental and personal. Hard to dismiss, though, in a way that was connected to Trevor's reluctance to go fortune hunting.

"How destitute are you?" Dorning asked.

Should one be insulted or touched at such rudeness? "I don't need a loan, thank you just the same."

"You need an heiress, though, suggesting your finances are structurally weak, not simply suffering a setback due to a drop in wool prices. My oldest brother tried to marry for money."

Trevor mentally flipped through Debrett's until he came to Grey Dorning, Earl of Casriel. A rusticating sort of peer whose seat was in Dorset. Well liked, horticulturally inclined, commended for seeing his army of younger siblings well and solvently settled.

"How does one *try* to marry for money?" Trevor asked for purely theoretical reasons.

"One spends the Season sporting about all the fashionable gatherings, title in one hand, charm in the other. Witty repartee helps, competent dancing comes into it, as does regular participation in the carriage parade. Most of all, one needs a willingness to accept decades of marital misery where joy, desire, and respect ought to be. Casriel came to his senses and married for love."

"And the earl is happy with his choice?"

"Grey is damned near jolly, and let me tell you, when a fellow relies on his eldest brother to be a sensible prig, jolly was quite an adjustment."

Trevor sipped his wine and cast around for a topic other than Casriel's connubial bliss. "Do you trust your solicitors?"

Sycamore finished his drink and set the empty glass on the sideboard. "Most of my business is handled by my brother Ash, who also takes care of our brother Oak's portrait commissions, our brother Valerian's publishing arrangements, and so on. Yes, I trust my brother, and I keep clerks on my payroll who can verify Ash's figures and are answerable only to me."

When one was raised as an only child, the finer points of sibling interactions were terra incognita, but Dorning seemed to be implying...

"Tavistock, if you have to ask whether to trust your solicitors, then you already question either their competence or their integrity. Jeanette kept a very close eye on Smithers and Purse Strings, and I suggest you do likewise."

"I thought I was. I read the damned reports, Dorning. Before I left for France, Jeanette made sure I grasped the fundamentals of my inheritance. I find all the ledgers and receipts and heretofores so much drudgery, though I nonetheless reviewed every document sent to me."

Trevor was hoping that Dorning, who ran a complicated business and also managed a large estate out by Richmond, would laugh, refer to the mystery of annual fluctuations in revenue, and tell Trevor the Tavistock ship would doubtless right itself.

"Do you have all those ledgers and reports?" Sycamore asked.

"Most of them are in Paris. I grabbed a few for light reading in the event I'm plagued by a bout of insomnia. I'm having the rest packed up and sent along. My decision to return to London was somewhat precipitous."

"You were afraid you'd lose your nerve."

If this was a sample of what having brothers was like, Trevor was almost glad to have been spared. "You asked why now?" He rose, the conversation having yielded little in the way of comfort and too much in the way of misgivings.

"Jeanette is in alt to have you back," Dorning replied, "but one does wonder at the timing. Had you made a quiet return in the autumn, or even summer, the matchmakers would have given you some time to find your feet. As it is, I regret to inform you that you will be the catch of the Season."

"Don't sound so pleased." Trevor finished his wine and set the glass on Dorning's desk blotter. The doodles thereupon included Jeanette's name with all sorts of floral embellishments. *Bon Dieu.* "I have tried to keep an eye on Jerome."

"Your... cousin."

"My heir. His sisters are all comfortably settled and adequately dowered."

Dorning collected the empty glass and set it on the sideboard. "Thanks to you."

"As is their right, given the familial expectation, but about two years ago, Jerome told me he no longer needed or wanted an allowance."

"One would hope he'd eventually find his way to independence, being several years your senior."

Trevor plucked his hat from the hook on the back of the door and took down his greatcoat. "Jerome found his way to Nice, Lisbon, Berlin... Border crossings on the Continent are often effected more easily than moving through London's turnpikes. Only in the capital cities and the ports does officialdom truly take much notice of anybody's country of origin."

"You lost him." No accusation colored that observation, but then, Dorning didn't much care for Jerome.

"Or he escaped. The primary benefit of keeping him on remittance was that I knew where he was. His letters were always cheerful recitations about weather, food, women, and accommodations, never any indication that he'd found a paying post. In January, I realized that I had not heard from Jerome for a year, despite having sent half a dozen letters to his preferred haunts. If my sole heir is that cavalier about remaining in touch with me, then I had best plan for contingencies, hadn't I?"

Dorning took Trevor's coat and held it for him. "I'm sorry. Jerome is your cousin, he was a friend of sorts at least for a time, and his disappearance must worry you. Has he written to his sisters?"

"I've sent inquiries to them, and I have contacts on the Continent looking for him. With any luck, he will turn up as the cicisbeo of some widowed Polish countess, and all my worry will be for naught."

"Or the cicisbeo of a Polish count, which might explain his taking French leave."

Interesting theory, though at variance with Jerome's observed behaviors, as far as Trevor knew them. "The French call it *filer à l'anglaise*." To leave English-style.

"When do you depart for Surrey, marquess-style?"

"Tomorrow, though I plan to start my inspection tour in Berkshire."

"What's in Berkshire, besides a lot of racing stables, forests, and an old castle or two?"

Trevor settled his hat on his head and accepted his walking stick from Dorning. "I'm not sure, but I intend to find out. I'll start by looking in on one of the marquessate's smaller estates near a village called Crosspatch Corners. I actually brought the Berkshire quarterly reports home with me, as it happens. My love to Jeanette."

"I'll tell everybody you're bound for Surrey."

"Why would... Oh. Thank you. Right. Surrey. The family seat. And I will go there, just not directly."

Dorning punched him on the shoulder, a gesture that imparted an odd measure of fortification, and Trevor was soon once again ignoring a London downpour and missing France badly.

CHAPTER TWO

The lady came galloping around the bend like the queen of the Valkyries running late for a ripping good battle. Trevor would have been knocked straight into the ditch had she not hauled hard on the right rein, aimed her horse at said ditch, and jibbed his quarters into the middle of the lane.

The horse, rather than leap the ditch and bound off into the adjoining meadow, went up on his hind legs, whinnying objections that should have been heard halfway to London. Had his histrionics been limited to a mere rear and a roar, the rider might have stayed aboard.

The beast was nimble, though, and embarked on a horsey country dance of bucks, dodges, and props that Trevor himself would have been hard put to manage. The lady's downfall came as the result of a hard buck followed by a side step and another buck.

The rider went overboard in a heap of skirts and profanity, and the horse cantered off down the lane, head high, tail wringing, bursts of flatulence punctuating his victory.

"*Madame, êtes-vous blessée?*" *Bon Dieu. Good God, rather.*

"Madam, are you injured?" Trevor had been walking his horse, who visually followed the miscreant's progress with a wistful expression.

The lady got herself onto all fours, then sat back on her haunches. "It's mademoiselle, and yes, I am the worse for that demon hell beast's bad manners. My pride is sorely bruised, my dignity fractured in two places, and I shall have a prodigy of a shiner on my feminine grace. Other than that..." She shaded her eyes and watched as the horse farted his way around a bend in the road. "Fricassee of fractious four-year-old colt might appear on this week's menu. The wretch was trying to bolt with me."

"He's quite muscular for four." Trevor offered the lady a hand, which she accepted.

She got to her feet a bit stiffly and shook out her skirts. "My thanks for your assistance, and you will forget my momentary lapse of decorum."

"I already have, and it was the horse who lapsed. You are truly hale?"

The word was too paltry for this magnificent creature. She stood at least five foot ten inches, though some of that height might have been attributable to riding boots. Her habit was a divided skirt, a style Trevor had seen from time to time on the Continent, but never before in England. She had eschewed—or lost—any sort of hat, and the setting sun turned Titian hair into a tumbling mass of dark glory.

"I should have known better than to get on that colt without working him first in the arena," the lady said, giving her skirts one last swat. "I didn't have enough daylight to do both. Roland is my brother's horse. Gavin backed him at two, and he's been allowed to languish since then. He's not a bad sort, just green. As you and I seem to be without mutual acquaintances, I'm Amaryllis DeWitt."

Her voice was a true alto, smooth and dark like a good Armagnac, with notes of humor, annoyance, and determination. Her physical nose was in proportion to the rest of her, and her curtsey was a brisk nod to protocol.

"Pleased to make your acquaintance, Miss DeWitt, despite the circumstances." Trevor bowed and offered the name he'd chosen to use for the sake of privacy on this excursion. "Trevor Dorning, at your service. We are within a mile or two of Crosspatch Corners, are we not?"

"That direction," she said, retrieving her whip from the side of the road and nodding to the east. "This road becomes the high street, and the Crosspatch Arms will be happy to put you up. If I'm not to cause a hue and cry at supper, I'd best be on my way."

"Take my horse."

She eyed Jacques dubiously, though he was a lovely seventeen-hand bay with excellent manners and a shameless fondness for apples.

"He's a perfect gentleman," Trevor went on. "We left London yesterday at noon, and I broke the journey into two easy days. He can get you anywhere you need to go and jumps five feet without hesitation."

Jacques sniffed delicately at the lady's gloved hand, his ears perked forward.

"He's up to my weight," she said, running a hand over Jacques's neck and down his shoulder. "Stands quietly. Somebody has kept a close eye on his feet."

"Somebody raised me with a modicum of manners, too, and I cannot abide the thought of a lady hiking home cross-county, alone, as darkness falls. Roland will soon be trotting into the stable yard *sans cavalier,* and that hue and cry you want to avoid will start up in earnest."

"You are attempting to reason with me." She gave the girth a tug. "Fair play requires that I warn you to desist. I do my own reasoning."

"One commends your good sense." Jeanette would like this woman. "I intend to be in the area for a few days at least and can use a livery hack if I need to be out and about tomorrow."

Miss DeWitt untied Trevor's saddlebags and passed them over. "You are proof that chivalry can yet be found on English soil, Mr. Dorning. My grandmother would have worried about me had I been late for supper, and I don't like to trouble her unnecessarily. She was a hoyden in her day, but tells me repeatedly that times are different now."

Miss DeWitt glanced about at the lengthening shadows.

"Even women of independent reasoning powers can use a leg up from time to time." Trevor offered that observation casually. Miss DeWitt was tall, but she was also wearing skirts, and Jacques was a tall horse. A mounting block would have come in handy.

She led Jacques to the fence on the opposite side of the lane and managed the delicate business of holding the reins, climbing the fence, and getting a leg over without anything approaching a fuss.

"I'll send him to the Arms tomorrow morning, and my thanks for the loan. What brings you out from London?"

"I'm looking for a country property within hailing distance of Town." A half lie, and even that much deception bothered Trevor. The whole point of the excursion, though, was to gather intelligence on his real estate holdings without alerting tenants or stewards—or solicitors. Announcing that the Marquess of Tavistock was on hand to play landlord would have put period to that goal.

"Most who have a choice prefer Kent or Surrey," Miss DeWitt said, smoothing a hand down Jacques's crest. "We're not as fashionable out this direction."

"A point in Berkshire's favor. Then too, there's the excellent company to be found here."

She favored him with an impish smile, circled the horse in a tidy pirouette, and trotted off into the sunset.

"Bring Jacques to the Arms yourself," Trevor called after her. "I could use some local knowledge before I begin my search."

She gave no sign that she'd heard him, which reassured Trevor that her pride, her dignity, and her feminine grace had recovered from the slightest of mishaps.

Trevor took his time on the walk into Crosspatch Corners, enjoying the chill in the air that came with evening's approach. The countryside slumbered under winter's lingering, frosty hand, but in a few weeks, the palette in the landscape would shift from browns to greens. The sky would yield up its pewter moods for cheerful blue and white. The livestock would start shedding in earnest, and birdsong would build into a morning and evening symphony.

"While I," Trevor muttered to no one in particular, "will be stuck in London, prancing about like a dancing bear for the delectation of the matchmakers and heiresses."

Unless, of course, he could sell some real estate, or otherwise devise a plan for rectifying his want of temporary revenue.

He was shortly ambling along a typical English high street, half-timbered homes and shops surrounding an open grassy square. The requisite fountain stood beneath what might have been a medieval pilgrim's cross. A pot of tulips had yet to bloom beneath the cross, but that day loomed close at hand. On the far side of the market green, the Arms rose to three stories, its stable yard off to the side and devoid of traffic.

The post would barrel through after dark, when other vehicles were less likely to be on the road. The locals, by contrast, would have headed home before the light faded. That much was the same in France, though—a grudging admission—the French post hadn't a patch on the Royal Mail.

Trevor was lounging in the common of the Arms, demolishing his second helping of trifle when the real reason for his invitation to Miss DeWitt occurred to him: She'd have got on splendidly in France.

Yes, she was a DeWitt, and thus probably associated with, if not a member of, the DeWitts who held the tenancy at Twidboro Hall. Trevor had noted that fact as soon as she'd introduced herself.

He'd noted other facts as well.

Napoleon's march on Moscow—part of one campaign in hostilities that had gone on for twenty years—had cost France an estimated half a million men before the remnants of the Grand Armée had staggered home. The great majority of those casualties had fallen to disease, starvation, and cold rather than any human enemy.

Several times that number of men were estimated to have died or suffered injury fighting Napoleon's other battles. Wellington had answered to Parliament and the public for every British life lost. Napoleon, by contrast, had operated without such constraints and had supplied his army in part by plundering the wealth of France's citizenry.

France would be a ruin but for the indomitable resolve of its womenfolk. The ladies, of sad necessity, now ran the villages and farms. They managed the markets and even some of the larger towns. A few successful vineyards had navigated the war years entirely in female hands, and even the largest charities relied almost exclusively on female supervision.

Miss DeWitt, attempting to school an unruly colt, riding *en cavalier*, and perfectly content to see herself home in gathering darkness, would have fit in easily among the French ladies of Trevor's acquaintance.

If she did bring Jacques to the Arms, he'd make an opportunity to tell her that.

~

Young Purvis, who hadn't felt young since he'd first set his bony arse on a clerk's stool as a boy some twenty years past, rapped politely on Old Purvis's door. Young Purvis had lately begun thinking of himself in the first person as Young.

Young hasn't had his nooning yet, again.

Young will soon piss in his breeches if he can't find a moment to step around to the damned jakes.

Young is ready to catch forty winks sitting in the damned jakes, but there's likely already a clerk occupying the same spot in pursuit of the same goal.

Young's given names were Giles John, which were Old Purvis's given names, and so on back through Purvis antiquity. Old Purvis claimed the use of Giles, leaving Young Purvis the dubious comfort of going by John. Should Young Purvis be so fortunate as to procreate—

though a man ought to leave his business premises to undertake such activity and remain awake for at least some of the proceedings—his son was foreordained to be yet another Giles John Purvis, Young and then Old in his time.

One of the clerks yawned hugely, scrubbed his eyes, and returned to whatever document he was copying. The boy might well have been on that stool since the previous evening.

Papa was getting worse, despite an exchequer that would be the envy of many a peer. Aunt Adelia said approaching senility might be part of the explanation. That Papa could grow worse was a feat of miserliness and ambition that Young Purvis would marvel at just as soon as he'd slept for a week straight.

He rapped lightly on Papa's office door. A low rumbling sound that might have been contented snoring ceased.

"Come in!" Papa called. "And state your business!"

Young Purvis had learned to effect brisk energy in Papa's presence. He closed the door smartly behind him and stood at attention before Papa's desk. A token document sat on the blotter, several pages of a draft marriage settlement that had served as evidence of industry for at least the last two years. Papa kept it in the top right desk drawer with his tin of peppermints.

A trimmed quill pen lay atop the papers, but Papa had forgotten to uncap the ink bottle, which sat on the silver standish. Close examination revealed a light coat of dust on that ink bottle, though the standish itself gleamed.

That dusty ink bottle was a small act of rebellion, probably perpetrated by Jones, whose jobs included tidying Papa's office.

"What is it?" Papa asked, rising and rubbing the back of his neck. "Has Viscount Thurston rescheduled his appointment yet again? I vow the man never knows what day of the week it is."

"His lordship is due at ten of the clock. I've brought you his files and reviewed them thoroughly myself."

Every Season, Thurston courted another beauty, and every Season he returned to the shires a bachelor. Old Purvis handled the settlement negotiations on his lordship's behalf, and every year, those negotiations went on swimmingly until the time came to sign documents. At that point, the bride's family became reluctant to execute the agreements.

"Who is it this year?" Papa asked, sounding as weary as if he'd been the one copying reports all night, when in fact he'd not been in the office above a half hour.

"No particular lady has had the honor of his lordship's attentions yet." Young Purvis passed over a thick sheaf of documents in a folder bound in red ribbon. "I thought you should know that Lord Tavistock left London the day before yesterday."

"That one." Papa grimaced. "I've the Brompton girl in mind for him."

Miss Hecate Brompton had left behind any pretensions to girlhood several years ago. "He'll need sons, and she's getting a bit long in the tooth, isn't she?"

"Still several years shy of thirty. Tavistock needs only one or two sons, and he does have a cousin rattling about on the Continent if all else fails. Miss Brompton's family is venerable and wealthy—there's an earl in the lot somewhere—and those are the prerequisites when it comes to wedding his lordship. If the Almighty is merciful to a poor, overworked solicitor, Tavistock will snabble the bride of my choosing, get her with heir, and decamp for France."

Young Purvis, who thought rather highly of Miss Brompton, couldn't see that happening, though one ventured to disagree with Papa at one's peril.

"Tavistock struck me as ready to take up the reins of his marquessate. His father was the determined sort, too, as I recall."

"The father had a sense of his own consequence and a proper respect for tradition. You young people and your radical ideas..." Papa resumed the seat behind his desk and pulled the draft settlement closer. "One despairs for the realm. Tavistock will likely kick his heels in Surrey playing lord of the manor, then trot back to Town in time for whatever social events his step-mother deems appropriate for a bachelor of his station. I never did care for her. A more uppish woman I have yet to meet."

The step-mother—Jeanette Dorning, and by courtesy still referred to as the Marchioness of Tavistock in some circles—had put old Smithers through his paces every quarter. When she'd remarried and Smithers had gone into retirement, Papa had lit upon Tavistock's accounts like a hog at his slops.

Careful observation of Papa's behaviors, a few pints with old Smithers, and close examination of the files in Papa's bottom drawer had given a dutiful son pause.

"That uppish woman married a Dorning," Young Purvis observed. "The Dornings are related by marriage to half the peerage and to Worth Kettering."

Papa produced a pair of spectacles and perched them on his nose. "If you value your inheritance, do not utter that name within these walls. Leave me to my labors, thankless though they are, and tell Tavistock's housekeeper in Surrey to send word when his lordship plans his return to Town. He stated a desire to tour all of the marquessate's holdings, but spring is when a young lord's thoughts turn to opera dancers. Not too many of those running about in shires."

"Sir, about Lord Tavistock..." According to Jones, the coaching inn closest to the Tavistock town house had sent his lordship's fancy trunk not to Surrey, but to the small Berkshire village of Crosspatch Corners. Which could only mean...

Papa looked up for one instant, enough to convey absolute, unbending resolve. "Young man, if you have the leisure to poke your nose into matters that do not concern you, then clearly, I haven't kept you busy enough."

What Young Purvis did not know—or could credibly claim to not know—could not land him in Newgate.

"Yes, sir."

Papa took up his quill pen and ran it slowly down the margin of the draft settlement. He could not read that quickly, he was merely pretending. More and more, Papa pretended to work, pretended to know the law, pretended to be concerned for his clients.

Young Purvis withdrew and closed the door. There was work to be done. There was always, always work to be done. He looked about at the dozen scribbling, ciphering clerks for one who could be tasked with taking notes during Lord Thurston's meeting.

The yawning lad, one Pennypacker by name, had fallen asleep on his stool, the pen still in his hand. A few words in a tidy hand were inked across his cheek mirror-fashion, and his snores gently fluttered the edge of the document he'd been working on.

"I doubt Gabriel's trumpet would wake Pennypacker," Jones said quietly, but then, Jones did everything quietly—moved, ate, wrote, and cursed without drawing any attention to himself.

"Let him sleep until half past nine," Young Purvis said, "then get him home until tomorrow." Papa would rouse himself to make a short inspection of the clerks' room before Lord Thurston arrived, but not leave his office before then. The clerks would anticipate Old Purvis's tour and bestir themselves to earnestly attend their chores before Papa could ambush them.

And somehow, this mutual exchange of performances was supposed to be how business was conducted.

"Jones," Purvis went on, "please send a note to the housekeeper at the Tavistock seat in Surrey. She's to notify us when his lordship is making preparations to return to Town."

Jones gently peeled the pen from the sleeping clerk's fingers. "But, sir, Lord Tavistock hasn't gone to Surrey."

"For all we know," Young Purvis said very softly, "Surrey has magically transported itself due west of Town. Old Purvis said to send the Surrey housekeeper a note, so a note we shall send. Tavistock might be looking up old school chums in Berkshire before turning south. He might be taking a scenic route to the family seat. Old Purvis was very clear that a note is to be sent to Surrey."

Jones carefully lifted the clerk's head, slid the document free, and let the laborer return to his slumbers. "I'll get right on it, sir, just as soon as I recopy the final page of Mrs. Peele's first-quarter report."

"Excellent, and see that Pennypacker has at least enough coin in his pocket for a decent meal before we send him to deliver that report." Clerks at Smithers and Purvis tended to slenderness.

Jones moved the ink bottle out of tipping range. "Send him to deliver...? Oh, right. Mrs. Peele is mad keen to have that report, I'm sure."

"Precisely. Mad keen. Mrs. Peele to the life." Though dear old Mrs. Peele was also still on a progress visiting her thirty-two grandchildren (eleven great-grands) and would not be back to Town until next week.

With any luck—Young Purvis was vastly overdue for some luck—Lord Tavistock would kick his heels out in Berkshire at least that long and then ride straight for the family seat in Surrey.

CHAPTER THREE

Mr. Dorning's horse had buttery smooth gaits and faultless manners. For those reasons—and not because Mr. Dorning stood several inches over six feet, had marvelous blue eyes, and had asked for Lissa's help —she cantered Jacques down the drive at a few minutes past eight.

An early ride was a wonderful way to enjoy the fresh air and sparkling sunshine of a spring morning, and—more significantly— allowed Lissa to sneak off before Diana or Grandmama could ask awkward questions at breakfast.

Roland, perhaps inspired by Jacques's good example, came along quietly with a groom, but then, Roland was always well behaved for the first mile or so.

Lissa nodded to Mrs. Raybourne, who passed her in a gig, though it was early for the vicar's wife to be on patrol. Coming home from a lying-in, perhaps. Mr. Dabney at the livery greeted Lissa with a wry smile.

"You're not aboard yon imp, I see," he said, taking Roland's reins from the groom. "Prudent, Miss DeWitt. They have the devil in 'em at his age." His speech bore a slight lilt brought with him from warmer climes. His smile was full of vintage Crosspatch deviltry.

"Roland's education has been neglected," Lissa said, "and I will do what I can to rectify that oversight. We'll need both horses at the Arms in a quarter hour or so, and they could do with watering first."

The groom would take his time walking back to the Hall and gather up the day's ration of gossip on his travels, once Lissa had made it plain he would not be accompanying her farther.

"I'll water the beasts. Will you be going up to Town any time soon?"

Mr. Dabney had a duty to the village to chat up any and all livery patrons. The whole shire knew Lissa was to take another turn in the marital lists, and bets placed at the Arms turned on the outcome of her Mayfair ventures. Last year, she'd talked herself into being excited to finally, finally have a full London Season.

This year, she'd rather risk a whole morning of Roland's tantrums than calculate the days of freedom remaining to her.

"Mama will decide when we leave for Town," Lissa said, swinging down from the saddle. "The weather hasn't quite turned, and one doesn't want to pay London rents any longer than necessary."

"Suppose not," Mr. Dabney said, taking Jacques's reins. "This is a handsome animal."

"He belongs to Mr. Trevor Dorning, a guest at the Arms. The gelding was lent to me that I might try his paces and assess his suitability as a lady's mount."

Mr. Dabney ran a practiced hand down Jacques's foreleg. "Good bone, quiet eye. Looks to be a steady sort. Big, especially to be a lady's mount, though."

Lissa was half a foot taller than Mr. Dabney, who'd been a jockey both on the Caribbean island from which he hailed and for a few glorious English seasons back in the day. She settled for peering down at him as if she hadn't heard him correctly, then waved a farewell to the groom and took herself across the green to the Arms.

"Is Mr. Dorning up and about?" she asked the middle Pevinger girl, Gerta by name.

"Aye, Miss DeWitt. Ate a prodigious breakfast, and you'll find him reading the paper in the snug."

The snug was usually appropriated by locals, while the private dining rooms were for the guests, but there Mr. Dorning sat, his blond hair turned golden in the slanting morning sunbeams, his hat and a teapot on the table beside his cup and saucer.

Lissa cleared her throat, and he looked up, then rose. "Miss DeWitt. Good day. A pleasure to see you."

"Mr. Dorning." She popped a curtsey in response to his bow. "The weather is fine, I'm keen to hold a rematch with Roland, and I thought you might like to get the lay of the land while the roads are dry."

His smile was a masterpiece of subtlety. An accomplished flirt could work his art while discussing the weather. Mr. Dorning flirted without saying a word, and without implying anything other than good humor and high spirits that encompassed Lissa and politely excluded all others.

His flirtation, in other words, was innate, an aspect of his personality rather than a set of skills he'd acquired of necessity. Lissa had forgotten there were such natural talents in the ranks of gentlemen.

"And here," he said, "I was hoping you'd allow me a crack at subduing Roland's antics. A steady diet of good deportment and platitudes allows a rider's reflexes to grow lax."

"You *want* to ride Roland?"

"Jacques wasn't always the pattern card of good conduct he's become in recent years. He and I have had some rousing disagreements."

Lissa was torn between the temptation to yield a responsibility—putting the manners on Roland was *her* job—and the anticipated pleasure of watching Roland work his mischief on somebody else.

Temptation won, for a change. "He has a dirty spook," she said. "A dirty buck, and a filthy bolt. You don't see it coming, and in hindsight, you never know what set him off. He can run like the wind when he's panicked, and then he gets the bit between his teeth and you're halfway to Windsor before he can be reasoned with."

"Better halfway to Windsor than halfway back to Town. Shall we?"

Lissa preceded Mr. Dorning from the common. "You truly do not care for London?" she asked when they'd reached the inn's front terrace.

"I spent most of my boyhood in London, and while Town life has its advantages, Mayfair never felt like home. Is Crosspatch Corners your birthplace?"

"I grew up here and have always dwelled in these surrounds, but for a year at a Swiss finishing school. I love Berkshire and wish..."

A groom was leading Roland and Jacques across the green. Both horses were large, elegant, and athletic, but one wasn't to be trusted.

"What do you wish, Miss DeWitt?"

That Gavin would come home. That Mama would cease fretting over Lissa's rubbishing settlements. That Grandmama wasn't so prone to repeating herself. That Diana wasn't doomed to disillusionment, as all girls whose grandfathers' fortunes had been made in trade were doomed to disillusionment.

"Here at home," Lissa said, "I can ride out with you, though we haven't been properly introduced. I need not pretend I'm a schoolgirl ignorant of life, or a fragile ornament who would shatter if you cited one of the Bard's more ribald jests. I am on familiar territory, such that you benefit from my escort, rather than conversely. I've helped out during foaling season, looked after my grandfather in his final illness. I can be myself here at home."

"You've been presented at Court?"

"When I was eighteen, which is beginning to feel like German George's day. Then my father died, and I was spared the rest of the Season. Grandfather died just as we were emerging from mourning, and there have been other... upheavals. My mother took it into her head to drag me back to London last year, and..."

I failed miserly. How to say that without admitting the resentment, bewilderment, and humiliation public failure had occasioned?

"You were not favorably impressed," Mr. Dorning said.

Roland made a try for a few bites of grass, and the groom, like an idiot, allowed that naughtiness.

"I was trying to figure out how to indicate that London was not impressed with me," Lissa said, "but your words are more accurate. My family has no title, my mother has only the most distant connection to some baron or baronet, but Papa was nominally a gentleman. The proper place of such a young lady is among the wallflowers and chaperones, looking anxious, pretty, and grateful."

"Pretty certainly applies. You there!" Mr. Dorning called to the groom. "You're letting Roland set a bad example for Jacques. Time enough for grazing when they aren't under saddle."

The groom touched a finger to his cap and hauled on Roland's reins. Roland, having established that now was the time to denude the green of every blade of grass, yanked back and tossed in a little hop to emphasize his point.

"Allow me," Mr. Dorning said, jogging down the terrace steps. He took Roland's reins from the groom, got a good hold close to the horse's chin, and set a course for the inn. Roland tried to protest, but Mr. Dorning wasn't having it. By sheer forward momentum, he towed the horse to the mounting block.

"Miss DeWitt, shall we be off?"

Lissa stood at the top of the steps, battling an uncharacteristic confusion. *Pretty certainly applies... Shall we be off?* She wasn't pretty. She was statuesque, Junoesque—detestable word—stately, imposing, substantial.

Big. Like Jacques and Roland, but less serviceable. Maybe Mr. Dorning knew what it was to be seen for only his height, though given those blue eyes and that smile, Lissa didn't put much faith in her theory. She came down the steps and got herself aboard Jacques. Mr. Dorning fiddled with his stirrup leathers and situated himself atop Roland.

"Are you interested in any particular sort of properties?" Lissa asked when she'd endured the groom's put-upon glower, resigned headshake, and muttered warnings.

"Peaceful properties. Pretty, bucolic retreats that retain the dignity and orderliness of self-sustaining manors. A conservatory is a plus, as are good pastures for the home farm and stable, some tenancies, a decent home wood."

He described half the holdings in Berkshire.

Lissa nudged Jacques into the street, and Roland ambled along beside him. "I meant, are you interested in any particular properties by name? Did some solicitor make inquiries on your behalf? My own home is under a ninety-nine-year lease, so we don't really own it, but Mama expects to grow old there, assuming we can pay the rent. Other properties in the area operate in the same way, but some are also available for hunt season, for shooting parties and so forth."

The village was quiet—no market this morning—but a few pedestrians and a dog cart idled along the perimeter of the green. Mrs. Wilson had her at home today, a jolly hen party very different from its sniffy Mayfair counterparts.

"I do have such a list," Mr. Dorning said. "Several properties west of the village caught my eye, both owned by some absentee lord or other. Does Twidboro Hall ring any bells?"

Unease slithered through Lissa's middle, but surely her anxiety was unwarranted. The Hall was technically a rental property, as she'd said, and a London solicitor might not know anything more than that.

"I've lived at Twidboro Hall my whole life, and as far as I know, my family has no intention of breaking the lease for the convenience of a greedy, prancing peer who thinks he can turn us out and raise the rent for a new tenant."

That was not the speech of a lady, but the DeWitt family had been through enough drama and upset in recent years, more than enough. To lose their home would be the outside of too much, and Lord Tavistock—whom Lissa had never had the misfortune to meet—

could learn to content himself on the pittance his dozen other properties doubtless earned for him.

"You live at Twidboro Hall? Well, that is interesting. I thought—"

Whatever Mr. Dorning thought, his whole focus was consumed
in the next moment by the rearing, bucking, and bolting of a horse
intent on eluding all the demons of hell, or—failing that—tossing his
rider from the saddle while all of Crosspatch Corners beheld the
poor man's undoing.

~

"Jeanette claims Tavistock is determined to take a bride," Sycamore
Dorning said, pouring himself a cup of gunpowder and lacing it with
honey.

"Tavistock's determination is not to be underestimated," Colonel
Sir Orion Goddard replied, taking up a green ledger book. "I have
never met anybody as keen to learn every detail of winemaking. Tavistock wasn't content to unravel the mysteries of champagne. He had
to stash himself in Fournier's pocket and learn the secrets of the
clarets too. He also spent nearly a year sailing up and down the
Rhine, and his German is flawless, provided he's discussing Rhenish
vintages."

In the light of a spring morning, The Coventry Club's gaming
floor might have been the gallery of any commodious country house
after a late-night card party. The carpets were spotless, the
windows sparkling, the chairs done up in matching velvets grouped
by table. Green for vingt-et-un, rose for whist, black for piquet, and
so forth.

The serenade coming from the kitchen, though, was pure corner
pub on darts night, and Sycamore would not have had it any other
way. A singing staff was a happy staff, and the Coventry thrived in
part because Goddard, who was Sycamore's brother-by-marriage,
kept the staff mostly happy.

Goddard's wife, Ann, in charge of the kitchen, kept the guests

well fed, and the Coventry's extensive cellars ensured the whole business sauntered forward on congenial and profitable footing.

"We've had a good week," Goddard said, jotting a figure at the
bottom of a column. "Isn't it about time you went out to Richmond
and oversaw the planting?"

"You'll have to try harder than that, Goddard. With Tavistock
home from France, Jeanette is resurrecting her mother hen skills, or
step-mother hen. His lordship's future won't be determined by the
matchmakers when Jeanette is on hand to see the job done properly."

"He's young." Goddard scratched another figure at the bottom of
another column. "Why the haste? Nobody would begrudge Tavistock
a year or two to enjoy the blandishments of Town."

Sycamore made himself attend the wine ledger, though he lacked
Goddard's head for figures. "He's not that young. My father had an
heir and spare in the nursery when he was Tavistock's age, and your
father was likely at least wed."

"Tavistock has an heir."

"Does he?" The ledger tallied down and across, which was a
small disappointment. Sycamore delighted in finding Goddard's rare
mistakes, though most of the time the error was with Sycamore's
eyesight, not Goddard's math. Continental sevens and ones were
confusing.

Goddard set down his pencil and poured himself a cup of tea.
"Do you know something I don't? Jerome Vincent is legitimate, at
least on paper, and he's Tavistock's cousin through a paternal uncle.
He'd be acceptable as an heir to the Committee for Privileges."

Sycamore totaled the last column and took a sip of his tea.
"Didn't it strike you as odd that when Tavistock made his flying
passes through Town in previous years, Jerome never came with
him?"

"Jerome likely had creditors to contend with, and they have long
memories."

In the morning light, Goddard looked weary and a little worn
around the edges. He'd been up until all hours overseeing the club's

busy evening, then he'd likely gone for a hack at dawn. That he could rely on himself to accurately balance the books at this hour suggested a former soldier's talent for forced marches.

"Why do we hold this meeting so early?" Sycamore said.

Goddard's smile was in his eyes, but it was a smile. "We were discussing Jerome Vincent, then it occurs to you that Jeanette is likely flitting about in her robe and slippers as we speak, and you—foolish fellow—could be flitting with her, but here you are."

"Dorning men don't flit."

The smile bloomed, imbuing Goddard's craggy, scarred features with an astonishing sweetness. "You flit mentally. I am happy to shift this meeting to later in the day—say five of the clock, when the kitchen is roaring to life, and the guests have yet to arrive. Or I could simply pass you a report, and you could drop by to look at the books at your leisure."

"God spare me another report. About Jerome."

"He took a passing interest in the making of champagne and became seriously fascinated with some prosperous publican's daughter. The next thing I knew, he was off to Copenhagen, or claimed that was his destination. When Tavistock removed to Bordeaux, Jerome appeared again like a bad penny, and thus it went. Jerome did put in an appearance at his father's funeral. I'm fairly certain he dashed home for his mama's funeral too."

"Tavistock has lost him and fears the worst. Hence, this sudden attack of matrimonial aspirations." That wasn't quite violating a confidence, but the next part might be.

"No other cousins?" Goddard asked. "Second cousins? Handy Americans bearing a strong family resemblance?"

"The Committee for Privileges wants documents for that sort of thing, and I don't believe any such heirs exist. The previous marquess took desperate measures to ensure the succession, and Tavistock, despite his many fine qualities, is the old boy's son."

Goddard stuck the pencil behind his ear. "Hence the determination. Jeanette is worried?"

"She's quiet, and that worries *me*. All she's ever wanted is for Tavistock to be happy, and a bad match can mean endless suffering." As Jeanette, who'd been married to Tavistock's father, well knew.

"Our marquess is sensible," Goddard said, closing the ledger books one by one. "He grew bored at university because so much of what goes on there is rank stupidity. He has the knack of being likable, despite his title and good looks. He might well make a match that is both lucrative and affectionate."

"Jeanette wants more for him."

Goddard and Jeanette had been estranged for a time, and both were by nature respectful of the other's privacy. A fine quality, until a sibling got into a spot of bother, which they both had.

"Dorning, I am tired. Not exhausted, but longing for bed, where my darling Ann is doubtless snoring like a stevedore. Such is my besottedness that I long to snore in harmony with her, so please stop attempting to be delicate—though I do find the spectacle entertaining —and convey your concerns directly."

Sycamore stacked the ledgers in a tidy pile before Goddard could do it.

"My dearest Jeanette says the Tavistock marquessate ought to be in good financial health. In Trevor's minority, she supervised the solicitors and bankers like I used to mind the last piece of cake at my mother's soirées. Jeanette made the investment decisions, checked the figures, and met with old Smithers quarterly. About the time Tavistock left for France, Smithers retired, Purvis stepped in, and Jeanette had no excuse for further meddling once she'd married me. Jerome's papa was Trevor's nominal guardian, and he was off to the Continent, too, there to shortly expire."

Goddard took to twiddling the pencil between his fingers. How could such a tough old boot of a man be so unselfconsciously dexterous?

"Not good, when nobody's on hand to do regular inspections," he said. "Discipline grows lax. Squabbling breaks out in the ranks. Officers are tempted to fraternize."

"Is that your way of saying the solicitors bear watching?"

Goddard flipped the pencil into the air, caught it, and set it atop the ledgers. "That is my way of saying you should go out to Richmond and ensure that your estate is in readiness for planting." He rose, stretched, and donned the jacket he'd draped over the back of his chair.

What the devil is this obsession with Richmond? "I don't want to go anywhere. The estate runs like a top, and we don't plant much corn when we're so busy with the market gardens."

"I am away to snore in harmony with my wife," Goddard said, "and you are away to explain your concerns to Jeanette, whatever those concerns might be. I fail to see how a young, handsome, well-mannered marquess can *be* a problem, but you were ever one for digging dungeons in Spain."

"Jeanette calls it a gift for strategic thinking. Consider Tavistock's situation, Goddard."

"For the record, young, unattached, handsome in a lordly way, fluent in maybe six languages, wealthy by the standards of most. Oh, and sporting a lofty title. A very sad state of affairs."

"Not that part." Sycamore rose and donned his own jacket. "The part about when Tavistock first went off to France. Jeanette made certain he grasped the marquessate's financial realities. The title was solvent and even comfortable. Jeanette saw to it. Away Tavistock goes, the old guard retires, Purvis leaps into the affray, and Jeanette can no longer guard Tavistock's flank."

"Don't dabble in military analogies, Dorning. Stick to horticulture and sweets."

Sycamore instead stuck to facts. "Jeanette put a lot of Tavistock's ready cash in five-year bonds, a lot in the cent-per-cents."

Goddard yawned behind his hand. "Low-risk investments, I grant you, but agriculture isn't the gold mine it used to be. It's not even a silver mine, what with rents falling and the wool market shot to hell without hundreds of thousands of military uniforms to make."

"The marquessate was in good health, and now, barely five years later, it's in sad straits. If you were the solicitors presiding over this disaster in progress, how would you behave?"

Goddard pulled a pair of gloves from a pocket and stared hard at the roulette wheel on the next table. "I would be very, very certain my client knew that trouble was brewing and that the client took responsibility for heading it off. I'd want all my direction from him in writing, and I would not move a penny without being able to document that the decision was his and his alone."

Goddard, in other words, would protect his own flank. "Precisely, like getting all orders from headquarters in writing so nobody is court-martialed for a superior's bad judgment. Tavistock was sent reports, little more than tally sheets, some of them no more than annually. He's a marquess, not some lowly baronet, and he was bound to come home sooner or later."

Goddard slapped his gloves against a muscular thigh. "You are saying the solicitors have behaved with gross negligence."

The man was tired, so Sycamore marshaled his patience. "It's worse than that. The solicitors are either unfit for their duties—after meeting Jeanette's exacting standards for years—or they have reason to believe that Tavistock's eventual ire at their incompetence will have *no consequences*. Tavistock, beneath all that handsome charm, is shrewd. He's had to be, and he'll be a peer of considerable consequence once he bestirs himself to vote his seat. He has connections all over the Continent thanks to you and all over Debrett's thanks to me."

"But," Goddard said, turning that gimlet gaze on Sycamore, "the solicitors have been fiddling while Rome burns. They ought to have been catching every other packet to Calais to warn Tavistock of impending disaster. We should get Kettering's perspective on this. Tavistock is in the middle of a money problem, and nobody knows money matters as Kettering does."

Nobody meddled in money matters as gleefully as Worth Kettering, who had the great good fortune to be married to the former Jacaranda Dorning.

"Before we haul out that artillery, we should consult the ladies, and then I might take a notion to jaunt out to Berkshire."

"What the hell is in Berkshire?"

"Tavistock felt compelled to start his royal progress in that direction, which is an odd way to begin a campaign as a fortune hunter, wouldn't you say?"

"Beyond odd. Give my love to Jeanette and send regular dispatches if you expect to live to a ripe old age."

"You aren't tempted to come with me?"

Goddard pulled on his gloves. "I'll be more useful here, picking up the latest gossip and floating a few innuendos. I might send a few dispatches myself."

Sycamore waved him on his way. Perhaps Jeanette would know what sort of dispatches her brother would send. Sycamore hadn't a clue.

CHAPTER FOUR

Out in the countryside, thoughts of London solicitors, ledgers, and heiresses faded from Trevor's mind. Berkshire was lovely, though had it been merely unremarkable, Miss DeWitt's regard for her home turf would have imbued it with bucolic splendor.

Trevor just had time to think, *I am Miss DeWitt's nasty landlord, and I must find a way to tell her that,* before Roland launched his first and—did he but know it—last bad-mannered salvo of the day.

Roland was a strategist. He assayed one tactic—a series of bucks—and when that failed to dislodge his rider, he propped, hopped, and then— yes, he bolted across the green, leaving a trail of flatulence worthy of a farting Congreve rocket.

When a fellow had Roland's reputation, though, these antics came under the heading of Predictable Nonsense. Trevor applied the tried-and-true prescription to the malady and hauled Roland's head around such that Roland's nose was compelled to enjoy a close acquaintance with Trevor's right boot.

The tantrum subsided into sidewise careening, until Roland nearly tripped himself by the pilgrim's cross. Much indignant tail-wringing and hopping about ensued. Around the green, shop owners had come out to stand on their stoops, and pedestrians ceased their progress along the walkways. The innkeeper watched from the top of the terrace steps, while Miss DeWitt and Jacques stood patiently by the inn's communal trough.

"Finished for the nonce?" Trevor asked the horse, easing the right rein experimentally.

Roland whisked his tail once more—give the colt points for pride —and walked placidly back to the street.

"He'll be good for a while," Miss DeWitt said. "I'd apologize on Roland's behalf, but I think you found that exchange diverting."

Trevor absolutely had. "Half of Crosspatch Corners enjoyed Roland's display. Always happy to do my bit for village morale. Don't pout. I have greater strength than you do, and Roland wasn't expecting me to react so quickly."

"You're being gracious in victory." Miss DeWitt gave Jacques leave to walk on, and Roland toddled forth as well. "That almost makes it worse."

Miss DeWitt was trying not to smile, and that made the whole morning better. "I suspect Roland dislikes his name."

"Then he will have to take that up with my brother, to whom Roland belongs. Gavin thought the name heroic." Miss DeWitt's almost smile had disappeared. She clearly did not think much of her brother's choice, or possibly of her brother.

"If the reference is to the legendary Roland of Carolingian deeds, that fellow died a martyr after being betrayed by family. I suspect the reference is more recent, to the Court of Henry II."

"You've read 'The Song of Roland'?"

"The French are justifiably proud of their literature, and I have an abiding affection for French culture and, in particular, French viticulture. I have read of Roland's bravery, though the Old French takes some determination. I also attended Eton, where I became acquainted with that historical personage referred to as *Roulandus le Fartere*."

Miss DeWitt steered Jacques around a puddle. "One has long suspected Eton to be a hotbed of puerile vulgarity."

"A normal boyhood is a hotbed of puerile vulgarity."

"You are telling me my brother named his horse for a... a..."

"I believe the term is flatulist. One who entertains with virtuosic displays of breaking wind."

Jacques ambled straight through the next puddle. Miss DeWitt's shoulders twitched. She dipped her chin, and then she burst out laughing, which caused Roland to dodge sideways, but surely out of genuine surprise rather than bad manners.

Miss DeWitt did not merely chortle or—God forbid—titter. She *laughed.* A big, booming cascade of merriment that turned heads and inspired smiles.

"Gavin would do that," she said when she'd regained her composure. "He was a jester. Is a jester. The best and worst of brothers. Have you any siblings?"

"I do not, alas for me. I have some cousins, but the ones closest to me in age are female. What of you?"

"Gavin is the only son, and I have two younger sisters, Diana and Caroline, ages sixteen going on eight and twelve going on eighty. They are very dear, though our mother despairs of the lot of us. My paternal grandmother lives with us as well, and if not for Grandmama, I would take up with the traveling players. We'll start with that bridle path to the left."

The track ran beside a quiet little river or a sizable placid stream. In an earlier age, the beaten trail had doubtless been trodden by barge horses, and on a spring morning, the way was sunny and pleasant.

"This is the River Twid," Miss DeWitt said, bringing Jacques side by side with Roland. "Our very own tributary to the Thames. It does some growing up on the way south. Many a paper armada has been sunk on the Twid and more than a few trout caught."

"Will you show me Twidboro Hall?"

"We'll ride past it. Lark's Nest adjoins, but the present tenant does not socialize with strangers."

The present tenant, as best Trevor recalled from Jones's annotations, was a Mr. Phillip Heyward, and he'd bided on the property for at least the past twenty years, though Jones had neglected to note what sort of rent Heyward paid. An honest mistake or another deliberate omission?

"Your neighborhood has its mandatory curmudgeon?" Trevor asked.

"Mr. Heyward is no sort of curmudgeon. He's simply shy and a bit backward by most people's standards. He's been a good neighbor, to the best of his ability. I doubt he has any interest in subleasing to you. I haven't known him to go farther than Crosspatch, and that's only on rare Sundays and market days. On the other side of Twidboro Hall, we'll come to Miller's Lament."

She rattled off names of estates, families, geological features, waterways, and historical incidents. Old Man Husey had claimed to see a witch beneath that enormous oak tree, though he'd been drunk, so nobody had believed him. But then, the squire hadn't been brave enough to chop the oak down either, and that had probably been Old Man Husey's objective. *That was his napping oak, you see...*

Amaryllis DeWitt knew her little corner of England as well as Trevor knew winemaking. He'd ridden down a thousand bridle paths and around countless village greens, but because this little tour of Berkshire was guided by Miss DeWitt, the surrounds acquired a dearness unique to this place, napping oaks and all.

She led him in a wide circle until, by Trevor's reckoning, they were pointed back toward Twidboro Hall along the same path beside the Twid.

"We really ought to race the next half mile," she said. "Roland has been a perfect angel, and Jacques is doubtless eager for a run."

"Jacques is?"

She patted the horse. "He's fit, Mr. Dorning, and he's been a good boy for the past two hours. Mightn't he have a bit of recreation before we part ways?"

Roland had been a good boy, too, within the limits of his scanty confidence. The horse's true problem was a lack of experience, and better for him to get a run in now, when he was likely to behave, than at some less opportune time of his choosing.

"We'll have a gallop, provided you introduce me to your family. I'd like to see your home, and the horses will need to walk some after their exertions."

That perfectly innocuous suggestion caused Miss DeWitt to twitch at her skirts, adjust the reins, and look over her shoulder.

"Mama will either be rude, because she thinks you will turn my head, or she'll fawn. I hate it when she fawns. Diana will try to flirt and make a cake of herself, Grandmama will be amused, and Caroline will blush."

And what, exactly, would be wrong with a little head-turning? Miss DeWitt had certainly made an impression on Trevor.

"To somebody raised without siblings, your dilemma sounds enviable, Miss DeWitt. Your family might well number among my neighbors if I can find a place to buy or rent hereabouts. I thought a passing introduction might be a way to get acquainted."

Also a way to look over Twidboro Hall from the inside, though that was a secondary consideration. Or tertiary. Maybe septenary.

Mostly, Trevor wanted to prolong this interlude with Miss DeWitt.

"Very well," she said. "We'll have a gallop and a spot of tea, but try to keep a straight face if Diana attempts her French with you."

Trevor tapped his hat more snugly onto his head. "*Je serai l'âme des bonnes manières.* And because I *am* the soul of good manners, the lady shall give the count. On three, and our finish line will be the Twidboro Hall turnoff."

He was certain Miss DeWitt translated the French easily enough, but she still peered at him curiously. "You're sure? My family can be a tribulation."

"I suspect that goes with the definition of 'family.' Are you putting off your defeat, Miss DeWitt? Jacques is fast, but he's not fresh, and Roland has youth and guile on his side."

She counted quietly to three and sent Jacques forward at a dead run.

~

Roland had youth, guile, and native talent on his side, and thus did Mr. Dorning, after hanging back for a quarter of a mile, leave Lissa and Jacques in the dust. Roland kicked up his heels when he had a two-length lead, but limited his high spirits to that understandable display.

Mr. Dorning won, fair and square.

In London, Lissa would run no races—on horseback or on foot— and if on an outing to Richmond or some other excursion from Town, there was a race, the gentlemen would "let" the ladies win and label the victors hoydens, bold baggage, and worse in the privacy of the clubs.

"Jacques tried," Mr. Dorning said as Roland pranced back from the finish line. "Since I made the decision to return to London, I've neglected his conditioning. My victory is hollowed by guilt."

"For a guilty man, you look mighty pleased with yourself." Lissa turned Jacques onto the farm lane that led to Twidboro's stable yard.

"Roland has real speed. I can see why your brother was reluctant to geld him, but now is when the horse should be competing over the shorter steeplechase courses."

In London, nobody would use the verb *to geld* in a lady's hearing, and even a gelded horse would likely be referred to as a steed, a mount, a beast, rather than allow any reference to a lack of testicles.

"Gavin liked the look of Roland's dam and sire, though Twidboro Hall has no pretensions to becoming a racing stud. Whenever Gavin took a tumble, Mama would go into hysterics..." Lissa knew Mr. Dorning only in passing, and disparaging her family—beyond the fair warning any visitor was due—was badly done of her.

"Might I ask what has become of your brother? One seeks to

avoid unnecessary awkwardness with your family, and your remarks have left me curious."

In London, Lissa could not be honest about Gavin's situation.

But I am not in London yet. "The whole shire is curious, as is Gavin's family. He jaunted off to Oxford to meet with some school chums and hasn't been heard from since. That was nearly two years ago." Almost exactly two years ago.

Mr. Dorning brought Roland to a halt just as the roof of the barn came into view. "Your brother has been missing for *two years?*"

Lissa brought Jacques to a standstill as well. To have this discussion in relative private was probably for the best.

"You'd hear it sooner or later at the Arms or at Dabney's Livery. Young Mr. DeWitt has gone missing, off to make his fortune or waste his fortune. The solicitors haven't heard from him either. We've made what inquiries we can, but of necessity, they've been quiet inquiries."

Mr. Dorning no longer exuded any charm or merriment. His good cheer had evaporated, leaving a serious and no less attractive countenance in its place.

"But you've no father, no grandfather," he said. "Is there at least an uncle or male cousin on hand? How are you managing?"

A year ago, Lissa might have been offended at that observation. A year ago, she hadn't endured her first full London Season and realized the complete legal disability visited upon an adult, intelligent person simply by virtue of her femininity. Prior to that Season, Lissa had been able to dismiss Mama's endless fluttering as overwrought imaginings.

Having to beg the solicitors for coal money every month put Mama's anxiety in a more understandable light.

"We are managing," Lissa said, the verb surely qualifying as a euphemism. "My mother's jointure, my allowance, Grandmama's dower funds, and some pennies winkled from the solicitors for Diana's and Caroline's needs suffice. Papa was nothing if not thorough regarding his finances, and he expected Gavin to be on hand to oversee our funds."

"But Gavin cannot be declared dead for at least another five years, and even then, the courts are likely to dither. This state of affairs must be exceedingly irksome. I'm sorry, Miss DeWitt."

"We don't talk about the possibility that Gavin has died," Lissa said, turning Jacques for the stable yard. "We don't talk about Gavin at all. He's away, he's traveling, he's enjoying a young man's freedoms."

"Is he dodging creditors?" Roland ambled at Jacques's side, docile as a lamb, though both horses were still breathing deeply.

The worst part about the purgatory that was London was the lack of plain speech. Thank whatever gods might be, Lissa hadn't encountered Mr. Dorning in Mayfair.

"Gavin is doubtless dodging creditors. Or he's dodging angry papas, note the plural, or he's married an unsuitable *parti* and is trying to avoid those consequences. He was of age when he disappeared, but the solicitors claim he's made no request to them for funds."

"Can you trust the solicitors?"

That was *very* plain speech, also a topic Lissa hadn't been willing to raise with even Grandmama. "Not in the least. Mr. Purvis and his partner made it plain they were doing Papa a favor by handling his affairs. If you bide in Crosspatch for more than a day, you will be told that Horace DeWitt's father started off as a chandler on an Oxford backstreet, selling tallow and rags to university students. That odor you detect on the Twidboro breeze is the taint of the shop, Mr. Dorning. Grandpapa was shrewd, hardworking, and successful, but his modest origins are what people discuss years after his death."

"I smell nothing but fresh Berkshire air, Miss DeWitt. A nation of shopkeepers disdains her lifeblood at peril of looking like a fool."

"The French call us that—a nation of shopkeepers—but ask anybody in a London ballroom, and we are a nation of squires, peers, lawyers, vicars, officers, and diplomats. One can also admit to an academic uncle or two, provided he isn't too eccentric."

"How fortunate that we are not in London, though I wonder how all those vicars and peers and whatnot expect to eat, dress, stay warm, and move about without the grooms, weavers, hod carriers, and other good folk to make a London life endurable. That is a pretty manor house."

Twidboro Hall sat in the morning sunshine, not a citadel on a hill, but a lovely honey-colored manor on a graceful rise.

"We are lucky to have a roof over our heads," Lissa said, "particularly that roof." Nine windows across a three-story façade, the requisite blue door placed in the center, painted to match blue shutters that nicely complemented pale limestone. Potted daffodils added a splash of color, though the flowers were fading and would soon need to be replaced with tulips.

"Is the house new?"

"About two hundred years old. Lark's Nest and Twidboro were one property. Some previous owner split them and put up this house, probably intending it as a dower property. The rent was reasonable until recently, and the maintenance fairly reliable as well."

Mr. Dorning regarded the Hall as if he saw more than shutters, windows, and drooping flowers. "No two-hundred-year-old dwelling maintains itself for long."

"What of your people?" Lissa asked before he spotted the lack of glazing on the higher windows. "Any chandlers or hod carriers on the family tree?" In London, everybody knew everybody's lineage, but Lissa preferred this more honest method of getting acquainted.

"I fancy myself something of a vintner. Family connections emerged from the war with vineyards in France, and I made a pest of myself learning that business. I've bought some land in France and hope to eventually produce a decent brandy. Here in England, beer and ale seem the better choice. We might stop burning coal one day, we might stop raising horses, but I cannot see the time when John Bull willingly gives up his pint."

"Then your people aren't nobs." Any man with means could hire competent tailors and buy good horseflesh. Manners were not the exclusive province of the peerage either. Mr. Dorning was successful, probably from wealthy gentry, but he did not move in the same circles as, for example, the Honorable Titus Merriman and Mr. Charles Brompton.

Lissa was inordinately relieved to reach that conclusion.

Mr. Dorning, on the other hand, for the first time looked nonplussed. "I haven't much in the way of people, to answer your question. I've mentioned my cousins, but that's about it, and the ladies are all settled. My step-mother remarried, and I am quite cordial with her in-laws. I am not a pauper, but I expect to have to earn my way like most other men."

A groom emerged from the barn, the same fellow Lissa had left grumbling outside the Crosspatch Arms.

"We've been sighted," she said. "Look harmless and a trifle dull-witted, and tea won't be so bad. You have a pressing engagement that prevents you from staying to lunch."

"One can have pressing engagements in Crosspatch Corners?"

"You seek to call on the vicar and must change out of your riding attire. Show some imagination, Mr. Dorning."

They handed off the horses with directions to unsaddle both and allow them an hour at what grass there was to be had so early in the season, and then Lissa was being escorted by her guest up to the house.

"Would it be a bad thing if I were a nob?" Mr. Dorning asked.

"I'm glad you aren't." Lissa could be that honest with him. "My experiences in London last year were not..." How to put it without exceeding all bounds? "I ran afoul of a young man when I first made my bow, years ago. He's an earl's heir now, though he was merely gentry then. That experience lingers in my awareness and apparently lingered in the memory of a few gossips. Titled Society strikes me more as a blight on the English landscape, rather than anything to boast of. They probably feel the same way about me."

"Then shame upon them," Mr. Dorning said, offering his arm.

When Lissa accepted that courtesy, she would lose the freedom of a friendly potential neighbor and become instead a lady constrained by propriety when in the company of a gentleman.

"The vicar is Mr. Raybourne," Lissa said, bowing to the inevitable and slipping her fingers around Mr. Dorning's elbow. "He's keen on the steeplechase and always rides to hounds in the first flight. We are treated to very brief sermons during hunt season, but alas, our reprieve is over for the year."

Mr. Dorning paused on the steps of the side door and took Lissa's hand in his. "I cannot recall when I have enjoyed a morning spent in the saddle as much as I've enjoyed today's guided tour. Please say I can call on you properly and that you will introduce me to a few of the neighbors."

I'm leaving for London soon. Mama has already started packing. Lissa pushed those dread thoughts aside.

"We don't stand on ceremony in these parts, Mr. Dorning. You could introduce yourself to the neighbors, or ask Vicar to send along a note on your behalf. Nobody would much mind, and if you're still here on Sunday, you'd be introduced in the churchyard as a matter of course."

"That's not the point." His expression was genial, but also... serious again. "You have been kind to a stranger and taken up a good portion of the day escorting me about. I know my way around now, and I will pay a visit to the vicar this afternoon. All that aside, I would like to call on you later this week."

The door flew open, and Diana, Caroline peeking over her shoulder, stood goggling. "Oh, Lissa. He's scrumptious. Who is he, and where did you find him? I quite like him. If you have no use for this gorgeous fellow, then please do introduce us. I'm Diana, and I'm not out yet, but I will be soon."

She held out her hand and batted her lashes, probably thinking herself very bold and sophisticated.

Mr. Dorning bowed over her hand. "Trevor Dorning, at your service, Miss Diana. Miss DeWitt saw me first, and thus by right of capture, I belong exclusively to her. I'm sure you will be the cynosure of all bachelor eyes—once you've finished growing up, of course."

Diana simpered and giggled, while Caroline blushed. Lissa wished she'd not risked this encounter between her sisters and her riding companion, but then Mr. Dorning winked at her, and that... that was an antidote to many tribulations indeed.

~

Trevor had learned more than winemaking in France. When he hadn't been marching up and down the terraced hillside of Bordeaux or reading old treatises on blending clarets, he'd been keeping an eye out for properties to buy, for rentals that would make a long-term visit in this or that region comfortable.

He'd developed an instinct for which chateaus were in good repair and which had been going to seed even before the war. A man's horse could grow fat on spring grass, but that man would have to put out coin for the harness maker to keep his saddle in good repair. Look at his horse, but don't forget to examine his saddle as well. So, too, were some signs of aging in a house merely cosmetic, while others indicated real difficulties.

Twidboro Hall was like the DeWitts who dwelled there. Sturdy —even the grandmother was stately and spry—and a bit down at the heels, but cheerfully determined to go on. Furniture in the guest parlor was placed somewhat oddly, no doubt to hide stains in the carpet.

Pictures, too, had been hung in unusual groupings, again likely to hide stains on the walls. An unfortunate splash of wax was one thing, but Trevor suspected water stains, which meant trouble if left unaddressed.

The Hall was spotless, though a little drafty. Some of the windows wanted glazing, and only half the sconces held lamps. The empty sconces sat across from lighter rectangles in the corridor, where—Mrs. DeWitt claimed—some of the older landscapes had been sent off for cleaning.

Of course they had.

"Lissa is going to London again." Diana sent her sister an arch look across the tea tray. "She's to make a fine match, and then Caroline and I can marry for *love*."

How did one converse with a creature who was half girl, half imp? "Do you imply that marrying for love would not be a fine match, Miss Diana?"

"Diana," Mrs. DeWitt said, "perhaps you'd best go practice your pianoforte."

"I already did my practicing for today. Don't you recall? You claimed Mr. Clementi was a minion of Satan in C major sent to plague all long-suffering mothers who needed a bit of a lie-in. Caroline heard you, but Grandmama—"

"Do you play?" Trevor asked Caroline. The girl hadn't said two words. She put him in mind of a hedgehog peeking out from beneath a thicket of fiery red hair. Round spectacles enhanced her air of timorous curiosity, as did blue eyes given to slow blinking.

"A little, Mr. Dorning. Lissa is the true talent in the family, though Diana is also very accomplished."

Mrs. DeWitt, occupying the center of the sofa like a biddy hen on her nesting box, beamed at her youngest. "The girls get their music from their father. He was always singing. We used to do little family musicales. Grandmama was very skilled with the violin. Do you favor any particular instrument, Mr. Dorning?"

Mrs. DeWitt wasn't exactly fawning, but neither had she attempted to toss Trevor out a window. Amaryllis had been quiet, presiding over the tray at her mother's bidding and forgetting to serve herself.

Or maybe there wasn't enough tea in the pot for her to have a cup?

"I am competent at the keyboard," Trevor said, "and I'm a passable baritone, but the only instrument I have any proficiency with is the flute."

"The flute!" Mrs. DeWitt clapped her hands. She was graying at the temples and matronly about the middle, but her smile was charming. "I adore the flute. Do any of the other Dornings claim musical accomplishments?"

Trevor popped a tea cake into his mouth, the better to give himself time to fashion a reply. He did not know if the Dornings were musical. They were horticultural by reputation, and resourceful. Also tallish, and one of them was notably fond of dogs. Another painted portraits, and then there was Sycamore, who specialized in mayhem and audacity.

"Mr. Dorning is not closely related to the Dorset Dornings," Mrs. DeWitt senior said. "He hasn't the Dorning eyes. I knew the previous earl in passing. Lovely man, always prosing on about flowers and herbs, but they weren't merely plants to him. They were medicines, poisons, tisanes. I recall him telling me that one could weave fabric from nettles. The result is stronger than linen, or so the earl claimed."

The Dorset Dornings were more numerous than renowned, but an earldom was unlikely to go unnoticed in this family.

"I am only passingly familiar with the titled branch of the family," Trevor said, "and not well acquainted with them. They do have the most interesting eyes, don't they?" Varying shades of lavender, violet, amethyst, lilac...

"You aren't closely related to them?" Mrs. DeWitt asked with studied diffidence.

"We are cordial, but I do not presume on the connection." Not quite a lie. Trevor's step-mother had married a Dorning, and that was a cordial connection of sorts, but still...

The earldom, the eyes, why hadn't he chosen his *nom du voyageur* more carefully?

"Have some more tea?" Amaryllis asked, holding up the pot. Her expression was horribly pleasant, not a hint of devilment or even intelligence in her gaze.

Trevor could think of no excuse to linger other than the socially acceptable second cup. "Just a splash, please, and am I correct that you enjoy a lovely view of the Twid from the east side of the house?"

"We do," Diana said, sitting up very straight. "I've sketched that view more times than you can count, Mr. Dorning, in all seasons, though the library gets quite chilly without—"

"Please don't bore our guest with a recitation of your artistic subjects," Mrs. DeWitt said. "Lissa has painted our prospect of the Twid to the satisfaction of all admirers."

"Mama, please don't boast." Amaryllis poured out the requisite splash, and only a splash. "I can play the pianoforte, Mr. Dorning, but my artistic gifts exist mostly in my mother's mind."

"Nonsense, Amaryllis. Compared to most girls, your watercolors are more than adequate. Tell us, Mr. Dorning, are you looking to buy property here in Berkshire or merely rent?" Mrs. DeWitt's smile had dimmed from gracious to polite.

"Either," Trevor said, finishing the tepid tea in a single swallow. "A long-term lease might suffice, though I'll need arable acres to go with a comfortable dwelling. Good acres, not neglected pastures that have to be tilled up, marled every year for the next five, and reclaimed from overgrown hedgerows."

He sounded even to himself as if he meant that—and he well might.

"Twidboro Hall has good acres," Diana said, which earned her a glower from both her mother and her grandmother. "Well, it does. Mr. Dorning could lease those acres from us and live in the gatehouse."

"Ignore her," Amaryllis said. "The gatehouse is a glorified hermit's folly."

Diana's chin jutted. "It is not. Grandmama lived there for years before Papa died. I used to visit her when Papa and Gavin got to arguing, and Grandmama would give me a biscuit and tell me a story."

"Bats like the gatehouse." Caroline offered that scintillating gem.

"Gavin told me they keep the mice down. He liked to rehearse his speeches there."

Silence descended, awkward and painful. The prodigal's name had been mentioned not once but twice, and the teapot was empty. Worse yet, Trevor had revealed that no earl numbered among his close relations.

"My friends who grow grapes in Bordeaux love bats," Trevor said. "Bats gorge themselves on moths, and vintners the world over abhor moths because they can ruin a whole harvest."

"Truly?" Caroline was clearly delighted in the nocturnal feeding habits of French bats, or maybe she was pleased that Gavin had been right about something.

"Truly. The wineries that can claim a bat cave near their vineyards are the envy of their neighbors, but if I start talking about wineries and vineyards, I will still be maundering on come Michaelmas. If you ladies will excuse me, I will thank you for your hospitality and take my leave."

Nobody made any effort to dissuade him from departing.

"I'll see you out," Amaryllis said, while Diana made a surreptitious grab for the last of the tea cakes.

Trevor waited until he and his escort had gained the corridor before speaking. "Might you show me the view from the library before we part?"

"Of course." Amaryllis was still impersonating a polite, blank canvas, though in her very reserve, she conveyed frustration. "This way."

"They aren't awful, you know. Your family."

"No, but they are desperate," she said quietly. "I tell myself it doesn't show, but then you stop by for a cup of tea, and we are nearly ridiculous. The sad thing is, we have pots of money, but we don't actually have it."

"The solicitors do?"

"Something like that. We have it, but mostly Gavin has it, and he's not around to approve expenditures, so the solicitors are acting in *anticipation of litigation.* I hate that phrase. It means they pretend some judge is looking over their shoulder, as if Gavin would sue them for letting me buy a pair of new boots, and every penny spent must meet the approval of that imaginary judge."

Amaryllis glowered at one of those paler patches on the wall of the corridor. "Mama's solution is for me to marry a man of substance —in the DeWitt dialect, that means from a landed, titled family, and better still if he is the titleholder—and he will sort out the solicitors while his mother and aunties help find splendid matches for my sisters. I shouldn't be telling you any of this."

As it happens, I have a title. The wrong title, though. When and how to convey that detail required careful thought. Amaryllis wasn't opposed to the peerage as a whole, but she had reasons for disdaining a certain marquessate, or thought she did.

She opened a door to a room full of light. Three sets of east-facing windows ran nearly floor to ceiling. Whitewashed fieldstone fireplaces bookended the room. Comfortable assortments of chairs were grouped around both hearths.

A wonderful place for reading, though lamentably few books were in evidence.

"We can't sell anything," Amaryllis said, "so the books are leased out. I am trying to put the manners on Roland in part so I can lease him out. Mind you, we will never see the books again, and I would send Roland on his way with a ninety-nine-year lease, but that's not selling, so Grandmama says the solicitors can't complain."

They would, though, did they learn of those leasing schemes.

"Is this the oldest part of the house?" The fireplaces suggested as much. No marble facing, no fancy pilasters, though the mantels were carved oak.

"How can you tell?"

"This is the central room, around which the rest of the house was likely built. The windows in the middle were probably a front door at one time, and you'd find the fittings for pot swings on both hearths if you looked hard enough. This is your famous landscape?"

He peered at a competent likeness of the Hall on its pleasant rise. The painting had been situated away from the hearths, which meant it would need less cleaning.

"I did that when I was eighteen. Papa had died, and we weren't allowed to go anywhere or do anything, so I painted. Mama has sold —leased—some of my better efforts. I hate that you know this about us and that you are probably noticing even more than you've admitted."

Trevor hated that a good, decent family, and that Amaryllis in particular, had been reduced to subterfuges and weak tea. His own prevarications seemed all the more dishonorable by comparison.

"I *am* indirectly connected to the Dorset Dornings. I consider two or three of them friends, in fact, and I am far from destitute."

Amaryllis ran a finger down the far mantel and rubbed the dust away with her thumb. "If you'd been destitute, Mama would have turned you away before you took your first sip of tea. We have enough funds for the present, but Mama is spooked. The past year has been difficult. The solicitors have dug in their heels at Gavin's continued absence, and I did not find success in London."

Amaryllis had found disillusionment—more disillusionment.

"May I propose a small collaboration in the name of thwarting the solicitors?" Trevor pretended to examine the view, window by window. He was relieved to see that the glazing was recent here, and these windows would not leak or let in drafts any time soon.

"Gentlemen proposing collaborations inspire me to caution, Mr. Dorning."

What would she think of a marquess telling lies? "Lease Roland to me for the duration of my stay here. I'll leave Jacques with you in Roland's place. Jacques is content in harness or under saddle. You could put Caroline on him, and he'd be the soul of patience with her."

"Why lend me your horse?"

Why was not a *no*. "Because Roland's besetting sin is a lack of confidence. He needs to hack out over hill and dale, around the market square, and back again day after day. He also needs to learn that his misguided attempts to control the direction of an outing will be consistently thwarted. I can do that. Jacques, on the other hand, will be expected to get me safely back to London, and he can use the rest he'll enjoy here at Twidboro Hall."

Amaryllis looked around the room, a library without books, but also without stains on the walls or rugs—yet.

"If you can settle Roland's nerves, he'll be more valuable."

"Gelding him would likely settle his nerves once and for all, but he's blazingly fast, and that's without anybody attempting to truly condition him. He might have value as a stud."

Something in that recitation, as ungenteel as it was, provoked Amaryllis into a subdued smile. "How long will you be at the Arms?"

"A week at least. It's a two-day jaunt back to Town if I'm to pamper my horse, and one doesn't typically travel on the Sabbath, so I'm here until next week." A voice in Trevor's head that sounded unpleasantly like Sycamore Dorning noted that calling at Lark's Nest would not take the better part of a week.

"We'll trade horses, then," Amaryllis said. "No lease, just a temporary trade to rest your gelding and put some manners on Roland. You are being kind, and I do appreciate it."

On that less than effusive note, Miss DeWitt saw him out the side door and accompanied him to the stable, where she explained the arrangement to the groom.

"I must get back to the house, Mr. Dorning. Mama and Diana will be rowing, Grandmama will have retired to her room, and Caroline is probably off to marvel at the bats in the gatehouse."

"Then you'd best return by way of the kitchen, Miss DeWitt."

"Why the kitchen?"

"An army marches on its belly, according to some old generals. If you are to sort out the warring factions, you will need some sustenance first. You ate not a single tea cake and forgot to pour yourself so much as one cup of tea."

Her displeasure was more evident this time. "Must you be so noticing?"

Apparently so, where she was concerned. "My apologies. Might we hack out again on Friday?"

She swished off across the stable yard. "Weather permitting, and assuming Mama hasn't whisked me off to London. Good luck with Roland."

Roland's situation was a straightforward matter of patience and consistency. Miss DeWitt's more complicated circumstances would assuredly have benefited from some luck.

CHAPTER FIVE

Lissa did not find her mother and sister squabbling. Diana was attempting a new sonatina, F major this time, and far from spiritoso. Her stumblings, fumblings, and repetitions were a worse trial to the nerves than even her party piece.

Lissa closed the door to the family parlor and prepared to be interrogated.

"How distant is Mr. Dorning from the titled branch of the family?" Mama asked, opening her workbasket. "Have you seen my gold thread?"

"I believe you gave the last of it to Grandmama."

"I most assuredly did not. Your grandmother would claim I loaned her my best bonnet because it looked so much more fetching on her, of all the ridiculous notions."

Lissa cast around for something innocuous to say, something placatory and cheerful, but that effort was beyond her. "I heard Grandmama ask for that spool and saw you pass it over to her."

"Don't be contrary, Amaryllis. Your failure to make yourself agreeable last spring is why we are facing such difficulties. If only you'd brought the Merriman boy up to scratch. He seemed quite keen on you."

The Merriman boy—age eight-and-twenty—had been quite keen on Lissa's settlements and even more keen to get under her skirts. "The less said about the Honorable Titus Merriman, the better."

Lissa ought to help Caroline with her French. She ought to look in on Grandmama, anything to put off this discussion, though sooner or later, Mama would have her say.

"But you and Mr. Merriman seemed so well suited. Not as well suited as you and Mr. Brompton, of course, though that's all water over the dam. What made Mr. Merriman change his mind?"

Lissa took the wing chair that had been Papa's favorite, back when the cushion hadn't been so lumpy. "Titus and I were not well suited. I was resigned to marrying him because, as you say, needs must. He changed his mind about courting me, and that is a gentleman's prerogative." At the time, Lissa had been relieved at his defection. A tittering husband would have made Diana's sonatinas soothing by comparison.

Titus was also an inept kisser with clammy hands. Worse yet, he lived for gossip and wagering and thought the most childish puns the height of intellectual sophistication. *The Prince of* Whales, *don't you know? Wink, wink.*

"You could have changed his mind back," Mama said, rummaging in her basket and producing an embroidery hoop. "A little friendliness always makes a courtship go more smoothly."

"Shall I stand on street corners showing off my ankles this spring, Mama? Will that solve our difficulties?"

Mama blinked at her embroidery, freed the needle from the fabric, tried for a stitch, then gave up.

"I know you think I'm awful, Lissa. I think I'm awful, to be so grasping and determined, so fixed on seeing you well matched, but your father did so hope you could marry *up,* and you have the settlements necessary to make that happen. Diana cannot be presented for another year at least, and that's assuming we have any funds to make the effort. She's not like you. She isn't stately, shrewd, or clever. She's like those sonatinas—pretty, amiable, forgettable—and I know what it is to have only those bland attributes."

Please, not the tears. Not today, not after such a lovely, impossible morning.

"You are not awful, Mama." Overbearing, desperate, and gauche, yes. Not awful. Gavin's disappearance was awful. The solicitors were heinous offenses against decency. "But dangling me before spares and fortune hunters is both awful and pointless. I was friendly to Titus, very friendly. He assured me he was talking to his solicitors about settlements, and I... Well, I would make different choices had I known that his handsome head could be turned so easily."

His handsome, empty head. Dear Titus had eloped with an opera dancer.

Charles Brompton, the suitor who'd defected during Lissa's first season, had at least proposed to a lady whose settlement was larger than Lissa's.

Society didn't hold that development against Lissa, but an opera dancer? What was wrong with her that Merriman had chosen scandal and penury rather than marriage to Lissa?

Mama studied her needlework, an intricate border of roses, leaves, and thorny vines. "That's why I married your father. We weren't a love match, but he was kind, loyal, and respectful. He was so cheerful, such a friendly husband, though he never once tried to dissemble with me. Marrying your father was to be my family's guarantee of financial security. He married well socially. My uncle was a baronet, let it be said. I married well financially. It can work, Lissa. Your papa would hate to see us in reduced circumstances."

In an earlier age, not as plagued by war and progress, Mama's formula had kept the squires, the cits, and the peers on nodding terms. Take one younger son or Honorable, marry him off to a cit's pride and joy or a wealthy squire's darling daughter. The products of that union could enjoy both standing and security as they took their turns marrying up.

"Times have changed, Mama, and even if they haven't, I am nigh elderly by Mayfair standards."

"You are also wealthy. Your father saw to at least that much. Your pin money, once you marry, will keep us all in fine style."

They aren't awful. Your family. Mr. Dorning had meant the words kindly, but they'd cut like the meanest gossip. Lissa was abruptly in anticipation of a megrim.

"Mama, instead of trying to find me a husband, why aren't we working harder to find Gavin?" That solution wouldn't require anybody to marry up, down, or sideways.

Mama stuffed her needlework back into the basket. "You know why. One cannot make inquiries without causing talk. If it becomes known that your brother is kicking his heels in Venice, then scandal is bound to follow. Perhaps he killed somebody in a duel or was led astray by a young woman with a jealous papa. Better to not know the details until the prodigal thinks it safe to return."

Lissa hadn't the heart to pose the logical question: And if Gavin had been killed in that duel? If Gavin was expiring somewhere of the pox, slowly losing his mind and physical health, but too ashamed to ask his family for help?

For those facts to erupt after Lissa had spoken her vows with some prancing lordling would make a difficult marriage hellish—and all the more necessary if Diana and Caroline were to find husbands.

"If only Mr. Dorning were more closely associated with the titled branch of his family," Mama said. "The Dorset Dornings are all married and doing well for themselves. One married an heiress that I know of. Perhaps your Mr. Dorning is a cousin of some sort?"

Of all topics, Lissa did not want Mama discussing Mr. Trevor Dorning. "He said he's cordial with the earl's family, but he would have told me if they were as close as cousins. I am coming to hate the key of F major."

"C major is the more villainous. No black keys to slow the child down and make her learn the notes correctly in the first place."

Diana was still a child, except for those rare flashes of insight that warned of impending adulthood. The Charles Bromptons and Titus Merrimans of polite society would corner Diana behind the potted palms before Lissa could say Muzio Filippo Vincenzo Francesco Saverio Clementi.

That thought restored a bit of Lissa's temper. "I truly do not want to go to London, Mama. Last Season was bad enough, and this Season will be worse." Brompton and Merriman both would give her smug smiles and leave innuendo wafting about with their cheroot smoke.

Their guilty consciences had so far stopped them from ruining her outright.

Mama rose and braced her hands against her lower back. "This Season might be worse, Lissa, but it had better be successful. The solicitors have kindly sent me a warning that Lord Tavistock will raise the rent at the end of summer."

Bollocks to Lord Tavistock. "He raised the damned rent after Papa died. That was only..." Well, five years ago. The marquess had waited until the DeWitts had finished second mourning, then cited rising prices, Twidboro's enviable proximity to Town, repairs to tenant cottages, and a lot of other twaddle. Gavin had approved additional expenditures for rent—a dwelling being a "necessity" and thus within his legal purview even as a minor—and life had gone on.

"Tavistock can raise the rent," Mama said, "but he cannot throw us out until we are in default. We are not in default, though your grandmother thinks we should stop paying rent at all. Save that money. It's not as if Tavistock has kept up with the repairs to the Hall."

But this is my home. This is Diana and Caroline's home. Grandmama's home. How much more forgetful would Grandmama be in new surrounds, where every neighbor was a stranger and every room unfamiliar?

"Then we will simply have to make the solicitors see that an additional sum for rent is the only reasonable course and the one Gavin would support, as he supported it five years ago."

Mama regarded her with a half smile. "You are very like your father, in some regards. He was cheerful and kind, but he was also determined. When that man took a notion to do something, it was as good as done."

"I have not taken a notion to marry just any old eligible title, Mama. I will do what I must to see that we keep a roof over our heads —preferably this roof—but I also think we should be searching most diligently for Gavin."

Mama pulled the window curtains closed, sunlight being the enemy of carpets and upholstery. "The solicitors have sent inquiries."

Lissa pushed to her feet, wishing she'd heeded Mr. Dorning's suggestion to stop by the kitchen. A good, hard ride had left her famished, and luncheon was an hour away.

"The solicitors are probably telling you that, when what they mean is, they added a footnote on some epistle to a factor in Marseilles last summer. I don't trust them, Mama."

"Nonsense. Smithers and Purvis is an old and respected firm, and they have given us nothing but loyal service since your father convinced them to accept us as clients."

"They have also given us generous helpings of condescension, sermonizing, and lectures about economy and expectations, while they help themselves regularly to our funds."

Mama shoved her workbasket behind a wing chair. "Riding out with Mr. Dorning put you in a bad humor, my girl, though he seemed taken with you. Should we ask the solicitors to investigate his prospects?"

Lissa knew how Roland felt when the compulsion to throw a tantrum bore down on him. "Mama, I've known Mr. Dorning less than twenty-four hours."

"I stood up with your father exactly three times before we began to form a closer acquaintance. *Gather ye rosebuds while ye may...*"

"Mr. Dorning is no rosebud. Please do not ask the solicitors to meddle, and don't you meddle. Mr. Dorning isn't looking for a wife, and he might well end up buying property nearby."

"Maybe he should be looking for a wife. Did you ever think of that?"

Well, yes. Somewhere between Miller's Lament and the majestic splendor of the napping oak, Lissa had thought that very thing. Also while trotting along the Twid, and while admiring Mr. Dorning's patience and skill with Roland.

"We should be searching harder for Gavin."

Mama's smile faded. "We'll leave for Town at the end of the month, Lissa. If we take Diana and Caroline with us, Mr. Dorning can sublease Twidboro for a few months. In any case, you shall remove to London, where you will exert yourself to charm the younger sons and fortune hunters into proposing marriage."

"Doomed," Lissa said, heading for the door. "We are doomed if our situation turns on my ability to charm anybody. Please listen to me, Mama, and don't wait lunch for me."

"Where are you off to now?"

"To call on Mr. Heyward. I will ask him if Lord Tavistock is raising his rent as well, and we can condole each other on our impending homelessness."

～

Not even in the friendly and informal surrounds of Crosspatch Corners would Trevor presume to call on the vicar at mealtime, so he took his nooning in the inn's common while reading yesterday's London newspapers.

A certain young lord, Marquess of T, was rumored to have returned from his Continental wanderings in search of a wife. The matchmakers were in alt, while the fortune hunters despaired.

"The news is seldom cheering, is it?" Miss Tansy Pevinger was the innkeeper's oldest daughter. She was pretty in a sturdy, tidy way. Her blond hair was neatly gathered beneath her cap, her apron damp around the hems but clean. "Hard times and getting harder, to hear that lot tell it."

"The London press delights in publicizing misery," Trevor replied. "I was looking for properties for sale or lease out this direction, and the paper is no help at all."

Miss Pevinger gathered his empty dishes onto a wooden tray. "We're not like Kent and Surrey, where all the fashionable folk like to bide in winter and summer. Berkshire is still a real shire, with real neighbors. The squires look after their tenants, and the tenants do a good job by the land. Closer to Windsor and Reading, we get the racing stables, but most of them have been here for generations as well."

She treasured her r's—harrrd times and getting harrder—but other than that, her diction would have passed muster in Mayfair.

"That is precisely why I'd rather bide here in Berkshire," Trevor said. "I'm keen to perfect the art of making beer. Do you know of any properties for rent?" At some point in the past two days, the inquiry had become half serious. Maybe more than half?

She finished collecting the dishes and set the tray on the next table. "Squire Holmes rents out his shooting lodge, but that's not what you mean. You mean a proper manor."

"With some land. I don't need a lot of acres, but they must be arable if I'm to experiment with hops, barley, and wheat." A place to tinker with his ideas perhaps, as French vintners tinkered with everything from which terrace best grew which grape varieties, to the angle at which wine bottles should be stored.

"I don't know that you'll find anything to interest you near Crosspatch." Miss Pevinger took a damp rag to the table.

"What of Lark's Nest and Twidboro Hall? My London solicitor claims those are rental properties."

Miss Pevinger began scrubbing hard enough to make the stout table jiggle. "Then your solicitors are right dolts, Mr. Dorning. Both of those properties belong to the Marquess of Tavistock, and a worse landlord you never did meet. The repairs don't get done, but the rents are always collected the very day they are due. Mr. Heyward looks after his place like he owns it—Mr. Heyward mostly goes his own way anyhow—but the DeWitts can't be so bold, can they?"

"I suppose not." Diana's brash attempts at sophistication did not qualify as boldness.

"Mr. DeWitt was barely cold in his grave, and what does Lord Tavistock do? Raises the rent by nearly half. Word is his rubbishing lordship is up to his old tricks, and with Mr. Gavin gone off God knows where and the ladies having barely a spare penny between 'em."

The table, clean to begin with, should have sported a mirror shine. "The DeWitts are good folk," Tansy went on. "Miss Amaryllis had a hard time of it in London because she doesn't know how to put on airs, and there's her ma, determined to wed the poor woman to some viscount's rackety spare. I'd rather slop the hogs and change the bed linens here at the Arms any day than trade places with Miss DeWitt, but you mustn't tell Ma I said so. I'm too forward by half."

She was dauntingly honest, a young woman secure in her place in the world. That honesty was denied Amaryllis DeWitt.

"You really don't think much of Lord Tavistock, do you?" She'd said as much, but Trevor apparently needed to add insult to invective.

"I've never met the man, Mr. Dorning, and I hope to die in that fortunate state. Most people are decent enough at heart," she said, lobbing her rag onto the tray with casual precision. "That one... Why treat people as he does? Off to the Continent for a jolly romp in Paris, they say. Gone for years at a time. If he can afford to kick his hand-some heels in Paris, he can afford to do right by the DeWitts."

Trevor's beef stew began to sit uneasily in his belly. "Tavistock sounds like a terrible person." Like every caricature of the greedy, irresponsible aristocrat who thought only of coin and self-indulgence. Like the previous Lord Tavistock.

"He's probably no worse than the rest of his kind, but I pray heaven keeps him and his ilk far, far from the Arms. Can I get you some cobbler for your sweet? Ma makes the best pear cobbler you ever did taste, and we serve it with a dash of brandy and a dollop of whipped cream."

"Perhaps later. I'm off to call on the vicar and stretch my legs a bit."

"You'll want to pop in at the vicarage smartlike. Vicar Raybourne likes a lie-down after his nooning. Getting on, he is. Ma says being holy all the time is hard work, but somebody's got to do it, because heaven knows that's certainly not a job for the likes of her."

Miss Pevinger hefted her tray and decamped on a smile, while Trevor wished he were a Dorning in truth. He nonetheless made the short jaunt around the green to the vicarage, rapped on the door, and was admitted by a plump, graying housekeeper to a cozy, if slightly worn, study.

King James held pride of place on a standing desk by the mullioned windows, open to the Gospel of Luke.

The Blessing of the Hounds was rendered with competent good cheer over the fireplace—Amaryllis DeWitt's work?—and a sofa liberally adorned with pillows suggested that Mr. Raybourne's devotion to napping was pursued here as well.

"Vicar will be along shortly, Mr. Dorning. He's working on Sunday's sermon. Mr. Raybourne is very conscientious about his sermons."

The twinkle in the lady's eye suggested Mr. Raybourne had already embarked on his afternoon slumbers.

Trevor was rereading the parable of the Good Samaritan and feeling wretched about his conversation with Miss Pevinger when Mr. Raybourne bustled in.

"I have a caller, I'm told. A Mr. Dorning. Shall I have Mrs. Pevinger bring us a tray, or do we indulge in a tot to ward off the lingering chill of departing winter?" Vicar was a spare man with thinning white hair and snapping blue eyes.

"Trevor Dorning, at your service." He bowed, which seemed to amuse Mr. Raybourne. "The air does still carry a slight nip, doesn't it? Despite the bright sunshine and twittering birds, spring hasn't yet arrived."

"You and I shall get on quite well, Mr. Trevor Dorning. Do have a seat. What brings you to Crosspatch, and can you help us put a new roof on the nave? Naves are always needing new roofs, it seems—every hundred years at least—but then, the weather in England would try the roof of heaven itself. And if you don't favor vicarage brandy, Mrs. P will be only too happy to bring us a tray. Gives her an excuse to linger at the door."

Raybourne tossed a square of peat onto the desultory fire. "Mrs. P's brother owns the inn," he went on. "Between them, they hear every bit of news Crosspatch boasts, and I daresay I do too. You did a fine bit of riding earlier today, for example. That colt should have been started over fences long since. He'd like the work too. I know his sire. Don't suppose you ride to hounds?"

He dusted his hands and gestured to the pair of reading chairs before the hearth.

"I can manage well enough in the second flight," Trevor said, "but blood sport in general has no appeal for me."

"You are a fine equestrian, as I have seen with my own eyes, but like me, you prefer not to be in at the kill. A gentleman of refinement." Raybourne poured a bumper of brandy into a plain tumbler.

"A tot will do for me," Trevor said, because indifferent brandy was not to be endured for any save dire medical purposes.

The vicar passed over a more modest portion. "To your health, a good growing season, and neighborly accord in the churchyard." He took the other reading chair and sampled his drink.

Trevor raised his glass. "And a new roof for all the deserving naves." He sipped and was pleasantly surprised. The brandy was far from flat, meaning Raybourne had either just opened the bottle, or he made short work of any bottle he did open. Trevor put the age north of four years—the oak came through, but politely—and the blend well balanced.

"Pevinger doesn't dare supply me with inferior spirits," Mr.

Raybourne said. "I will wax loquacious in the pulpit, and the faithful do so enjoy my talent for brevity. I'm partial to Luke the Physician because he raises uncomfortable questions. Did you know we find the Good Samaritan and the Prodigal Son only in Luke's gospel? Two of my favorites, but you did not come here to discuss Scripture."

"I didn't?"

"Of course not. You rode out with Amaryllis DeWitt and are smitten. We are all smitten with our Lissa. Then I see you trot back to the Arms aboard the self-same juvenile miscreant you rode out on, meaning Miss DeWitt at least nominally approves of you."

Never underestimate a country parson or his housekeeper. "I understand the DeWitt ladies are in an awkward situation."

"Lissa doesn't mince words, does she? If I were twenty years younger... but I'm not, and Mrs. Raybourne has my undying devotion." Raybourne took another sip of his brandy. "Lissa told you that her brother has gone missing, didn't she? We don't mention Gavin DeWitt around strangers, or much at all, but the boy needs to come home soon if the ladies aren't to face dire consequences. Mourna DeWitt has got it into her head that Lissa must marry some fellow with enough consequence to take the solicitors in hand, though short of the Almighty and His holy thunderbolts, I've yet to meet the young fellow up to that task."

To discuss the DeWitts' situation beyond generalities struck Trevor as disloyal and indiscreet. "I'm actually in the area looking for a property to lease or purchase. Miss DeWitt was good enough to acquaint me with the surrounds and to introduce me to her family. She gave me to understand that Lark's Nest and Twidboro Hall are both rental properties with some acreage."

"You don't want either one, sir, though you will excuse an old man's blunt speech. The Marquess of Tavistock owns both, and he holds the living here at St. Nebo's. He's young, so we can hope that he learns some responsibility and compassion, but so far, he bears far too close a resemblance to his late father."

Trevor took a fortifying taste of the brandy and prepared to be castigated in effigy once again. "You knew the previous marquess?"

"One doesn't *know* a fellow like that, not if one is merely a rural vicar. We might politely refer to the late marquess as old school. An uppish, titled prig with no concern for anything but his own consequence. One pitied his wife, a mouse rather than a marchioness. The present lordship is said to be on something of a grand tour, though I wish he'd tour St. Nebo's nave. The roof leaks right over the front pew, and with luck, we could host his lordship on a rainy Sabbath. My parishioners would forgive me any long-windedness on that occasion. Have you considered Miller's Lament?"

Did anybody have *anything* positive to say about Lord Tavistock? "I want to grow grain for beer-making, and a miller's lament would seem ill-suited to the venture."

"Not that sort of lament. The land is all well and good, but the lament part relates to a marital situation dating from the time of Good Queen Bess." Raybourne prosed on, about three daughters and three parcels of land, and the miller ending up with the best parcel and the homeliest daughter, with whom he had eleven children, et cetera and so forth.

Raybourne echoed what Amaryllis had said about introductions and social calls. Nobody stood on ceremony, and word of Trevor's arrival in Crosspatch had already traveled all over the neighborhood in any case.

As Trevor got up to leave, he hazarded a question he would never have put to a new acquaintance in London—or Paris.

"Do we know anything of Gavin DeWitt's possible whereabouts?"

"We know young Mr. DeWitt is likely enjoying himself, wherever he is. He has his father's gift of a light heart. We like and respect Lissa DeWitt, but we dote—doted—on Gavin. A good-looking devil who always has the right word, the right smile, the right silence. Mrs. P called him a natural-born charmer, and he was our best baritone too. Very musical. His mother's pride and joy, though his father was forever after him to take more of an interest in the family business."

"Candles?"

"DeWitt and Son probably does still sell candles, but they also did quite well supplying the army with lanterns, fuses, whale oil, and I know not what else. The business prospers, but all the profits are turned over to the solicitors, and being a man of God, I will lapse into pious silence rather than give you the benefit of my thoughts on that arrangement."

"Then nobody has any idea where DeWitt has gone off to? No duel, no ruinous gambling, no scandals involving women?" None of which would have forced Trevor himself into hiding, but then, he was a useless, titled, fribbling lord.

"Gavin DeWitt is jolly, but he isn't stupid, beyond the stupidity we are all heir to in our youth. He might have fallen afoul of highwaymen, but it's a rare gentleman of the high toby who commits murder these days. The press-gangs have been outlawed, Britain is more or less at peace, and DeWitt has a gentleman's usual accomplishments."

"He was literate?"

"Literate, well-read, musical, mannerly, a fine equestrian, and not too proud to take part in the amateur theatricals and musicales. We all miss him."

Trevor took his leave on that wistful note. The afternoon was sunny, if not quite mild, though testing Roland's improved manners with another outing seemed ill-advised. The horse was not in regular work, and overtaxing him would be a sure recipe for a histrionic display of the equine variety.

The thought of returning to the Arms to read more gossip and tattle held no appeal, and yet, Trevor wasn't in any frame of mind to call at Lark's Nest, where he'd doubtless hear himself vilified yet again. He had no recollection of raising the rent at Twidboro Hall—the opposite was the case, if memory served—but twelve properties, travel, the unreliable mails...

Perhaps Purvis had confused one tenant with another, one property with another. In any case, Travis would *un*-raise the DeWitt's rent, of that he was certain.

He trod the path along the Twid until he came to a boulder situated along the riverbank. He perched upon that boulder and mentally composed correspondence to his solicitors. After that exercise had exhausted his stores of lordly imperiousness, he turned to drafting a note to Sycamore Dorning.

When his bum had grown stiff and cold, he yet remained on the boulder long enough to mentally dispatch an epistle to Worth Kettering. As he rose and took the path in the direction of Lark's Nest, he added a short postscript to the last missive.

By then, he'd realized that somebody half secreted in the undergrowth was watching him and had been for some time.

CHAPTER SIX

Jones, whose self-possession rivaled Wellington's legendary calm on the day of battle, passed Young Purvis a single folded piece of paper.

"Troubling news, sir." A slight quaver in his voice indicated the news starting Young Purvis's day was dire. The blob of wax clinging to the edge of the paper was of a particular purple color, suggesting the dire news had come from Berkshire. "His lordship sent this by express yesterday afternoon and to my attention."

"Most unusual." On the reverse of the epistle, in the same elegant, confident hand as the letter itself: *John Jones, Senior Clerk. To be opened by addressee only, at the firm of...* "I take it we had no direction from his lordship requiring the rent at Twidboro to be raised in the first place?"

"None, sir. I double-checked the files to be sure. Tavistock has never given us leave to raise anybody's rent. Shortly after he went to France, he indicated that, in particular, no rents are ever to be raised on any family in mourning."

In France, Tavistock would have seen one dispossessed widow after another, and the current marquess was a decent sort, more's the pity.

"We must do as our client says." Young Purvis passed the letter over. "Make a copy of that and file the copy. You may return the original to me."

Jones folded the letter carefully. "And the funds for a new roof on St. Nebo's? It's a modest house of worship, but a new roof...? The bankers will want a Purvis signature on that dispersal, sir."

"Battle stations!" Young Pennypacker sang out the warning from his desk along the window. He jammed the last bite of a hot cross bun into his maw, took up his pen, uncapped his ink bottle, and bent over a half-finished copying exercise. The other clerks followed suit, and by the time Old Purvis strolled into the office, the clerks' chilly chamber was a hive of quiet, focused industry.

"Good morning, all," Old Purvis said, ambling between the desks. "A fine day to be gainfully employed on the business of the great and the good. Jones, I'll want a word with you."

Jones discreetly handed Lord Tavistock's express back to Young Purvis. "Of course, sir."

"I'd like a word with you as well, sir," Young Purvis said, tucking the letter into his breast pocket. "About the Tavistock Berkshire properties."

Pennypacker exchanged a portentous look behind Papa's back with the assistant head clerk, Northam.

Papa began unbuttoning his greatcoat, a work of sartorial splendor sporting five capes. "What of them?"

"A word in your office would be appreciated, sir."

Papa gave his only begotten son a dyspeptic look. "Very well. Pennypacker, off to the sweet shop with you. A man needs a bit of sustenance if he must toil in legal vineyards the livelong day. I fancy an apple tart if they have any. Pear will do, or even cherry."

"Yes, sir." Pennypacker carefully capped the ink bottle he'd just uncapped, threw sand on a document with exactly two words of fresh writing on it, and trotted for the foyer.

Papa passed his coat and hat to a yawning Northam. "Young

Purvis, you first, then Jones, and I am not in the mood for bad news, gentlemen."

Young Purvis entered his father's office with every intention of putting the whole increasingly complicated Tavistock mess squarely on the desk of its originator, but where to start?

"See to the fire, young man. Old bones can't be expected to cope with a frigid office."

Young Purvis closed the office door and dutifully tossed a scoop of coal onto the flames, though Papa's office was on the enviable side of toasty.

"What's on your mind, boy?"

"Miss Hecate Brompton," Young Purvis said, surprising both his father and himself. "She is due to return to Town tomorrow." Young Purvis was on good terms with the Brompton house steward and had made it his business to know of Miss Brompton's impending arrival.

Papa settled behind his desk. "Send her our felicitations on a safe journey from Hampshire. Request a meeting at her earliest convenience, and be sure to invite her father. If Isaac Brompton runs true to form, he'll try to bribe an advance on his allowance from us, but he'll leave any actual meetings to the girl."

Miss Brompton hadn't been a girl even when she'd been a mere adolescent and new to her wealth.

"Mr. Brompton," Old Purvis went on, "will be happy to know that we've at long last found an appropriate suitor for his daughter's hand. I've been saving Miss Brompton these several years past for a special suitor."

Oh, Papa... "For Lord Tavistock?" Miss Hecate was a fine figure of a woman, but she had to be in at least her seventh Season, and that was rounding the math in the direction most flattering to the lady.

"Her fortune, under our careful management, has grown considerably in recent years. She can afford a marquess, and for all Tavistock knows, he needs Miss Brompton."

Miss Brompton had all but managed her own funds. She read foreign newspapers, talked to herbwomen, dowsers, and strolling

players, and ran a sailors' charity. Sailors, according to Miss Brompton, noticed the most interesting developments in foreign markets.
Her curiosity was nothing short of rapacious, and she somehow took
all these bits and bobs of information and turned them into wealth.

She put Young Purvis in mind of a female Worth Kettering,
though she hadn't been cursed with the prominent beak Kettering
stuck into all manner of businesses.

"Miss Brompton might have a thing or two to say about whether
Tavistock will do, sir. He's passionate about winemaking, not exactly
of a staid demeanor. Miss Brompton takes divine services very seriously, by contrast." She collected information in the churchyard as
well and called her reconnaissance *being neighborly.*

Papa assembled his props—draft settlement agreement, ink
bottle, quill pen, spectacles. "Tavistock will go to church once the
Season begins because the churchyard is a prime place to flirt.
Besides, eternal salvation and securing the succession are separate
undertakings. If you've no other—"

"But, sir, Miss Brompton notices details. She reads every line of
our reports and sometimes even corrects our figures." And those
corrections—*trivial inaccuracies*—were always brought to Young
Purvis's attention in the most polite, roundabout correspondence. "I
daresay married to Tavistock, Miss Brompton will read *his* reports,
and Tavistock is not in the habit of gainsaying his womenfolk."

Papa donned his spectacles. "I much preferred the old marquess.
That fellow knew how to go on. Brooked no dramatics. Made a decision, and that decision was respected. If he was given sound advice,
he followed it, and there was none of this... this... unbecoming intru-
siveness into the minutiae of business that the younger generation
favors. Why did the Heavenly Arbiter put solicitors on earth, if not to
see that business is properly conducted?"

*When had fleecing clients become synonymous with proper busi-
ness, and who ever said that lawyers were sent by heaven?*

"Miss Brompton does have those lamentable intrusive tendencies, sir, and she will surely notice that St. Nebo's has been requesting

funds for a new roof for the past decade. That is the only living Tavistock holds, and his father was parsimonious toward it. If Tavistock is
to make a good impression on the lady, then neglecting the only
house of worship in the marquess's care will not do."

This whole discussion was vexing. Tavistock ought to look after
St. Nebo's because that's what a decent fellow with a title and means
did, but then, nobody had shown his lordship the myriad letters from
old Mr. Raybourne, so how could his lordship even know the matter
had been neglected?

And none of this was convincing Papa of the foolishness, the
utter absurdity, of attempting to tell Hecate Brompton whom she
should marry.

"My boy, you surprise me," Papa said, taking out a silk handkerchief
bordered in gold embroidery. "Your attention to such a detail suggests
you have the potential to one day make me proud to call you my son." He
polished his spectacles with the handkerchief. "A gesture in the direction of St. Nebo's is the very thing. I will mention his lordship's conscientious attention to even an obscure rural parish when Miss Brompton
calls upon us. Of course, we had to nag him into doing his duty, but he
did heed our guidance now that he's preparing to take a wife."

Forgive me, Miss Brompton. "I'll prepare the bank draft for your
signature, sir."

"Do that, and don't stint. Don't be lavish, but don't stint. Any
excess goes to the poor box, and so forth."

"Very good, sir. Shall I send Jones to you?"

A triple rap on the door suggested Pennypacker had returned
from the bakery.

"Not just yet. A hardworking man intent on legal complexities
wants to start his day in peace and quiet, and you've given me something to consider. Perhaps his lordship should make a few other
gestures in anticipation of his nuptials. Donate to a few charities of
my choosing."

Papa, no. One of those charities would doubtless be the Foundation for the Improved Circumstances of a Certain Undeserving Solicitor.

"I can discuss charities with his lordship if you like, sir, though I'm sure he'd rather start with the organizations supported by his Dorning connections."

"Come in, boy!" Papa bellowed. "Nothing is less appealing than stale pastry."

Pennypacker set the parcel on Papa's desk and withdrew. The scent of cinnamon reminded Young Purvis that breakfast had been three long, busy, worrisome hours ago.

"Get the new roof on St. Nebo's," Papa said, "and go back through the correspondence. See to the tenant repairs and so forth. Miss Brompton will doubtless concern herself with those."

"We keep tenant properties fairly spruce, sir, but the rentals... Twidboro Hall, for example, is overdue for reglazing, the chimneys need attention, and the brickwork of the terrace and the walkways has been neglected."

Papa extracted an apple tart sticky with glaze and redolent of every boy's fondest holiday memories.

"I'll want coffee to wash this down. No repairs to Twidboro for the nonce. The DeWitts might well vacate if they can get Miss DeWitt fired off, though one doesn't hold out much hope of success in that regard. Amaryllis DeWitt has been an object of talk, and no fortune, however large, can salvage a woman's reputation when that happens."

What heiress only two generations removed from the shop wouldn't be an object of talk? Heiresses with blood bluer than the Aegean Sea in summer were the objects of talk.

"The glazing at Twidboro Hall is becoming urgent, sir."

Papa took a bite of his tart and made happy shoat noises. "Do the glazing, then," he said around a mouthful of tart. "I'm sure there's some case law somewhere to support the necessity of periodic glazing. Water at large is the common enemy and so forth."

Delightful. Papa had taken up inventing case law. "I'll send Pennypacker in with your coffee."

"Do, and let me know well in advance when the Brompton antidote is coming by. I shall prepare most thoroughly."

Meaning Young Purvis, who withdrew on a bow, should prepare most thoroughly, but then, he took a personal interest in safeguarding Miss Brompton's legal wellbeing.

"Coffee," Young Purvis said to Pennypacker. "He's in a decent mood, thanks to the tarts." And thanks to the prospect of wrecking Miss Brompton's life while shifting her fortune closer to Papa's paws and continuing to fleece the marquess.

Pennypacker scurried off—heaven help the clerk who served a tepid cup of coffee—and Jones sidled nearer.

"Well?" Jones asked quietly.

"St. Nebo's acquires a new roof the better to impress Miss Brompton when Tavistock gets around to courting her."

"Clever of you, but Old Purvis is getting worse, or my name's not John Jones."

"He also approved glazing for Twidboro Hall, and for reasons unknown to a mere solicitor, that glazing will involve repairing walkways and chimneys. I'd forgotten your given name is John."

"Biblical, easy to recall, and nobody else in the family has it. Why should my given name be of any significance to you?"

"No reason. You are right that he's getting worse. I meant to tell him that Tavistock is inspecting Twidboro as we speak, but the moment never arose."

Jones watched Pennypacker weave between desks, a full cup of steaming coffee in his ink-stained hands. "Lord Tavistock is not the same sort of marquess his father was, sir. Old Purvis has too many schemes of the wrong sort afoot, and this cannot end well."

"Please warn me if you intend to give notice, Jones."

"Likewise, sir."

Pennypacker's foot caught on the worn edge of the carpet, and the boy went tumbling, spilling coffee all over himself, the rug, and the document Northam had spent the last half hour copying.

~

"I don't have to remain seated in Mr. Dorning's company, the better to allow him to loom over me." Lissa hadn't realized she liked that about Trevor Dorning until the time had come to escort him from the house after tea yesterday.

She'd popped to her feet without a second thought, a small but telling freedom.

"You get loomed over?" Phillip Heyward asked as he and Lissa ambled along the fence of the mare's pasture. "Am I guilty of this offense?"

"You are sufficiently tall that I need not try to be diminutive with you. Loom all you like, or try to. With too many of the Mayfair Honorables and eligibles, I must stoop, wear flat slippers instead of the heeled variety, and remain seated. Diana won't have that problem."

Phillip paused at the stile and offered Lissa his left hand. "We should have a closer look at Pearl."

Lissa did not need Phillip's assistance to navigate the steps of a stile, but neither did she resent the courtesy. Phillip was a neighbor and a friend. He'd been at Lark's Nest as long as Lissa could recall, intensely shy, bookish, a few years her senior. He was happiest out of doors and happiest of all in his sprawling home wood.

By London standards, Phillip was probably eccentric, sticking so close to home and burying himself in books and birdsong, but to Lissa he was just Phillip. Dear, reliable, steady—when not distracted by some flower or bug—Phillip.

"Pearl looks the same to me," Lissa said as they crossed one of the best pastures in the whole Crosspatch neighborhood. The fenced area belonged half to Lark's Nest and half to Twidboro, and the whole ran parallel to the river. Good bottom soil with plenty of shade near the water and full sun on the upward slope.

"Her eye is different," Phillip replied, stopping a few feet from an elegant gray mare with a notably drooping belly. "She's bagged up, but she's still keeping company with her friends." He walked around behind her, gently lifting her tail. "No changes back here."

Lissa took a closer look at the mare's udder. "She hasn't waxed up. No signs of dripping. We have a few days at least. Let's have a look at your Dove."

Dove, a dapple gray draft cross, was in the same state. Getting closer, but not close enough to move either mare into a foaling stall. The other expectant mothers had some time to go yet.

"You worry for them," Phillip said as he and Lissa returned the way they'd come.

"I want to be here, Phillip. I do well with foaling, even Dabney admits as much, but instead I'll be parading around London, trying to catch the notice of some fellow who hasn't heard that my morals are questionable, my antecedents are questionable, my brother's where-abouts are questionable..."

Phillip again offered Lissa his left hand at the stile. "People make life so complicated. You are kind and honest. You care for your family. Any man should be able to see that. Your banker tallies your coin, a figure any man ought to be able to read."

He'd failed to note the involvement of the solicitors, bless him.

"There speaks a fellow who has avoided Mayfair Society." Phillip had also avoided having any family. As far back as Lissa could recall, Phillip had dwelled alone at Lark's Nest. He'd had tutors and gover-nors, and now he had staff, but he was the king of his private fiefdom and accepted by his neighbors as such. He paid his tithes, though he seldom went to services, and he cooperated with neighboring proper-ties at planting, shearing, haying, and harvest.

He was friendly in casual encounters, but those encounters were always brief, unless somebody sought to tap Phillip's knowledge about fertilizing peas or building a fruit wall.

To a very great extent, Phillip Heyward went his own way.

"If you don't want to spend spring in London, you shouldn't go," he said. "I have some money, and you are welcome to it."

"You will need that money someday," Lissa said, "for your experiments."

He was forever importing seeds and plants, crossing this breed of sheep with that. Dove was a result of one of his experiments, a horse comfortable under saddle and tireless in the traces, though she wasn't as refined as a saddle horse ought to be or quite up to the heaviest demands of the plow.

"You like Mr. Dorning," Phillip said. "You complain about all the others, but you say nice things about Dorning."

Mrs. Dabney claimed *our Mr. Heyward* was a touch slow-witted, but Mrs. Raybourne contended that Phillip was instead a careful thinker. He'd been raised without siblings, without schoolroom politics, without public school pecking orders and competitiveness. He felt no compulsion to be hasty in his thoughts or movements, though he was without doubt socially backward.

"Mr. Dorning is ambitious, Phillip. He isn't waiting for some heiress to rescue his finances so he can continue to waste his days and nights in dissipation. He wants to build something."

"Build a house? I thought you said he sought a rental property."

"Build a business, as my grandfather did. Build a life. I can't always tell what he's thinking, and he doesn't laugh much—the man has a certain irksome dignity foreign to Crosspatch Corners—but he isn't a fop."

"Gavin isn't a fop."

That Phillip spoke easily of Gavin, whom he'd regarded as a somewhat bothersome younger brother, was a comfort. The rest of the village had politely dropped Gavin from conversation, though Lissa was certain they kept him in their prayers.

"Gavin is stylish," Lissa said. "Also given to dramatics, and that vexed me past all bearing, but now I hope he's simply involved in a grand tantrum rather than lying in some pauper's grave."

They walked up the bridle path toward Lark's Nest, the day trying for spring and falling short. In bright sunshine, when the breeze was still, a hint of mildness touched the air. Two hours hence, that warmth would flee as the sun inched lower.

"You have not described Mr. Dorning's appearance," Phillip said, "other than to note his height. Describe him for me."

This was a game Lissa and Phillip had played for years. Grandmama had taken her to Bath the summer before Papa's death, and on Lissa's return, Phillip had quizzed her for weeks. What did the air in Bath smell of? Why did the spa waters taste of rotten eggs? Were the seagulls larger? Did they use the same cries as the seagulls who occasionally visited Crosspatch?

His curiosity had subsided only when Lissa had hit on the notion of sketching her memories for him, and then she'd found a handsome bound book full of drawings of Bath and its surrounds. Phillip had pored over the book for hours at a time.

"Mr. Dorning's appearance is not that remarkable," Lissa said. "He wears standard Bond Street attire, and it fits him exquisitely. A bit more lace than the usual squire, less than a fribble prefers. Sober colors, nary a wrinkle or stain to be seen. I'd say the clothes are new, but he wears them so comfortably that they likely aren't new, but rather, well cared for."

Phillip waited for her to open a gate and pass through ahead of him. She closed the gate behind them, and they resumed walking.

"Describe the man, Lissa, not his clothing."

"Tallish, broad-shouldered, muscular without being brutish—like you. He's clearly fit but doesn't need to show off his vitality. He was patient with Roland—very patient—though his reflexes are devilishly quick, at least in the saddle."

"You let him ride Roland?"

The path led between rows of rhododendrons a dozen feet high, a rare splash of green in a landscape still inching out from under winter's browns.

"Mr. Dorning offered, and... he wants to help, Phillip, but he hasn't tried to tell me what to do." And everybody told Lissa what to do, from Mama to Grandmama, to Diana, to the solicitors, to Mrs. Raybourne, and even Phillip.

"Then Mr. Dorning is a dolt," Phillip said, shoving Lissa's shoulder gently. "He should tell you to bide in Crosspatch, running everything from the assemblies to the market committee to the altar society, because that makes you happy."

The committees and whatnot made her busy and tired. "Mama mostly runs the altar society." A knitting club for gossips, though nobody in the neighborhood lacked a warm scarf or new stockings come winter, and St. Nebo's was always clean and tidy. "The market runs itself."

"Except when Dabney gets to squabbling with Pevinger, or Squire Jonas takes a notion to criticize Mrs. Henry's jams and jellies."

"They squabble for the joy of squabbling, like children." And yet, Lissa would miss the sound of raised voices on a sunny Wednesday morning, followed by the moment when all heads on the village green turned to the steps of the inn, and a few quiet bets were exchanged. Which man would let a profanity slip first? Would Mrs. P or Mrs. D appear to support her champion?

Then Lissa would wade in, sort out the misunderstanding, and everybody would have a little something to talk about over their nooning.

"Mr. Dorning would never lower himself to squabbling," Phillip said primly. "He *has a certain dignity foreign to Crosspatch Corners*, but so far, nobody will tell me what color his hair is."

A certain *irksome* dignity, as if he was keeping his own counsel about some weighty matter far above the petty concerns of an obscure village. A loftiness, for all his correct manners and pleasant conversation.

"He's blond. Blue eyes. Entirely standard English coloring."

"As far as I know, I'm English," Phillip observed as they rounded the bend in the path that brought Lark's Nest into view. "Not a blond hair on me. Black Irish, as best Mrs. Raybourne can describe me.

You're English, as are Diana and Caroline, and again, not a blonde among you. Why does Mr. Dorning's coloring win national honors, I wonder?"

Gavin had teased Lissa like this—gently, annoyingly. The part of Lissa that wasn't worried witless about him, or furious with him, missed him. Why was it so hard to admit that?

"Oh, very well," Lissa said. "Mr. Dorning is handsome. Handsome in a substantial way, not in the pretty, fribbling manner of a London dandy. I didn't realize at first how different he is, because it's mostly a matter of what's absent. He doesn't make florid gestures. He doesn't raise his voice to draw notice. He doesn't talk about people I've never met as if I should know who they are and be impressed that he's acquainted with them."

"And Mr. Dorning walks with a certain easy confidence," Phillip said, "that draws the eye despite a lack of military bearing or fashionable affectations. No quizzing glass, no gloves dyed to match a green top hat, no tassels on his boots, no jeweled walking stick."

Well, yes. "You've seen him."

Phillip leaned close enough that Lissa caught his lavender and scythed grass fragrance. "He's pacing on my terrace, and if you turn tail and run now, I will send him after you. I will not endure a caller, Lissa DeWitt, unless you endure him with me."

Phillip had no hostess, but he didn't need one. He never entertained formally and seldom entertained informally either. Vicar Raybourne might stop by twice a year, and Lissa came and went on casual terms, but Phillip was no sort of host.

And there was Mr. Trevor Dorning, taking up a lean against a porch pillar and looking... Damn and blast, the man was *scrumptious.* Diana had chosen the right word. He was polite, well spoken, ambitious, and all that other twaddle, but he was also *physically attractive,* and that realization both pleased and puzzled Lissa.

"Did I tell you that Lord Tavistock is raising our rent at Twidboro?" she asked, waving in greeting to Phillip's caller.

"You did not, and you know it," Phillip said, falling in beside her as she headed for the house. "That bastard. This is why you are so grimly determined to return to London, isn't it? Mourna is going quietly daft, and your grandmama has simply grown quiet. Take my money, Lissa, please."

"Thank you for the offer, but I doubt you have enough to solve the dilemma that we're facing. Gavin might not return for years, if he returns at all. I must marry well if we're to have any sort of regular income and any hope of seeing Diana and Caroline properly fired off."

"You'll support your family once you're married?"

"If need be. The loftiest husband in the realm does not interfere with his wife's pin money." Mama was very certain on that point.

Phillip maintained a silence that might have been intended as diplomatic, but instead felt pitying.

Mr. Dorning allowed Lissa to make the introductions, and he shook left-handed when Phillip proffered his left hand. The gentlemen embarked on a discussion of whether spring was early or on time for Berkshire while they waited for the tea tray.

Lissa added the occasional remark—the crocuses were early, but the daffodils had been less precocious—and considered what if anything to do about the inconvenient fact that she, who had disdained heirs and dandies, was physically drawn to Mr. Trevor Dorning, whose ambition in life was merely to brew a good pint of beer.

CHAPTER SEVEN

Amaryllis had come striding along the path from the stable, her gait easy, her smile genuine. She was the most self-confident woman Trevor had met, and that sat uneasily with him. In polite society, diamonds could be confident, originals could be forthright and even outspoken, but a chandler's tallish, red-haired granddaughter had best exhibit unrelenting humility.

The appearance of self-doubt would have served Amaryllis well in Mayfair.

A hint of uncertainty might have gained her a few more dance partners.

Some diffidence might have quieted a few whispers.

And Trevor would have hated to see that, but...

Squire Heyward, by contrast, was a notably shy fellow. Tall, rangy, sable-haired, blue-eyed, he barely glanced at Trevor, instead examining the terrace flagstones, the clouds, the spot over Trevor's left shoulder.

What a refreshing change from all the bonhomie, toadying, and backslapping of the London clubs.

Heyward appeared to favor his right arm, holding it closer to his body than his left and at a slight angle. He was a stranger to lace and starch, instead preferring creased boots damp at the toes, breeches worn to the softness of velvet, and a battered hat that might have been new when Mad George had been in leading strings. Heyward's neck-cloth was plain, limp cotton tied in a lopsided mathematical.

Amaryllis rattled off the introductions and suggested a spot of tea. She presided over the tray again, making no effort to steer a conversation that would have bored Trevor even in French.

"An early spring is not necessarily a good thing," Heyward said. "Drought can follow, then a ruined harvest. I prefer a late spring. The beasts have winter coat well into April, and the crops make up the difference as the days lengthen. What of you, Mr. Dorning?"

This was what the gentry discussed instead of fashion and match-making? "I know little of growing corn, but for grapes, a rainy winter and a long, warm summer work best. We sometimes get the summers here in England, but our winters are too harsh to be ideal most of the time. Tell me, do you grow hops?"

"I do, and after some experimentation, I find the Spalter variety does quite well on my land—Bavarian in origin—though the Saaz is also successful."

"And have you tried any of the hops originating along the Bodensee?"

Heyward waxed eloquent, all shyness gone, about the bittering qualities of the Tettnanger hops and the aromatic tendencies of the Spalter hops. The Saaz strain, to which the Tettnanger could well be related, was also quite aromatic, but more susceptible to rusts than the German varieties.

Amaryllis nibbled shortbread and let the discussion gallop on. Her expression was bemused, as if she'd heard much talk of mildewed crops, the oniony scent of a hop cone ready for harvest, and the papery sound that cone should make when rolled between the fingers.

Trevor had had a few such conversations, but he hadn't expected to find a hops expert in Crosspatch Corners.

"Phillip reads everything," Amaryllis said when Heyward had paused to gather his thoughts about how tall exactly to leave the hop bine after the second-year harvest. "If the neighbors have difficulty with a patch of ground, or a brood mare isn't doing well, they stop Phillip on one of his rambles, and he usually has a solution."

The Dorning family—the *real* Dorning family—would love Heyward and his horticultural acumen. He offered Amaryllis a bashful smile, and she topped up his tea cup. They were easy with each other, without pretense, and that was mildly puzzling.

Heyward gave off no I-saw-her-first warning signals in his conversation. He did not presume to touch Amaryllis in the manner of a familiar. Nothing in his deportment suggested possessiveness toward a woman Trevor couldn't get out of his imagination.

"You are taking young Roland in hand, I hear," Heyward said. "Had him out for a gallop this morning, according to Mr. Raybourne."

"That horse is *fast*," Trevor said, nearly as fast as the Crosspatch gossip vines. "And he's not in condition by half. If he ever learned to focus on his schoolwork, he'd be formidable."

Heyward was off again, discussing shoulder angles, oats versus wheat in an equine's winter diet, the muscling of the neck, and the optimal construction of a horse's stifles for both speed and smooth gaits. Heyward looked like a handsome bumpkin, but on agricultural topics, he was an articulate, protean intellect.

Trevor had met many Heywards in France and along the Rhine. Men who sat about the village square looking unprepossessing in their homespun fashion, smoking their pipes, sipping their wine. Ask these same humble fellows when the Merlot strains ought best be harvested, and they became lions of wit and wisdom, bringing passionate intelligence to the most detailed debates.

The parallel brought an odd comfort, along with the admission that Heyward knew grains as well or better than Trevor knew grapes.

"Bring Roland around tomorrow," Heyward said when Trevor had thanked him for discussion that turned surprisingly enjoyable and enlightening. "There's a half-mile straight stretch along the Twid just past the mill. I'll time you an hour after first light."

"Phillip will do so discreetly," Amaryllis said as she accompanied Trevor and their host to the front door. "You won't find half of Crosspatch cheering you across the finish line."

Trevor was inclined to accept and not only because a hard gallop was great fun. Heyward was... just plain good company. So comfortable in his own skin that he didn't need to put on any airs or lace his conversation with gossip and bons mots.

That settled, self-accepting quality made him easy to be around, as if he and Trevor had been great friends earlier in life and were taking up where they'd left off, rather than meeting for the first time.

"Roland would run faster against a competitor," Trevor said, which was very bad of him.

Heyward took an inordinate amount of time to pass over Trevor's hat. The shy bumpkin was back on duty, or the *sly* bumpkin.

"I'll bring Jacques." Amaryllis straightened a shooting jacket hanging from a peg along the wall and moved on to tidy up a plain wool cloak hanging beside it. "A hack before breakfast starts the day off on the right foot, but I'm not up for a public race. Phillip, you will keep an eye on Pearl?"

"And Dove and the lot of them. I'll send word if there's any change."

"Thank you." Amaryllis kissed his cheek. Heyward settled a cloak over her shoulders, and they smiled at each other like... cousins or something, though Trevor's lady cousins had never smiled at him quite that sweetly.

"Come, Mr. Dorning," Amaryllis said. "I'll walk with you to the gateposts, and you can regale me with all the latest tattle from the Arms."

She jaunted out the door and down the steps, leaving Trevor to bow a farewell to Heyward and join the lady as she set off along the drive.

"For a recluse, Heyward is friendly." Also quite good-looking. His house, from what Trevor had noted, was also devoid of the recluse's requisite cobwebs, bats, and lurking cats. Lark's Nest appeared to be in better trim than Twidboro Hall.

"You asked about barley or hops or winter wheat," Amaryllis said. "I forget which, and Phillip cannot help himself on topics such as that. His head is full to bursting with knowledge. He says he travels between the pages of his books."

"Had I been in the slightest manner rude or condescending to Heyward, you would have put me in my place, wouldn't you?" Like Jeanette had done to Trevor's tutors when they had presumed to criticize the boyish imperfections of his penmanship.

Though Heyward wasn't a boy and could probably have handed Trevor a tidy set-down without any assistance from anybody.

Amaryllis's gait acquired a marching quality. "Had Phillip been rude to you—he can be very direct—I would have chided him as well. I feel as if my feet have been cold since Michaelmas. I'm ready for spring to get on with itself."

A change of subject in any language was a change of subject. "You'll miss him when you go to London," Trevor said, thinking back to those old fellows lighting their pipes in France. "He's a part of home for you."

"Phillip is kind and sweet and a good neighbor, but every time I'm around him, I think, 'Those dandies and diamonds in Mayfair would never see him for the treasure he is. They would ridicule him because he isn't fashionable and he doesn't lisp his gossip in French. I want to take a horsewhip to the lot of them."

The lady was not complaining entirely on Phillip Heyward's behalf.

"Mayfair Society includes some decent folk, Miss DeWitt. Good souls who behave with kindness and generosity toward others." Jeanette was such a soul. Sycamore might be, too, beneath all his bluster. Goddard of a certainty was a fine specimen, and Trevor could name others.

The present Marquess of Tavistock, for example, wasn't such a bad fellow, once you got to know him. He was putting a new roof on St. Nebo's and making repairs at Twidboro Hall.

"You are right, of course," Amaryllis said as the Lark Nest's gateposts came into view. "Not everybody in Town is a backbiting tattler or an overdressed wastrel, but that seems to be the Society I found myself in most frequently. I truly dread returning to London."

"Then don't go. The solicitors cannot allow you to starve, and an independent investigator ought to be able to turn up some clue as to your brother's whereabouts."

"One must pay such investigators, Mr. Dorning, and Mama hoards every groat against our London expenses. Grandmama has written to every friend and acquaintance she can think of. I have made inquiries of Gavin's friends, to the extent I could do so discreetly."

She stopped at the bend in the lane and looked back toward Heyward's manor house. Lark's Nest was a half-timbered, white-washed Tudor dwelling of three stories atop a sunken basement. The interior had been full of light owing to an abundance of mullioned windows, the flagstone floors had been uneven with age, and the hearths small.

A modest, aging jewel, but a jewel nonetheless.

"Papa tried to buy Twidboro," Amaryllis said, shading her eyes with her hand, "but the old marquess would not sell. An offer on Lark's Nest was similarly rejected out of hand, and now we can be tossed into the street at the new marquess's whim. His lordship has a dozen properties, but he would not sell the least of them to us, not even for excessively generous coin. I loathe a snob, Mr. Dorning, but thanks to Lord Tavistock's intransigence, I'll likely have to marry one."

Now that was... That was unfair. "Lord Tavistock did not snatch your brother away or decide the terms of your father's will, Miss DeWitt."

She rounded on him, and Trevor was both impressed and glad she hadn't a horsewhip to hand. "You haven't been paraded through half the ballrooms in Mayfair while the same men who sampled your wares ruin your chances of a decent match, the same men who promised to *be* that decent match as they were pawing at your skirts. Lord Tavistock may not number among those knaves, but he is of their world and one of the authors of my family's distress."

They were in view of the house, so Trevor resumed walking around the bend, where they would have more privacy.

"Do you know what annoys me the most about you?" he said as Amaryllis stalked after him. "You are so confident, so competent, so capable and self-possessed. You can ride astride with no self-consciousness whatsoever. According to Raybourne, the village goes into a collective decline when you remove to Town. Your family clearly pins all their hopes of salvation upon you, but you have no idea, not the least dim inkling, how magnificent you are, how breath-takingly lovely and dear, and if you tell me who those blasted lordly arsewipes are, I will see them ruined in the next fortnight."

She took him by the arm, forcing him to slow his pace. "How can a mere mister ruin an earl's heir or a viscount's spare?"

She ignored the lovely and dear part of his outburst. Of course, she did. "The same way they'd seek to ruin you—with talk. London runs on talk and money, and please recall that I'm connected to the Dornings and, through them, to the Haddonfields, who are on conspiring terms with the Windhams. The former Miss Emily Pepper is among the Dorning brides—she is quite the heiress—and one of the Dorning sisters married a viscount of her own."

He stopped short of mentioning that the other Dorning sister had married Worth Kettering, and Kettering's brother was an earl. Goddard and Jeanette had a Shropshire earl among *their* cousins-by-marriage, and a Welsh knight or baronet or something of the sort...

"You should throw more tantrums," Amaryllis said. "One would almost think you are a peer when you're all self-possessed and articu-late. I like the fellow who splutters better."

I do not splutter was immediately shouted down in Trevor's heart by *She likes me.* "I meant what I said, Amaryllis DeWitt. You are magnificent and dear, and to blazes with anybody who can't see that. Take your verbal horsewhip to London with you, if you must go, and be sure to give the solicitors a taste of the lash before you've unpacked the first trunk."

She laughed that gorgeous, warm laugh, and when she half hugged his arm, Trevor knew himself to be a man in deep, deep trouble. The way out of the trouble was simple—shovel aside a barrow full of lies, sort out some apparently crooked solicitors, undertake a proper courtship, and convince the lady that her fortune had nothing to do with Trevor's besottedness.

Nothing whatsoever.

~

Lissa could not have said which of Mr. Dorning's salient qualities— ambition, good looks, horsemanship, helpfulness—most held her attention, but it was his subtle dignity that threatened her composure.

She longed to have such self-possession, to know instinctively which remarks to ignore, which to meet with a witty riposte, and which to quell with a frigid stare. Trevor Dorning intuitively sensed how to carry himself such that he drew the eye *respectfully*. He was by nature quiet, with his words, his posture, and his gestures, and rendered himself all the more interesting for making less noise.

Even when he lectured Lissa, he remained self-possessed. Even his *tantrum* was lordly, for pity's sake, and that...

"You are provoking me," she said as they ambled along. "You don't mean to—your sentiments are purely honorable—but you are most provoking nonetheless." His sentiments had been *protective*, outraged on her behalf. Whatever was she to make of *that*?

"A gentleman does not provoke a lady. I am trying to... I don't know what I'm trying to do. You provoked me first."

Lissa examined the gauzy honeysuckle hedges rather than allow Mr. Dorning to see her smile. "Are there no competent, capable, confident ladies where you come from?" She wanted him to say no, that she was the first he'd met, and he was dumbstruck by her wonderfulness.

"As a matter of fact, I know many such women. I was mostly raised by one, and you would like her. My step-mother has the knack of being formidable while appearing to merely pour the tea and remark on the weather."

"You have the same quality, and that is what provokes me." Provoked and beguiled her. His innate self-possession and his protectiveness. "I want to throw you off stride, challenge your assumptions." She wanted, more to the point, to break rules with him. Not because he importuned her to do so, not because a small compromise of propriety might result in a large gain in security, but because... he purely, joyously, *tempted* her.

To muss his hair, to wrinkle that pristine cravat or, better still, get it off him. He inspired her imagination to canter down alluring trails that led into dense thickets of longing and self-indulgence. To impossible kisses and satisfied sighs.

When was the last time Amaryllis had been tempted to do something sweet, pleasurable, and flirtatious? She'd been endlessly tempted to deliver set-downs to presuming bachelors or to tell uppish dowagers what she really thought of their bonnets. She'd been tempted to tell Mr. Pevinger and Mr. Dabney that their squabbling made them both look foolish.

She'd been tempted to plead a megrim to avoid Sunday services.

Now, she wanted to learn if and where Trevor Dorning was ticklish. *Ye cavorting cupids.*

"Are those men you referred to," he said, "those knaves, still at large in Mayfair, Miss DeWitt?"

Mr. Dorning also apparently tempted Lissa to be much too forthright. "You cannot ruin them. Charles Brompton was an earl's spare when I met him during my first Season. He's the heir now, the older brother having succumbed to consumption. I was young and foolish, and he was... I had to leave Town when Papa grew ill, and Mr. Brompton's attention was drawn elsewhere."

"He used you." Three words had never conveyed such utter contempt for a peer-in-waiting.

"'Use' implies some scheme, some forethought. I was simply an amusement to him. 'Get the cit's daughter to go for a stroll behind the conservatory...' I thought he and I were courting. He was probably winning a wager or merely passing an idle quarter hour."

"A quarter hour." Three more words that summoned an arctic wind of judgment. Whyever...?

How many quarter hours did Mr. Dorning regard as adequate for the same pursuits? How many *hours*?

"Titus Merriman beat that record," Lissa said, determined that Mr. Dorning hear the extent of her folly from her first. "We were most definitely courting. He'd asked Mama's permission, and the solicitors were negotiating. I wasn't about to make the same mistake twice, but I did exactly that."

Lissa had tormented herself with the past, reviewing every conversation and glance, always looking for the exact moment when she'd tossed caution aside. A tactical blunder dissected was one that could be avoided in future.

"I forbid..." Mr. Dorning stopped walking and stared at the distant gateposts while the breeze teased at the lace of his cravat. "You *must not* blame yourself. You trusted that assurances of respect and affection were honestly offered, not lies meant to manipulate you. The scurrilous behavior of a pair of randy jackanapes is no fault of yours."

Lissa stood in the middle of the road, savoring those words. She had needed for somebody to absolve her of responsibility, or at least ease the burden, and yet, she was to blame as well. *Fool me once...*

"Men lie, Mr. Dorning. Sometimes to be kind, sometimes to keep the peace, and sometimes for their own benefit. I know this now, and I will not forget it. Papa told us he was merely suffering a little head cold. He was dead two weeks later. Gavin claimed to be jaunting off to Oxford to meet some old school chums. One doesn't pack a full trunk to nip up the road for a weekend gathering. One doesn't send that trunk on and hire a livery hack for the journey when one could take the family coach and have shelter from the elements."

Mr. Dorning took off his hat and ran a hand through blond hair. "Do you know these friends he was supposedly meeting?"

"I'd been introduced to one. Peter Cleverly's parents own a lot of land around Reading, and he and Gavin shared a passion for Restoration comedies."

Mr. Dorning tapped his hat back onto his head. "Did they share a passion for each other?"

As awkward as the question was, to leave Charles and Titus in the conversational dust was a relief. "I doubt it. Gavin made a nuisance of himself to the serving maids at the Arms. I suspect he was smitten with Tansy Pevinger for a time—all the young fellows are—and I know he had flirtations with various landladies and so forth at university."

"One proclivity does not necessarily exclude the other." Trevor Dorning could say that—polite words aimed at shocking facts—and sound merely considering.

"Cleverly married the daughter of some fellow who owns a dozen coaching inns. Gavin is godfather to their firstborn, though that also proves nothing." Lissa walked on, the better to gather her thoughts. "We've considered that Gavin might have formed a mésalliance, married or loved inappropriately. We have no evidence to support that supposition."

Mr. Dorning fell in beside her and offered his arm. Lissa took it, though she was perfectly capable of walking without assistance.

"I meant what I said, Amaryllis. You are impressively confident, competent, and self-possessed, but that doesn't mean you should have to carry every burden on your own."

He'd left out *capable*, though he'd said that too. "Mama is at her wit's end. Grandmama is fading. Diana and Caroline are children. To whom should I surrender my burdens?"

"Don't *surrender* them to anybody, but you might share them with friends, mightn't you? I have contacts on the Continent, mostly in the wine-growing regions, but also the occasional factor in the capitals. I can make inquiries regarding one Gavin DeWitt. What does he look like?"

"I'll give you a sketch. He looks like a cross between me and Caroline with Diana's brown hair. An intelligent face and a winsome smile. Tall, athletic, graceful. In any amateur theatrical, he always played the dashing hero."

Gavin was playing the villain now, did he but know it, but how lovely to be able to discuss Gavin even more honestly than Lissa did with Phillip. How lovely that Mr. Dorning again offered to help rather than try to dominate the situation with his infallible male judgment.

"I meant those other things I said, too, Amaryllis."

"I'm capable." A solid, simple word that encompassed much pride.

"And you are magnificent and dear. Merriman and Brompton were idiots to abuse your trust. I won't call them out, only because they were also unfathomably dim-witted to let you slip through their fingers. One cannot pity them—they didn't deserve your trust—but one can leave howling bunglers to their miserable fates."

"Charles will be an earl." Mama would have been so happy being his mother-in-law. "Titus has been restored to good-catch status. His older brother shows no signs of marrying, and he'll likely end up with a title too."

"Merriman will wed some ambitious twit whose uncle is a banker. She will pretend to adore him in public, while in private pleading a megrim six nights out of seven. They will be desperately miserable, because that viscountcy means they must somehow muddle through those seventh nights for years to come. Their lives will be a purgatory of public manners and personal frustration. Trust me on this. I saw the same pattern in my father's marriages."

Lissa considered Mr. Dorning's words, spoken with even more weight and conviction than he brought to most of what he said. The union he described was... bleak. Worse even than Lissa had imagined when she'd packed up her dancing slippers and attempted to take Mayfair by storm last year.

"You are telling me I had two near misses." Not blunders, not disasters, not missteps. Near misses, and Mr. Dorning seemed very sure of his conclusion.

"Precisely. Near misses. Brushes with disaster, and thank the merciful powers you are unscathed."

"My reputation got a bit scathed." Lissa wasn't ruined—Titus and Charles would blot their own copybooks if they were too specific in their innuendo—but she hadn't *taken* either.

"Nor is your trust unscathed," Mr. Dorning replied, "but your heart remains whole. Take courage from that and be proud of your fortitude."

She wanted to kiss him, to know the feel of his embrace, to lose herself in Trevor Dorning's boundless confidence, competence, and capability. His kisses would be delightful, his hands marvelous.

That way lay mischief and foolishness, and Lissa was not at all sure she'd escape with her heart whole. She was attracted to Mr. Dorning when she'd thought no man could ever tempt her in that direction, but she was also...

Smitten? The word felt too giddy, too irrational. Trevor Dorning offered something Lissa hadn't thought to find, ever, in a man or elsewhere. Aside from his inconvenient physical allure, he was part champion, part confidant, part companion, which all added up to... *friendship*.

At some point in the past twenty yards, Lissa had slipped her hand into his, and he'd given her fingers a light squeeze without breaking stride or remarking her presumption.

To walk hand in hand with Trevor Dorning, merely that, was dear and magnificent and gave Lissa much to think about.

How glorious to have a friend, and how awful to know he would soon be lost to her.

CHAPTER EIGHT

"You told these fine folk that you are Trevor *Dorning?*" Sycamore Dorning paced the confines of Trevor's private parlor, his boots thumping a tattoo that echoed in Trevor's skull. "I am torn between horror and hilarity. The name is respected, of course, but you lack our lovely eyes, you are blond, you are all Frenchified and lordly, and not half impecunious enough to be a bachelor Dorning. Whatever were you thinking?"

"I was thinking," Trevor said *quietly,* "to enjoy some anonymity, which I will cease to do if you continue to shout my particulars to the rafters. If I'd come to look over these properties as Lord Tavistock, nobody would have been honest with me. As it is, I wish the fine folk had been a little less truthful."

"I seldom shout." Sycamore toed off one dusty boot, then the other. "Jeanette says raising my voice is unbecoming of my station and ought to be kept in reserve for truly vexatious situations involving at least three of my siblings at once."

"You were nigh crying the watch." Trevor stationed himself at the window overlooking the green. "The Arms is considered the rival of the churchyard for collecting gossip. Crosspatch Corners is a close-knit community, and any suspicions you raise will make the rounds before sunset." *If they haven't already.*

Dorning tossed himself into a chair by the hearth. Even travel-worn and rumpled, he exuded style and a certain... Dorning-ness that Trevor envied.

"You have become an expert on this village in three days?"

"Villages, be they English, French, German, or otherwise, have the same basic attributes if the place is in good working order. The denizens close ranks against outsiders and live in each other's pockets. I don't know how it is with brothers and sisters, but I suspect a village is like a big family. Half exasperating, half wonderful."

Like Miss Amaryllis DeWitt was half exasperating and half wonderful, though the feel of her hand in Trevor's had surpassed even wonderful and left magnificent sitting in a dazed heap by the side of a thoroughfare leading to breathtaking destinations.

"Do go on," Sycamore said, propping his stockinged feet on a hassock. "I have a mere eight siblings, well, nine and counting if we bend the rules a bit. They each bring in-laws into the picture, and I'm an uncle a dozen times over. Pray enlighten me about the qualities of a family life."

Trevor would rather smack dear Sycamore, though the man was wicked fast with his fists and carried more knives than he had siblings.

"Using an alias was nearly unavoidable," Trevor said. "Admittedly, I should have chosen something other than Jeanette's married name."

"Which is also my name, the Earl of Casriel's family name. The name of the increasingly famous Hampshire portraitist, the successful children's author, the renowned trainer of canines who—"

"Pour l'amour de Dieu, ferme ta bouche."

"If you must tell me to shut my mouth—*en français*—at least address me politely."

"I will politely dunk you in the Twid if you let on in any fashion that I am a peer. Lord Tavistock is universally reviled in Crosspatch, and for good reasons."

Sycamore leaned back his head and closed his eyes. "His lordship never bothered to check on the chickens, for one thing, and when he should mince about, dispensing repairs and new breeding rams, he instead lurks behind the Dorning name, sneaking about the hedgerows."

"I'm too blessed tall, blond, and well dressed to sneak anywhere. I learned that in France. What, by the way, brought you to this bucolic little Eden just as Town is preparing for the annual madness?"

"My instincts bring me here, and I trust them utterly. Why do the locals dislike you, beyond the obvious?"

Trevor lowered himself to the window seat. "What obvious? I am certain I forbade the solicitors to raise rents before I left for France. I also directed them to mind the repairs, but plain English clearly defied their comprehension."

Dorning, eyes still closed, crossed his feet at the ankles. "Say on. You've inspected your properties and found them approaching ruin?"

"I haven't managed inspections. I'm supposedly looking for a small estate where I can perfect my beer-making skills." Though there was less and less *supposedly* about it. Why not? Why not brew up the best beer John Bull had ever tasted and offer it to him at an affordable price? Why not bring the same dedication and science to making beer that had for centuries been brought to the making of wine?

"Every butler and housekeeper knows how to make beer," Sycamore said. "Every estate has its own little distillery or shares one with the neighbors. *I* know how to make beer, more or less, and you already own thousands of acres. Besides, I thought your passion was wine."

The less talk of passion, the better. "The Continental climate offers better conditions for growing wine grapes, but we do a solid job by our grains here, and *everybody*—duchesses, dressmakers, dancers, drummers, and drovers—enjoys a good beer. *Dornings* enjoy a good beer."

"That, we do. You see a larger British market for beer than wine and without any importation bother, but the beer market is also crowded."

"Correct, thus one must distinguish one's product by its quality and affordability, as the winemakers long since learned to do, but all this has no bearing on why I came to Crosspatch Corners."

"By the time I'm fast asleep, you will surely get around to that part."

Trevor was tempted to kick Dorning's feet off the hassock, but a braver, more honest part of him admitted that he was glad to see a familiar face. Sycamore did have formidable intuition, and he was formidably well connected too.

"I've made the acquaintance of the DeWitt family," Trevor said. "They are my tenants at Twidboro Hall. Got myself invited to tea, had a casual look around the public rooms. The repairs are behind by several years, and the DeWitts are a household of women. The scion of the house went missing some two years ago, and the family finances are growing muddled."

"Damsels in distress are notorious for having muddled finances," Sycamore observed, settling lower against the cushions. "Not their most endearing trait."

"The DeWitt ladies haven't the authority to muddle their own finances—lest we forget that detail—and the news grows worse. They have been warned that the rent will go up this autumn, and I have given no instructions to raise any rents. The peace created all manner of economic havoc, then the harvests were thin. The DeWitts have been good tenants, Twidboro Hall is home to them, and yet... I cannot trust my solicitors, Dorning. Lark's Nest, by contrast, is occupied by a Mr. Phillip Heyward, though my solicitors forgot to include Lark's Nest on my list of holdings. The dwelling is older and more modest, also in better repair than Twidboro, with which it shares a property line."

"You suspect Smithers and Purvis of taking advantage of the DeWitt ladies?"

Trevor rose, turned, and stared across the shadows lengthening on the green. St. Nebo's leaky roof was on display in the fading light, standing seam tin grown rusty over most of its surface. A roof took years to yield to the elements like that.

"I suspect the solicitors are preying on the ladies and other vulnerable tenants, which is to say, the weasels are taking advantage of me."

"And?" Sycamore was the picture of masculine repose, eyes closed, hands folded on his flat belly.

"*Why* does Purvis think he can play skittles with a marquess's money? Yes, he knew me when I was a lad, but I'm clearly not a lad, and thanks to Jeanette, I'm not stupid. Gullible, but not stupid."

"But you are worried?"

Down on the green, Mr. Dabney got into a discussion with Tansy Pevinger at the pilgrim's cross. Tansy busied herself lifting the spent daffodils from a pot, gathering them into her apron. Dabney lent a hand, digging bulbs out of the second pot.

"Something in Crosspatch Corners is amiss," Trevor said. "The DeWitts are desperately hoping to make a socially advantageous match for their eldest daughter, because without a son or father on hand, their money is kept from their reach. If Miss DeWitt can marry up, that situation is likely to improve. The ladies should not have to scheme to ensure access to their own pin money. The vicar claims to have dunned me ceaselessly for a new roof, but I've never received a single letter from him. Phillip Heyward is the next thing to a recluse, though his knowledge of agriculture is exhaustive."

"All very interesting," Sycamore said around a yawn, "but I thought every self-respecting English village had a requisite number of eccentrics. Drunks who can foretell the future, white witches, ponies that do math, that sort of thing. A recluse and a dissembling vicar aren't so far from the norm, are they?"

"Smithers and Purvis handle the DeWitts' business, and Heyward was my maternal grandmother's maiden name."

Sycamore opened his eyes, and Trevor was struck again by that peculiar amethyst hue unique to the Dornings. Amaryllis's grand-mother had known about those eyes. What else had she noticed about Mr. Trevor Dorning, and when she would mention her suspicions to Amaryllis?

"You took a *nom de guerre*," Sycamore said, "and now you are seeing false monikers everywhere. Heyward is a fine old English name, the origins having something to do with a protected enclosure. What of it?"

How would Sycamore know that? But then, his handsome head was stuffed with obscure information and strange facts, just as his knives were secreted about his person in unlikely locations.

"Heyward has a portrait of my mother in his parlor," Trevor said. "I about fell on my arse when I saw it. The likeness is wonderful. She's young, pretty, and happy in that likeness. The painting might well be something Heyward retrieved from the attics—my family has owned the house for centuries—but Heyward also stood in the woods watching me for a good hour yesterday. When he and I were properly introduced this morning, he made no mention of it."

Dorning sat up. "He *watched you* for an hour?"

"Stood so still I thought the birds would perch on his shoulders. I tossed pebbles into the Twid and waited for him to show himself. He never did, though at that point, we hadn't been introduced. He was there, hidden in shadows, and then he wasn't. Why do that?"

"I used to sit in trees and spy on my brothers," Sycamore said, rising and rubbing his backside with both hands. "They never did anything that merited a solid hour of my attention, though they got up to some fascinating mischief. I learned a lot, sitting in trees, and not about how to toss pebbles into streams. This Heyward person bothers you."

Amaryllis DeWitt bothered Trevor more. "And I apparently unsettle him, though we conversed with astonishing amiability for nearly an hour over tea. Miss DeWitt says he reads voraciously but never leaves the Crosspatch Corners neighborhood."

"Until recently, most of Britain's villagers never strayed far from the home patch, unless they joined the military. What else does Miss DeWitt say?"

Trevor was not about to stroll into that ambush. "Darkness is falling. The inn has a worthy kitchen, and all this country air has me famished. Shall we eat in the common, or ask for the private dining room?"

"Wherever we eat," Sycamore said, resuming his seat and pulling on his boots, "you will tell me about your Miss DeWitt. Unless I'm much mistaken, Trevor *Dorning* has turned her head, and from what I've heard—assuming this is Miss Amaryllis DeWitt—she does not suffer fools, and I doubt she's very keen on liars either."

A surmountable problem. The situation wanted a bit of strategy and timing, was all. "How soon will you be returning to London?"

Dorning smiled the smile that Jeanette, for reasons Trevor would never understand, found so charming.

"I have all the time in the world to enjoy the—what did you call it?—fresh country air, and I would not think of returning to London without you."

I was afraid of that. "You must suit yourself, of course, though I'm sure Jeanette will miss you. London's loss is Berkshire's gain. Please recall that for as long as you bide here, I am a distant cousin. Very distant. We are cordial. Perhaps you are on your way down to the family seat in Dorset?"

"I'm here to discuss investing in your beer venture. Have you done any budgets yet?"

Trevor had, as a matter of fact, while rambling out to Lark's Nest and trying to push the image of Amaryllis DeWitt, tall, laughing, and lovely, into the farthest corner of his mind.

With no success whatsoever.

"We can discuss budgets over supper." Trevor donned his jacket and ran a comb through his hair. "If you were a young man surrounded by female family, adulthood breathing down your neck, no real interest in your father's legacy, and even less interest in stepping into his shoes, where would you hide?"

Sycamore was for once not smiling. "I'm told one can hide on the Continent for years at a time and for very little coin."

Trevor did not punch him, did not even smack him, though the temptation was nigh overwhelming.

~

Phillip waved the red handkerchief Lissa had brought for the purpose once, twice, and on the third wave, he dropped it.

"Go, you ruddy bugger!" Sycamore Dorning shouted as Trevor, whom Lissa privately distinguished from his London cousin as *my* Mr. Dorning, gave Roland his head.

Horse and rider made a dashing sight, racing along the Twid as wisps of mist rose from the water and morning sun slanted along the hard-packed path. Songbirds fell silent as Roland thundered closer, and some small creature bolted away into the bracken.

Roland was moving so quickly that his individual hoofbeats blurred into a sort of vibration on the ground, and less than a minute later, he was streaking past Lissa and Phillip, Trevor crouched close to his neck.

"Beast has odd form," Phillip said as Trevor slowed Roland to a canter and then to a trot. "Not many horses run with their heads that low."

"Eclipse did," Lissa retorted. "He won a race or two in his day."

"Eclipse?"

Lissa was reminded that Phillip, for all he could prose on about manure and marling, had gaps in his gentlemanly vocabulary.

"Eclipse was a thoroughbred sire who retired undefeated after eighteen starts. Nobody would compete against him by that point, so he was put out to stud and died at the venerable age of twenty-four in 1789. I wonder if Roland comes from that line."

Roland looked pleased with himself, trotting along the riverbank, and Trevor looked... magnificent and dear, also windblown, ruddy-cheeked, and exhilarated. He'd passed Lissa his hat before taking his place at the starting line half a mile on, and the morning sun loved those golden, tousled tresses.

Drat the man, he looked eminently kissable.

"Time?" he called, which sent Roland skittering sideways. "Settle, silly boy." The affection in Trevor's voice, if not his competence in the saddle, had Roland recalling his manners.

Phillip looked at the pocket watch in his hand. "Forty-eight seconds, maybe a hair more."

Trevor patted the horse's sweaty neck. "You're sure this is a half-mile course?"

"Dabney swears it is," Lissa said. "Is that a fast time?"

Trevor nodded. "He's carrying a lot of weight, he's not been conditioned, and it's a mere hop by racing standards, but put some strength and stamina on him, and he'll be formidable."

"Time?" Sycamore Dorning asked, trotting up from the starting line on a handsome bay.

"Fifty-two seconds for the half mile," Lissa said.

Sycamore Dorning looked to Trevor. "Fifty-two seconds. You're sure?"

Phillip passed up the watch. Dorning peered at it, then handed it back. "How much do you want for that colt, Miss DeWitt? One of my brothers is the best animal trainer in the land. Willow prefers to work with dogs, but he's no slouch with horses or even ravens. We Dornings are countrymen at heart and know how to bring a beast along so he can grow into his speed. Roland would have the best care and spend his days doing what he clearly loves to do."

Trevor seemed amused at this offer, while Lissa was annoyed. "Are you always so impulsive, Mr. Dorning?"

"I know what I saw, Miss DeWitt. Heyward had no reason to keep inaccurate time. True, the horse is largish and runs with irregular form, and he'd be getting a late start, but that colt can cover ground."

Lissa expected either Phillip or Trevor to respond to those observations. Trevor let Roland amble in a wide circle around the finish line, and Phillip had lapsed into one of his characteristic silences.

"Eclipse was largish," she said, "and ran with irregular form— the same irregular form Roland apparently prefers when his rider has the confidence to yield the reins. Any number of champions haven't started racing until they were four or five years old. Be that as it may, you cannot buy that horse from me, because I don't own him. My brother does, and Gavin has expressed no wish to sell Roland."

"What about a lease?" Mr. Dorning asked as Roland snatched at the grass along the towpath. "A long-term lease. I tell you, Miss DeWitt, that colt is going to waste here in the shires. He has potential."

"Desist," Trevor said, swinging from the saddle and loosening the girth. "You are attempting to talk business with a lady before breakfast. Bad form."

Sycamore looked tempted to persist with negotiations, which inclined Lissa to think poorly of him. Not only was it bad form to talk business with a lady before breakfast, it was worse form to argue with her at any hour of the day

"I thought..." Phillip stashed his watch into his jacket pocket. "Rather, I had hoped..."

He wasn't blushing, but he was staring hard at the dark surface of the Twid, which he'd likely seen every day of his life.

"Phillip?" Lissa murmured.

"I can offer breakfast," Phillip said, "should anybody care for some food. Nothing fancy, but... I can offer breakfast."

If Sycamore Dorning was impulsive, Phillip was the soul of deliberation. He'd spend three years considering whether a field ought to be switched from oats to barley and then take two more growing seasons to swap the field one half at a time. He'd dither all the while over the wisdom of the change, measuring and recording the resulting crops to the ounce.

Phillip was cautious to the point of peculiarity, and while he might occasionally trot out a tea tray for a caller, he had never, in Lissa's memory, entertained guests for a meal.

"I'm famished," Trevor said, "and I can truthfully say that Sycamore Dorning's appetite is legendary. Takes his sustenance very seriously, don't you, Dorning?"

"I do," Sycamore replied, "and breakfast is one of my eleven favorite meals of the day. To horse, Heyward, Miss DeWitt. We have eggs and toast to vanquish."

"I'll walk with Roland and his jockey," Lissa said. "You and Phillip can go ahead. If I recall correctly, Mr. Dorning has market gardens on a Richmond property, Phillip. Quiz him about medicinals and spices, why don't you?"

A gleam came into Phillip's eye. "Market gardens require a fair amount of labor."

"And manure," Sycamore said, his bonhomie fading. "Tons of seasoned horse manure if we're lucky. Are you much in the vegetable line, Mr. Heyward?"

Phillip mounted his gray, collected Jacques, and disappeared in the morning mist with Sycamore, their voices trailing behind them.

"Who knew that aging horse manure is as much an art as aging brandy?" Trevor said, stuffing his riding gloves into a pocket and offering his arm to Lissa.

He was being gentlemanly, the wretch. Lissa took his free hand, glad in her bones that she'd removed her gloves when she'd dismounted.

"Sycamore Dorning annoys me," she said, getting a firm hold on Trevor's hand. "I doubt I've stood up with him. I'd recall that too-charming smile, those too-knowing eyes, though his height would have appealed to me in a dancing partner. He's probably a decent fellow beneath all the bluster, but he's a bit much for Crosspatch first thing in the day."

Roland was content to plod along behind them, and Lissa was acutely aware that in London, this little gathering would never have taken place. She might hack out in the morning in a crowded park, her mother or some other matron along to chaperone, a groom one horse-length back, and all of Society watching to ensure that she didn't converse too familiarly with any gentlemen even on horseback.

She would have no opportunity to hold hands with a fellow to whom she wasn't engaged, no chance to speak her mind to him in private unless he was proposing to her. For her to hold his hat while he walked along bareheaded would have caused gossip.

"Sycamore has a fear of being ignored," Trevor said. "He's the youngest of seven sons, and his two sisters commanded attention by virtue of their novelty. For years, he was the smallest, the least skilled, the least educated. He struggles now to remind himself that he's not seven years old and watching his brothers gain inches of height each year while he is still sitting atop the atlas at table. For the most part, I like him, and I respect him."

"You understand him. Why is that, I wonder, when you and he are of different stations?"

The question was simple enough, but Trevor took his time answering. "I have no legitimate siblings, and the one possible half-brother—raised as a cousin—has, like Gavin, taken French leave. Maybe a poverty of siblings makes me sympathetic to a man with so much family. Sycamore loves them, but he sometimes doesn't know what to do with them."

Trevor had given the matter of Sycamore Dorning some thought. Lissa had given a different topic extended consideration.

"I want to kiss you, sir."

He didn't drop her hand, didn't step away and announce a sudden need to return to London. He didn't sweep her into his arms either, and he was too substantial for even Amaryllis to sweep him anywhere.

"Why, mademoiselle? I'm just a fellow passing through, for all you know. A gentleman of modest means with a modest dream."

Why kiss him? Because he was patient with everybody—Caroline, Diana, Mama, the fractious horse, Sycamore Dorning... Because he wasn't demanding Town manners on a Crosspatch bridle path. Because he held hands without assuming he was welcome to go buccaneering beneath Lissa's skirts.

Though he probably was. She was still mentally sorting that out.

"Sycamore Dorning," Lissa said, "assumes that a quiet country life, for horse or human, is not to be compared with the glamor of worldly success and Town life. If I'm keeping my Dornings straight, he owns some fancy club in London and takes a keen interest in it, despite his claims to be a countryman at heart. You say his Richmond property is a wonder, where—skirting the acceptable limits of agricultural wealth—he grows everything from tomatoes to tarragon..."

"He wasn't trying to insult you, Amaryllis. He's just... Sometimes Sycamore doesn't think before he speaks."

"His view, that the shires are synonymous with boredom and obscurity, was all too often expressed to me overtly last year. Wasn't I delighted to get away from Berkshire, which is far more beautiful to me than any manicured London park could ever be? Wasn't I lucky *at my age* to be dragged from all I love to wear uncomfortable fashions and stay up all night drinking dreadful punch? What is *wrong* with those people, that they criticize the way of life that makes their frolicking and fashion possible? Does Mr. Dorning think his precious horse manure falls from the sky?"

One corner of Trevor's mouth twitched. "Will you kiss me for revenge on all the fops and dandies and matchmakers?"

Oh, maybe that had something to do with it, but not much. "If I kiss you, it will be because, on this lovely, rural spring morning, I'm in the company of a man I esteem, I'm in good spirits, and I am honest enough to admit an attraction. Does that make me a strumpet?"

The hint of amusement died in his eyes. "Of course not. It makes you honest, and possessed of good taste in kissing partners, but, Amaryllis, you barely know me."

That he'd remind her to stop and think, to be sure of her course, made Lissa that much more confident of her feelings for him.

"I've spent more time in your exclusive company than I ever did with..." She refused to mention her near misses by name. "I know you well enough, Trevor Dorning, and I also know that in five minutes, Tansy Pevinger will come down that path, swinging her egg basket and humming the Sumer Canon, though summer won't be a-coming in for months. Lawrence Miller knows by her tune whether she's alone or not, and he'll be lurking just this side of the mill. I also know that in the next minute..."

"Yes?"

"I will lose my nerve and feel foolish, and, Trevor, I am tired to my boots of feeling foolish."

He drew her off to the side of the path. "The only fool in this company would be me, if I denied us what we both long for."

He took his top hat from her and settled it on her head, then regarded her with a seriousness that brought the moment to a still point. The robins offering an aria to the new day, the sun touching all with slanting light, the peaceful murmur of the Twid burbling toward the sea...

So lovely and so different from a dimly lit ballroom stinking of sweat, perfume, and beeswax, so quiet and peaceful. No matchmakers, no hovering chaperones, no—

No *thinking*, as Trevor's bare hand cradled Lissa's jaw, and his thumb brushed over her cheek. She closed her eyes and purely reveled in the sunrise of yearning pouring through her.

"God help me," Trevor muttered before pressing his mouth gently to first one cheek, then the other. He grazed his nose along her eyebrows—a ridiculous caress—but intimate and sweet. By the time he touched his lips to Lissa's, she was wrapped around him and oblivious to anything save the need to be closer.

His kisses were deceptive, easy at first, but by degrees bolder, until Lissa offered him a dare with her tongue, and he met that challenge and swept her off into realms of adventure that suggested her near misses had been... blundering, bumbling, bungling *nincompoops*.

Trevor had called them dim-witted, and he'd been right.

Lissa eased free of Trevor's mouth, too pleased and stunned to bear more. "I was right," she said, hands fisted on his lapels. "I was right. Kissing you is right, and I *knew* it would be."

He held her loosely, though he seemed a trifle winded. "You know something. I envy you that. I don't know what day of the week it is. I suspect that if you let me go, I'll topple onto my backside."

"Likewise, I'm sure."

They stood, hugging each other and hugging the moment and all its wonder close, until Roland nudged at Lissa's arm.

"He probably hears Tansy coming," Lissa said, stepping back to pat the horse's neck. "Good boy, Roland."

She expected Trevor to aid her struggle to regain her composure by offering his arm and taking up the subject of, say, the ideal soil for growing hops or whether coffee, tea, or chocolate went best with eggs and toast.

Instead, he offered his hand, and Lissa took it, and that aided her heart to commence dreaming in all sorts of marvelous directions. She even forgot to hand Trevor back his hat until they were standing in Phillip's foyer, and Phillip himself took the hat from her head.

CHAPTER NINE

Breakfast for Trevor was an ordeal and a delight. While Sycamore and Phillip chattered on about holy basil and horse manure, Trevor ate—he had no idea what—and alternately castigated himself for kissing Amaryllis and yearned to repeat his folly at greater length.

Amaryllis sat across from him, looking serene and delectable, nibbling toast, and sipping tea as if nothing momentous had happened on that towpath.

Trevor, for his part, had endured three cataclysms. First, the barrowful of lies he had to shovel aside had turned into a barge-load of untruths. His previous dissembling, at least as an adult, had been limited to white lies told to preserve somebody's dignity. His aptitude for dishonesty had apparently blossomed, and that bothered him terribly.

Second, he'd kissed a pretty lady.

He'd kissed many pretty ladies, and more than a few had kissed him, but not... not *like that*. Not as if the heavens were shaken, the earth had moved, and the very seasons had paused in their march, all to wake him up, mind, soul, and—very much—body, to a state of awareness that... that...

Amaryllis had kissed him witless. Trevor hoped he'd returned the favor with interest.

Third, he'd lost his heart, and if anybody had told him that the fabled *coup de foudre* was more than fable, he'd have politely smiled and changed the subject. Lightning strikes were a regular and documented element of weather in most corners of the realm, and on the Continent too. He'd do well to remember that.

The sight of Amaryllis in the sharp morning light, his hat perched on her head, determination shining from her eyes... Determination to share a sweet moment not with the wealthy, titled peer, but with the common man who relished a dawn gallop on a lively colt, with the same fellow who understood why Sycamore Dorning could feel invisible while topping six feet, dropping bons mots, and turning heads.

Trevor had lost his heart, and his wits, and that made airing the truth with Amaryllis all the more imperative.

"Jam?" Phillip said, offering the lady a little ceramic pot with a cluster of berries painted into the glaze. "This is from the batch you put up in autumn, raspberry with the last of the cherries."

"The lady needs butter for her toast if she's eschewing the eggs," Sycamore said, passing over the butter dish.

Phillip's table was small, and yet, dining alone, meal after meal, it probably felt too large. Trevor hadn't realized the kindness Jeanette had done him when she'd insisted that he take his meals with her after Papa's death.

"Would you care for some eggs, Miss DeWitt?" Trevor asked. "I've served myself more than I should have."

"A few bites." Amaryllis held out her plate. "The morning air has given me an appetite."

God help me. God help me. Trevor effected the transfer while Sycamore pretended to stir honey into a cup of tea, and Phillip poured himself more tea.

"Where is your brother, Miss DeWitt?" Sycamore asked. "If he's Roland's owner, I want to have a word with him."

Sycamore was interested in the horse, but he was also, Sycamore-fashion, stirring up trouble.

"Gavin is traveling," Amaryllis said, taking a bite of eggs. "Has been for some months. When next we hear from him, I will forward word of your interest in Roland, but truly, Mr. Dorning, I doubt you have a prayer of owning that colt."

"Then I'd like to put some mares to him. Spring is upon us, now is the time, and all that. Instead of investing in a beer venture, I can make a fortune with a racing stud."

"And is that your definition of a successful life?" Trevor asked, crossing knife and fork over a now empty plate. "Turn a spare coin at every opportunity?"

Trevor's father had certainly been concerned with coin—and with the self-indulgence that saw so much of that coin spent.

"My family is vast," Sycamore said, "as you well know, sir. By the time we get all the nephews educated and the nieces dowered, the pensioners looked after, and the cottages repaired, no coin of mine will consider itself spare. Is there any more cream on the table?"

Phillip set the cream pot by Sycamore's elbow. "Will you invest in Mr. Trevor Dorning's beer venture? He's taking a rather scientific approach to the matter. I admire that."

Heyward spoke quietly and without the thread of pugnacity Sycamore so often defaulted to. The support was even more effective for being rendered in polite tones.

"Science is all well and good," Sycamore replied. "My father was quite the botanical investigator, but intuition and imagination should also receive due respect."

"I agree with Mr. Sycamore Dorning," Amaryllis said, finishing her eggs. "Science can be so many excuses for a ruthless parody of reason that ignores all but the most convenient evidence. There is no evidence, for example, that girls are less intelligent than boys—and plenty of evidence to the contrary—and yet, as Mr. Sycamore Dorning notes, it's only the men who get the education, and thus only men who define what constitutes science and decide where that science will poke its nose."

Phillip groaned, Sycamore's brows drew down, and Trevor saluted with his tea cup.

"If you must hoist me on my own petard," Sycamore said, "then please do call me Sycamore, or Cam, as my friends do. With this fellow at table,"—he gestured in Trevor's direction—"we'll be Dorning'd to death ere we rise."

"If we were in London..." Amaryllis began.

"We're not," Trevor said, "and if this presuming bounder is your new bosom bow Cam, then I am Trevor." He wanted Amaryllis calling him by name not only for the bold familiarity of it, but also for the honesty. He was no sort of Dorning, but in very friendly company —say, when private with Jeanette—he was still Trevor.

Though even she had taken to milording him.

When every crumb of food had been consumed and the teapot was empty, Trevor rose. "Thank you, Heyward, for a fine meal and for rousing yourself at an early hour to indulge in a lark. Might I trouble you for a tour of the house? I do enjoy these old Tudor dowagers. They stand the test of time for the most part, and you've taken good care of this one."

"I've seen the house," Amaryllis said, getting to her feet. "If you gentlemen will excuse me, I'll collect Jacques and be on my way."

"Nonsense," Sycamore said, coming around the table. "You showed Trevor half the shire, I'm told. You can tolerate my company on the hack back to Twidboro Hall. You might not need the escort, but I suspect we will enjoy a lively conversation about the rights of women, Miss DeWitt."

That was Trevor's cue to elbow Sycamore aside, though being Sycamore, he'd not yield without a verbal tussle, and Amaryllis and Heyward would witness the whole stupid exchange.

"Any of the three of us would enjoy seeing you home, Miss DeWitt," Trevor said. "Choose your escort, and we will graciously yield to your decision."

Amaryllis crooked her finger at Sycamore. "Come along, sir. Mr. Heyward and Mr. Trevor Dorning will get into a fascinating discussion about oak beams and thatching methods. You and I will spare them an audience."

Damn and blast, though Amaryllis had chosen the best course. If Trevor was to properly inspect Lark's Nest, he didn't want Sycamore underfoot causing trouble.

He also didn't want to let Amaryllis out of his sight, but now was not the time to burden her with awkward revelations.

"We'll see you off," Heyward said, leading the procession to the front terrace.

The sun had gained strength, and the day was making a good bid to be mild, if not warm. Trevor wanted nothing so much as to spend the whole of it walking hand in hand with Amaryllis, talking with her, and kissing her. That the kissing was only a complement to the talking and hand-holding gave him pause, in a good way.

"A leg up, if you please," Amaryllis said, taking Trevor's arm. "Jacques is wonderfully steady, but Lark's Nest is in want of a ladies' mounting block."

Sycamore was blessedly occupied with the stirrups and girth on his own horse, and that gave Trevor a moment to...

Whisper something witty and endearing, though nothing inspired came to mind.

Arrange another private walk by the Twid, though how did one do that?

He boosted Amaryllis into the saddle and got her skirts sorted out while she took up the reins.

"I hope we meet again soon, Mr. Dorning."

"I will sustain myself with the same ambition, Miss DeWitt. Don't be too hard on Sycamore. Whatever else is true, he means well."

"Thus do all busybodies excuse their meddling." She clucked to Jacques, who ambled down the drive at a placid walk. Sycamore steered his mount beside Jacques, and Trevor watched a piece of his heart disappear around the bend.

Au revoir, ma chérie.

"Here," Heyward said, passing over a square of red silk. "You can return that to Lissa for me."

Or Heyward could have passed it to her at any time in the previous hour and a half. "This is her handkerchief?"

"What use would I have for a red silk frippery, Dorning? Come along, and you can pretend to marvel at my humble abode."

Heyward *knew.* He at least knew that Trevor and Amaryllis had been kissing—the blasted hat had given that much away—and he might well know more than that.

"Your humble abode looks to be in excellent repair," Trevor said some thirty minutes later.

Heyward had taken him not quite from the attics to the pantries, but through all the public rooms and into the cellars. The kitchen was an old-fashioned half-sunken marvel of vaulted stonework with a hearth large enough for a man to stand in upright.

"I keep after it," Heyward said, twisting off a few leaves of mint from a potted specimen in the windowsill over the copper sink. "I do, after all, spend most of my time on my own property."

"I haven't spent enough time on my property," Trevor said as the mint filled the kitchen with a pungent aroma. "Why don't you rely on your landlord to manage the repairs?" That was the law—the landlord alone had the right and responsibility to maintain his asset.

Heyward crushed the mint between his palms and tossed it into a pot of water simmering over the coals in the hearth. "I do as I please here. Were you doing as you pleased with Miss DeWitt?"

Heyward moved around the kitchen not like the lord of the manor, which he was, but like the head stable lad come in for a pint between chores.

"The boot was on the other foot," Trevor said. "Miss DeWitt made up her mind that I was worthy of her notice, and she has certainly earned my esteem."

Heyward's smile was fleeting and sweet. "Good for Lissa, then, but mind your step, Dorning. Lissa did not have an easy time of it in London, and now Mourna is determined to drag her back there. I have only the one strong arm, but if you forget your manners where the DeWitts are concerned, you'll learn that I have strength enough to cause you a few regrets."

"Thank heavens somebody is bestirring himself to make threats on the ladies' behalf. Where the hell has the brother got off to?"

The smile came again, this time bringing with it a fleeting hint of familiarity. Somebody else Trevor knew smiled like that, a private amusement given momentary expression. A little mischievous, a little rueful... That smile was charming, implying goodwill in the face of life's many conundrums.

Heyward led the way up the steps and took Trevor to the parlor where Amaryllis had presided over the tea tray the previous day.

"Gavin DeWitt was discontent in Crosspatch," Heyward said, gesturing for Trevor to take the chair nearest the fire. "He had no interest in managing the family business, which I gather is actually a network of businesses. The lot is run by competent managers, from what I can tell. Gavin would have been in the way, and worse, he would have directly associated himself with the shop, when his grandmother and parents were dedicated to distancing him from it."

Amaryllis's words came back to Trevor, about fashionable Society disdaining the classes that made all their finery and frolic possible.

"That tells us what Gavin did not want, but where did his ambition lie?"

Heyward poked up the fire, tossed another square of peat on the flames, and took the opposite wing chair.

"Gavin was an excellent storyteller," Heyward said. "You might think that a mere party trick, but here, where we've no theater, no gentlemen's clubs, no social whirl, the fellow who can sit in the common and spin an old yarn into new entertainment is valued. He spent time with all the elders, listening to them reminisce. He was great friends with the herb lady, who knew all manner of miraculous tales. Gavin is the reason the witching oak still stands."

"He made up that story about the tree being haunted?" The chair was well cushioned, the parlor cozy, and the company inviting, but the portrait over the mantel prevented the moment from being entirely comfortable.

Mama to the life, but a more lighthearted version of the lady than Trevor had ever known.

"The witching oak story might have been languishing in the Husey family's fading memory," Heyward said. "Gavin dusted it off, reenacted the drunken particulars, and turned it into our local version of Tam O'Shanter. The tree is safe for another hundred years at least."

What did this story say about the man who'd seen its potential and saved the tree? "He's clever, then, and likes being the center of attention."

The fresh fuel caught, and the fire blazed a little higher. "Not quite, but close. Gavin was the only son, then the only male, in the DeWitt family. He was quite the center of attention, more than any fellow could enjoy, though Lissa has always run Twidboro. When she was a child, she'd drop by the kitchen and suggest dishes to the housekeeper on menu day. She looks after the tenants, settles their squabbles, fusses over the new babies, and takes tea with the elders."

"Gavin should have been doing that?"

Heyward swiveled keen blue eyes on Trevor. "Precisely, Gavin, Mourna, Mrs. DeWitt senior... Lissa became the unpaid steward when her father began failing. Now she's the man of the house. The family, staff, and tenants are fine with that."

"You are not fine with that." For which Heyward was to be commended. No wonder Amaryllis had been tempted to snatch a kiss for herself by the stream, if the rest of her life was so much drudgery and duty. Trevor well knew how unappealing such a prospect could be.

"I have little power to intervene where the DeWitts are

concerned," Heyward said. "I offered Lissa a loan—she would be insulted by a gift of money—and she refused. Said she doesn't need cash so much as she needs to get the solicitors out of the picture, and only the right husband could do that effectively."

"Miss DeWitt doesn't speak well of the family lawyers."

"Smithers and Purvis. Elegant offices in the City, I'm told, titled clients dropping by on fine days, a pedigree among the partners that doubtless goes back to the conqueror's royal weasels. I pay my nominal rent to them, and if their correspondence is any indication, they are self-important poseurs."

For the same firm to represent both landlord and tenant was probably unethical, now that Trevor considered the matter. That conflict could perhaps be waived by the parties, though Trevor had certainly not waived it. More to the point, if Smithers and Purvis felt free to abuse the trust of a marquess, how much less respect would they show a household of ruralizing, untitled women?

"Will you be returning to London soon?" Heyward asked, apropos of nothing Trevor could discern.

"My plans are flexible. At some point, I am expected back in London, but I've yet to find a property in the shires that will suit my beer-making ambitions. I don't suppose you are interested in leasing me some acres?"

"Why beer, Mr. Dorning? Everybody makes beer."

Trevor rose, because he'd promised Sycamore a detailed look at some budgets, and those budgets yet resided mostly in Trevor's head. Also because Heyward felt no compunction to limit his questions to the weather and Trevor's state of health, and despite Heyward's peculiarities, he was no fool.

"Everybody drinks beer," Trevor said as Heyward also got to his feet. "I thought I'd give winemaking a go and spent years studying the various Continental vineyards. Then I noticed that the Germans make both excellent beer and good wine. I became interested in the beer, some of which is nigh ambrosial. High-quality wine is delightful, but beyond the reach of many of us. John Bull should always be able to enjoy a good pint, and I want to offer him an excellent pint."

That speech was both spontaneous and true, to Trevor's surprise.

"My acres are all spoken for," Heyward said, "but Twidboro has plenty of good bottom land along the river, and the ladies need income. They've put that ground mostly into pasture, so you'd have to break sod, but sooner or later, one should rotate from pasture to crops and back again."

Heyward would know all about that, while Trevor had much to learn. He liked Heyward, though—liked the unapologetic left-handed handshakes, the honesty, the protectiveness toward the DeWitts, the curiosity toward all things agricultural.

Heyward had also, in a quiet way, put Sycamore Dorning in his place, which was difficult to do. Amaryllis had managed the same feat, though without any semblance of subtlety.

"Thank you again for a fine meal and for good company," Trevor said as Heyward handed him his hat. "I will see the handkerchief returned to Miss DeWitt."

"Try to save that errand for tomorrow, Dorning. A man ought to bring some dignity to the business of esteeming a particular woman."

"Ah, but the lady inspires eagerness, Heyward. Wish me luck."

Heyward's smile came again, a little merrier and lighting a sober countenance for more than an instant.

"Luck, then, and you will need it."

Trevor jaunted down the steps and collected his mount from the stable lads. He was trotting back to Crosspatch, in charity with life, if a little troubled by the need to sort out a few muddled factual prevarications with Amaryllis, when he nearly fell off his horse.

Phillip Heyward's smile was familiar because it was, to the last detail, the masculine version of the same smile captured in the portrait of Trevor's own mother.

≈

"You're going too fast, Diana!" Caroline's accusation bore a hint of inchoate tears, audible even in the next room. "Allegro doesn't mean vivace or prestissimo. You always want to show off!"

"You simply can't keep up, *as usual*," Diana shot back. "You didn't study your part, and now you want me to plod along and ruin the music."

The bickering continued while Amaryllis tried to stitch a border of pink lace onto one of last year's bonnets. Pink wasn't preferred for redheads, but Amaryllis liked it, and they had plenty of pink to work with.

"Your grandfather and I always did enjoy the four-hands pieces," Grandmama said, her embroidery resting in her lap. "He's wicked good at the pianoforte and manages to jostle me in the most distracting manner. Grandpapa prefers Mozart to Clementi for a rollicking duet."

Lissa sewed a few more stitches, debating, not for the first time, whether to take issue with Grandmama's lapse into present tense regarding a man who'd played nothing but a celestial harp for years.

"Why did Clementi have to write so many pieces in C major?" Lissa mused. "Diana does go too fast, and then she can't manage the hard parts at the tempo she chose for the easy parts."

"A common failing in life. Your brother's horse apparently distinguished himself with some speed earlier today, and yet, the colt's education in other regards has not kept pace with his innate talents."

Luncheon had come and gone, and Lissa had hoped that the particulars of her morning hack had escaped the notice of Crosspatch's various town criers.

"Who tattled?"

"Tansy Pevinger caught the finish from upstream and politely waited for the path to clear before relaying the news to her mother."

Well, of course. "She relayed the news to Lawrence Miller, who told his aunt, Mrs. Patsy Miller, who conveyed word to her cousin, Mrs. Holly Pevinger, when she took the day's eggs to the vicarage. Mrs. Holly P might have mentioned something to Mr. Dabney when he put up her gig, and from thence, getting news to the inn was the work of a mere five-minute chinwag beneath the market cross."

"London is no different, Lissa."

"London is worse, but I live in the hope that Mr. Clementi won't be accompanying us." The squabbling from the music room had escalated to the I-hate-you and you-are-not-my-sister phase, so Lissa set aside her bonnet and prepared to speak peace unto the heathen.

"Put them on bread and porridge for a week," Grandmama said. "A good smack to the fingers wouldn't go amiss either, and no fire in the nursery until they recall their manners."

Neither Diana nor Caroline had set foot in the nursery for years. "They are anxious because we will soon leave home for Town. Mama hasn't decided whether the girls are to come with us or bide here."

Diana delivered her signature and entirely mendacious, "I will never speak to you again!" Which was met with Caroline's familiar, "Let the rejoicing begin!"

Lissa opened the door to the music room in time to catch Diana sticking out her tongue and Caroline brushing at her cheek with her cuff. They stood six paces apart, so the final phase of the hostilities— hair pulling—was still a few minutes off.

"Why is Di so *mean?*" Caroline wailed. "I try to practice, and every time I do, Di comes around and says she has to practice, and she's older, so she gets first crack at the piano, and then Mama says she has a megrim and no more pianoforte for the day, and I hate stupid duets anyway."

Lissa wrapped her arms around Caroline, who was still enough of a child to accept the embrace. She was gaining height, though, and Lissa prayed that a merciful God would not visit too many more inches on a girl who already bore the burden of bright red hair.

"Diana," Lissa said, "you have hurt your younger sister's feelings."

"Caroline can't keep up. She doesn't practice nearly as much as I did *at her age,*"—delivered with a nasty little emphasis—"and the piece is in the simplest possible key."

I am ashamed of you. The words begged to be spoken in the most disappointed and imperious tones, but that would engender more spatting. Caroline tried hard, but she lacked Diana's appetite for attention, and thus her playing was more circumspect.

More plodding, truth be told. More cautious and dull.

"You were a fiend at Caroline's age," Lissa said, "while Caroline is more drawn to the natural world. I will practice the duet with Caroline until we're confident of the fingering, but you have to admit you set a blazing pace."

Diana sank onto the piano bench facing outward. "I love to go fast."

Caroline pulled away from Lissa and sat beside Di. "But you stumble on the difficult passages because you don't make yourself work out the fingering. I don't want to trip and fall at the cadenza. That's the last, hardest flourish, and everybody will recall that I couldn't manage it no matter how many arpeggios I played correctly."

"Who is everybody?" Diana countered. "Grandmama? Lissa? The cat?"

Insight struck with painful certainty. *Everybody* did not include Gavin, who'd always encouraged Diana's music and admired the wild flowers Caroline collected along the river.

"Gavin has been gone two years," Lissa said. "Two years *this week*. We miss him." She'd attributed the same upheaval last year to her impending Season and realized only in hindsight that the anniversary of Gavin's disappearance had complicated matters.

"We worry about him." Caroline plucked at her damp and wrinkled cuff. "I am tired of praying that God will keep him safe, but I'm afraid to pray that God will send him home, because if Gav doesn't come home, maybe he can't come home, and w-won't ever."

"I said I'd never speak to him again when he made fun of my bird bonnet," Diana said. "A fortnight later, I spoke to him for the last time."

They both looked so young and so forlorn. "Not the last time.

England has rules about recording deaths and notifying the home parish and so forth."

"Do highwaymen and cutpurses follow those rules?" Diana asked.

"He's not dead." Caroline for once sounded more mulish than Diana. "I'd know it. He said he could not wait to see how beautiful I was when I grew up, because I was so lovely in girlhood. He will come home."

Oh, Gavin. "I agree," Lissa said. "He will come home, and when we are done rejoicing at his return, we will stick out our tongues at him and never speak to him again for at least an hour. Until he does come wandering back to us, though, somebody has to sew the new trimming on my old bonnets, and I nominate you two."

"Caroline sews straighter seams than I do," Diana said. "She has more patience."

Caroline was concerned that not even her stitchery reflect poorly on her, and that broke Lissa's heart, but Diana was apologizing after a fashion.

"Perhaps you can serenade us while Caroline and I work at our straight seams. Mama says every bonnet must be retrimmed."

"Only poor people retrim their bonnets," Diana said. "Are we poor, Lissa?"

"We are frugal. Our only poverty is a lamentable lack of menfolk to deal with the solicitors. We are, in fact, wealthy, though we would never be so ill-bred as to mention that beyond ourselves, would we?"

Diana twirled on the piano bench and laid her fingers on the keys. "Of course not, but retrimming bonnets never fooled anybody."

"Play the F major, Di." Caroline rose and shook out her skirts. "I like retrimming bonnets."

Lissa hated it. As Diana had noted, retrimming last year's millinery was the hallmark of straitened finances, also tedious beyond bearing. "Come along, then, Caroline, and we will festoon my hats with rainbows."

They found Grandmama asleep, her mouth slightly open. Lissa

gently eased the embroidery hoop from her fingers, tucked the needle into a corner of the fabric, and draped a lap robe over Grandmama's knees. In sleep, Grandmama looked more frail than usual, more vulnerable, and she was dropping off in the middle of the day more frequently.

She had yet to fall asleep at table, but that day was doubtless close at hand. The London tabbies would not let that behavior go unremarked.

"When did you plan to tell me that Mr. Heyward timed Roland over a half mile this morning?" Caroline asked, taking up the half-completed pink ribbon project. "Cook says Mr. Dorning let Roland have his head, and he ran like a hound with his nose halfway to the ground."

"We actually had two Mr. Dornings present," Lissa said. "One of Mr. Trevor Dorning's distant relations—Mr. Sycamore Dorning—has come out from Town. They are mad keen to brew beer commercially or something."

Grandmama's hand twitched, and then her eyes opened. "Where is my...?" She patted around her lap. "Who took my hoop?"

Lissa fished the requisite item out of her workbasket. "You were resting your eyes. I didn't want this to fall to the floor." She passed over the embroidery,

The look Grandmama gave her was odd. A little wary, a little suspicious, as if she might not have heard Lissa clearly.

"I don't suppose you have my spectacles in that workbasket, young Lissa?"

Caroline looked up from her stitchery. "Your eyeglasses are about your neck, Grandmama. You always wear them on a chain about your neck." Caroline shifted so she was closer to the window light, while Grandmama donned her eyeglasses and pretended to assess her embroidery.

We are going mad. We are all going slowly mad, and all I can think about is kissing Trevor Dorning again, and...

"Will you two excuse me?" Lissa said, rising. "The hem of my riding habit has doubtless dried enough to be brushed out, and one mustn't put that off."

"Sooner begun is sooner done, your grandpapa always says."

Caroline rolled her eyes and kept stitching, and Lissa departed with as much dignity as tattered nerves and tried patience could muster. As she brushed at her hem, hard enough to remove any trace of mud and then some, tears threatened.

Grandmama would continue to fade, Caroline and Diana would fret, and Mama would insist that the solution lay in finding Lissa the right husband. A husband of sufficient standing to take the whole situation in hand—solicitors be damned, Gavin's troubles be damned with them—and with a wave of his magic, husbandly *wand*, all would come right.

Though Mama's proposed solution was all wrong.

Trevor Dorning wasn't a courtesy lord or an heir-in-waiting. He was a common mister with some ambition and education. His connections were not spectacular, but they were good—witness an earl's younger brother had come racketing out to Berkshire to talk business with him.

Lissa absolutely agreed with Mama that Papa had meant for his oldest daughter to marry a title and open the door for Diana and Caroline to make fine matches. Papa had made no secret of his ambitions or of Lissa's role in them.

Mama was also correct that Giles Purvis would attempt a hundred delays and dodges before parting with an extra shilling of DeWitt money. In Gavin's absence, not just any fellow would be up to the challenge of outwitting such schemes.

But Trevor Dorning would deal summarily with legal ditherers. He'd make a few pointed, polite comments, let silence speak volumes, and achieve more from Purvis without drama than Mama and Lissa ever achieved with tears, threats, lectures, and scolds.

Lissa left off scrubbing at hems that needed turning and fresh trim, though they were more than adequate for Crosspatch Corners.

"If Trevor Dorning asks to court me," she muttered, "I will

consent." He wouldn't be like the dimwits, making overtures in bad faith, taking liberties, and sauntering on his way. In fact, with Trevor, Lissa had taken the first liberties...

He had certainly joined in the spirit of the undertaking.

She cracked the laundry room window and hung up her habit to dry, then returned to the family parlor. Grandmama was stitching away, and Caroline was fastening the pink ribbon into place with a series of French knots done in matching thread.

"I didn't realize you liked pink so much," Caroline said.

"It's not fashionable, but we have plenty of it, and one doesn't want to run out halfway through a project. Grandmama, shall we ring for a tray?"

"No, thank you, dear. I'm at a good stopping point, and I do believe it's time I had my lie-down."

When had Grandmama taken to napping so much? She spent more time in slumber than an infant did.

"I'll see you up to your room."

"Don't bother. I might forget my glasses, but I do know where I sleep." She pushed to her feet and made a stiff progress toward the door. "Thank heavens Diana is taking an intermission. I don't know which is worse, when she rushes through a passage and bungles it, or when she finally slows down enough to play it correctly—over and over."

"We will applaud her newfound patience," Lissa said, "though I suspect it will be short-lived. Pleasant dreams, Grandmama."

"Cook says there's another Dorning racketing about Crosspatch. One of the trees. The late Earl of Casriel named all his children for trees and shrubs and whatnot. Daft notion, but we can't all be George, William, and Edward, can we?"

"His name is Sycamore Dorning," Caroline said. "He's out from Town."

Grandmama put a hand on the door latch. "One of those Dorset Dornings married old Lord Tavistock's widow, if I'm not mistaken. This would have been... oh, before your father died, certainly. Years ago. The poor woman wasn't well liked, but then, she was married to a difficult man and was many years his junior. Society was quite surprised that she'd remarry and give up the title. Perhaps she wished it good riddance. That's all getting to be ancient history, I suppose."

She wafted out the door, muttering about Old George and a proper court and your grandpapa always said...

"She's getting worse," Caroline said.

"She's getting older." But Grandmama's distant memories were still for the most part reliable. Lissa went to the window, where afternoon sunshine gave the oaks a pinkish cast. Green leaves would soon follow, and then...

If one of Trevor's distant relations had married the former marchioness of Tavistock, Trevor might keep that to himself rather than get off on a bad foot with potential neighbors in Crosspatch. More likely, he had little idea to whom a distant cousin's wife had been married to ten years ago.

Trevor would have been a schoolboy, and what schoolboy concerned himself with fashionable matches?

Lissa would nonetheless ask him about it, some fine day when she'd run out of other ways to spend time with him. Maybe.

And maybe not.

CHAPTER TEN

Trevor spent a week pretending to school Roland while, in fact, lecturing himself on the folly of indulging impulses and the necessity of charting a deliberate, well-reasoned course in life.

Between lectures, he indulged in kisses with Amaryllis. She accompanied him on his hacks, though sometimes they spent more time walking the horses along the Twid, holding hands, and arguing —discussing, as Amaryllis put it—than they did in the saddle.

The weather moderated, the birds built their nests, and Trevor tried—inasmuch as a smitten man could—to make sense of his situation.

All to no avail.

"How much longer will you bide at the Arms?" Amaryllis asked as they walked their horses along the lane leading to Twidboro Hall.

"How long until you must remove to London?" Trevor replied. "I'm supposed to return to Town myself, Sycamore made that quite plain, but I'd rather bide here."

"What pulls you to London?"

How to answer that? "My solicitors need at least a stern lecture, if not sacking." One could sack solicitors by letter, and one probably should, though Trevor would still have to return to Town, so he offered the rest of the explanation. "My step-mother bides in London, and she has social ambitions for me. I have been traveling much in recent years, and she has missed me."

Did the errant Gavin miss his family? Trevor had discussed a few ideas with Sycamore about Gavin's possible whereabouts, because clearly, directions to the solicitors would yield no results.

"You care for your step-mother?"

"Very much. She was all that stood between me and my father's worst tempers. He never beat me— he left the birchings to the tutors— but he could slice a boy to ribbons with a few well-placed insults, and his rejections cut worse than any lash. I learned to be a very good boy and to avoid his notice. My step-mother wasn't as lucky."

The Twidboro gateposts came into view, and Trevor's heart sank. Another parting loomed, and one day soon, either he or Amaryllis would travel on to Town. There would be no avoiding the fact that he'd misled her as to his identity. Their paths would cross in some ballroom or on some Hyde Park bridle path, and with all of Mayfair looking on...

He could not risk the injury such an encounter would do to Amaryllis's pride, of that he was certain.

"Spring is supposed to be a time of hope," Amaryllis said. "When I'm not with you, I feel mostly dread. My father was the sweetest of men—cheerful, kindhearted, grateful for life's many blessings—but he was determined that I should marry as well as possible, and thus my settlements are outlandishly generous. If my sisters are to have a future, I must try to make a good impression in Town."

"Unless your brother turns up."

"The London newspapers go to every corner of the realm, Trevor. If Gavin is in Britain, he must have read about a certain delicate *flower* from bucolic Berkshire whose attractions were apparently inadequate even years ago to secure an offer from a *titan* of gentle-manly *merriment*, and so forth."

"I am seized by an abrupt desire to burn down the penny press." Soon enough, they'd be remarking the doings of the Marquess of T...

Roland attempted a halfhearted spook at a large blue butterfly fluttering about his face.

"He's much calmer than he was even ten days ago," Amaryllis said. "You've given him some dignity."

What was she saying? "We all grow up eventually. Roland simply wanted for some guidance and experience."

They turned through the gateposts, and the sinking sensation spread to Trevor's gut. He'd be welcomed at the Hall for a cup of tea, and Amaryllis's family would flutter about like human butterflies, chattering, laughing, and vying for attention. Amaryllis would grow quieter and quieter, until she saw him off with a wan smile.

He enjoyed her family—enjoyed their noise and warmth and humor—but today's looming separation sapped his social stamina.

"Show me the gatehouse," he said, before Amaryllis could extend an invitation to take tea. "Your mother mentioned that I might rent the place as temporary quarters, and it's certainly more commodious than a room at the Arms."

Amaryllis turned Jacques off the carriage lane onto a short drive. "Gavin liked to rehearse here. Caroline sneaks away to read in Grandmama's old parlor. I come to the gatehouse and pretend I'm dusting, but mostly, I'm finding solitude. The gatehouse was the first dwelling on the property, where the original owner lived when Lark's Nest was being built."

Trevor expected her to launch into a discussion of the building's provenance—who built it in what year, of stone from which quarry—but she instead remained quiet. They pulled off the horses' gear and turned them out in a grassy paddock behind the gatehouse proper. Amaryllis took a key from beneath a boot scrape and led Trevor into a sunny kitchen with mullioned windows and a flagstone floor.

"When the kitchen is spotless," Amaryllis said, taking Trevor's hat from his head and setting it on a counter, "the house must be deserted or for sale." She stripped off her riding gloves and set them in the crown of Trevor's hat. "My father used to say that. Come, I'll show you the rest."

The rest consisted of four other rooms—a dining room and parlor on the ground floor and, according to Amaryllis, two bedrooms upstairs. The topmost floor was a garret for housing staff. The whole was furnished, though the parlor sofa and chairs were under Holland covers, and the china cabinet in the dining room was empty.

"Empty houses have a different kind of quiet," Trevor said, "as if they wait rather than slumber. I toured many empty homes in France, some of them pathetically grand. They'd survived the famines, the Revolution, the Terror, and the wars, but their occupants had not been so lucky."

"Were you tempted to buy any of them?"

The clock on the mantel had stopped at noon or midnight. The sunshine coming through the windows was bright, but the Holland covers gave the parlor a sad air.

"I bought one of the most modest properties," Trevor said, "not for the house. I have land in France, and the dwelling came with the acres. A friend manages it for me. We grow claret grapes, mostly." Fournier was a friend, for all he was also a business partner.

Trevor saw the question his disclosure raised: He could afford land in France. He had toured *pathetically grand* homes with a view toward buying them. He had means, so why not...?

"Is there somebody else, Trevor?" Amaryllis asked, leading the way up the steps. "Somebody to whom you are obligated?"

He was obligated to the Marquess of Tavistock and to a thousand other somebodies—tenants, factors, staff, cousins, pensioners, Parliament—though nobody save Jeanette would miss him if he resumed traveling for another five years.

"I am free of romantic entanglements—of other romantic entanglements." He followed Amaryllis up the narrow steps and emerged onto a landing that boasted a window seat. The horses cropped grass below, and the roofline of Twidboro Hall was barely visible through the luminous green of the emerging canopy.

Two doors opened off the landing, the bedrooms presumably, and a visual metaphor for choices Trevor faced.

"Might we sit for a moment, Amaryllis?"

"You are the only person to call me that, other than Mama when she's vexed with me." She settled on the window seat and studied the dusty toes of her riding boots.

"Your name is lovely, and you are lovely, but you are too reserved to ask me what my intentions are. Had you a father or brother on hand, they would sort me out, but since no such worthy is available, you must sort me out yourself."

She patted the place beside her. "Are you in a muddle?"

"I am. You?"

"I know very clearly who and what I want, Trevor."

A secluded gatehouse was a fine place to have a difficult discussion, though it struck Trevor belatedly that it was also a fine place to... effect a mutual seduction.

"You don't know the whole of the who," he said, taking her hand. "You know me as Trevor Dorning, and Trevor is my forename."

"Which you gave me leave to use, of all the shocking familiarities." She sounded pleased.

Trevor took courage from that. "We're in Crosspatch, where friendliness comes as no shock to anybody, but, Amaryllis, you should know that my father was the late Marquess of Tavistock."

The fellow everybody, including Trevor, had disliked. If Trevor's lineage cost him Amaryllis's affection, he might graduate to hating the old shade.

"Lord Tavistock was your father?"

"And I hold him in as low esteem as the rest of the village does, but I cannot deny my patrimony."

Trevor expected Amaryllis to leap off the window seat, or at least rise, make a brisk remark about the time, and state a pressing need to rehearse some duet or other with Caroline.

Amaryllis put her head on his shoulder. "You cannot help who your father was any more than I can help that mine was the son of a prosperous shop owner, not that I'd want to change that. We are not our parents, Trevor." She took a firmer hold of his hand, and Trevor wrapped an arm around her shoulders.

"He was awful to my mother, awful to women generally, but not much better to any man who didn't outrank him. He demanded toadying, then insulted those who toadied because they lacked a spine. He excelled at giving other people nothing but bad choices."

"Like denying my father ownership of Twidboro. Papa could continue on as a tenant subject to his lordship's whims when it came to maintaining the property, or Papa could uproot us and admit that Tavistock had rejected a shopkeeper's coin."

An extraordinary thought emerged from the relief coursing through Trevor: Amaryllis not only took no issue with Trevor's station, she *sympathized* with him.

"I was to be an obedient son, but if I was too obedient, then I was, in his lordship's words, a disgraceful invertebrate," Trevor said. "I was to be smart, but if I was too smart, then I was an arrogant little bookworm. I was to be polite, but if I was too polite, then I was a disgusting little prig. I was never what he wanted me to be, but then, he was never what I wanted him to be either."

"He's dead," Amaryllis said in the same tones she might have noted that the pansies beneath the market cross were wilted. "You are quite alive and apparently thriving. I do not hold your patrimony against you, Trevor, and nobody else in Crosspatch will either. The old marquess was a blight upon society and apparently a blight upon your life as well."

The situation wasn't as simple as that. Papa had also been conscientious about managing his marquessate. He'd had cronies, if not friends. He'd been denied the nursery full of sons he'd longed for, and he'd seen his legitimate heir well educated and more than adequately fed, clothed, and housed.

He'd done his duty, however begrudgingly.

Amaryllis kissed Trevor's cheek. "This has been weighing on your mind, hasn't it?"

"Terribly. Would you want to claim a connection to a man who's universally reviled in the village?"

"No, but neither would I dignify that connection with subterfuges meant to hide it. I have not been riding out with the late marquess. I haven't been turning my family loose on him to test his manners and patience. I certainly haven't been kissing him, and it's not the late marquess I'm dreaming of."

Trevor's dread of this conversation was replaced by a sense of lightness and joy, and—it took his mind some groping about to find the word—*hope*.

Amaryllis's great good sense, her pragmatism and inherent kindness, were seeing him through. "You dream of me?"

She nuzzled his shoulder. "I ought to know better, but there you have it. When I should be stitching a new pair of gloves to match my retrimmed bonnets, I'm instead wondering, 'What does Trevor look like with his shirt off? Does he have a favorite poem? Where did he learn to ride so well?'"

"My riding skills were honed on every back road and farm lane in France, for the most part. Do you truly dream of me?" He dreamed of her, though he knew the lanes and paths where she'd learned her riding skills, and he'd already memorized her favorite Shakespearean sonnet.

Not the romantic flights of Sonnet 18 or the pretty comparisons of Sonnet 116, though Amaryllis granted them honorable mention. Her favorite was the sober and reflective Sonnet 29.

When, in disgrace with fortune and men's eyes, I all alone beweep my outcast state... Haply I think on thee... For thy sweet love remembered such wealth brings / That then I scorn to change my state with kings.

"I think of you," Amaryllis said. "I think of matters a young lady doesn't admit to dwelling on."

He hugged her. "How you flatter me."

She drew back and regarded him with a focus that tossed Shakespeare's pretty rhymes right out the window.

"I am not asking for a commitment, Trevor, but I am asking for a memory. We have time, we have privacy, we have—"

He silenced her with a swift buss to the cheek. "When it comes to the commitment, I do the asking. I put my entire future and my heart into your hands. Then you decide whether to accept or reject my proposal. If you want the bended-knee bit, I'm happy to oblige, but your mother, grandmother, and sisters would probably like to eavesdrop on that exchange."

Amaryllis leaned against him and was silent for a fraught moment. "They would, but I'm not sure I can allow that. Some conversations should be private. Before we get to the pretty speeches, Trevor, I'd like to..."

He felt the heat of her blush because they sat cheek to cheek in the window seat.

"You want to try my paces?" he suggested.

"You aren't a horse."

"I am a prospective husband." He'd never thought to say those words so joyfully. "You have been disappointed by others, and you are entitled to sample my wares if you please to before we get to the pretty speeches, though I warn you, Amaryllis, they will be short speeches, however heartfelt."

"Do you suggest I might have to yield my crown as the most plainspoken member of the family?"

Family—he was to be a member of her family, as she was to become nearly the sum total of his.

"I'll have a tiara made for you instead of a crown," he said, though the Tavistock jewels included at least four tiaras. "Shall we make love, Amaryllis?" He could pose the question without any agenda other than acceding to her wishes. They'd all but agreed to be married, she knew who she'd be marrying, and all was right with Trevor's world.

She stood and held out her hand. "I've kept the second bedroom dusted. The balcony has a nice view of the Twid, and I like to read and nap here when the weather is fine."

Trevor took her hand, kissed her knuckles, and rejoiced to recall the day he'd decided to see Crosspatch Corners for himself.

"Before we yield to passion—because I will yield, Amaryllis, and will do my utmost to see that you do as well—I have one very short speech to make."

Her expression said his speech had best be the shortest in the history of speeches.

"I love you," he said, though he wanted to throw open the window and shout the words to the world. "I love you and—"

She bundled him into a ferocious hug. "I heard you the first time. Thank you for the words, now show me that you mean them."

She was shy, bless her. Trevor felt shy, too, also pleased, proud, and determined to prove that Amaryllis would never, ever regret her choice.

"Let the wild yielding to passion begin," he said, opening the bedroom door and bowing her through, "and may it never, ever end."

～

Amaryllis sailed into the bedroom on wings of rejoicing.

Trevor's illegitimacy explained so much. A peer's by-blow had a foot in the fashionable world and a foot in the common man's realities. He'd be a canny fellow accustomed to keeping his own counsel. He would be well educated, well dressed, and well mannered, but also cautious, never presuming he's welcome and always aware of the appearances. Fashionable Society would receive him, though an invitation to show his face at Court would have been unusual.

She could well understand why he'd enjoy Continental society, which operated with fewer strictures and conventions. His titled half-brother apparently did too.

Trevor's enviable self-possession had clearly been learned early and well, in a world that had frequently judged him for matters beyond his control.

Amaryllis knew how it felt to be held accountable for the

previous generation's choices. Her grandfather had been a shop-keeper—a shopkeeper!—and her father was still regarded as little better. How much more complicated if her father had been a titled, philandering martinet disregarding his marriage vows?

"I want to hurry," she said. "To tear your clothes off before you succumb to a sudden attack of propriety."

"If you succumb to such an attack, Amaryllis, or to an under-standable bout of cold feet, I will respect your decision."

Because he respected *her*. That was what made Trevor different. Other men had found Amaryllis attractive. Other men had been taken with her settlements, or her figure, or her agreeable conversation.

Trevor relished their disagreements and even incited the occa-sional argument out of sheer deviltry.

He closed and locked the bedroom door—a nice bit of gallantry, though nobody would intrude here—and gestured to the vanity stool.

"My lady's boots should be removed."

Trevor meant for them to undress. That realization dashed a bit of cold water on Amaryllis's fog of delight.

"I've done this with my boots on, you know."

"As have I," Trevor replied, "but those were passing moments, while what we undertake now *matters*, Amaryllis. If we are to be inti-mate, I'd like for our first time to be more than a quick interlude against a sturdy wall." He studied the room, a particular gleam coming into his eyes. "Unless you'd prefer a sturdy wall?"

Gracious. "The bed will do."

He patted the back of the vanity stool, and Amaryllis's heart gave an odd leap. She'd dreamed about him, speculated, wondered, and hoped, and he was right—this mattered. She settled on the vanity stool and held out her right boot.

Trevor made quick work of her footwear and remained on his knees before her. "You're sure, Amaryllis?"

"Are you?"

"Never more certain in my life. Let's get you out of that riding habit, shall we?"

Part of Amaryllis was happy to follow Trevor's lead, to let him be the one thinking logically and managing the practicalities, but she'd been entirely passive in her previous encounters, and Trevor merited more from her than mere acquiescence.

"What of your boots?" she asked, rising. "What of this cravat? I'd hate for it to get torn in a moment of enthusiasm."

"Then you best remove it from my person, hadn't you?"

She took her time, and not because her hands shook ever so slightly. With Charles, she'd watched the cobwebs wafting about in the corners of the Breadalbane library's coffered ceiling. Somebody had neglected the dusting sorely.

She could hardly recall the details of her encounter with Titus Merriman. A conservatory rendered aromatic by virtue of a barrow of horse manure awaiting use in the rose garden. Damp air and a cramp in her right thigh while Titus... jiggled away.

Trevor would brook no inspection of the ceiling, though Lissa very much wanted to inspect him. She slid the cravat from his neck and draped it neatly on the vanity. Next, she undid the buttons of his waistcoat and shirt, then relieved him of his jacket and slipped his sleeve buttons free.

"Enough for now," Trevor said, sitting on the bed and pulling off his right boot then his left. "My turn."

He unbuttoned the jacket of Lissa's riding habit, and though she had on several other layers—shirt, chemise, jumps—she felt every brush of his fingers, every undone hook. As he eased her clothing off, he indulged in small caresses—a hand brushed over her hip, a finger drawn along her shoulder, a kiss to her nape.

All lovely, and yet, disconcerting. "You are taller when we take our boots off." Inane observation.

He leaned close. "I am dying to learn how our heights match in bed, Amaryllis." He kissed her lips, and that became a whole bouquet of kisses.

Lissa wrapped her arms around him, the better to kiss him back. She'd known he was solid muscle, but to have only a thin lawn shirt between her fingers and his naked flesh...

"Shirt off, please."

"How polite you are." He stepped back and pulled his shirt over his head. "Skirt off, please."

Lissa managed the hooks and tape and stepped free. With a traditional sidesaddle habit, she would have worn breeches beneath the skirt. With the divided skirt, she wore only plain stockings gartered above the knee and a summer-length chemise.

The stockings were darned, the chemise worn, and yet, the way Trevor regarded her made her feel lovely. His gaze held longing and desire, but also tenderness, reverence even.

"I am," he said, "the most fortunate of fellows. I am anointed by fate to endure more wonder and delight than a mortal man can describe."

Rather than withstand that gaze, Lissa turned back the bedcovers. Thanks to her bickering sisters, she'd kept this room as a sort of retreat, and thus the bed was made, the windows clean, the linen lightly scented with lavender.

"You are loquacious," Lissa said. "Will you murmur sweet nothings to me the whole time we're frolicking?"

"I will murmur whatever your please, Amaryllis, or maintain a rapt silence, the better to savor a sensory feast. I am yours to command."

She sat on the bed and undid her garters. What commands did one give? Tallyho? View halloo? She was abruptly feeling in over her head and at risk for bungling.

Bravado would not serve, and retreat would not do *at all*. That left... Lissa cast around for strategies. Changing the subject, trying for a jest, small talk... Nothing in her social arsenal would get her past the growing puddle of self-consciousness occupying the place where her enthusiasm had so recently been.

That left... honesty?

Well, yes. With Trevor, she could be honest. "You find me at something of a loss. I know how to organize the sack races at the village fete, but this... I am at sea, Trevor. I have no desire to row in to shore, but I haven't... That is, I'm not as experienced as you might..." She gathered her courage and leaped. "I don't know what to do."

The words cost her. If he laughed, if he gave orders, *if he lost interest* because of her ineptitude...

He sat beside her, tucked an arm around her, and spoke near her ear. "We do as we please, my love. We come together in a rapture of shared, private indulgence, but, Amaryllis?"

"Trevor?" How she loved the feel of him, warm and naked and close.

"Please be patient with me. I am unsure of myself in this new venture, and I need time to find my way."

Of all the words he could have murmured in her ear, those were unaccountably dear. "You aren't in the least unsure of yourself."

"Oh, but I am. I have frolicked, as you put it, but this will be love-making, and I am determined to exceed your expectations, though I am as new to the venture as you are."

The knot of self-doubt Amaryllis had been worrying eased. Trevor would not lie to her, not about this. He was telling her she was different and that he was at sea with her too—in the same boat.

"I like the cuddling part," she said, yet another inanity, "and you are a good kisser." Also a dear, desirable, breathtakingly brave man who'd said he loved her and apparently meant it.

Trevor rose and came around the other side of the bed, flipped back the covers, and undid his falls. Amaryllis had to twist about, but she witnessed the moment when he stepped free of his breeches and tossed them onto the vanity stool.

Ye pagan gods of pleasure.

"Come here," Trevor said, lying back against the pillows and holding out his arms. "I have it on good authority that my kissing is merely good. If you are amenable, I'd like to work on my technique."

Lissa heaved herself back and halfway across the bed, bundling into his side and drawing the covers up.

"I am amenable."

Trevor shifted over her. "Thank whoever the patron saint of lonely bachelors is for that."

Soft lips pressed against her throat, and a warm hand glided slowly over her hip. Trevor touched her in only those two places, and Lissa retaliated by running her toe up the side of his calf.

"I like this," she said. "We fit."

"We have not begun to fit, mademoiselle."

What Trevor could do with his lips, his tongue, his *weight*... Lissa did her best to return fire by exploring his back, shoulders, and arms. She got a fistful of his hair—that was technique too—and kissed him until he was panting on all fours above her.

"Please get back here," she said. "You are my new favorite blanket, and—"

He sat up, and she was treated to the sight of Trevor Dorning fully aroused. He perched over her hips, his hair tousled, his chest rising and falling with each deep breath, his smile wicked and sweet.

"You were saying?"

He stroked himself idly, and Lissa touched the tip of his cock with one finger. "I said, please..." Please... something...?

He let her explore this, too, let her learn his contours and sensitivities, let her look and stroke and consider. No dark conservatory or faffling about in a dusty library for Trevor Dorning...

And no more for me either. Lissa gave him a soft pat. "My expectations are exceeded, Mr. Dorning."

He seized her hand and crouched over her. "No, they are not. Not by half. Not yet. Kiss me."

These kisses were bolder, more carnal, and laced with French. *Je t'adore... Je te desiré* ... Other words were spoken too softly for Lissa to hear. She arched up, needing to be closer, and then he was there—right there—and the moment of joining was upon them.

"*Es-tu*... Are you certain, Amaryllis?"

She replied by taking him in her hand and putting him where she needed him to be, then angling forward.

"Wait." He hung over her, their bodies barely joined. "Wait, please. A moment."

Another man would have begun thrusting away, ready to yield any semblance of restraint or consideration. That Trevor refused to seize that pleasure for himself touched Lissa unbearably.

"I will wait until Domesday."

He cuddled close and drew her into his arms. "And I will make the pleasure worth your sacrifice."

She held him and resisted the temptation to gallop off with his good intentions. When he did start to move, he did so slowly, setting up a rhythm Lissa could counterpoint. She wanted to bolt, to break stride and kick over the traces, but Trevor kept inexorably to the slower tempo.

"Damn you, Trevor. There's no need…"

"There is every need." He brushed his finger across her brow, and even in such a small tenderness, he moved with deliberation.

When Lissa would have argued, she was distracted by a sense of gathering desire, a drawing up of all her yearning and wishing into an impossibly intense longing.

I cannot bear this had formed as a thought in her mind, and she was marshaling the effort to speak the words aloud when Trevor increased both the tempo and power of his thrusts.

And truly, Lissa could not bear what came next. She endured, she shook, she rejoiced, she marveled, and endured some more, until a deluge of pleasure receded to a roaring torrent, and then a steady current of satisfaction, surprise, and joy.

Trevor stilled above her, holding himself just far enough away that Lissa could breathe freely.

"That was…" She cast around for words—French, English, dog Latin, any words at all. "That was…"

"That was merely a prelude."

CHAPTER ELEVEN

Joy had given Trevor the self-restraint of a god, though come to think of it, the gods hadn't been known for their self-restraint. That thought drifted through the happy mists of his mind as Amaryllis drowsed in his arms and satisfaction burbled through his body.

Along with a dawning awareness that he could soon be aroused again.

Lissa had gone two rounds with him before declaring herself at the limit of her endurance. Trevor had spent on her belly and used a handkerchief on the resulting mess. He'd expected to wrap himself around Amaryllis and drift into the contented sleep of the lover who'd *exceeded expectations*—and had his own exceeded as well—but instead, he hovered just out of reach of sleep.

In the name of all that was lovely, this moment was too precious to spend snoring.

A special license would take a week or so to arrange, but then again, Amaryllis deserved to be courted.

Publicly.

In the parks, in the ballrooms, at Gunter's Tea Shop, and in the travel section at Hatchards. At rubbishing Almack's too. Out at Richmond, in the churchyard of St. George's, and in every fashionable shop in Piccadilly.

For starts.

And she deserved to be courted for more than the three weeks necessary for crying the banns. They'd be married at St. Nebo's—the new roof ought to be finished in a couple of months—and if nobody else was on hand to see Amaryllis to the altar, Trevor would prevail on the nearest handy duke to attend to the honor.

Moreland would oblige. He was famously besotted with his duchess. Anselm was a closet sentimentalist when it came to weddings. Quimbey was a Dorning connection who'd married for the first time late in life...

Trevor was mentally choosing the flower arrangements for the altar—the amaryllis could symbolize pride and strength as well as determination—when his prospective bride stirred.

"I slept," she muttered. "What time is it, and... Oh, you, you... I like that. When you kiss me there, I go all shivery."

He'd merely kissed her nape. They were spooned together in a cocoon of warmth, and—Trevor hoped—joy.

"You merely dozed for a few minutes," he said, "felled by a surfeit of passion. For your information, I like the cuddling part too."

She aimed a look at him over her shoulder, a little wary, a little impish. "You excel at cuddling, sir. One would not have suspected this." She subsided on a sigh. "I have some latent talents, too, it seems."

Trevor took the span of two more leisurely kisses—shoulder, biceps—to realize he was being asked for reassurances.

"You knocked me so far off my horse, Amaryllis DeWitt, I'm still flying somewhere above Hampshire. Ours will be a passionate union."

"You haven't proposed yet."

Oh, but he would. "The matter wants some thought. You may rely on me to make a proper job of it."

"You sound so determined, so serious about a mere formality. I'm not a high stickler, Trevor." She seemed to think he hadn't noticed that lovely attribute, when he was all but wrapped around her naked abundance.

But then, some of the patronesses at Almack's were both high sticklers and... notably frolicsome.

"Don't spend too much time planning your speech," Amaryllis went on, rolling over to face him. "Mama thinks to drag me off to London by the end of the month."

Trevor caught her hand in his and kissed her knuckles. "What do you think?"

"You have no idea," she said, cradling his hand in both of hers, "no earthly, human idea, how that question warms my heart, but I am torn, between dread at facing the Season again and a petty, niggling desire to swan about Town knowing that I am spoken for, and by a man whom I deeply esteem. If I do go to Town, I can finally deal with those people on my own terms."

Trevor suspected she would smile at Titus Merriman and honestly pity his wife. She would watch Charles Brompton turning down the room with his Eglantine and silently thank the woman for sparing Amaryllis that duty and many others.

"You want to return to the scene of battle," Trevor said, tucking the covers up over her shoulder. "We will do as you wish, and I would enjoy the opportunity to show you off. Shallow of me, I know, but I'd also like to introduce you to my step-mother and her family."

"You are about as shallow as the North Atlantic. I would like to meet her as well. You speak so highly of her, and I hope she will visit us often. Where shall we live, Trevor? I don't want to be too far from my family, but I can't expect you to settle in Crosspatch because of them."

"Yes," he said, pulling her into his arms, "you can. I'm honestly considering buying Miller's Lament, though we will have to change the name, of course. Something cheerful and beery, if we're to grow hops and barley there. I have some properties I can sell in York, and we'll need a Town residence for business purposes and to see your sisters properly presented. I would never steal you from your family."

They spent another half hour in bed, cuddling, talking, and laughing. Amaryllis cataloged his few scars and imperfections—a mishap with an oil lamp when he was eleven had left a fading white streak on his right wrist. His left earlobe had been nicked in an early fall from his first pony. He was ticklish about the ribs, though he saved for another day an investigation of where Amaryllis might be ticklish.

The lovemaking had been wonderful—a revelation—but planning a future together was marvelous in a whole different way. Trevor shared his opinions as only that—opinions—and Amaryllis answered him with honest replies. She listened to him, and he listened to her, and that was wondrous too.

She truly *listened* to him, and her every word commanded his attention.

They settled nothing, other than that Amaryllis would go to Town as planned, and Trevor would be in London as well to court her. No special license, no announcement in the papers, not even a disclosure to her family—not yet, anyway. She doubtless wanted some time to rehearse that announcement and to adjust to her changed circumstance before family stuck their oars in.

Trevor was doing up the hooks at the back of Amaryllis's blouse when he realized that since leaving the bed, she'd grown quiet. He looped his arms about her waist and drew her against his chest.

"You've gone silent, my love."

How he adored holding her. She turned in his arms and embraced him as well. How he loved—loved—her embrace. Secure, affectionate, *present*. She listened with her embraces, too, and he would be a long time adjusting to the notion that his words mattered to her.

Not his title, not his consequence, not his wealth or standing, but his thoughts and needs and words.

"I'm thinking of Mama and Grandmama. They are both widows.

I've labeled them flighty, silly, sentimental... How ignorant of me, when they've both suffered an unfathomable loss. I will be kinder in future."

"They also had decades of joy, Amaryllis, and children to love. I wish that for us too." Not an heir and spare, for God's sake. Sons and daughters, fascinating little people with curious minds and devilish humor and all manner of imagination.

Amaryllis mashed her nose against his throat. "Centuries would be better. Eternities."

Trevor stroked her back and marveled that beneath all the brisk competence and family loyalty, he'd found the real Amaryllis. The lady who could spout fanciful effusions and whimsical wishes. The lady who could hold the prospect of eventual sorrow in her heart even as joy became more abundant.

Where had she been hiding and for how long? What parts of himself had he hidden away, only to find them on a dusty lane leading to Crosspatch Corners?

"I don't want to leave here," Amaryllis said when they were both dressed and had returned to the sunny kitchen. "I'm afraid I will wake up in my own bed and realize I've been napping away a pretty afternoon that I should have spent stitching new ribbons onto old bonnets."

"I am so smitten," Trevor said, "that I look forward to choosing your new bonnets with you."

"Very smitten indeed, and I'm smitten enough that I might even allow you to escort me."

Trevor permitted himself one more hug, one more moment to revel in Amaryllis's warmth and affection, before he stepped back, passed over her gloves, and tapped his hat onto his head.

"When will you return to London?" she asked.

"Soon, I suppose." He had a scoundrel or two to sort out at Smithers and Perjury. Either Worth Kettering or Ash Dorning could handle the settlement negotiations for him, because he wasn't about to entrust them to Purvis.

"You will have my direction," he went on, "and you will remain in possession of my heart—in fee, simple, absolute. I don't want to go, but the idea that I will see you in Town, ride the bridle paths with you, share an ice with you... I have never had much good to say about London, but I suspect all that is about to change."

Amaryllis kissed his cheek—she doubtless meant that as a consolation rather than a temptation—and accompanied him out into the bright afternoon sunshine. The day was gorgeous, spring was on the way, and Trevor had never been happier or more full of hope.

~

"My German is rusty," Jeanette Dorning said. "I hope yours is in better repair."

Jeanette's brother, Sir Orion Goddard—he'd dropped the colonel part at some point in the past year or two—was certainly in good repair. Marriage had put the spring back in his step and the gleam in his eye, and running The Coventry Club had given him an outlet for his considerable administrative skills.

Rye had also traveled extensively on the Continent and had business contacts in several of the German states.

"I will never forget how to give commands in German," he said, ushering Jeanette into a comfortable parlor.

Ann's influence was evident here. A sampler on the wall held not some old quote from Proverbs, but a quote from the Bard: *Love comforteth like sunshine after rain.* Another hung beneath it: *When love speaks, the voice of all the gods makes heaven drowsy with the harmony.*

Potted herbs basked on the windowsill—thyme, tarragon, basil— and a letter from the great Carême complimenting one of Anne's sauce recipes had been framed under glass and hung beside the quotes.

On the opposite walls were sketches of children, ranging in age from toddlers to adolescents. Rye's urchins, many of whom were on the way to self-sufficient adulthood thanks to positions at the Coventry.

Jeanette had been estranged from her brother for years, but Sycamore had given her back her family, that family being Rye and some cousins plus the urchins, the staff at the Coventry, a forest of Dornings...

The list grew year by year.

"Please read this," she said, extracting a folded letter from her reticule. "I'm fairly certain of the meaning, but I want confirmation from somebody whose skill with languages exceeds my own."

Rye gestured to the sofa and took the place beside her. He withdrew a pair of spectacles from an inside pocket and examined the letter. The moments ticked by, and Jeanette prayed her German had misconstrued the letter's contents.

Rye folded up the missive and passed it back to her. "Jerome Vincent has apparently gone to his reward."

"Oh blast. Jerome was no prize, but he was Trevor's heir and something of a friend to him." And a burden and a vexation. Jerome was also—had also been—the only other Vincent male and thus a theoretical buffer for Trevor against sole responsibility for the marquessate. If nothing else, Jerome had been able to commiserate with Trevor regarding the old marquess's many shortcomings.

"What else does it say?" Jeanette asked.

"Jerome was engaged to be married to the widowed Countess of Raffensburg. She writes that she had never been so happy as she has been for the past half year. They went out riding. Jerome's horse spooked at a rabbit, and he took a tumble and smacked his head."

The rabbit part had eluded her. "I got most of that, but the rest of it...?"

Rye rose and crossed the room to pour two servings of brandy. He passed one to Jeanette and resumed his seat. "To Jerome's memory."

Jeanette sipped, because she appreciated good libation and because she needed the fortification.

"I have so much family," she said. "Sycamore got you back for me, and you have added Ann and your urchins to our lives. I have the Dornings—a veritable army—and through them so many friends and in-laws. Trevor ran off to France as soon as I married, and somehow, my family has not become his family. Jerome was, in a way, all he had."

"He will be comforted to know Jerome didn't suffer."

"I'm afraid I didn't pay as much attention to the rest of the letter. What does she say?"

"He seemed fine at first. Laughed at his mishap, got back on, rode home all in fine spirits. By suppertime, he had a headache, and he seemed tired. He was lapsing into English when he couldn't recall a German word or phrase. He went to bed early and did not rouse when the countess joined him. By morning, she could not wake him, and he expired peacefully while she and a physician kept vigil."

"He died in his sleep. Who could have predicted that?"

Rye took a sip of his drink. "Damned head wounds. They are notoriously fickle. A fellow can think he's fine, and three hours after the mule kicked him or he got tossed into a ditch, he drops into a coma, and that's the end of him. I've seen it a dozen times."

"Why did the countess contact me rather than Trevor?"

"Because you would know where Trevor was, while Jerome might well have professed to have lost track of him somewhere along the Rhine."

Jeanette sipped her brandy and considered what she knew of young men, and of Trevor and Jerome in particular.

"Jerome was dodging Trevor's letters, and for some reason, he didn't want the countess to be able to contact the head of his family. I do believe Jerome managed to die before he grew up."

Rye crossed his legs at the knee. He was not an elegant man to appearances—he was too scarred, craggy, and worn for that—but he was mannerly, tidy, and at ease with himself in a way Jeanette associated with Frenchmen.

Sycamore had some of the same quality, as did—oddly—Trevor.

"Perhaps," Rye said, "Jerome did not want Trevor telling the countess the old stories, about that time Jerome lost his first pony in a schoolyard bet, or that time Jerome had to catch a ride out of London on a fishmonger's cart, or that time Jerome lost his membership in some club. If the countess was in love with Jerome, he might have wanted to keep that joy private for a time."

Jeanette studied the letter, though penmanship told her nothing. "She loved Jerome. That's good. He was charming and shrewd, and I'm sure Trevor will grieve at his passing. Trevor perfected the art of being friendly without forming friendships, and I think Jerome was a sort of exception to that rule."

"Trevor is no longer a schoolboy longing for a basket from home, Jeanette."

"He liked school. I had to argue with his father that twelve was old enough to risk the rigors of public school, particularly when Trevor had already conquered the entire curriculum. He was bored at university, and—he never said this, he was too damned polite—disgusted by the debauchery he saw there. He called it boredom, but I used to know my step-son well. University boys reminded him too much of his father."

"And he was unimpressed with London Society," Rye observed. "But when word of Jerome's death gets out, the matchmakers will swarm Tavistock like bees searching for a new hive."

"Why couldn't Jerome die after Tavistock has taken a bride?" Jeanette tried to find labels for her feelings. Sadness for Jerome's sisters, who'd been fond of him, but who'd never crossed the Channel to visit him on the Continent. Worry for Trevor. Sadness for Jerome, though he apparently had not suffered and had died in the company of a woman who loved him.

Nowhere, though, among those feelings could she find shock or dismay. Jerome had always been a rascal and a wastrel. That he hadn't been sent to his reward by frustrated creditors or some young lady's furious family was the real surprise.

"Jerome is dead," Rye said, "and I doubt you can keep the news quiet for long. Somebody should warn Tavistock—in person—that his cousin and heir has passed away. Don't trust the information to the post. No black-banded epistles to get the staff talking or the posting inn taking notice."

Rye had been a fine strategist and still was. "I'll send Sycamore out to Berkshire. He had no excuse to linger in Crosspatch, but I can tell he's itching to see how matters for Trevor are progressing."

"You are itching to see how matters are progressing. More brandy?" Rye rose and collected her glass.

"No, thank you. The right marchioness could do much to brighten Trevor's days. He was self-possessed, even solitary, at the age of eight. He was nine when I married his father, and in some ways, Trevor was already more adult than the marquess. It took me years to earn my step-son's trust, and I never felt I had the whole of it."

"The right *wife*," Rye said, finishing his drink and setting the glasses on the sideboard, "could do much to brighten his lordship's days and nights. If he can find that wife among Society's belles and diamonds, I will be surprised."

"Sycamore says there's hope, though the situation in Crosspatch is a tad complicated. Tavistock told nobody there of his title, and by doing the equivalent of listening at keyholes, he's heard nothing but bad about himself."

"According to Sycamore," Rye said, "Trevor has made a complete shambles of his first attempt at wooing a lady. Perhaps I should go myself."

Sycamore and Rye had a complicated relationship. Sometimes they were brothers-by-marriage, other times they were employer and agent. Occasionally, they were partners in mischief, and sometimes they were friends. Jeanette didn't pry, and she didn't take sides, and neither her brother nor her husband put her in a position where she had to.

"Sycamore," Jeanette said, rising, "was amazingly adept at wooing me, and he counseled Tavistock to confess his duplicity at the first opportunity. His lordship is stubborn, though, and stubborn men seldom heed the best advice."

"A hit," Rye said, smiling the roguish smile he usually saved for Ann. "You haven't lost your touch, sister mine. Send your loyal vassal, and we will somehow muddle on at the Coventry in Sycamore's absence. If he leaves in the next hour and gets good horses at the changes, he can be in Crosspatch before sundown."

CHAPTER TWELVE

The past three days had been the realization of every ridiculous girlish fantasy Lissa had ever denied herself. Sweet hours with Trevor, sweet dreams of Trevor, sweet moments thinking of Trevor and when Lissa would next see him.

They'd taken to riding out at midmorning, trysting in the gatehouse, and picnicking by the river. Trevor had come for supper the previous evening, and Grandmama had most certainly not fallen asleep. Even Mama was losing some of the pinched, distracted quality that had haunted her for the past two years.

And yet, life went on too. As Lissa made her way along the bridle paths to Lark's Nest, the Twid burbled by, the birds chattered, the sun brought a hint of warmth to the air.

"Spring is here," Lissa murmured, patting Jacques's neck. "Or as good as."

She handed her mount off to a groom and rapped on Phillip's door.

"No change," Phillip said, stepping back and smiling. Lissa had only recently noticed how unrelentingly plain Phillip's attire was. Unstarched cravat, creased boots, worn breeches. He was always tidy, always fastidious, but it was as if he'd decided to wear the same costume—contented country squire—for every scene.

"I went down to check on the mares at first light," he said. "They toy with us, and when our backs are turned for an instant, we'll have a pasture full of foals. Do come in. You can watch me finish my breakfast."

"I'll join you," Lissa said. "I left Twidboro before my sisters came down to eat. Mr. Dorning joined us for supper last night, and Diana and Caroline outdid themselves trying to be grown up." And they'd done that for Lissa's sake, a touching display of support from an unexpected quarter.

"He's bold, your Mr. Dorning." Phillip ushered Lissa into his dining parlor and passed her a plate at the sideboard. Trevor would have filled that plate for her, which was neither here nor there.

Trevor absolutely was *Lissa's* Mr. Dorning. "Bold, because he accepted a dinner invitation? If I thought you'd accept, I'd send you one, but we can't even get you to dance at the assemblies on the rare occasions when you attend them."

Phillip gestured to the sliced ham, indicating that his guest should help herself first. "Not every lady would be enthusiastic about taking my hand, Lissa, and I'm not sure what a lot of linked arms and hands-held-high would do to my shoulder."

"*That's* why you never dance?" She speared a slice of meat and felt like a fool. "You worry about your arm?" They never discussed a weakness that, as far as Lissa knew, had been present since Phillip's birth. What else had Phillip been keeping to himself?

"I worry about my shoulder, but I also don't know the steps. I've watched them enough times, but watching, or studying a diagram on a page, and capering about are different undertakings."

Well, blast and botheration. "Phillip, you could have asked me to show you the movements."

He became absorbed in heaping eggs onto his plate. "And then we would have needed an accompanist, and another couple to form a square, and somebody to call the tune, and soon half the shire is watching me fall on my arse."

He'd certainly thought about learning to dance. "Half of London watched me fall on mine."

That apparently wasn't what he'd expected her to say. A slow smile spread upward from his lips to his cheeks to his eyes, and for the first time in her life, Lissa saw Phillip not as her friend, not as a pleasant and reliable fixture in her life, but as a handsome fellow with depths she'd never guessed at.

"You did not fall on your... your backside, Lissa DeWitt. We would have heard about that, even out here."

"Leave me some eggs. What Crosspatch heard was that I did not *take*, I was not popular, I received no offers. At my age, and with my infamously generous settlements, that amounts to the same thing as going top over tail at Almack's."

They took their seats at the table, Lissa at Phillip's right hand. Trevor would have somehow found a way to hold her chair, though Lissa managed easily enough.

"Why go back there again?" Phillip asked, sprinkling a pinch of salt on his eggs. "Why give them the satisfaction of an encore?"

"This year will be different." Lissa shoved a bite of ham into her mouth rather than explain to Phillip why this year—why the rest of her life—would be different in the best possible way. She was kinder, happier, and more full of hope and joy for having become Trevor Dorning's intended. They were not officially betrothed, which was even better than if she'd been sporting an engagement ring.

Trevor would propose at the perfect moment, after wooing her for the duration of the perfect courtship. The feelings he inspired, with his combination of private passion and public rectitude, were so different from what Lissa had felt with her near misses.

Titus buttoning up his falls, consulting his watch, and expecting Lissa to precede him from the library. "Ladies first." Meaning she took the risk of discovery while he restored his hair to its coiffure *à la Brutus.*

Charles touching a mere finger to his hat brim in the park, while he urged his horse to all but gallop past her.

"That is an alarming smile, Lissa," Phillip said, passing her the salt dish. "Determined and somewhat lupine."

"I made a mistake thinking I had to deal with polite society as if a shopkeeper's granddaughter had no place in Mayfair. I have as much right to turn down the room in my pretty frocks, or to sit up at night with a restless mare, or to while away an afternoon reading sonnets as the next woman. My home is here in Crosspatch, and it's the opinions of our good neighbors that matter to me."

Phillip paused in the midst of demolishing his eggs. "I'd say it's your opinion of yourself that should matter most. I have found you magnificent, if a bit overwhelming, should you be planning to inquire. I'd rather have you for a friend than an enemy. Might you pass the butter?"

That comment was surprisingly personal, even for plainspoken Phillip. "Has something changed for you, Phillip?" Lissa buttered two slices of toast and passed over the dish.

He scraped butter onto his toast, then drizzled honey over the butter. Such was Phillip's inherent sense of focus that when he was done, a perfect spiral of sweetness adorned the bread. He spread the honey evenly before taking a bite.

"Something has changed," he said, dabbing at his lips with his napkin. "Perhaps I have changed. I offered you a loan, and you thanked me kindly, probably believing that I could spare the equivalent of a summer's egg money."

"You were very generous, regardless. Thank you for the gesture."

He glowered at her over a forkful of eggs. "Not a gesture. Never that." He downed the eggs and took a sip of tea. "Dorning and I got to talking, about hops and barley and the best cooperage and so forth, and I realized... I am a good farmer, Lissa."

"You are a very good farmer. A walking almanac. You know farming better than Vicar knows his gospels, better than Dabney knows his farriery." *But not better than I know the feel of Trevor Dorning in my arms.*

"I should be a good farmer. I've done little else, and the subject lends itself to endless study and experimentation. Dorning has set his cap for you. He's taken Roland in hand. He dreams of possibilities at Miller's Lament I never imagined. He toured this house, asking me about this deal table or that painting, and I realized I am not attending to my own life. I'm drifting, a rudderless skiff bobbing along on the tide of changing seasons, not a man pursuing worthy ambitions."

The words were simple and honest and, from Phillip, profound. "Is that why your foyer smells of beeswax, lemon, and camphor? You see your dwelling with new eyes as well?"

"I've turned the housekeeper loose on the spring cleaning early, authorized her to hire as many village ladies as necessary to scrub the place from eaves to foundation. We're going through the attics room by room, I'm considering adding a conservatory, and I might even have Mrs. Peeksgill make me up a new suit or two."

"Have her make you a new wardrobe, Phillip. Tell Vicar you'd like his company on a jaunt into Reading. Visit a mercer's and take your time choosing the fabric."

Phillip grimaced. "Reading." His tone implied a large cache of putrid eggs immediately upwind.

"I'm not suggesting you go on a market day," Lissa went on, "but neither should you allow Crosspatch to hold you captive forever." Why had she taken so long to tell him that?

But Lissa knew why: She'd liked having Phillip on the next property over, a dependable, if shy, knowledgeable neighbor. Phillip had been a comfort, in his way, and Lissa hoped he'd say the same about her.

He finished his toast. "Are you a captive here?"

"I felt more like a prisoner in London." A prisoner to Papa's ambitions, Society's games, Gavin's absence, Mama's schemes... Did Trevor ever feel like that, as the illegitimate son of a lofty peer?

"But now you are free?" Phillip asked. "Do I conclude Mr. Dorning has been the agent of your liberation?"

"You conclude I don't answer rude questions." She spoiled her scold with a smile.

"I like him," Phillip said, finishing his tea. "Dorning is busy up here." He tapped his temple with a finger. "A fashionable gent to appearances, but he pays attention."

That last was said while Phillip peered into the dregs of his tea cup. He swirled the cup, and something about the gesture struck Lissa as familiar. She'd seen Phillip make the same gesture previously, of course, and examining tea leaves was more than a metaphor, but still...

"Phillip, how did you come to be at Lark's Nest?"

He set down his tea cup. "In the usual fashion. I was born here, by all accounts. My mother's health was delicate, and she did not want to compound the challenges of childbed with the ordeal of London in summertime. Lark's Nest was suited to the purpose."

"What happened to your mother?"

He rose, though Lissa still had a piece of toast to finish. "Died, I'm afraid. Her health was never robust, though she apparently had a lively mind. Granny Jones recalls Mama fondly, as do I. Will you and Mr. Dorning be riding out again today?"

Lissa stood and took her last piece of toast with her. "Have you been spying, Phillip?"

"I've heard laughter drifting up from the path along the Twid. I've seen evidence of two riders passing by Lark's Nest side by side. I know Roland's particular whinny, and he does greet the mares when he's in the vicinity."

"Are we that obvious?"

Phillip paused in the dining room doorway. "Methinks you are that besotted, but if Dorning ever gives you cause to regret his acquaintance, you can count on me to hold him accountable. I am a dead shot, in case he has a need to inquire."

"I suspect he is, too, and not only with an antique fowling piece."

"Details."

Lissa munched her toast as Phillip led her through the public rooms, explaining his plans for new curtains here, a reupholstered love seat there. In the parlor, he'd taken down the portrait of the blond lady and propped it against the sideboard. Another painting rested on the mantel, not yet properly hung.

"The same woman," Lissa said. "The late marchioness?" And a solemn little blond boy standing beside her. "Is that the heir?"

"I suppose so. Mrs. Peeksgill thought an informal portrait ought to grace the informal parlor, but I've asked her to give the painting a cleaning and find someplace else to hang it."

Phillip had spoken sharply, for him. "Someplace like the cow byre?" Lissa studied the boy, who was past the age of breeching, but not by much. Such a serious little lad, and for the second time in an hour, she had a sense of elusive familiarity. "That would be the present marquess?"

"I know not who he is, but he's too superior for my parlor."

Not superior, the lad looked... stoic, beyond the patience demanded of a child holding a pose for a portraitist. That boy had already learned some of life's harder lessons and was resigned to learning more.

"A proper little man," she murmured, moving closer. The child's attire was exquisitely made for such a small person, right down to a tricorn hat trimmed with gold braid and silver buckles on his Sunday shoes. "His mother loved him."

The lady had a hand on the boy's shoulder, and her expression was the epitome of maternal devotion. Pride, joy, a touch of worry, and tremendous fondness. The child's expression, by contrast, was devoid of emotion.

Sad little creature. Lissa looked for a signature. "Good God, this is a Reynolds, and it has been gathering dust in your lumber room?"

"I didn't commission it, for pity's sake," Phillip said, pacing for the door. "Haven't you a handsome swain to meet by the mill?"

"We meet at the Arms, in broad daylight for all of Crosspatch to see."

"And you kiss by the mill."

Among other places. Lissa grinned. "You've seen us?"

"Tansy Pevinger has made a few comments that suggest she might have. Be careful, Lissa. Dorning is apparently a lovely fellow, but we aren't all who we seem to be."

"Precisely," she said, turning her back on the mother and child. "Polite society says I seem to be a shopkeeper's uppish granddaughter with more settlements than refinement. Little do they know that I am the belle of Crosspatch Corners."

Phillip offered her a swirling bow, gesturing with his left hand. "Tell it to Dorning. I've seen you with straw in your hair and manure on your skirts."

"And yet, I can still be a belle, can't I?" And the woman Trevor Dorning loved most in the whole world. "Who are you, Phillip?"

Lissa expected a flippant reply, a reference to the walking almanac of Berkshire, the Crosspatch expert on sheep breeds, a knight of the foaling shed...

Phillip's gaze went to the portrait, his eyes bleak. "I am nobody of any consequence. I'll keep vigil over the mares, though, and you can give Dorning my regards."

Lissa studied the portrait one last time, seeing a resemblance between Phillip's expression and that of the serious boy. She visually reviewed the child's features, one by one, until she reached his left ear.

Reynolds favored flattering his subjects, but perhaps with this small boy, the artist thought evidence of a typical childhood mishap might humanize his subject. The child had recently suffered a laceration to the earlobe, hinted at by the artist.

Everything in Lissa focused on the painting as a sense of dread congealed in her middle. The hair was too blond, but then, blonds were often lighter in childhood.

"Do you know who that child is, Phillip?" Lissa knew. She didn't want to admit that she knew, but her body confirmed the boy's identity. Peculiar sensations skittered down her arms, and a strange quality of mental distance came over her.

"I don't know anything," Phillip said. "Let it go, Lissa. Please."

"You know that is the late Marchioness of Tavistock, and she is posing with her son, the present marquess." The chin was the same, the line of the mouth, the resolution in the jaw, the reserve in the gaze... All unchanged by the passing years. "Trevor told me the marquess was his father. I assumed plain Trevor *Dorning*, who has little use for doing the fancy in Town, would be one of the old man's by-blows. I am apparently in error."

"You don't know that. Brothers often bear a resemblance, even half-brothers."

Lissa stalked from the parlor. "Don't take up the false art of empty platitudes now, Phillip. I have very nearly made a fool of myself over a man again, but the situation yet has a remedy."

Lissa wanted to pound her fists against the ancient bulwark of the napping oak, to shut herself in the cavernous safety of Crosspatch's watermill and curse down the rafters, and she wanted to pummel Trevor Dorning flat. Beneath those impulses, understandable in the circumstances, was also a howling sense of loss.

No dream, no future, no marriage worth the name was built on a lie, and as surely as Mr. Pevinger and Mr. Dabney would argue on market day, Trevor Dorning—*if that was his name*—had lied to Lissa and then taken her to bed.

~

"I simply cannot fathom that Jerome is gone," Trevor said as he and Sycamore waited on the steps of the Arms for the Dorning coach to be brought around. The morning sun still rose in the east, and a daring rabbit had ventured onto the green from the shade of the vicarage's oaks. The vicar himself was taking a constitutional outing about the green, his wife and housekeeper bookending him.

Daffodils bloomed beneath the market cross, and the village went about the start of its day just as it had been for centuries.

But Jerome Vincent—cousin, companion, traveling partner, aggravation, and heir—was no more.

"The notion of his death is difficult because you haven't seen him in ages," Sycamore said. "You weren't there when he passed, never shared a final pint with him, probably can't bring your last conversation with him to mind."

"My last conversation with him was the same as many others. I tried to discreetly inquire if he needed funds as he prepared for another jaunt across the Continent, and he'd say, 'No, thank you, my dear. But the inquiry is appreciated.' He'd offer a casual wave farewell, and then I'd worry for weeks."

"Like when my papa hared off on his horticultural sorties," Sycamore said, slapping his gloves against his thigh. "He'd be gone for eternities by a small boy's reckoning, and the longer he was gone, the more fretful Mama became, which made me fretful because grown-ups are not always forthcoming with children. I'd worry that Papa had gone away to die, like a cat that seeks solitude in its final days."

Trevor bestirred himself from his grief—because that's what this bewildered ache was—long enough to realize that Sycamore, ever confident, irreverent, and resourceful, had just disclosed more than he'd meant to.

"You asked your brothers, didn't you? You made certain your papa wasn't behaving like an old mouser." Such a wealth of brothers Sycamore had, and some sisters too. If Trevor had a regret, it was that his wedding day would see so little in the way of family present on behalf of the groom.

Here in Crosspatch, that would not matter, but if the wedding were held in Mayfair, the lack would be endlessly remarked. Though to blazes with Mayfair, provided its denizens showed the future Marchioness of Tavistock a proper welcome this year.

"I asked my sisters," Sycamore said. "The ladies had the ear of the staff, and my brothers started trooping off to public school when I was still toddling."

And that, Trevor realized, had also been a source of grief for a very young Sycamore. Maybe a large family wasn't the unqualified blessing Trevor supposed it to be.

"*Où diable est...* Where the hell is the coach?" Trevor wanted to pace, to fiddle with his hat, to slap his gloves as Sycamore was doing, but nervous behavior had been scolded and birched out of him decades ago.

"We aren't the Royal Mail," Sycamore said. "Jeanette would have sent an express if the news had hit Town. Jerome apparently died at some obscure *schloss* in the Bavarian forest."

"A castle. My cousin died in a castle, a countess to mourn his passing. Jerome would have been pleased to know that." If he'd ever regained consciousness, though drifting into oblivion after a passing tumble from the saddle was probably the kindest death possible.

That thought steadied Trevor. Jerome had led a rackety life as an impecunious spare barely supported by his expectations, but he'd had a kind death.

"Isn't that Miss DeWitt up on your Jacques?" Sycamore asked, gloves going blessedly silent.

"Indeed it is." The sight of her, trotting so calmly around the green, brought peace to Trevor's heart. "They get on splendidly, and Jacques is a discerning fellow."

Sycamore peered at him with those peculiar gentian eyes. "Have you gone and proposed?"

"Don't sound so hopeful. I esteem the lady greatly and hope to further our acquaintance in Town this spring, though I have a spot of mourning to do first." Four weeks of full mourning for a first cousin, but Jerome's demise would buy Trevor a longer period of reduced socializing after the initial month.

All the better if he limited his outings to escort duty for the lovely Miss DeWitt.

"Thank you, Jerome," he murmured as Amaryllis brought

Jacques to a halt at the foot of the inn's steps. She wore no hat, and the sun caught every fiery highlight in her hair. She apparently perceived that Sycamore had not returned to Crosspatch on a frivolous errand. Her expression as she mounted the steps was nearly solemn.

Trevor longed to sweep her into his arms and hold her, but had to settle for doffing his hat and making a stupid bow.

"Miss DeWitt. Your arrival is fortuitous."

She curtseyed as if they were at some damned Venetian breakfast. "Mr. Dorning, and Mr. Dorning. Are you preparing to depart?"

"We are," Sycamore said when he ought to have kept his mouth shut. "Urgent business. No time for delay. Urgent *family* business."

Amaryllis flicked an annoyed gaze at Sycamore. "*Family* business? Dorning *family* business?"

This was Crosspatch, so of course some youthful Pevinger of the female persuasion was making a great production of scrubbing the inn's spotless steps. A groom had materialized to hold Jacques's reins, though Jacques would stand on command until Kingdom Come.

The vicar and his honor guard had taken up a bench directly across the road, and several older women had congregated near the cross.

"There's been a death in the family," Trevor said quietly. "In my family."

"My condolences."

Amaryllis had lost her father and grandfather, she feared her brother had followed them to the grave, and those two words, uttered with the next thing to detachment, were all wrong.

"A cousin," Trevor said. "Once entangled with my expectations. I'll have to settle the resulting affairs and..."

The maid on the steps was frankly gawking, as were Vicar and his housekeeper.

Amaryllis cocked her head. "You were saying?"

"This is not the time or the place to go into details, but my return to Town has become urgent. I've left a note for you with Mrs.

Pevinger, though the message is brief in the interests of discretion. The livery will send Roland to you later today, and I will dispatch a groom to retrieve Jacques by the first of the week."

Amaryllis's features still showed no relenting, no warmth, but then, she was likely as shocked by Trevor's sudden demise as he was.

"You could keep Jacques for me," he said, taking a step closer to her. "Bring him with you when you remove to Town at the end of the month?" He needed for her to approve that plan, to light upon it as a means of staying connected through a silly, sentimental gesture. Jacques had been one of their chaperones, along with Roland and the placid waters of the Twid.

"Why don't you take him now?" Amaryllis said. "Your saddle and bridle are on him, and he was at grass all night. That will simplify matters."

"Worthy suggestion," Sycamore said when he again ought to have kept his rubbishing mouth shut. "One less detail to tidy up. Miss Dewitt can ride the other gelding home."

Trevor felt as if the reins of his situation were slipping through his fingers, and he was powerless to gain them back. The separation from Amaryllis would be temporary, but the parting was going badly.

The coach chose that inopportune moment to lumber around the corner, four matched grays in the traces.

"Let's be off," Sycamore said, a shade too brightly. "*Tempus fugit* and all that." He passed a pair of saddlebags to a groom, who stowed them inside the coach.

"Is that the Dorning crest?" Amaryllis asked, giving the coach a baleful inspection.

"Sycamore wanted to ride out here hotfoot with the sad news," Trevor said. "My step-mother made him pack properly and take one of our traveling coaches. The crest is mine."

Amaryllis nodded as if Trevor had confirmed a suspicion. "Then I will wish you safe journey, my lord, and offer repeated condolences on your loss." For the first time, she looked at him with something approaching warmth, or hope, or longing.

Trevor did not care for the milording from her, but he'd told her himself of his title. "You will come to Town, Amaryllis?"

Sycamore stood by the coach, all but pawing the earth and wringing his tail with impatience, about which Trevor cared not one French profanity.

"Yes," she said very calmly. "Yes, I shall. Safe journey, and thank you for some interesting memories." She kissed his cheek, and Trevor felt as if she'd kicked him in the cods.

"Amaryllis, are you well?"

"I will manage." She offered him a bright, false smile. "You must be off, of course. At least you have fine weather for the journey. I'll see about having Roland saddled."

She strode down the steps and around the corner of the innyard, divided skirt swishing briskly.

"Not the farewell you'd anticipated?" Sycamore asked, taking Trevor by the arm and half hauling him down the steps.

Trevor shook free, resisting the mighty temptation to send Sycamore sprawling on his backside. "I'll ride with John Coachman on the bench," he said as a groom ran up Jacques's stirrups and let the girth out two holes before tying the reins to the back of the coach. "You may enjoy your own company inside, or bide here for all I care."

"Miss DeWitt is angry to see you go," Sycamore said. "I know the look. She can't argue with a death in the family, but the lady had plans for you this morning that did not include a public fare-thee-well."

"Her plans for me and mine for her involve the rest of our lives. Stop dawdling, Dorning. *Le temps passe* and all that."

"You only speak French when you're upset."

"*Va au diable.*" Trevor scaled the coach and took the place beside the coachman, who nodded a greeting, his hands full of reins. Sycamore climbed into the coach, and the moment arrived for Trevor to take his leave of Crosspatch Corners.

Amaryllis stood at the corner of the innyard, tall, composed, bare-headed. As the coach rocked forward, Trevor swept off his hat and waved, then blew her a kiss in parting while half of the village looked on.

She barely nodded, and Trevor came to the very puzzling conclusion that Sycamore was right: Amaryllis wasn't merely annoyed at this sudden change of plans, she was angry, possibly even furious.

And that made no sense at all, given what Trevor knew of her general good sense, compassion, and—most especially—her stated regard for him.

The coach clattered away from the green, and Crosspatch Corners was lost to Trevor's view.

CHAPTER THIRTEEN

The damage done by a lie was rarely limited to the falsehood itself.

Everybody, from Mama, to Grandmama, to Vicar, to the fancy deportment instructors at Lissa's finishing school had agreed on that. The greater harm was to one's reputation when the lie was revealed. A fib told to spare a neighbor's feelings or flatter a friend was tolerable in moderation, but nobody respected self-serving dishonesty.

Nobody trusted a liar. Except, apparently, for Amaryllis DeWitt, if the liar was a fashionable bachelor.

Lissa patted Roland soundly on the neck, dismounted, and handed the reins to the Twidboro groom. "He was a perfect gentleman, and I gave him every opportunity for bad manners."

"Roland needed to get away from the Hall for a bit," the groom replied, loosening the girth and running up the stirrups. "See the sights, learn a few lessons that the home pastures can't teach. The lad has a sense of himself now. You can see it in the eye. Mr. Dorning did right by him."

Mr. Dorning had not done right by Lissa, and yet, he also hadn't acted like a man caught in a betrayal. She knew *that* look only too well. She pondered the conundrum of Trevor's behavior at the Arms as she made her way up to the Hall.

"Lissa!" Caroline was sitting on the side porch with a book in her lap, and for once, the child was smiling. "Has Roland graduated from finishing school?"

"Something like that. What are you reading?"

Caroline held up a tome bound in morocco leather. "Wordsworth. Mr. Dorning recommended it at supper last night. Did you know Mr. Wordsworth went to Paris to support the anti-royalists when he was a youth? Mr. Dorning told me that."

"The poet is hardly doddering now, and he seems to have settled his spirits." Or the unmitigated savagery of the Revolution had dissuaded him from radical tendencies.

"Mr. Wordsworth settled his spirits by communing with nature," Caroline said, her smile taking on a smug quality. "Mr. Dorning said the contemplatives have always sought the wisdom and solitude of nature. Are there female contemplatives, Lissa?"

Mr. Dorning... Mr. Dorning... Diana was similarly afflicted with a need to quote Trevor, while mention of him left Mama looking thoughtful and Grandmama smiling.

Lissa took the place beside her sister on the sun-warmed bench. "If we haven't any lady contemplatives, you can be the first. You certainly love to wander the out of doors. Your bluebells will soon be blooming."

"I might miss them, if Mama lets me go to London."

Why had Trevor inquired about Lissa's London plans? Had that been for form's sake? Had he realized his dishonesty had been revealed?

Grandmama emerged from the house, a paisley shawl about her shoulders. "Greetings, children. I do believe spring has finally arrived. Amaryllis, how fare our mares?"

"Phillip gave an all's well report."

Grandmama propped her cane against a wrought-iron chair

shaded by the overhang of the portico and settled onto the cushion by deliberate degrees. "And is all well with our Mr. Dorning?"

He's not ours, and he's not Mr. Dorning. "No, actually. He claimed that a death in the family required his immediate remove to Town."

"One cannot argue with death," Grandmama said, closing her eyes. "I will miss him. He was a lovely fellow, and he seemed to take to Cross-patch as few of the Town tulips do. The air in spring smells so hopeful. If one must be commended to the earth, it should be on a day such as this."

"The air smells like manure," Caroline said. "Phillip always cleans out the loafing shed on his home farm when the weather warms up. Who died, Lissa? Was it Mr. Dorning's step-mother?"

His step-mother, the former marchioness, of whom he'd spoken so fondly, the one who'd married a Dorning.

"He wasn't specific," Lissa said, thinking back. "A cousin." One entangled with Trevor's expectations—a fiancée sort of cousin, perhaps? A fictitious sort of cousin?

Though Trevor's upset had seemed real.

"He's going to London, though, right?" Caroline set her book aside. "And you are going to London. You can resume your friendship in Town."

Any interest Lissa had had in a return to London—little enough to begin with—had clattered out of sight along with Trevor's sump-tuous traveling coach. Crests displayed, matched grays in the traces, liveried coachman and grooms...

Ye gods, he was the Marquess of Tavistock. Their *landlord*, a notorious pinchpenny until recently, and he'd... Why had he come to Crosspatch, and why had he lingered?

"I'm off to have a look at the bluebell wood," Caroline said. "Maybe it will bloom early this year if the weather stays mild."

"Fetch a hat," Lissa said, though Caroline's hats ended up hanging from tree branches, floating down the Twid, or pressed into service as a trug for flowers and medicinals.

"Your father loved to roam the countryside," Grandmama said, opening her eyes as Caroline dashed into the house. "Gavin and Caroline get that from him." Grandmama was being kind, offering Lissa a change of subject if she wanted one.

She wanted for Trevor to be who he'd said he was. "Grandmama, I can't abide the thought of setting foot in London again."

"But your Mr. Dorning will be there. Has he played you false, Lissa?"

"In a sense." She took up Caroline's book, lest it be forgotten out in the elements. "The man who told us he's Trevor Dorning is, in fact, the current Marquess of Tavistock, Grandmama. The peer. Our landlord. Son of the strutting popinjay who would not sell Twidboro to us twenty years ago. He's the fellow who threatened to raise our rent."

"And who apparently changed his mind, at least about the rent." Grandmama rearranged her shawl. "I did notice a resemblance, but then, the old marquess was something of a Lothario. Many of his ilk behaved no better, and nobody remarked it as long as they supported the fruits of their diversions."

What sort of society regarded siring hapless children born into scandal as a diversion? "You noticed a resemblance, but you didn't say anything to me?"

"Lady Cowper's paternity is a mystery, apparently even to her, and she's a patroness at Almack's. I thought it quite possible Mr. Dorning—the fellow we thought was Mr. Dorning—was old Lord Tavistock's unacknowledged by-blow, or an acknowledged one. Does it matter?"

"I wish you'd mentioned that." Though Trevor had said in plain English that the marquess was his father. Lissa had assumed Trevor was illegitimate, and he had not corrected her error. She could not recall her precise words, though she could conjure up every detail of what had followed Trevor's disclosure.

"Will you cower here in Crosspatch so you can strike Tavistock from the rolls of eligibles too, Lissa? He seemed like a charming

young man, though every bounder in Mayfair claims a full complement of charm."

He'd said he meant to propose, but then he hadn't proposed.

He'd said he was Tavistock's son, but had not admitted that he
himself was the marquess.

He'd said his remove to Town would be soon, but then he'd
planned to depart without a farewell.

"I cannot trust him," Lissa muttered. "I did trust him, and he
wasn't who I thought he was."

Grandmama took up the Wordsworth. "Dearest child, nobody is
who we think they are. This is the real challenge in any marriage. You
speak your vows, perhaps having known each other for years, perhaps
for weeks, but there are always disappointments and surprises. Your
grandfather snored—loudly. He was not prepared for me to be
peevish about limitations on my pin money."

She smiled at the closed book. "We rowed," she went on. "We
sulked, we made up, until we rowed again. It took us years to reach
smooth sailing, and then your grandfather got up to the sort of foolishness men of a certain age are infamous for. He was wealthy by then,
and his coin allowed him to be a very great idiot indeed."

"Opera dancers?" Lissa asked, half fascinated and half fearing the
answer.

"Two in particular, upon whom he lavished his generosity all the
way to Ludgate and back. Your father became aware of the situation
and delivered a stern set-down to his sire. The foolishness stopped."

And this memory caused Grandmama to smile fondly?

"I don't want to be foolish, Grandmama. Not again. I was certain
that Trevor was different, that he was his own man and a good man,
but what marquess sets out to marry a shopkeeper's granddaughter?
A veritable village girl? I ride astride here at home. I help with the
foaling. I scrub my own hems if it's half day for the maid. How could
a marquess possibly...?"

"Then you don't distrust him—or not just him—but also
yourself?"

Lissa rose. "Of course myself. My judgment where suitors are concerned has been notoriously bad."

"Or your mother's vigilance as your chaperone has been inadequate. Those rascals in Town knew you had neither father nor brother to defend your honor, and Mourna relaxed her guard. All most vexing. If you don't want to go to London, then don't, but we've let down Caroline's hems as far as they'll go, and Diana's opportunities to attend tea dances in Crosspatch are sorely limited."

Lissa leaned against the porch post, which could have used a fresh coat of paint. "You are saying I must not think only of myself."

Grandmama opened the book to a random poem. "You are constitutionally incapable of thinking only of yourself, and Lord Tavistock probably has obligations he can't shirk either. As I see it, you have understandable questions, and his lordship has answers. If you don't like his answers, you are free to reject his suit."

"And if I *do* like his answers?"

"The harder question, by far, and only you know the answer."

"I haven't any answers at the moment. Phillip had suspicions."

Grandmama closed the book with a snap. "You and Phillip would not suit. He's very dear, and that business with his arm or shoulder, or whatever plagues him, is of no moment, but please don't set your cap for that one."

"I like Phillip." More significantly, Lissa could *trust* Phillip.

"You respect him, but Phillip is no fool. He's seen you with Mr. Dorning, and what man wants to go through life knowing his wife chose him because she could manage him?"

"It wouldn't be like that." It would be exactly like that, with Lissa doing all the trips into Reading and Phillip burying himself in pamphlets and agriculture. They would rub along well enough, and children would probably arrive, and all the while...

"Trevor lied about his name and sustained that lie until very recently. He's no more a Dorning than I am a marchioness." Though Grandmama had a point too. The solicitors were in London, and something had to be done about their miserly meddling. "Perhaps Trevor has an explanation for his dissembling."

Lissa wanted him to have one, and she wanted to hide in Crosspatch until she was as venerable as the napping oak.

"Then you're going to London?" Grandmama asked.

Lissa pushed away from the peeling post. The air did bear the tang of the loafing shed, and the view of the Twid was slightly obscured by the emerging leaves. Crosspatch was lovely, and it was home, though for a moment, Lissa understood exactly why Gavin had needed to escape it.

Some answers were to be found only by leaving home pastures. "The DeWitt ladies will go to Town to enjoy the Season. Mr. Clementi will doubtless accompany us, and while we are in London, I will have a very pointed discussion with the blasted solicitors."

"One takes on solicitors cautiously, Lissa."

"If I have to ride half naked through Hyde Park, all of London will know that Giles Purvis has begrudged us even money for decent wardrobes for the past two years. That is *our money*, Grandmama, and he behaves as if it's his. Society will view that presumption dimly."

"I've said as much to Mourna, but she keeps hoping Gavin will come home and sort matters out discreetly."

"We cannot wait for Gavin, and we cannot toady to Purvis. Trevor lied and deceived us and waved a false flag, but he was right about at least one thing: What we need and want matters." Not quite what he'd said, but close enough. "Purvis has no excuse for keeping us in embarrassed circumstances, and I mean to make that point very clear to him."

"Mourna will object. I suggest you glower at her as you are glowering now. Puts me in mind of your grandfather on the subject of taxes."

"Do you still miss him, Grandmama? Foolishness and all?"

"Every day, my dear. Every single day."

Lissa's decision made, she left Grandmama on the porch with

Mr. Wordsworth and asked for a bath to be run. She was choosing a day dress—a rich green rather than the pale shades she was expected to don in London—when the maid brought her a folded note.

"From the Arms, miss."

"Thank you."

The handwriting was exquisite, worthy of a professional scribe. *Miss Amaryllis DeWitt* was neatly penned on the outside, the wax seal impressed with the same crest she'd seen on the traveling coach.

Did he think the Pevingers wouldn't notice *that* seal? For that matter, what was Lissa to make of such a bold acknowledgement of his status? What exactly had he said about his patrimony, and why had she assumed he was illegitimate?

Miss DeWitt,

Please forgive the presumption of correspondence addressed to you personally. The press of business requires my presence urgently in London. My thanks to your family for their generous hospitality, and I pray our paths will soon cross in Town.

I remain your obed serv,

T.

Well, there was another lie—he'd never been her obedient servant—but their paths would cross in Town. Lissa would make sure of it.

～

"Not the done thing, to spy on one's solicitors," Worth Kettering said, showing Trevor into a room that blended the qualities of an office with those of a genteel parlor. The round Louis Quinze table by the window would serve equally well for a spot of tea or some reading. The elegant desk was discreetly tucked in a corner, and the carpet, curtains, and pillows were coordinated around a cheery theme of irises and restful green foliage.

The purpose of the room, Trevor realized, was to send a message of social welcome that relegated any financial discussion to the status of afterthought and detail. Only clients from the upper reaches of Society would crave that fiction. The rest of the world—the good folk of Crosspatch Corners, for example—dealt pragmatically with commercial realities.

"Not the done thing to spy, period," Trevor replied as Kettering closed a solid oak door. No eavesdropping through those intricately carved planks, and the mechanism was a latch-and-lock. No listening at keyholes either. "But how does one catch a thief without bending a few rules of etiquette?"

"Valid question. I'll ring for a tray, shall I?" Kettering's tone implied that he would enjoy a spot of tea and a biscuit, and if Trevor wouldn't mind obliging him...?

The trick of a gracious host or a shrewd solicitor.

"Tea would be appreciated." Trevor had been in Town for more than a week and was still having trouble sleeping. Too damned noisy, and the wrong sorts of noise, the wrong sights, the wrong stinks, the wrong everything.

Kettering tugged a bell-pull twice. He was an impressive figure, tall, lithe, and exquisitely kitted out. Touches of silver at his temples only added to an air of formidable self-possession. He'd married the oldest Dorning daughter—Lady Jacaranda—and was legendarily besotted with her.

"Your wife was at one time your housekeeper, was she not?" Trevor asked as Kettering pushed back curtains to let in what passed for afternoon sun in the metropolis. Dingy, desultory illumination compared to what graced the countryside.

"She was," Kettering said, "though we rarely refer to the particulars of our courtship outside of family. You qualify—Dorning-by-association."

"Honored, of course. Why was an earl's daughter in service?"

Why had her ladyship lied about her antecedents, as Trevor had lied about his to the whole village of Crosspatch, save for one exceptional lady?

"Jacaranda was on a sort of holiday from her family. The Dorning brothers have mellowed with time. They aren't all in Sycamore's league when it comes to being a pest, but they can be—I know this will surprise you—a lot of overbearing louts."

Then Lady Jacaranda was well prepared for marriage to an overbearing lout? A real Dorning would have posed that question aloud. "You rescued her from them?"

"More the other way around. She rescued me from my own loutishness, though I'm still a work in progress." A work in progress who sported a fatuous smile at the mention of his courting days.

The tray arrived, and Kettering poured out. He'd chosen to fulfill his office as host at the table by the window, and Trevor was honestly grateful for the tray of sandwiches and cakes accompanying the service.

"What have you learned of Jerome Vincent's affairs?" Kettering asked, helping himself to a raspberry cake.

Trevor took two sandwiches. They were minuscule, and Kettering wasn't having any. "Jerome had apparently grown up after all, in his fashion. He had established a thriving venture that imported and exported bawdy prints across the Channel. The French appreciate our particular brand of political satire, while we English have an eye for the Continent's more ribald art. Jerome wasn't wealthy, but he was well on the way to comfortable."

And that news had been beyond gratifying.

"What will you do with the business?"

"I've sent an inquiry to the countess. She could take over the business in partnership with Jerome's Paris factor. Too soon for a reply yet, but she intended to marry Jerome, and despite dwelling in a castle, she might enjoy the connection to him."

"Or the income," Kettering said, dipping his cake into his tea. "Widows are all too often in want of income. Now, about Purvis."

Trevor swirled his tea, prepared to hear bad news. "Say on."

"He's a snake—you are entirely correct about that—but he's a shrewd snake. I sent a fellow to your larger manor in Kent—Solvang. Odd name, but the place prospers. Excellent land, and the tenant knows how to care for it. His subtenants adore him, and his missus is the neighborhood's granny-at-large. I gather they intended to live out their years in gracious contentment on your property."

"But then they got word that the rent was being raised," Trevor said, "and Lord Tavistock, believing that the rent is quite modest and has been for years, would support that notion if they were so bold as to query him on it. The place is doing well after all. The name means 'sunny field' in Danish, and the land is lovely."

Kettering helped himself to a second raspberry biscuit. "According to my man, who could charm the keys of heaven from Saint Peter's grasp, the rent on Solvang is nine hundred pounds per annum and has been raised three times in the past twelve years."

Of course it has. "Your man's report varies significantly from what Purvis is telling me. The rent is four hundred pounds per annum and hasn't been raised for the past fifteen years. A sad overindulgence on my part, not to demand the coin I'm due as the owner."

Kettering finished his biscuit and dusted his hands over the tray. "Shall I send somebody to York? You have two properties up there, if I recall correctly?"

"I'll sell those," Trevor said. "I'm fairly certain Purvis took out mortgages on them during my minority, or reborrowed against a mortgage my father had all but paid off, all without telling me a thing until recently. I want nothing to do with mortgages and the bankers who profit from them."

Kettering munched his biscuit. "I can make quiet inquiries of the tenants. They might not be as disdainful of the bankers as you are. The current tenants are the logical buyers."

Trevor chose a third sandwich. Plain fare was preferable to the delicacies Cook was determined to serve him at his town house, no matter how many hints he passed along to the housekeeper, no matter how many of the delicacies were returned to the kitchen to be devoured by the footmen.

"Bankers in the general case are likely above reproach. My bankers apparently can't tell my signature from that of a forgery."

Kettering sat back, making the chair creak. "Purvis likely started out clerking for his father. He would have learned at an early age how to skillfully wield a pen. If you spend your formative years learning how to reproduce perfect copperplate, you also acquire the ability to replicate signatures. My clerks explained this to me in the most delicate terms."

"Forgery is a hanging felony."

"But the client's signature is not always easily obtained, and in some legal offices, signing *for* a client is regarded as acceptable, with the client's permission in writing and provided one doesn't make a habit of it."

"Purvis has apparently made a regular fortune from appropriating my signature. When Purvis isn't putting my name on mortgage documents, he's raising rents at my imaginary direction. My priority now is to disentangle myself from him and his schemes."

Kettering crossed his legs at the knee, a posture acceptable on the Continent, but considered too informal for Mayfair's drawing rooms.

"You are riding a tiger," he said. "I've given the matter some thought, and your situation confounds even me."

"Purvis has stolen from me and from my tenants. He has misrepresented me, abused his office, likely forged my signature, and... I can't prove any of this, can I? If he can forge my signature, he could forge a note from me approving his various schemes. A few words, my name, my seal—which he doubtless has had since my father's day —and his crimes become invisible."

"It's worse than that," Kettering said. "If you bring down the law on him, he will let it be known in polite circles that you are sadly pockets to let. The pathetic bankrupt peer, pointing fingers at everybody but himself to hide his disgrace."

"I'm not bankrupt." Jeanette had put as much of Trevor's funds as she could into the cent-per-cents, and Trevor had insisted that those funds be left to slowly and safely accrue interest.

"Tavistock," Kettering said gently, "one need not *be* bankrupt for whispers of pending insolvency to soon render one a bankrupt. If you are rumored to be in dun territory, the trades demand payment in full rather than wait for a December reckoning. The banks accelerate the mortgages based on justifiable insecurities. The vowels all come due, and Purvis has seen to it that rents are not paid to you directly. They are paid to his offices, and thus you haven't even pin money."

The DeWitt ladies had been managing with very little in the way of pin money. Trevor had sent three notes by special messenger out to Twidboro Hall and hadn't received a single reply. Young ladies typically did not correspond with bachelors of short acquaintance, but Amaryllis was Trevor's intended, and her silence ate at him.

When he wasn't dwelling on that unhappy development, he was instead focused on his finances.

"If I reveal Purvis's scheming, but bring no criminal charges, then he's ruined, too, isn't he?"

"Without doubt. Rich but ruined. Not a bad compromise in the opinion of many."

Trevor rose and took the place behind Kettering's fussy desk. The chair was at least comfortable. "But if I ruin Purvis, then his clerks, his son, his other clients, all suffer as well. Then too, he will doubtless turn the tide of gossip against me. I was gullible, careless, and easily duped, or he'd never have been able to pull off his schemes."

Kettering rose and took himself to a wing chair. "You were young, trusting, and without champions. You did nothing wrong."

"And yet," Trevor said, "Purvis has me in a corner. If I accuse him in a court of law, then I cause a great scandal that reveals me to be a fool too lazy to mind his own ledgers. If I confront Purvis without involving the authorities, he quietly ensures that I become the bankrupt he's nearly made me. Either way, the scandal lands on me. I can be ruined for either stupidity or insolvency, or—if Purvis is feeling lively—both."

More to the point, Amaryllis was expecting a proposal from a properly set-up marquess, not some titled, destitute bumbler. She had no use for fortune hunters, she'd made that clear. Trevor hadn't any use for them either.

"Purvis won't want to kill the goose laying all the golden eggs," Kettering said. "He had to know you'd catch on to him sooner or later. Until a few years ago, your finances were in the hands of old Smithers. He was a plodder, but honest within the limits of his clientele. Some stray comment from Jeanette, a casual encounter with a tenant... Sooner or later, you'd start asking questions."

"You do not reproach me for frolicking on the Continent?"

"You weren't frolicking. Fournier and I are cordial, and he was much impressed with you. A problem five years in the making might be five years in the untangling, but even Purvis has to eventually retire. The whole scheme falls apart when he's no longer in practice."

"Wait him out?" Amaryllis would never support such a passive course. "With my luck, he'll live to enjoy a spry and well-heeled five score years."

Kettering's air of savoir faire faltered. "I honestly don't know what you should do, Tavistock. Your finances can eventually be brought right. The properties are solvent, and you are no wastrel. Your good name, though, once stained by scandal, will never shine quite as brightly. Mayfair has a deuced long memory. Your grandchildren will pay the price if you are rumored to be bankrupt."

"What if I should sell the properties, one by one, and shut down Purvis's game by inches?"

"That... might... work."

And Kettering hadn't thought of it. A small consolation. Trevor rose, still hungry, still tired, and still very much missing Amaryllis and the bucolic splendor of Crosspatch.

"If I wanted to buy a farm out in Berkshire, could you finance the transaction?"

"Of course."

"You know I'm teetering on the verge of scandal and possible bankruptcy, but you would essentially buy me a whole farm on my word alone?"

"I am known for my ability to choose sound investments," Kettering said, coming to his feet. "More significantly, you have a firm grasp of commerce, and I cannot say that about any other peer of your rank. You were not idling about the Continent. You were scouting opportunities, learning the languages, and staying well clear of Mayfair's man-traps—or marquess-traps, as the case may be. I have faith in you, and Sycamore and Jeanette have faith in you."

What did one say to such... such... effusions? "Thank you. I haven't made up my mind about Miller's Lament, but I do like the place."

"Don't do anything precipitous," Kettering said, tugging the bell-pull again. "Suggest to Purvis that you want to sell off the Yorkshire properties and see how he reacts. He might be smart enough to content himself with the fortune he's already stolen from you."

"Test the waters. Good advice, though I am plagued by two questions."

"Greed is the answer to the first question," Kettering said, swiping another tea cake from the tray. "Purvis saw a way to better his situation, to do a bit of Robin-Hooding on his own behalf, though he'll tell himself he did it for the sake of his family's security. You were born with more wealth than you need, he was born having to work hard. Ergo, you owe him. He stole from you because, in his mind, he's the victim of undeserved misfortune."

"He should have been a marquess, of course. Granted, we all should be marquesses and marchionesses, and I even understand that, but the other question... Why does he think he can get away with this?"

"Because the peerage loathes scandal above all things. Your father was apparently haunted by the fact that he had only one son. That is hardly an affair in the hands of mere mortals, and yet, he was shamed by his inability to sire more than one legitimate son. Imagine how much worse bankruptcy or madness or some other infirmity would have haunted him."

"He was a terrible husband to Jeanette. He should have been haunted by that. I don't think my mother fared any better with him." Because the old blighter had been ashamed? A theory of some merit, but no sort of excuse.

"Times were different then," Kettering said, escorting his guest to the front foyer, "but masculine pride is ageless."

"Purvis has certainly given mine a drubbing." Trevor accepted his hat and coat from Kettering. The meeting had solved nothing, but at least the horrible magnitude of the problem had been clarified. "Have you made any progress on that other matter?"

Kettering passed him his walking stick. "Not yet, but I expect word any day. Even no findings tell us something we didn't know before."

Trevor pulled on his gloves. "I will content myself with that bit of wisdom, put please persist. The issuance is of significant importance. Good day, and thank you."

"My regards to Jeanette and Sycamore. Take heart, Purvis might convince all of Society that you are a dunderhead and a bankrupt, but you have family, and we'll stick by you to the last."

Trevor bowed and departed, though he had the odd notion that Kettering's parting comment, despite the jaunty tone, had been in all seriousness.

How unnerving.

And... touching too.

CHAPTER FOURTEEN

The light triple rap on Purvis's door signaled an interruption from Jones. Better Jones than Purvis the Younger. Jones had some tact and discretion, while the boy was too fretful by half. Purvis turned his newspaper from the Society pages to the financial news, separated his unopened correspondence into three piles, got out his trusty settlement agreement, and took the cap off the ink bottle.

"Come in."

Jones bore a tea tray, proving that the man had a brain in his head. "Sir, apologies for intruding, but Lord Tavistock has presented himself without an appointment. His lordship begs a word with you, if it's not too much trouble."

"The marquess hasn't begged for anything since his nurse denied him a second helping of pudding." How rude to simply drop by when his lordship had been told that the offices were unbearably busy. "Popped into Town for a fitting, no doubt. Needs must, I suppose. Two cups on the tray? Well done, Jones."

Jones set the tray on the low table nearest the hearth. "Shall I take notes, sir?"

"You shall sit over there,"—Purvis nodded to the bench by the window—"and open these letters. I vow one cannot keep up with the news, the work, and the post these days, much less with marquesses who eschew basic manners."

"Very difficult, sir, I'm sure."

"Fetch him in here," Purvis said, perching a pair of spectacles on his nose. "And please let the Surrey housekeeper know that she's disappointed me. A peripatetic client is a trial to the nerves."

"Consider it done, sir." Jones scampered out—he would have made a decent footman, though he wasn't half handsome enough—and Purvis waited behind his desk. Perhaps his lordship was preparing to sail back across the Channel. That would not do, not when the Brompton fortune was going begging, but an extended honeymoon on the Continent might serve.

His lordship appeared a moment later, attired in the finest Bond Street plumage and gracing the air with some delicate Parisian scent. He hadn't nipped up from Surrey to see his tailors, then. He was in Town to call upon some ladybird. Fast work, even for a robust young peer.

"My lord." Purvis rose and bowed, affecting the stiffness of a man who'd been sitting for too long. "An unexpected pleasure."

"I do apologize for the lack of notice, but the matter is urgent."

With Tavistock's kind, a missing handkerchief was urgent. "I am here to serve you, sir. Shall we discuss this urgent matter over a spot of tea?"

"No, thank you. Jones, if you'd excuse us and close the door behind you?"

Jones sent Purvis an apologetic look, bowed, and withdrew, and Purvis's resentment edged a little closer to rage.

"Jones is my most trusted amanuensis, my lord. He is fast, accurate, and discreet."

"No doubt he is a paragon among clerks, but I thought my news ought best be delivered to you alone, and then you can decide with whom to share it. Jerome Vincent is dead. My cousin, my friend, and my traveling companion expired after a fall from a horse. Taken much too soon, though I'm told he did not suffer. I have notified his sisters by post. I am his heir, and his factor in Bordeaux has been in communication with me."

"The man was a pauper." Purvis ought not to have said that, but lack of means had been young Vincent's most salient feature. A bon vivant who would have been a wastrel if he'd had anything to waste.

In his case, a fall from a horse might well be a euphemism for dueling or worse. How... interesting.

"I admit that Jerome was occasionally in want of funds," Tavistock said. "You are concerned that I might well have inherited his debts. An understandable worry. My cousin, for all his many fine qualities, was not always prudent with his finances. I have alerted you to the situation so you will be prepared if his creditors apply directly to you rather than to me."

Purvis's mood took a turn for the better. "The creditors with a sense of your station will do exactly that, my lord. You cannot be bothered with invoices for boot black and beer."

"I *should* not be, of course, but on the Continent, protocol is often sacrificed to commercial exigencies."

Purvis gestured to the chairs by the hearth. "How long since Mr. Vincent went to his celestial reward?"

Tavistock settled into a wing chair. "A month, give or take. The post across the Channel is slow and unreliable."

Purvis took the second seat, though he did not like having his back to the door. "Mr. Vincent's sad demise changes your situation, my lord. If I might be blunt, you have no heir. Your sainted father would be unhinged in such circumstances, meaning no disrespect. He took his responsibility to the succession most seriously."

An understatement of a magnitude the present marquess could not possibly appreciate.

"And here I am," Tavistock said, "dutifully presenting myself in Town for the express purpose of finding a bride and compelled to observe several weeks of mourning. If I were in the running for an heiress, I'd find myself beginning well behind the starting line."

The day abruptly bloomed with possibilities. "You have it backward, my lord. The matchmakers are hobbled, but Smithers and Purvis can discreetly advance your cause. Have you made the acquaintance of Miss Hecate Brompton?"

The lordly nose wrinkled. "The name is familiar. One doesn't come across many Hecates. Goddess of magic and spells, if I recall correctly."

"Goddess of inherited wealth in this case, and a very agreeable lady. She does not suffer fools, and she will understand the benefits of a mutually advantageous match. I believe you and she would get on splendidly."

Tavistock rose, and he was even taller than his reprobate of a father had been. "I won't be getting on with the ladies at all until I've done my bit for Jerome's memory. One violates mourning protocols at one's peril."

Purvis got to his feet, though he could not let Tavistock jaunt off quite yet. "Your cousin has been dead the requisite month, my lord. Mourn him in your heart all you please, but he of all people would understand why you must attend to your social obligations."

"The four weeks of mourning are required of me nonetheless, Purvis, and there's one other matter that has been nagging at me. I will in no wise have time to visit my properties in Yorkshire and can't see why I should have to make the effort. Please arrange to sell them on whatever terms are necessary to liquidate the mortgages. I cannot abide being obligated to a lot of nosy bankers."

The acorn had fallen directly at the base of the tree. "I'd advise against selling those estates now, sir. The tenants will make a poor job of planting and haying, knowing they might well be turned out by harvest. Agricultural properties are put on the market in autumn and change hands on the first of the year. Much cleaner that way."

That was mostly bunk, of course. The leaseholds would convey with the property, and for the tenants, nothing would change until the leases expired or were renewed. To most tenants, the identity of the landowner mattered far less than the terms of the rental agreement.

More to the point, the Yorkshire tenants paid two hundred pounds per annum apiece over the amount Lord Tavistock believed himself to be owed. Negotiations to sell the properties might reveal that slight discrepancy in his lordship's ledgers.

Tavistock swiped a biscuit from the tray. "Shall I engage a factor in York to see to the transactions, Purvis? York is hard farming, and the wool market has died. I don't see it reviving when every yeoman from America to Australia can raise his own sheep."

He crunched the biscuit into oblivion, and Purvis debated strategy. The Brompton fortune, or a tidy slice thereof, hung in the balance. For now, Purvis would be patient.

"I have excellent connections in York," he said. "We will begin readying the properties for sale, if you're sure that's what you want. A house in good trim makes a better impression on a prospective buyer, particularly if he has a wife and family and most especially if his mama is on hand. If comparable properties are for sale in the area, we will want to consider price carefully."

Tavistock consulted his watch, a gold article that might well have been willed to him by his father. "I am not asking for delicate maneuvers, Purvis. I am giving you an order: Sell those damned farms. If Jerome's creditors do come crawling out of the Continental swamps, I want to pay them off without delay. We have no idea how many losing ventures Jerome backed, how many by-blows he left behind. Liquidate the properties at the first viable opportunity."

Tavistock sounded exactly like his father, and Purvis would manage him exactly as he'd managed the previous marquess.

"If my lord wants to alert all of Mayfair to his lack of ready cash," Purvis said, adopting a martyred tone, "then selling two properties that your family has held for generations will achieve the purpose nicely. That they are the most distant properties from Town will only underscore to any gossip that you are trying to raise funds without attracting notice."

Tavistock took another biscuit. "Given that my solicitors pride themselves on their discretion, how will anybody know I'm selling?"

He was as proud as his father, thank the Deity, and almost as thickheaded. "Land records are public, my lord. Tenants complain. The buyers will crow over their new acquisitions. Later in the year, when many other properties are changing hands, the matter would not be as obvious, but if you are determined to ignore my advice, then I will have those farms on the market by this time next week. Don't blame me when speculation about your financial situation starts up the week after that."

And how gratifying it would be to start that speculation. How easy.

A muscle in Tavistock's jaw twitched. "Oh, very well. Get both estates caught up on repairs, and stand by for further orders. I'll wade through Jerome's affairs and defer decisions affecting my own holdings. Bad timing on Jerome's part. As usual."

"Terrible, my lord, and so very sad. I do appreciate your bringing the news to me directly." Though a note would have served as well and been one-tenth the bother.

"When it becomes known that I have no heir, I will have no peace. I will spend the next few weeks treasuring my privacy. You are not to thrust Miss Brompton in my path, Purvis. Your word on that."

Idiot. "You have my word, sir, though I cannot control the lady or her dear mother. I will do my best."

"I'll see myself out. Must alert the household. Crepe on the knocker, black armbands, and all the other whatnot. Jerome is probably vastly amused on whatever celestial cloud he occupies."

Why did the aristocracy always assume a heavenly fate for their departed loved ones? "Shall I make some charitable donations in Mr. Vincent's memory, sir? Soldiers' widows and orphans, aged seamen, the Magdalen houses?"

"I'm putting a new roof on St. Nebo's?"

"You are."

"Then I'll donate a new organ as well, in Jerome's memory. He loved music and had a fine tenor singing voice. If I ever attend services while visiting my Berkshire holdings, I'll at least be spared the bleatings of an ancient wheeze-box."

Of all the brainless impulses... "Lavish of you, my lord, though commendable." An organ? An *organ*? Purvis had had in mind a handsome bank draft made out to bearer...

"I'll be off. My thanks as always for your time and expertise, Purvis. Don't know what I'd do without you."

"You flatter me, my lord." Purvis let his client strut as far as the door before dropping the critical question. "My lord, that factor in Bordeaux who might present Mr. Vincent's unpaid bills—can you give me a name? We get all manner of correspondence from the Continent, but if you give me a name, I'll have the staff bring those epistles to me directly, unopened."

"Good thought. The firm is..." His lordship stared at the tea tray, upon which one biscuit remained. "*Marchand et Fils*. Probably trying to sound English. Offices on the Rue du Vignoble. Back a few streets from the harbor."

"Very good, my lord, and again, my condolences."

Tavistock took the last biscuit, sailed through the door, and bellowed for Jones to bring him his hat.

High-handed, just like his father. Exactly, precisely like his father.

∽

"Are you sure, Lissa?" Diana murmured, fingering the rim of a straw hat trimmed with embroidered ribbons. Tiny birds in shades of blue, cream, and brown flitted about on intricate green satin boughs, and a bouquet of silk bachelor buttons adorned the right side of the brim. "I've never seen such delicate work."

Because Diana had never shopped anywhere save the Crosspatch shops and markets. "I've never seen trimming that so effectively flatters your coloring. To replicate this pattern would take us weeks."

"Maybe you could do it," Diana said, lifting the hat off its stand, "I haven't the patience for it."

"Try it on, miss." The clerk was young, handsome, and doubtless half the reason for the millinery's sales. "Is this your first Season?"

"Stop that," Lissa said, leavening her scold with a smile. She didn't blame the fellow for flattering the customers, but even flattery needed limits. "We are in Town to see the sights, and you know quite well that if we buy the hat, we'll need matching gloves and a shawl to go with it."

Diana perched the hat on her head and allowed Lissa to do up the ribbons in a trailing bow tied off-center.

"Let's have that blue silk shawl," Lissa said, "the one hanging in the window, and we'll try a pair of blue gloves the same shade as the bachelor buttons."

The clerk scurried off like a man carrying news of victory back to his general, while Diana beheld herself in a cheval mirror.

"I never realized how blue my eyes are."

"And you probably thought your hair was plain brown rather than a lovely dark chestnut." Lissa watched as her sister turned to the left, then to the right. Diana's fascination with her reflection revealed a depth of wonder both touching and painful to behold.

She was attractive, in her liveliness, youth, and robust spirits, but she did not know that.

Mustn't be vain.

Mustn't be uppish.

Mustn't draw too much notice.

Until speeding through the nearest sonata became a weapon against invisibility. Diana was also naturally social, had a fine sense of humor, and was fiendishly talented at maths. She spoke French with Mr. Dabney as if it were her native tongue, and all of these wondrous abilities—to say nothing of her fiery skills at the pianoforte—were of no use to her, because she lacked confidence in her own worthiness.

"Very fetching, miss," the clerk said, holding up the blue silk shawl. "May I presume?"

Diana nodded and allowed the man to drape the blue shawl around her shoulders. He was deft, probably would have made a fine valet, and stepped back when he'd arranged the shawl just so.

Loose, graceful, the perfect wrapping for a lovely pair of shoulders and a pale throat. Diana's eyes positively glowed when she wore that hue.

"And the gloves?" he said, offering a crocheted pair in a lighter shade of blue.

To assist a lady to put on her gloves was a personal office, and Diana was bearing up well under the fellow's attentions.

She turned to the mirror again. "Is it too much blue? Is the blue too *intense*? I thought I was required to wear pastels until... until I'm older."

Until she'd secured a proposal of marriage. "You are required to wear clothes that flatter you and cover you decently," Lissa said. "Clothes you enjoy wearing. What do you think of the gloves?"

"I like them well enough."

Faint praise where an honest opinion should have been, and that was Lissa's fault. When had she stopped seeing her own family? Probably just about the time Gavin had disappeared, taking with him financial security and all of Mama's good humor.

The clerk cocked his head as if studying some Renaissance masterpiece. "I agree with Miss. Maybe a bit too much blue?" he asked with just the right degree of self-doubt. "The shawl provides a heavenly complement to your eyes, but a touch of contrast might also draw attention to your exquisite complexion. Brown gloves might work, or cream, perhaps? Tan?"

There followed an earnest and protracted discussion of all the colors of glove that might suit—even green came under consideration—while Lissa let the shop clerk begin repairs to Diana's self-regard that were at least two years overdue.

Diana eventually followed his advice—cream gloves, blue shawl, the perfect straw hat—and Lissa considered the cost well worth the goods.

And the service.

"If you have the stamina to shop for slippers," the clerk said, wrapping Diana's new treasures in brown paper, "I can suggest Madame Celeste's two doors down. Her selection is unrivaled and her prices—if I might be so bold—competitive. Shall I summon a porter?"

"Please say we can peek at the slippers, Lissa." Diana struggled to hang on to her newfound dignity, though she was clearly on the verge of begging.

"Of course we'll have a look at the slippers while we have your shawl and bonnet with us, and then we can send the lot home with a porter, along with any additional purchases." They would carry their own parcels. Ticket porters in London came dear.

"Very sensible," the clerk murmured, though the smile he sent Lissa was pure cheek. "And where shall I send the bill?"

"To the attention of Mr. Giles Purvis, Smithers and Purvis, on Peebles Street, to the account of Miss Amaryllis DeWitt."

The clerk jotted the direction on some ledger or other and congratulated Diana on having made a tasteful and original purchase.

Diana did not clap her hands and spin with joy, but her eyes sparkled, and when she left the shop on Lissa's arm, her step was bouncy and her parting wave to the clerk coy.

"He reminded me of Gavin," Diana said. "As if he was playing the part of a shop clerk on a lark and having a jolly time with the role. My job was to be the inexperienced customer, and I was to have great fun with that, too—which I did. Do you recall when Gavin would challenge us to pretend we were attending a funeral rather than Sunday services? His little farce kept Caroline from tucking a book between the pages of the hymnal for nearly a month."

They strolled along the walkway, which was busy, but not thronged as it would be a fortnight hence.

"You do know all the clerk's charm and flattery was intended to bring you back for your next purchase, Di?"

"Oh, I suppose most of it was, but I hope a little was also because he enjoyed making me smile and helping me look fashionable."

"You don't look merely fashionable in that bonnet and shawl, you look lovely. Beautiful, fetching, delightful. I can see a resemblance to Grandmama when you tilt your head just so, and she was quite a beauty."

Lissa expected a demurral, a reversion to the brittle testiness Diana favored in Crosspatch Corners.

"That hat would make anybody look scrumptious. If Caroline had a hat like that, she might not be so prone to freckles. The next time we visit that shop, we're buying new millinery for you. Roger said with your height, you could carry off the boldest styles."

Roger? "Diana, I'm glad you enjoyed making your selections, and it's wonderful to have such an abundance of choice, but please be careful. He's a clerk whose fortunes rise or sink on the strength of his charm." And Lissa had passed him a generous tip for his efforts.

"Were you careful with Mr. Dorning?"

Not careful enough. Lissa debated strategy and decided if Diana was old enough to flirt with shop clerks, she was old enough to hear the truth.

"He's not Mr. Dorning, Diana."

"Well, he's certainly not Mrs. Dorning. Who is he?" Diana stopped outside the shoe shop and all but pressed her nose to the glass. "Oh, Lissa. Just look. Every color, and the buckles!"

To Hades with the buckles, which sparkled in the afternoon sun like so many jewels. "Mr. Trevor Dorning is the current Marquess of Tavistock. His given name is Trevor, and the family name is Vincent." Debrett's had confirmed that much. "He might well have been skulking about Crosspatch with a view toward selling Twidboro Hall and Lark's Nest." Lissa had been haunted by that possibility through many sleepless nights.

Trevor's behavior—familiarizing himself with the surrounds, inspecting both houses to the extent a guest could, riding over the tenancies and grounds—supported the theory of an inspection tour prior to sale. Even his wooing could have begun as part of a campaign to acquaint himself with his pretty estates not too far from Town.

"Our Mr. Dorning is a lord?" Diana said, slanting a look at Lissa. "I don't understand."

"I'm not sure I do either. He hasn't explained his use of a fictitious name to me, but then, I did not ask him for details when I had the opportunity."

Did she want those details? "He lied to us?" This possibility was of sufficient enormity that Diana ceased goggling at the shoes. "He seemed like a true gentleman, Lissa. The genuine article. Why would he be dishonest?"

"I don't know. I suspect had he swanned into the village exhibiting the full regalia of his station, we'd have closed ranks against him. St. Nebo's has been sorely neglected, he raised our rent the moment we'd put off mourning for Papa, he has begrudged us basic maintenance for the Hall, and nobody has anything good to say about the old marquess either."

A coach clattered by, high-stepping bays in the traces, plenty of gold trim. Crests on the doors and boot.

Not Trevor's crest. Lissa had been watching the traffic since they'd arrived in Town three days ago. She'd been watching the mail, hoping for a knock on the door. She was on edge and homesick and out of sorts.

Expecting another ambush, spoiling for battle, and—the heaviest burden—hoping Trevor could explain himself.

"I tell you, Lissa, your Trevor is a good, decent fellow. Patience and good humor like his could only be sincere. Are you sure he's the marquess?"

"He all but told me himself, and when he left Crosspatch, his traveling coach—which was half the size of Crosspatch's assembly rooms—displayed the Tavistock crest. The former marchioness of Tavistock married a Dorning, and that's probably where he got the name."

"You said he left the village because of a death in the family. Was that a lie too?"

"We should choose a pair of slippers for you. The ones on the end —brown velvet—might do. Brown won't show wear as cream would."

"Lissa, hang the perishing slippers. Did Mr. Dorn—Lord Tavistock toy with your affections? Is he even in London?"

The lending library was across the street, and they'd left Grandmama there perusing fashion magazines. Crosspatch had no lending library. Trevor had probably thought the place pathetic.

"How would I know if he's in London or France or darkest Maryland?"

Except that he'd sent her two expresses by private messenger, and the riders had mentioned riding out from Town. The notes had been little nothings.

Safely arrived, hope your upcoming journey is similarly uneventful. T.

Anticipating your arrival, matters here complicated and tedious. T.

Why pay for an express that said nothing? Though the notes also had said that Trevor was thinking of her and biding in Town, as he'd said he must.

"Well, what *do* you know about him?" Diana asked. "He seemed smitten, Lissa. He put up with me and Caroline at supper, he rode out with you all over God's back pasture, he put some manners on Roland, and he even called on Phillip."

Those facts had also featured in Lissa's sleepless nights. "I know there truly was a death in his family. We passed his town house on the way here, and the knocker was done up with black crepe." A detail on an otherwise elegant and imposing façade.

A small detail, and an enormous relief.

Diana leaned near and lowered her voice. "Amaryllis DeWitt, were you *spying* on his lordship?"

"Perhaps. All I know for certain is that I am in London to get our solicitors sorted out and to do some shopping. Other than that, I have no earthly notion what I'm doing here."

Diana straightened and patted her shoulder. "Most of us find ourselves in that posture the majority of the time, Sister dear. You were long overdue for a turn at muddling along. Let's find Grandmama, shall we? I do believe the situation calls for an ice."

Diana took Amaryllis by the arm and led the way across the street, and what did it say about Amaryllis that she was willing for once to go where her younger sister directed her?

CHAPTER FIFTEEN

Trevor had considered many a scheme for crossing paths with Amaryllis.

His first thought was an apparently chance meeting on the bridle paths at dawn, though a discreet chat between grooms confirmed that Amaryllis hadn't brought a riding horse to London.

An encounter at Gunter's came under consideration—except a peer in mourning ought not to be treating himself to an ice, much less turning the occasion social while all of Berkeley Square looked on.

A rendezvous feeding the Serpentine's ducks at some quiet hour might have served, but for the fact that in spring, Hyde Park was never entirely deserted, and ducks made a deuced lot of noise, which would attract notice. They also left disagreeable mementos all over the grass.

The solution had come from the only person Trevor truly considered an ally: Jeanette had mentioned that she was presuming on Sycamore's acquaintance with the DeWitts to invite the ladies to tea.

Even in mourning, Trevor was permitted to call on family.

He did so at precisely two of the clock on Tuesday afternoon, after having fussed over the propriety of showing up with an amaryllis blossom on his lapel and discarding the notion as beef-witted and fatuous.

Instead, he wore a black armband and the most subdued morning attire Bond Street offered.

"Tavistock." Jeanette took both his hands and let him kiss both of her cheeks. "A pleasant surprise. You might be acquainted with my guests."

Amaryllis, attired in a flattering ensemble of raspberry trimmed in gold, sat between her mother and Sycamore on a sofa flanked by enormous ferns. She rose as Jeanette ran through the introductions, curtseyed at the appropriate moment, and held out her hand for Trevor to bow over. Her bare hand, because the ladies were at tea.

"You must join us," Jeanette said. "My guests have been in Town for only a week, but Sycamore had lovely things to say about Berkshire. I want our friends to have lovely things to say about London hospitality."

Sycamore had risen to shake Trevor's hand, and the scheming bounder now found it expedient to take the place beside his wife on the love seat. Unless Trevor wanted to occupy the escritoire by the window—which he did not—the only available seat was beside Amaryllis.

Not subtle, but appreciated.

"How are you finding London, Miss DeWitt?" The impulse to take Amaryllis's hand with her mother looking on and Sycamore smirking nineteen to the dozen was nigh overwhelming. Trevor denied himself that pleasure not only because propriety demanded it of him, but also because Amaryllis's military bearing suggested she'd dump her tea in his lap for presuming.

"London is an adjustment, my lord. I imagine you endured something similar in reverse when you sojourned in Berkshire."

Had Amaryllis put a slight emphasis on the honorific? Was she in some way offended that he'd intruded on this tea?

"I found Berkshire very congenial after years spent more or less in the French countryside. Like you, I find a return to London an adjustment."

Amaryllis shoved a tea cake into her mouth. Sycamore's smirk had turned into a puzzled half smile, and Mrs. DeWitt was eyeing the door.

Dieu au paradis.

"Sycamore," Jeanette said, "might you show Mrs. DeWitt your latest botanical album? I believe you left it in the family parlor."

Sycamore popped to his feet. "Oh, do indulge me, Mrs. DeWitt. The illustrations are exquisite, and I can ask your opinion on a pair of ferns that are turning up contrary. The family parlor is this way."

He had Mourna on her feet and out the door in the next instant, with Mourna looking more bewildered by the moment.

"If you'll excuse me briefly," Jeanette said after a few more minutes of isn't-this-marvelous-weather. "I will inquire after a second pot and have the kitchen send up some sandwiches. Tavistock enjoys a healthy appetite, even in the blighted confines of London."

The only sound in Jeanette's wake was Amaryllis munching her tea cake. Trevor swirled his tea and decided on the direct approach. Neither Sycamore nor Jeanette would leave him alone with Amaryllis for long.

He took Amaryllis's hand. "I've missed you dreadfully."

That was her cue to buss his cheek and offer reciprocal assurances.

"I've missed Mr. Trevor Dorning," she said, "and I've wanted to administer the Marquess of Tavistock a sound drubbing."

What the hell was going on? "Has his lordship given offense?"

She rose and began to pace, arms folded, hems whispering of feminine upset. "Why did you lie? You presented yourself to us as Mr. Trevor Dorning. Then you told me otherwise, but I was too muddled... I was not focused on proper terms of address, I was... I thought you were Tavistock's by-blow."

Trevor stood because the lady was on her feet. He grasped the plain meaning of her words—Amaryllis had been mistaken about his antecedents—but his pride snagged on the word *lie*. He'd told her...

What, specifically had he said? Not that he was the marquess, but that the previous titleholder was his father.

"You thought I was the marquess's bastard?"

She nodded once. "Your name—the only name you gave us—was Trevor *Dorning*. The shires are full of aristocratic by-blows. The young ladies get sent to select academies. The fellows are given a patch to go shooting on. They become vicars and squires, and nobody thinks anything of it, and I... I *don't like* that you are Lord Tavistock. I don't like it at all."

"I'm not too keen on it myself," Trevor said, which was the rubbishing damned truth. "I needed to not be the marquess when I nosed around Crosspatch. I had thought to salvage some of my honor by ensuring you knew of my birthright before we... before our expectations advanced beyond a certain point. I apologize for causing confusion."

Amaryllis looked ready to hurl blunt objects at his head, or perhaps to cry. He'd withstand any and all domestic missiles she wanted to pitch at him, but he could not bear to see her in tears.

"I apologize," he said more softly, "for causing you any upset at all. Badly, badly done. I am sorry I hurt your feelings. That is the last thing I'd ever intend. I can explain."

Amaryllis's chin came up. "This had better be the best explanation in the history of explanations, sir. I do not enjoy being made a fool of."

She hated feeling like a fool. Trevor started there. "I am the fool. When I went to France, I thought only to escape the stupidity that amounts to polite society. Nobody *does* anything. The young men get drunk, make stupid wagers, and dangle after heiresses or expect heiresses to dangle after them. The social entertainments are deadly dull, and Parliament is a farce."

"Do go on."

She was listening. Trevor took heart from that. "I served no purpose here, and Jeanette had started a new chapter of her life. The Continent loomed as my salvation, and for a time, it was."

"You learned about winemaking?"

"Jeanette's brother makes champagne. Another family connection blends exquisite clarets. Then I became interested in the Rhenish vintages. Languages are much easier to learn if one has a purpose for learning them. Travel becomes more meaningful if undertaken for a reason. I was half serious about brewing beer commercially when I went to Berkshire. I'm in earnest about it now."

"Do not," she said, "prose on to me about beer. You lied to the whole village, and the truth you eventually gave to me was easily misconstrued. Explain that."

I was somewhat distracted at the time struck Trevor as an imprudent observation, though he'd never forget the hours spent in the Twidboro gatehouse.

If Amaryllis regretted those hours... He'd make it up to her, somehow.

"I am being made a fool of," he said. "While I was kicking my heels in France, my solicitors were having a fine time looting my coffers. They still are. They didn't even tell me that I owned Lark's Nest, and the rent they claim I am receiving from Twidboro is substantially less than the rent you are paying."

Some of the starch went out of her posture. "Is that why you tried to raise the rent again? Because you didn't know about the last increase?"

She sounded merely curious, not appalled—not appalled *yet*. "It's worse than that, Amaryllis. I had no hand in establishing the rents. I thought only to flee Town before the matchmakers got ideas, to gain some time to sort myself out, to indulge my own whims and fancies after doing as I had been told since birth. I bid farewell to Merry Olde, told my solicitors where to reach me, then contrived to not be at that address for months on end."

She dropped her arms and resumed her seat. "What does all this belated self-castigation have to do with lying about your name, station, and connection to Crosspatch?"

"I have created a mess. Cleaning up that mess is my responsibility. Twidboro and Lark's Nest are only two of my holdings. The solicitors have likely left the family seat largely unmolested. The staff and tenants there are loyal to the Vincents, but in Yorkshire? Derbyshire? The ties are attenuated, and I'm sure Purvis has been lining his pockets handsomely with those properties."

"Purvis." She spat the name. "Mama and I have an appointment with him next week, and if he'll steal from a marquess, he's likely been looting our funds too."

"This has occurred to me and makes my determination to see him foiled all the more pressing."

A peal of feminine laughter sounded from a few rooms away, followed by, "Oh, Mr. Dorning. You are so naughty!"

Amaryllis looked as if she'd charge to her mother's rescue—or something—though Trevor wasn't yet ready to let her go.

He'd *never* be ready to let her go. "Sycamore collects political prints. Satires, bawdy sketches, cartoons. Pastes them into collections. I don't understand it, but his other hobby is playing with knives."

Amaryllis brushed her hand over the fern. "I was afraid that your hobby was... toying with the affections of aging rural spinsters. Making light of their virtue."

He ached to hold her. To go down on his knees and wrap his arms about her. To swear all manner of undying everythings in three languages.

"I am profoundly sorry to have misled you as to my identity," he said, forcing himself to sit across from her rather than beside her. "That I have caused you any distress, any distress at all, wreaks calamity upon my soul. I was spying on my solicitors, hoping discretion would yield truths that dozens of quarterly reports have obscured, and my hopes were justified."

I love you. He kept that part behind his teeth, because a man in disgrace with his beloved hadn't the right to burden her with declarations.

Also, Sycamore and Jeanette both had acute hearing.

"You've caught Purvis at his pilfering?"

"Thousands of pounds of embezzlement happened right under my figurative nose. If you are distressed to learn that I am a marquess, you will be even more displeased to know that Purvis has tried to render me a bankrupt as well."

Amaryllis caressed the damned plant again. "And now you are to marry the heiress of his choice?" Her tone clearly said she would not be that heiress.

"He's certainly offering suggestions and has been since I returned to London. I have no intention of gratifying his greed any further, though."

For the first time, Amaryllis's self-possession seemed to falter. "He can ruin you, can't he?"

"He's apparently a skilled forger in addition to being a cheat and embezzler. He has endless examples of my penmanship, should he want to create salacious letters over my signature, for example. I suspect his attack will be financial, though, a few muttered asides at the club, some pointed silences over supper with his counterparts at other firms. If he chooses to gossip with his fellow solicitors, they will gossip with their clients."

"And to think," Amaryllis murmured, "the king believes himself the highest power in the land. In the midst of all this intrigue, looming scandal, and criminal lawyering, how will you find time to do the pretty?"

Jeanette's voice, an indistinct patter, drifted in from the corridor.

"You mean how will I find time to court you?"

Amaryllis gave him a look severe enough to make his insides go all crozzled. "Precisely. We had discussed a courtship, my lord."

He had been mendacious before—no escaping that fact—and the antidote was unflinching honesty now. "Does that courtship still interest you as dearly as it interests me?"

"Courtship with Mr. Trevor Dorning did interest me," she said. "A very great deal. I am torn now between dismay at the circumstances you face, my own smarting pride, and... the need to absorb all that you've told me. Embezzlement is a hanging felony, and I understand why you resorted to subterfuge, but I cannot like how you went about it."

"Can you still like me?"

"Liking has never been at issue, Trev—my lord. The difficult issue is trust."

Jeanette sailed into the room, all smiles. "My apologies, but Cook started going on about the sauces for tonight's dinner, and deserting the royal navy on the high seas is easier than escaping Cook's raptures. Another pot is on the way, along with some sandwiches. What do you suppose Sycamore is getting up to with Mrs. DeWitt?"

Amaryllis spared Trevor the effort of a reply. "I heard Mama laughing a moment ago. She hasn't laughed in ages, so let's leave them to their amusements, shall we?"

The second pot and the sandwiches arrived, Sycamore and Mourna returned, and Trevor chatted about the blasted weather for twenty interminable minutes. He kept telling himself that the difficult discussion with Amaryllis had been progress, but perhaps, larking about in Berkshire, he'd grown a little too facile with falsehoods.

Or much too facile.

~

"Gracious." Mama peered at the stack of mail just pushed through the slot. "We've had more mail in the past week in Town than we get at Twidboro in three months."

Lissa bent to gather up a half-dozen missives and felt a sense of unreality. Three of the six epistles had been sealed with a crest, two had been franked by peers: Casriel—he was the Dorning titleholder—and... She squinted at the corner of the folded letter.

Bellefonte, another earl. Two of the earl's sisters had married into the Dorning family, Lady Susannah and Lady Della.

"Lady Della made good on her threat," Lissa said, setting the stack on the foyer's sideboard. "The Countess of Bellefonte has apparently seen fit to invite us to some function or other."

Mourna passed Lissa the bonnet trimmed in pink ribbon. "You know, I've longed for just this sort of reception for you. Invitations piling up, the best people getting to know you. I suspected that your Mr. Dorning had some good connections."

Mama tied the pink ribbons as if Lissa were still eight years old, and Lissa wanted to fidget as badly as an eight-year-old too.

"I never suspected Mr. Dorning *was* the best people," Mama went on. "A good fellow with good prospects, yes, but a marquess! Such a pity about his cousin."

Mama was not offering condolences on the passing of a man taken much too young. She was lamenting the hiatus mourning put on a peer's social schedule.

"I doubt Lord Tavistock feels the loss of a few weeks' prancing around at Almack's, Mama, and he truly does mourn for his cousin. Let's be on our way, shall we?"

Lissa wanted to be moving, to walk off the restlessness that had plagued her since Mrs. Sycamore Dorning's cordial tea six days ago. The invitations had started up two days after that, another from Mrs. Sycamore Dorning, this time for a picnic at Richmond. Lady Della Dorning had started off with the requisite chat over tea.

Lissa had been rendered speechless to see an invitation from the Duchess of Moreland for a musicale at which her son, the composer and conductor, would offer a few selections at the pianoforte. Then an invitation had come from the Duchess of Quimbey for a Venetian breakfast, and Mama's joy had been complete.

While Lissa wondered what Trevor thought all these invitations were in aid of, because they were surely his doing.

Mama donned gloves and bonnet and squared her shoulders. "I

am glad I allowed you girls to add a few items to your wardrobes. One can be *au courant* without spending a fortune."

Allowing hadn't come into it. Lissa had announced the need for some fripperies, and Grandmama had started making suggestions.

"I will do the talking with the solicitors, Mama. You are to be very much on your dignity, the widow who is too ladylike to speak candidly."

"I *am* too much of a lady to tell that wretch Purvis what I think of him. I loved your father dearly, but he made a grievous error when he decided to entrust his business to Smithers and Purvis."

That was as much disloyalty as Mama had ever expressed regarding her late spouse.

And it was enough. When they were ushered into the solicitor's office, Mama glanced around as if somebody needed to empty the dustbin. The room exuded the same staid opulence it always had—these audiences were annual rituals for Lissa—but she was struck by the extent to which Purvis's place of business resembled a stage setting.

Legal tomes marching in height order along the shelves, Blackstone quotes framed on the walls.

That the king can do no wrong is a necessary and fundamental principle of the English constitution.

The husband and wife are one, and that one is the husband.

A portrait of some bewigged lord justice imperiously pointing to what was intended to be the Magna Carta, symbolic scales at his elbow, a statue of blind Justice in the shadows behind him.

Though no actual work appeared to be ongoing in Purvis's sanctum sanctorum. None of the books were open. No documents were being drafted on the table closest to the window. No briefs, red ribbons trailing, were open on the desk.

"Do be seated, ladies," Giles Purvis said. "How lovely to see you back in the capital. I trust you're settling in?"

Lissa took a chair by the hearth, though Purvis had gestured to the reading table. "We cannot settle in, Mr. Purvis, and we lay that sad fact at your feet. Tea would be appreciated. China black for me. Mama prefers gunpowder."

Mama took the second wing chair on a rustle of lace and muslin. "If you have gunpowder, Mr. Purvis. Not everybody does. You mustn't go to any trouble."

"No trouble at all, ma'am. Happy to oblige." He stalked out, and Mama aimed a placid smile at Lissa.

"The DeWitts have a talent for playing roles," Mama said. "You see before you the Duchess of Crosspatch Corners."

"Then I suppose I'm Lady Amaryllis."

"Just so."

Two clerks returned with Purvis, one carrying a chair, the other a tea tray. Purvis's opening salvo was to ask Lissa to pour out.

"You are our host, Mr. Purvis. I leave management of the service to you, and perhaps that good fellow,"—she nodded at a sandy-haired, freckled young man who looked too friendly to be immured in a law office—"will take notes, because my list is lengthy, and I do not have time to repeat myself."

Purvis nodded at the clerk, who set the tray on the low table between the wing chairs and scurried off, presumably to find pencil and paper. Purvis took his seat directly facing the hearth and checked the strength of the tea.

"What sort of list, Miss DeWitt?"

"Modifications to our financial situation necessary to honor the spirit and letter of the documents which control your legal duties."

Mr. Purvis poured out two cups of black tea and one of gunpowder. "Mrs. DeWitt, how do you take your tea?"

Mama peered at the cup, a delicate little affair that looked to be French provenance. "Stronger than that, sir. You must allow the green teas especially to steep properly. And one doesn't pour out three cups at once, or pour into tea cups sitting on the tray. One holds the cup and saucer up to the pot to minimize the risk of spills." Mama sighed. "In the shires, we recall our manners, but I suppose in London, all must be hurry and expedience."

Ye heavenly choruses. Mama had always been a good sport about participating in Crosspatch's amateur theatricals, but truly, the stage had lost a talent.

"Best fetch a fresh tray," Lissa said, gesturing to the sandy-haired clerk, who bounced up from his post and headed out the door. "Mama has her standards, and they are a significant motivation for this call. The price of bread has tripled since my father's death, Mr. Purvis, and Mama's settlements require that her pin money *be increased from time to time as economic necessity may require.* We require you to adhere to the terms of those settlements. Triple will do. We can be thrifty."

Purvis's eyebrows and mouth worked in a disjointed dance of disapproval, or perhaps dismay.

Lissa had considered this meeting since the day she'd realized that Trevor was not an aristocratic by-blow. She had lost the luxury of assuming a prospective spouse would deal with Purvis, and thus she must see to the business herself.

She was good at seeing to matters herself, and she'd forgotten that all too easily when faced with a London solicitor's posturing.

"Miss DeWitt," Purvis said, sitting back, "I cannot simply... That is, you will exhaust your funds, and it would be most intemperate of me to approve any expenditure at triple the rate... Ladies, the world of finance is complicated, and you must rely on me—continue to rely on me—to guide you safely along its many twisting byways."

Not blessed likely. "Mr. Purvis, we've called upon our banker. Not the banker Papa used for his business, but young Mr. Wentworth, with whom Mama's settlements were lodged by Mr. Smithers. In the past five years, my personal fortune has increased by twenty-five percent. Mama's portion has done even better, and that doesn't take into account the income the family businesses generate, which falls into your capable hands. If you triple our pin money to keep pace with rising prices, we could spend every penny each month for the next one hundred and twenty-seven years and not have exhausted half our principal.

"That assumes," Lissa went on, because Mr. Wentworth had done the calculations for them, "that our principal earns no interest in all that time. You shall triple our pin money, or we will ask our banker to take a very close look at the document you use to keep our fortune from its appointed purpose."

The majority shareholder in Mama's bank was a duke, and he'd been a banker before he'd been a duke. Not a friendly man, by all accounts, though one who took the welfare of his widowed clients seriously. Lissa had never met him, but she'd seen him up on the bank's mezzanine, surveying the busy lower floor like a ship's captain watching for bad weather on the horizon.

Had she been a squall, she would have fled far across the northern sea rather than face down that gimlet gaze.

"For pity's sake, why involve the bankers?" Purvis said. "They get above themselves all too easily and can't see beyond the numbers, when it's the legalities that must control the situation."

"Precisely," Lissa said as Mama dumped the poured-out tea back into the respective pots. "The legalities require that Mama's pin money be tripled. Retroactive to the first of the year will do. Economies, to those living in the country, are second nature after all."

Purvis was looking at Mama as if she'd burst out singing a bawdy ballad.

"Economies," Mama said gently. "If the clerks are to have that tea, Mr. Purvis, there's no need for them to drink it both weak and cold."

"Quite," Purvis muttered. "I'll see what I can do about your pin money, ladies, but these things take time, and I will want to review the documents Miss DeWitt has alluded to."

Lissa was at once pleased—Purvis was stalling rather than denying their demand—and frustrated. Why hadn't she confronted him with the legal wording of Mama's settlements two years ago? Four years ago? Why hadn't Gavin or Mama?

"I have a copy of Mama's settlement agreement with me," Lissa said. "Shall I read the relevant portion to you?" She fished in her reticule and brought out a sheaf of papers bound in a ribbon faded to pink.

"That will not be necessary," Purvis retorted. "One must read these agreements as a whole, not simply pick and choose language at will from this or that paragraph."

"Only one paragraph deals with Mama's pin money, sir, and you will either write us out a bank draft before we depart this office, or I will take the matter up with our banker *and his superiors*. The Season is already upon us, and because you have been remiss regarding our finances, we are quite behindhand. We have no Town coach, for example, nor do my sisters and I have riding horses. How does one honor invitations from the peerage when one has no appropriate means of transportation?"

Purvis sat back, sighed heavily, and looked from Lissa to Mama.

~

"The DeWitt ladies appeared ready to sack London," Jones muttered.

Young Purvis would have described matters less delicately. The DeWitts had arrived looking ready to sack their solicitor, and Young Purvis would not have blamed them.

"No shouting. That's encouraging." Papa raised his voice if he thought the moment called for it. He didn't bellow so much as he appropriated the role of barrister being emphatic for the sake of the jury.

"Perhaps the shouting will occur when Lord Tavistock comes in for his next appointment." Jones passed over an elegantly penned note, signed by Tavistock and requesting the favor of an appointment. He'd specified the day and time because that was what a marquess did, when he wasn't dropping by unannounced to create havoc and riot.

The other clerks were sending uneasy glances at Old Purvis's closed door.

"This cannot end well," Young Purvis muttered, a refrain that should have been the Smithers and Purvis motto.

"Tavistock has been out in Berkshire," Jones said, speaking very quietly. "He has come home from years abroad with a view toward getting his finances in order prior to choosing a marchioness. That could end disastrously."

"I meant the DeWitts' appointment isn't likely to end with smiles all around." Though still no voices had been raised. No irate women had stalked from the office in tears threatening to involve Uncle Lord Methuselah or Great-Auntie Lady Dragon.

"I meant," Jones retorted, "Smithers and Purvis can't end well. How much do you know about the situation in Berkshire, sir?"

Jones ran the place. Young Purvis had known that for years, and thanked God for it. Should Young Purvis feel a pressing need to admire the Continental capitals, Jones would keep the firm muddling forward.

"Tavistock's situation in Berkshire?" Young Purvis replied, taking Jones by the sleeve and hauling him into the foyer. "What I know is that Smithers told me when he retired to leave Tavistock, and especially the Berkshire holdings, entirely to my father. Said it was worth my freedom to remain in ignorance."

"And have you?"

Young Purvis felt a bolt of something go through him—homesickness, perhaps, for a law firm where nobody intrigued, nobody fell asleep at his desk, nobody wished for a different patrimony. Aunt Adelia had told him he'd always be welcome to her guest room, and that offer had become an inordinate comfort.

"Smithers was emphatic with me about keeping my distance from Tavistock's files," Young Purvis replied, "and I respect old Smithers." Not the answer Jones had sought. Young Purvis had nightmares about his father's more ambitious schemes, but they were nightmares resting on a bed of supposition and conjecture, as far as anybody would ever be able to prove.

"I haven't the luxury of ignorance," Jones said. "My granny was on the staff at Lark's Nest before I was born. Tavistock—the old lord —tossed her out when she took him to task for what was afoot there. Turned her off without a character, raised his hand to her, and told her to expect worse if she defied him."

"Do not, I pray you, burden me with particulars, Jones. Whatever scheme my father has hatched, I want no parts of it."

Jones leaned against the door, arms crossed. "Goes back to before your pa had the file, I know that much. Smithers knew. He had to have known. I don't think the marchioness had any idea—the second marchioness. She would never have countenanced—"

Young Purvis put his hand over Jones's mouth, which earned him the oddest smile.

"Stop talking. Grannies are prone to fanciful maunderings. You *know* nothing, I *know* nothing, and we can pray to a merciful heaven that young Tavistock knows even less. I have written out characters for every clerk on staff, glowing, honest recommendations. Smithers has done the same, and he's the one who suggested I follow suit."

Jones pushed way from the door. "But who will write a character for you, sir? His lordship is not a fool."

What a good fellow Jones was, and kind. "Perhaps Tavistock will simply leave things as they are."

"I sent Tavistock to Lark's Nest because that's what my granny would have insisted I do. What Old Purvis has afoot is wrong, and Tavistock can go along with it if he pleases to. I wasn't referring to Lord Tavistock, who might well be a fool. I was referring to his lordship in Berkshire. He's mentally quite sound, to hear Gran tell it, and long since of age."

Bloody, bollocking hell. Who would look after Miss Brompton's affairs when Young Purvis was living in some Parisian garret? Who would listen patiently to old Mrs. Peele natter on about her brilliant grandchildren? Who would nearly swoon with pleasure over a plate of Aunt Adelia's Sunday roast every week without fail?

Who would make sure the clerks weren't worked into early graves, and who, who on earth, would look after dear Jones?

"I know of no lordship at Lark's Nest," Young Purvis said, "and you don't either. The whole business has nothing to do with us, at least until we've packed our bags, collected our savings, and put our affairs in order."

"What of the clerks, sir? They work themselves to exhaustion and barely see the light of day."

Young Purvis had been such a clerk, and Jones still was. "God bless you, Jones, for your nobility of spirit, but generous wages that they have had little opportunity to spend and a pair of glowing characters might be the most they can hope for."

Jones shook his head, and that reproach stung bitterly. Jones could go larking back to the provinces, his savings considerable, his London cachet standing him in good stead in Reading or Oxford.

While Young Purvis's only hope was that Aunt Adelia wouldn't disown him.

CHAPTER SIXTEEN

"We're off to a Richmond picnic next week," Mama said, beaming at Purvis graciously, "assuming we can find a conveyance by then. The Countess of Casriel prefers informal gatherings apparently, and Mr. Sycamore Dorning is proud of his property. Her Grace of Moreland is starting off the Season with a musical entertainment, and the Duchess of Quimbey is taking her chances on the weather with a Venetian breakfast. I forget what Lady Bellefonte's do will be. We haven't accepted that invitation yet, have we, Lissa?"

"Not yet, Mama."

The odious legal carbuncle sitting upon his lawyerly toadstool underwent a transformation. Purvis had been getting a beady-eyed, testy, governess-filling-her-sails look, but Mama's commentary inspired a crafty smile.

"Ladies, I bow to your importuning. You'll have your bank draft, and subsequent disbursements will reflect your requested increase. Now, if that will be all?"

"No fresh tray," Mama muttered. "I suppose it's hard to find good help among all the riffraff flocking to London these days."

"We'll need a second bank draft to cover increased expenses for

Diana and Caroline," Lissa said, not at all trusting Purvis's capitula-
tion. "If Diana is to make her come out next year, she needs to begin
attending the informal calls and gatherings where appropriate this
year. Tea dances, strolling the park, the carriage parade, and so forth.
She cannot do any of that wearing turned hems and the last century's
bonnets."

Purvis rose and went to the door, and the clerk returned, bearing
a new tray. "But, Miss DeWitt," Purvis said as the clerk exchanged
trays, "I was under the impression that before Miss Diana could grace
Town with her presence, *you* had to find a husband. Is there some
happy news in the offing about which you and your dear mama are
being overly discreet? A solicitor needs to know these things if we're
to spend adequate time drawing up any settlements."

Lord, he was tiresome. "Don't be antiquated, Mr. Purvis. The
highest sticklers might insist that daughters marry in age order, but
the gentry have never been so foolish. Diana will have her turn
regardless of my situation, as will Caroline. You will triple the funds
disbursed for their welfare, and we will take that bank draft with us
as well."

The clerk fussed with the tea things, stepped aside, and put his
hands behind his back like some liveried footman. Lissa was certain
the fellow was eavesdropping, and she hoped he'd sing the news of
Purvis's defeat in the streets.

"Jones," Purvis snapped, "fetch the ledgers and printed bank
drafts. We'll be making a disbursal from the DeWitts' account at
Wentworth's."

Lissa went to the window, which—like all London windows—
could have benefited from daily scrubbing at least on the outside. A
handsome coach and four—matched blacks—pulled up, and a fashionable lady was handed down by a liveried footman. The woman
glanced up at the window where Lissa stood, her expression...
resolute.

Miss Hecate Brompton frequently wore a resolute expression,
though she also had an astonishingly mischievous smile.

"If you are expecting Miss Brompton," Lissa said, "she has arrived."

"If so, then she's early," Purvis said, accepting some papers from the clerk and retreating to his desk. "Not a habit that endears a client to her man of business. I much prefer the punctuality that you ladies favor."

He was filling out what were presumably bank drafts, or some sort of order to release funds, so Lissa did not chide him for his rudeness. She knew Hecate Brompton, had sat out many a dance with her among the potted palms and drowsing dowagers. Lissa couldn't quite call Miss Brompton a friend—her fortune eclipsed Lissa's by a wide margin—but Miss Brompton didn't put on airs or suffer fools.

She had Lissa's respect, and Lissa hoped the sentiment was mutual.

"There you are," Purvis said, tossing sand on his signatures. "I trust you ladies have concluded your business with me?"

Mama collected the bank drafts and shook them gently over the dustbin. "For the nonce. The list of repairs needed at Twidboro can be handled by mail, and it is lengthy, sir. I don't suppose my son has contacted you in the past few months?"

He capped the ink bottle, laid his pen in the tray, and set the ink bottle back on the silver jack. Purvis was not a man to tidy up after himself, and yet, there he was, putting all to rights and sweeping a stray bit of sand into his palm.

Dithering, delaying, organizing his lies.

"No word, Mrs. DeWitt, though I have alerted my associates in Paris, Rome, Vienna, and Copenhagen to be on the lookout for him."

Not Edinburgh or Dublin, which were more likely locations for an Englishman with an indifferent command of Italian, much less Danish or German. And Lissa sorely doubted Purvis had any associates in foreign capitals, come to that.

"We'll be on our way," Lissa said, pulling on her gloves. "We will expect the next disbursements at the end of June, and we will provide you a complete list of pending repairs at Twidboro Hall at that time. The feeble gestures you've approved thus far are just the beginning."

Purvis had taken a post by the other window, and the gaze he turned on Miss Brompton's coach and four was almost fond.

"Of course, Miss DeWitt." He couldn't be bothered to see them out apparently, casting more doubt on the state of good manners in London. "I am at your disposal should it be necessary to draft any settlement agreements. We take particular joy in that happy task."

Lissa decided that she and Miss Brompton needed to share an informal cup of tea in the very near future.

"I'm sure you do," was all Lissa said.

"Is Miss Brompton here to discuss settlements?" Mama asked, which was atrocious of her.

"That one." Purvis's smile boded well for somebody, probably him. "She's to marry a certain handsome young marquess newly returned from the Continent, but you didn't hear that from me. A very agreeable match for both parties."

No, it was not. Though clearly, Purvis regarded such a match as agreeable for him.

Lissa left his offices feeling as if she needed a long, hot, soaking bath and a scrub from head to toe.

"Odious rodent," Mama muttered. "You dealt with him splendidly, Lissa. I wish we'd brought him to heel much sooner."

They walked along a street lined with maples unfurling gauzy green leaves and pigeons strutting about the pavement like so many burghers and dowagers. London wasn't so awful, not when the weather was decent.

"So do I," Lissa said, "but I hadn't thought to invoke the scorn of the bankers. Mention of Wentworth's worked like a magic incantation." And Trevor had been the one to suggest that tactic.

They paused at a streetcorner while a dray laden with barrels lumbered past. Pickled herring, from the scent on the air.

"Did you get the impression," Mama murmured, "that Purvis became bored with us? Miss Brompton commands a much larger fortune, and her lineage in no wise leads to the shop. Purvis is clearly expecting a match for her in the near future."

They crossed the street and angled northwest, toward the wide avenues of Mayfair.

"You need not be so delicate, Mama. Purvis expects Tavistock to offer for Miss Brompton." He'd all but opened the window and shouted that scheme to the world.

"But you and his lordship... You don't seem upset, Lissa, and the bank drafts in my reticule are not the reason for your calm."

Lissa inventoried her feelings, which were many and varied. A touch of glee, to have argued funds out of Purvis's undeserving grasp. Relief, because if he'd wanted to be difficult, the meeting might have gone very differently.

"You might well be right, Mama. We have served our purpose for Mr. Purvis and his greedy schemes. I was prepared to call in reinforcements from the bankers, and Mr. Purvis made a tactical retreat after offering barely any resistance. He has larger geese to pluck, or so he believes."

"What do you believe?"

They came to another corner, and Lissa considered Mama's question. "Trevor has no intention of marrying Miss Brompton, and I daresay he's not her cup of tea either." Miss Brompton could be a bit of a stickler where the male of the species was concerned.

She would never ride astride.

She would never yield liberties to a prospective suitor and know the pleasure of passions fulfilled out of sheer joy rather than duty.

She would never know the delight of a neck-or-nothing gallop along the Twid, or a victory kiss claimed at the conclusion of such a match.

"You aren't in the least bit concerned that Tavistock has once again exercised a bit of, um..." Mama waited for a dog cart to rattle by, a pair of dowagers aboard.

"I am curious," Lissa said, "regarding Purvis's schemes, but Trevor told me Purvis is trying to marry him off to some well-heeled bride of Purvis's choosing. Trevor had reasons for his deceptions in Crosspatch Corners, but he would not dissemble about his intentions toward Miss Brompton."

The dog cart was followed by a pair of high-perch phaetons, ridiculously unsteady vanities, one with yellow wheels, the other with red.

"You're sure of that?" Mama asked as they started across the street.

"I am, oddly enough." A comforting realization.

As Mama chattered about new frocks, an evening at Vauxhall, and the outlandish pleasure of having received invitations from two duchesses—two! In one day!—Lissa thought about Trevor.

She'd trusted him enough to follow his advice where Purvis was concerned, and the meeting had gone splendidly. Trevor had fibbed about his name, for understandable reasons. He was also a marquess and in need of funds.

That did not make him a habitual liar or a fortune hunter. Lissa trusted him that far, at least, and was relieved to reach that conclusion.

He still wanted to marry her, and he'd been the soul of patience with her family. He'd been kind to Phillip. He'd been both patient and kind with Roland, and the horse's future was much brighter for it.

But I am not a flatulent horse who lacks confidence.

Even in Crosspatch, Lissa would not have spoken that observation aloud, nor would she have voiced the real question that followed:

I was prepared to be Mrs. Trevor Dorning, but can I possibly be Lord Tavistock's marchioness?

That she could ask the question was progress, though toward what, she still wasn't certain.

$\sim$

Trevor's four weeks of mourning were slipping by, the reprieve from socializing a parting gift from Jerome more precious than Trevor could have anticipated.

"I'm consolidating my forces," he said as he and Sycamore gave their horses a chance to blow at the crest of a rise overlooking the Thames. "Marshaling resources."

The day was lovely as only a spring day could be. All of the earth rejoicing, the river a sparkling expanse, the heavens a perfect blue canvas dotted with puffy white clouds. Sheep and cattle cropped lush grass, and the road was in that splendid condition that allowed of neither dust nor mud.

"You are marshaling resources for the Great Courtship?" Sycamore replied. "I thought a fellow had to rely on native wit and courage for that undertaking, not minions and vassals."

"Marriage has made you slow-witted. Of course I will court Amaryllis myself. I was referring to my campaign to rid the marquessate of Purvis's embezzling influence. I have a meeting with him next week, and I intend to sack him. He sent me Hecate Brompton's social schedule, which is the outside of too much and a violation of the lady's privacy."

"Unless she herself urged that measure upon him. Who would name a child Hecate?"

Trevor liked Hecate Brompton, the same way he appreciated a Canova sculpture—from a respectful distance. "She probably wonders who would name a child Sycamore."

"Could have been worse," Sycamore said, patting his horse. "I could have been Nettle or Henbane. I'd rather be Sycamore than, say, Worth."

"Kettering will be at this gathering?"

"You say that as if you'd like him to be present, while the rest of us... He's family, and he generally means well. Yes, I know: He would say the same of me. Are you thinking of moving your finances into his capable hands?"

"Some investments, yes, if he'll take them on, but for day-to-day business, I was hoping your brother Ash would lend a hand."

Ash Dorning, married to Lady Della, was as good-looking as Sycamore and possessed of the famous Dorning eyes, but he was a more subdued fellow. He and Sycamore were surprisingly close, given the difference in their personalities. But then, all the Dornings were close in a way Trevor could sense without exactly understanding.

They communicated with glances and elbows to the ribs, made humor out of the most unlikely topics, and had thirty-second arguments that nonetheless made Trevor fear for the king's peace.

"Ash handles the club's business," Sycamore said. "He's responsible for Valerian's publishing contracts, Casriel's estate finances, Oak's commissions... Anything he turns his hand to is soon better organized, more precisely worded, and more thoroughly accounted for. He and Della do like to spend their winters in sunnier climes, though. Kettering steps in then, if a matter becomes urgent. Ash does the same when Kettering rusticates."

Trevor had spent plenty of winters in sunnier climes. He wanted to spend the coming winter snuggled up with Amaryllis in the snowy wonderlands of Berkshire.

"You're sure the DeWitts are coming?" he asked.

"You doubt the word of a Dorning?"

"I doubt your infallibility, certainly. I also doubt my luck when it comes to courting Amaryllis. We got off on a splendid foot, but she takes a dim view of dissembling."

"Lying, you mean. About your title, your standing, your expectations, your name?"

"But not about my devotion. She hasn't sent my flowers back."

"Mrs. DeWitt probably hid the card before Amaryllis saw it."

Trevor shoved Sycamore's shoulder. The horse took a step sideways, but Sycamore's seat remained secure.

"The problem," Trevor said, "is that Amaryllis thinks I don't need her. Everybody needs her, and she's comfortable in that role. She's occasionally out of patience, often bored, and growing exhausted, but she will never shirk her duty, and I am not a duty for her, so she doesn't know what to do with me." Hours spent tossing and turning though the din that passed for a London night, and Trevor had finally landed on a sensible theory.

"Love has made you philosophical, my lord."

"Love has made me determined."

"Or daft. Might Amaryllis think you need her money?"

"You have blundered into *even a blind hog* territory, or perhaps you are purloining Jeanette's insights. I will give the possibility some thought."

A lot of thought.

"*Do* you need Miss DeWitt's money?" Sycamore asked. "And before you put up your fives, know that I inquire because I might be in a position to help, if you need a loan, say, for that beer business. The Dornings are in a position to help. Hawthorne's herbals and whatnot are selling faster than new hats, Valerian's little stories are the sine qua non of every nursery bookshelf, Willow can charge a king's ransom for training the aristocracy's mutts, and Oak has more commissions—ouch. No more pugilism, please. Jeanette grows testy if I don't show up where I'm expected, and sorting you out would take more than a moment."

"Is this what you *do*?" Trevor asked, bringing Jacques to a halt. "Lend each other money, advise on courtships, exchange insults, and meddle? Is that how the Dornings go on?"

"Yes," Sycamore said, rubbing his shoulder. "That is precisely how we go on. 'For better or for worse' isn't just for the mama and the papa. Goes for the whole family, but you have no way of knowing that, given that you were saddled with a titled ninnyhammer for a father. All you had when he cocked up his toes was Jeanette, and then I stole her away from you. You will allow a fellow to offer reparations, because I have no intention of parting from her. I was and am in the grip of true love, for which we must all *make allowances*."

Sycamore urged his horse into a canter, and Trevor was left to ponder whether he'd just been scolded, apologized to, hugged, or spanked. Maybe all of the foregoing, because that, too, was how the Dornings went on.

He cued Jacques into a brisk trot, the gateposts of Sycamore's Richmond estate having come into view. More to the point, the Dorning traveling coach was turning through those gateposts, meaning Trevor would soon once again be in the company of his beloved.

~

"They aren't even subtle, are they?" Lissa asked, slipping her arm through Trevor's. "One would think a game of hide-and-seek was in progress, so quickly did the Dornings disappear after tea."

"'Strolling the gardens to admire the view of the river,'" Trevor said, resting his hand on Lissa's forearm. "What they lack in subtlety, they make up for in the agreeableness of their schemes. Jacques has missed you."

The Dornings en masse must have been strolling the gardens at Kew, because as Lissa surveyed the expanse of tulips, irises, and greening beds at the foot of the terrace steps, she saw not a single Dorning.

"Jacques has missed me?"

Trevor smiled down at her, and oh, how she'd missed that smile. Friendly, a little mischievous, *personal*.

"Missed you terribly. He has paced his stall by the hour, wishing we could call on you, sent up little horsey prayers for your wellbeing, and counted the hours until he could trot himself out here to this family gathering."

"I am not family to these people, Trevor."

"That is only partly up to you. They can't help it, so you'd best yield gracefully. I'm trying to. Let's put an end to Jacques's pining and take a stroll through the stable, shall we?"

Trevor was up to something with that suggestion. Well, so was Lissa.

She'd had a long talk with the former marchioness on the coach ride out from Town. Mama had traveled out with the Ketterings in a carriage that had made Sycamore Dorning's conveyance look like a pony cart by comparison.

Jeanette had explained to Lissa about a small boy, born with a courtesy title slung about his neck and raised by a man with impossibly high expectations of his son. Trevor was never to complain, never to show fatigue, bad manners, impatience, ignorance, vulgar laughter, temper, or foolish smiles.

He'd become adept at playing roles from a young age out of sheer necessity. Of course he'd put aside the Tavistock title when he'd wanted tenants and villagers to be honest with him. He'd probably put the title aside permanently if he could.

"I have missed Jacques too," Lissa said, letting Trevor steer her toward the fieldstone stable sitting downwind of the gardens on another slight rise. "I spent many happy hours in his company."

"Did you?"

"Yes, and we can continue to mince about if your sensibilities are too delicate for direct speech, Trevor, but even the Dornings won't leave us endless privacy."

"I didn't want to presume, and I did want to be... swainly. Considerate. Not rush my fences."

He was adorable when he was on his dignity. "I am not a stile in muddy footing that you need to check your speed when approaching me. I was upset with you."

"One notes the past tense with cautious hope."

"You lied to me, and I don't like that, but your reasons were sound, and you thought you'd put matters right with me before... the critical moment. I lie, too, Trevor, though not as convincingly."

They passed a paddock of mares, some with foals, some drowsing in the shade of a maple hedgerow and clearly still in anticipation of motherhood.

Lissa shifted her grip on her escort so they were hand in hand. "When I came to Town this year, I decided I would not be old Tom DeWitt's granddaughter, with the stink of tallow clinging to my skirts. I would be instead the DeWitt Heiress, who had already passed over two crops of eligibles, including an earl's heir. The DeWitts have always excelled at amateur theatricals, and London is nothing if not one big theatrical."

"Hadn't thought of it that way, but you're right."

"Diana and I were shopping for bonnets, and as we made our way home, it occurred to me that if I could have arrived in Town credibly claiming to be a marquess's granddaughter, I'd have done it. Not for myself, but because of how Mama, Diana, and Caroline would be treated if I could make the claim convincing. Sooner or later, my ruse would have been discovered, and that's probably all that keeps more people from putting on assumed names and fictitious antecedents."

"But you did not lie, and I did. I'm sorry for that, and I hope we can get past it."

"We are past it. I am past it. Just don't do it again."

"I won't."

They had reached the stable, and given the midafternoon hour, the yard was quiet. Crows flitted around the rim of a stone trough. A particularly grand specimen perched atop the pump. A fat tabby tom lazed on the ladies' mounting block, watching the crows through slitted eyes.

Swallows darted about when Lissa and Trevor entered the barn, and the scent of hay and horses thickened the air.

"A country smell," Lissa said, wrapping Trevor in an embrace. "A good smell. You brought me here so we could greet one another properly, didn't you?"

She felt the surprise and relief go through him, and his arms settled around her like homecoming and springtime in Berkshire and all good things.

"I wanted privacy to talk, Amaryllis. I could not presume beyond that."

"What shall we talk about?" The feel of him was the same—muscular, elegant, solid, and dear.

He pulled off his gloves with his teeth, finger by finger, while Lissa held him. "I'm not a fortune hunter, for one thing. Purvis has looted the marquessate's coffers, but I wasn't idle on the Continent, and Jeanette had much of my personal money put in the cent-per-cents. I don't need or want your money."

Lissa purely hugged him. Not the declaration most women would long to hear, but precious for its insightfulness. "Purvis thinks he has you by the pence and quid, but he doesn't?"

"That is very likely his scheme, but he's sorely in error. The boot might well be on the other foot."

How she had yearned for these conversations undertaken at close quarters, confidences freely traded. The situation called for kissing, too, so she planted a smacker on Trevor's lips.

"Purvis thinks to see you married to Miss Hecate Brompton."

"I'm sure Miss Brompton is a lovely person—we've stood up together a few times—but the only woman I'll be marrying is in my arms at this very moment. If she'll have me."

"Is that a proposal?"

Trevor stepped back and took hold of Lissa's hands. "That is a request from Trevor, Marquess of Tavistock, to court Miss Amaryllis DeWitt, late of Crosspatch Corners, Berkshire. If you look with favor upon my request, I will approach your mama and make a proper job of stating my intentions. Then I will swan about Mayfair, ogling your hems and looking poetical, and to blazes with Giles Purvis. I'm giving him his congé next week."

"He'll hate that."

"He'd hate a cell at Newgate more, and that's what he deserves. I chatted up Ash Dorning over tea, and he's willing to serve in Purvis's stead. Kettering will help with the investments, if I ask very, very nicely."

Lissa treated herself to a more lingering kiss this time. "I don't want to discuss investments, Trevor, and I don't want you making any announcements or stating any intentions until your mourning month is over. Don't give anybody any excuses to look askance at us."

He seemed to grow taller in the stable's gloom. "Very well, but what *do* you want?"

"You, Trevor. No titles or last names allowed. I tried to be angry with you, I tried to convince myself that you'd played me false, I tried to rehearse all the set-downs I'd deliver to you when we met in Town. To no avail. I could not convince myself of your villainy, and the evidence was mixed at best anyway."

"I gave you a bad scare," Trevor said, "and you have been played false in the past. I'm sorry for that."

"You've apologized enough, and you are not one of my near misses. Does this stable have a saddle room?"

"Amaryllis DeWitt, I am not making love with you in a saddle room."

"Why not? You made love to me in a gatehouse."

His expression, one of fierce concentration, suggested he truly had not brought her to the stable for *that* kind of privacy. He had not presumed, hadn't even planned for the contingency. Clearly, a country upbringing had been denied him.

"The summer cottage," he said. "It sits closer to the river and just over the lip of the hill, so mostly out of sight of the house. Sycamore doesn't keep it locked."

"A redeeming quality," Lissa said, taking Trevor by the hand. "How refreshing to know even Sycamore Dorning has a few."

She wanted to bolt down the path and find this summer cottage, but two things stopped her. First, she had no idea where the summer cottage was, and second, Trevor had a firm grip on her, and he was not one to hurry what mattered.

So she strolled along at his side and vowed to make him pay for his perishing decorum, and pay dearly.

CHAPTER SEVENTEEN

A very kind fate indeed had sent Trevor home to England, ready to seek a bride and even readier to take the marquessate's affairs in hand. Amaryllis DeWitt was meant to be his best friend, lover, wife, the mother of his children, and his marchioness.

In that order.

Trevor now grasped why Jeanette had abandoned her title and standing to become a mere missus: She and Sycamore were compatible on so many levels, in so many ways, that remaining apart had been unthinkable.

Trevor strolled along hand in hand with Amaryllis, a wonderful sense of rightness pervading him. She had considered the whole business with the assumed name, gone hat shopping, put herself in Trevor's boots, and decided to overlook the subterfuge.

He had not assumed she would come 'round—being a marchioness would daunt any woman of sense—but she had. She'd not let him down, she'd not cast him aside, and life was lovely.

"That's the summer cottage?" Amaryllis asked as the path wound over a rise. "Lovely view of the river."

"And yet, you miss Berkshire."

She bundled close, though they were still within view of the house. Trevor steeled himself for the wonder and delight of an affectionate as well as passionate marriage.

"How did you know?"

He kissed her cheek and resumed walking, his arm around her shoulders. "Because I miss Berkshire. I miss Roland. He's a fine conversationalist, by the way. I miss the calm that seems to flow along with the Twid and the stories everybody knows and tells each other again anyway. I miss the gossip competition running between the Arms and the vicarage, and I want more opportunities to argue irrigation and drainage with Phillip Heyward."

"I do miss Phillip," Amaryllis said. "He demands reports of our travels, as if we're junior officers who've been out on reconnaissance."

"Did you miss me?"

"I missed Trevor Dorning. The prospect of marrying a peer..."

They climbed the steps of the cottage porch. "Yes?"

"I will have to do as you did and assume a role. The gracious lady in her jewels."

"You are a gracious lady, and the jewels... Don't wear them if you don't please to." He led her to a bench facing the river. When they sat, he again tucked his arm around her waist, because simply touching Amaryllis made his heart rejoice.

"My father was obsessed," Trevor went on, "with his privileges and the deference due his station. He was vain about social standing he'd done nothing to deserve. I cannot be that sort of peer. I want to be the peer who pulls his share of the load and then some. A marchioness concerned with which parure to wear to the opera could never hold my heart."

Amaryllis kissed him, which was the outside of too much when he was trying to be sincere and manly, so he kissed her back, and this resulted in stirrings—more stirrings than usual when in her company—and thus he escorted his darling to the sunny bedroom on the far end of the cottage.

Amaryllis made short work of his clothing, sparing him only breeches.

"I've missed the gatehouse," he said, working his way down the row of hooks running down the back of her dress. "The hours to touch and talk and drowse and love. I hadn't realized..." He drew her against him, tenderness engulfing him without warning.

"Trevor?" Amaryllis turned in his arms and embraced him.

"Years ago, I saw what Jeanette had discovered with her second husband," he said, wrapping Amaryllis close. "Saw that she was enthralled, as was he. I was emphatically *de trop*, and more to the point, I could barely stand to look on them. My own father hadn't been capable of that closeness and joy. What did that mean for me? Would I ever find anything similar, and would I know enough to appreciate it if I did?"

He kissed Amaryllis's bare shoulder, for courage and for joy. "Then you came galloping along, determined as hell to stay on your panicked horse, unruffled even to find yourself in the ditch, ready to get right back on as soon as you'd caught the beast. You caught me instead, and thank God for that, because I am never letting you go."

He'd made a vow to his prospective bride with those words, and she seemed to know it, because her mood turned patient and sweet. Her hands entreated rather than demanded, and her kisses promised rather than insisted.

The bed was comfortable and sunny, and so were the preliminaries to the loving. Trevor wanted to give Amaryllis his whole heart, all the desire and cherishing and wonder, but he had a lifetime to deliver those sentiments.

Today, he'd taken another step toward that lifetime with the woman he adored.

"I want to be on top," Amaryllis said, giving his backside a brisk, get-a-move-on pat. "We don't have hours to indulge ourselves today, and you have too much self-restraint."

He tucked closer, hoping for another little spank. "You are complaining about my vast consideration for your pleasure?"

"Never that." A stroke instead of a pat, then a luscious squeeze. "But we will be missed, and there will be smirks and smiles, and—not fair, Trevor."

He'd changed the angle of their joining, aiming straight for his target. "If we're to be subjected to smirks, let us at least earn the penance and give ourselves ample reason to smile as well."

"Oh, very well, but I want—botheration."

A slight increase in tempo had earned him a *botheration*. "You wanted to be on top?"

Lissa locked her ankles at the small of his back. "Soon."

"But if it's what you desire, my dear, what would please you, then surely, as the soul of gentlemanly—?"

A slap that ended in a caress. "Drat you." Amaryllis was laughing, a curious pleasure when he was intimately joined to her. "Drat your dratted, dratting self-restraint." She hitched herself more tightly around him—ye gods, riding astride did marvelous things for a woman's leg strength—and set out to defeat Trevor's willpower.

He lost the contest, though the struggle was glorious. A steeplechase of the passionate variety, and not—he hoped—the last such race they'd have.

He levered up onto his elbows and knees and crouched over his intended, dealt with the mess he'd left on her belly, then rolled to his back and wrestled her atop him. He drew the covers over her shoulders as her sigh fanned his chin.

"We must work on your managing tendencies, my lord."

"Must we really? What of my lady's managing tendencies? I am rather besotted with them, and if you'd like to hone those skills yet further, I will be your willing accomplice in about five minutes." Or ten. A quarter hour, if he was honest.

"Hush, I must hone my napping skills, and I have found the most agreeable, if somewhat talkative, pillow."

Trevor kissed her crown and let her doze, though he was too happy to sleep. He'd thought to abandon the joys of France, sort out his estates, and resign himself to the quest for a marchioness.

He'd had it all wrong. With the right wife, all that other sorting and accounting and inspecting was a mere afterthought. Mostly pleasant duties undertaken on the scaffolding of a supremely satisfying and challenging relationship.

As Amaryllis became a warm weight over his heart and a breeze stirred the bedroom curtains, Trevor assured himself that within a week, he'd be free of the only real blight on the family escutcheon. Sacking Purvis would not be pleasant, but it would a relief.

And then would come the public courtship and that would be a very pleasant business indeed.

∾

"Lord Valentine *Windham*," Mama said in the same tone she might have referred to a visitation from the archangel Gabriel. "Stopping to chat with you right here in the park. *Such* a pleasant fellow. Of all of Moreland's sons and daughters, Lord Valentine is said to be the most like His Grace."

"I didn't know His Grace was musical," Lissa replied, giving her mare another nudge. The creature was pretty enough—chestnut with four white stockings—but a plodder. A lady's mount, meaning comfortable to sit on while going in a sidesaddle at a very sedate pace. A fine choice, if the point of a Hyde Park hack was to see and be seen and not to start the day with an invigorating gallop.

"Lord Valentine has his father's charm," Mama said, nodding graciously as Lady Stephen Wentworth tooled past at the ribbons of a smart gig, her husband lounging at her side. "Not that even Lord Valentine can hold a patch on your marquess."

Since returning from Richmond last week, Mama referred to Trevor exclusively as Lissa's marquess.

He was her marquess. Also her lover, her best friend, and her companion of first resort. Trevor had arranged another family tea earlier in the week, courtesy of Sycamore and Jeanette, and yesterday he'd contrived to cross paths with Lissa while she and Mama had enjoyed their morning hack.

Today, he was occupied sacking London's most unworthy solicitor.

"This is what I wanted for you," Mama said. "The most-sought-after invitations from the best hostesses, the finest fashions, all the right people greeting you with proper respect. You are a fine young lady from a good family, and you deserve no less."

Mama's confidence in Lissa's deserts had bloomed along with the irises adorning the park. Trevor's patronage and the resulting invitations were part of the transformation, but so was having enough coin to conduct life with some semblance of ease.

Damn Purvis to perdition. Lissa could not sack him—only Gavin had the authority to move the DeWitts' affairs to another firm—but she would certainly watch Purvis with the vigilance of a barn cat at a winter mousehole.

"Miss Brompton." Lissa brought her mare to a halt and nodded. Hecate was turned out in stylish good taste and sat her elegant bay as if to the sidesaddle born. "Delightful morning, isn't it?"

"Mrs. DeWitt, Miss DeWitt. A spring sunrise does lift the spirits, particularly in such lovely surrounds. I do hope the season continues to bless us with such lovely weather. That is a fetching hat, Mrs. DeWitt. May I ask where you came upon it?"

Hats, weather, the lovely flowers, last night's musicale, more weather... Yesterday, Lissa had indulged in a gallop with Trevor, or a canter, given the mare's limitations. Mama had waited patiently beneath the maples and chatted with acquaintances only too happy to acknowledge her.

Today's outing was merely an excuse to get out of the house on a pretty day, but even that was a vast improvement over last spring's horseback excursions. Small talk was no longer a trial to Lissa's nerves, passing smiles weren't barbed with innuendo or pity, invitations had ceased to be ordeals to be dreaded.

Life was sweet, and next week, when Trevor's mourning was well and truly behind him, life would become sweeter still.

"You ladies will excuse me," Mama said. "I see my dear Agatha Prufrock is out with her oldest. We haven't spoken in ages, and one does want to catch up." Mama, who was a fine horsewoman, gave her mare a nudge with her heel and trotted off a few dozen yards.

"My mother has found her element," Lissa said. "I don't doubt that Mama might capture a few hearts before we leave London this year, and nothing could make me happier."

Hecate arranged her skirts to drape more smoothly over her boots. "You mean that. You wouldn't begrudge your mother a proposal before any have come your way?"

What to say? Miss Brompton had a reputation for stickling and vinegar, but Lissa hadn't found her to be anything but pragmatic. Her wit was a bit dry, true, but never mean.

"Mama has been widowed for some time, and while she misses my father, I hope she would not put loyalty to his memory above her own happiness."

"Let's walk, shall we? Admire the sunlight on the Serpentine, or pretend to." Miss Brompton signaled with her chin, and a sizable young groom rode up on a cob. "Miss DeWitt and I will enjoy a short stroll, Benjamin. If you'd see to the horses?"

"Of course, miss."

Lissa dismounted, curious as to what Hecate Brompton could possibly have to say to her. They were cordial, but not... not friends. Lissa's only friend in London was Trevor, though she certainly enjoyed the company of many of the Dornings.

"That bench," Hecate said, striding off, skirts draped over one arm. "You must not take me to task for presuming, Miss DeWitt. My intentions are good."

"Why would I assume they were anything else?" The bench was deserted, set apart from both walking paths and mounted traffic, suggesting the conversation required privacy.

"Because I saw you and Lord Tavistock yesterday morning."

"We were in plain sight." Except for a short moment behind a clump of rhododendrons, when Trevor has stolen a kiss, and Lissa had reciprocated his larceny.

"He kissed you," Miss Brompton said, settling on the bench. "You kissed him. Don't worry. Nobody else saw, and a kiss in the park is hardly enough to get much of a scandal going."

"But you are willing to try?" Was this why Miss Brompton was unpopular—she lectured people on their lapses, or worse, threatened to expose them? What a silly, pitiful thing to do.

"I have no wish to bring scandal down on anybody, but I don't like to see a lady ill-used. Lord Tavistock will shortly be offering for me, and given your past... I owed you a warning."

Lissa sank onto the bench, feeling herself abruptly out of charity with the day. "Lord Tavistock will not be offering for you." Lissa spoke with more confidence than she felt. Hecate was nobody's fool, and she seemed quite convinced that she was to become the next Marchioness of Tavistock.

"He will, and for the same reason, I will accept. To do otherwise is to be ruined. I am at the point where I almost relish the thought of ruin—the Antidote Heiress is my latest sobriquet—but scandal has a way of contaminating the innocent, and that I cannot abide."

Such a lovely day, and Miss Brompton spoke with such bitter conviction. "Is Giles Purvis the reason you are willing to marry a man you don't love?"

Miss Brompton had an elegant profile, and her features were well proportioned. Straight nose, firm chin, generous mouth, and eyes that brooked no foolishness. For the first time, though, Lissa noted that those eyes were sad. Behind all the propriety and dignity, Hecate Brompton was both lonely and sad.

"I try not to speak that man's name." Sad, lonely, and *furious*. "You know my cousin Charles. His side of the family got the title. We got the money. What you do not know is that Charles intended to marry you. He was genuinely fond of you, though for him and his brothers, fondness will always include an element of pecuniary appreciation."

"He was fond of my settlements."

"And of you, but Eglantine found herself in a scandalous condition, courtesy of a titled bounder. Purvis mentioned Eglantine's situation to Charles and negotiated the settlements, which were outlandishly favorable to Charles and his many creditors. Eglantine's son—in line to inherit the title—is not Charles's offspring."

In Crosspatch Corners, this would be passing gossip, and of no particular moment if everybody was happy. This was Mayfair during the Season, where no personal problem could solve itself without somebody pointing fingers.

"Is Purvis threatening to tell all? That would violate every tenet of his profession."

Hecate turned her face to the sun, something a London lady could do without much fear of freckles, because the light in Town was weak compared to its rural counterpart.

"The only tenet Giles Purvis adheres to, Miss DeWitt, is greed. Some lordling or peer made untoward advances on his sister years ago, and he's used that excuse to wreak vengeance on his betters ever since. My companion explained it to me when Charles and Eglantine married. She warned me, but I thought I was safe."

"I am sorry. As we speak, Lord Tavistock is preparing to give Purvis his congé, and his lordship is confident he can do so without repercussions. If you were hoping for a proposal, you'd best adjust your expectations."

Miss Brompton's smile was wan. "I gave up hoping for an acceptable proposal years ago, Miss DeWitt. Once you reach our age, you realize that marriage is society's way of ensuring women never question their powerlessness. We're too busy hoping the next baby doesn't kill us. I have funds of my own, and now that I'm such a fossil, I have control of them. The last thing I want is to marry and have that independence taken from me. Tavistock seems a good sort, if a bit too tall, and if he proposes, I will accept him nonetheless."

"But legitimate by-blows are a fact of life, Miss Brompton, particularly a fact of aristocratic life. We need look no further than Devonshire House or Almack's for examples."

Miss Brompton rose, and while she was not tall, she had a commanding presence. "My nephew bears an unfortunate and nearly exact resemblance to his sire, while his younger brother is Charles to the life. I don't much care what befalls Charles—his treatment of you earns my disregard of his fate—but Eglantine was seventeen when he married her. She had been out for half a Season, and that philandering varlet could not keep his hands off her. He was and is married, of course. For her and the children, I will become Tavistock's marchioness, and from that lofty perch, I can make life very difficult for the author of Eglantine's misfortune."

Amaryllis rose as well and linked her arm through Miss Brompton's. To appearances, they must be two young ladies having a pleasant chat while they strolled back to their waiting horses.

"You'd marry for revenge?"

"Not precisely. More for the sake of my nephews. You think a legitimate by-blow ought not to be of any moment, but Society never lets those by-blows forget their status. Lady Cowper's patrimony followed her to London, and her frolics outside of wedlock will follow her children and grandchildren. Society has a long and malicious memory."

"And Purvis would unleash that fate on innocent children?" He would. Lissa knew instinctively that he would.

"Of course, and if he'll threaten children, then he'd think nothing of using the Vincent family's dirty linen to get Tavistock to the altar."

"So that Purvis can rob you blind, when he's finished robbing Tavistock blind."

"Precisely."

Lissa accepted her mare's reins from the groom and climbed aboard, a slightly awkward undertaking, though the mare stood placidly while Lissa sorted out her skirts. Miss Brompton accepted a leg up and gathered up her reins.

"I'll see you back to your mama's side, Miss DeWitt."

"I can find my way, and I appreciate your honesty, Miss Brompton, but I fear Purvis's scheme is doomed."

Hecate turned her mare back the way she'd come. "Why is that?"

"The Vincent family closet has no dirty linen. The old marquess was a martinet and a bore, but everybody passes that off as indicative of a less genteel era. The present marquess is honor personified."

Miss Brompton looked like she'd argue with that conclusion—*let her try*—but instead, she saluted with her whip.

"Let's hope, for the sake of all concerned, that you are correct, Miss DeWitt. Good day."

She cantered off as Mama's laughter floated across the lush grass, and Lissa's breakfast threatened to rebel.

~

The years away from home had taught Trevor a few skills he'd never have picked up slouching from one London club to the next or idling away his evenings at the Coventry. On the Continent, he'd done *business*. Competed, collaborated, bargained, and bluffed his way into agreements that he'd hoped were beneficial for all parties.

As plain Monsieur Vincent, he'd bought and sold land, equipment, grapes, barrels, expertise, and even donkeys for the sheer joy of doing work his father would never have disdained to handle himself.

Thank God for that spate of mercantile rebellion, because Giles Purvis was likely more wily and unscrupulous than any competitor or foe Trevor had faced in his travels.

"I'll take your hat, my lord," the sandy-haired clerk, Jones, said. "Fine weather we're having, isn't it?"

Trevor passed over his high-crowned beaver. "Lovely. Jones, you will please leave Purvis and me our privacy, no matter what your employer demands of you. He and I will be having a conversation today that nobody should overhear."

Jones hung Trevor's walking stick on a hook and draped the hat over it. "Old Purvis is a great one for having witnesses about, sir. Says it keeps everybody honest."

"He's aspiring to honesty now, is he?"

Jones colored up about the cheeks and ears. "I take the man's coin, sir. That obligates me to not speak ill of him."

"The pittance you call your wages does not obligate you to go to Newgate for Purvis's sake, Jones. Deliver a message, take the post down the street to the inn. Do not involve yourself, or Young Purvis, or the lowliest apprentice clerk in the exchange between me and my solicitor today. He will accuse the charwoman of wrongdoing if he thinks that will exonerate him."

Jones looked unconvinced, and Trevor had the unsettling thought that Jones's concern was for the client rather than the solicitor.

"You called at Lark's Nest, my lord?"

"I did." Whatever that had to do with anything. "A lovely little estate."

"If you'd someday like to meet my granny, sir, she was on staff there years ago. Has a sharp memory, though her eyes aren't what they used to be."

Trevor had no earthly idea what Jones was going on about, and he had a lawyer to sack. "Most kind of you, Jones. Now be off. I'll see myself into Purvis's office."

"But, my lord..."

Trevor waved a hand toward the door. "*Vite, vite!*"

He crossed the room full of clerks all nose-down over their scribbling. A very young lad in the corner appeared to have fallen asleep, head bent, pen in hand, arm curled protectively about his document. The boy could not have been more than nine years old, and he'd been worked to exhaustion.

Trevor opened Purvis's office door and sailed through, finding his hardworking solicitor fast asleep at his desk, snoring audibly. The blotter was bare, the pen in its tray, the desk devoid of correspondence. A plate holding an empty mug and a half-eaten hot cross bun sat on the corner of the desk.

The temptation to have a look around was compelling, but a gentleman did not snoop when he was intent on evicting squatters.

"Have I come at an inconvenient time?" Trevor affected the sneering drawl he'd heard so often from his father. "I do beg your pardon, but I was under the impression this is the appointed hour for our meeting."

Purvis's eyes opened, and for a moment, he looked like a cranky old man clutching at the flailing ends of his wits. The ship of lawyerly dignity righted itself in the next instant. Purvis rose, tugged down his waistcoat, and bowed.

"My lord. You have literally caught me napping. I was up late last night with a flood of correspondence. I'll see Jones's pay docked for failing to escort you into my office."

"Jones was nowhere about, and neither was Young Purvis. Pressing business, apparently." Trevor took a wing chair by the fire. "It's you I wanted to see. I have questions, and you had better have answers."

Purvis took the second wing chair. "Has anybody told you, my lord, that you put one in mind of your late father?"

Too many people had done exactly that. Trevor had Papa's height, his blond hair, his nose, his title. Surely that list was not the entire measure of a fellow?

"Thank you for the compliment, however unoriginal. Why did you fail to list Lark's Nest among my unencumbered holdings?"

Purvis was not good enough at his deceptions to hide a small start of surprise. "An oversight, my lord, nothing more. You have seen for yourself that the offices are kept very busy this time of year, and one tends to think of Lark's Nest and the adjoining property as one estate."

"Though they've been separate tenancies for two hundred years. I see. Was it also an oversight that Twidboro Hall has been paying hundreds of pounds more in rent than you listed on the tally sheet for that property?"

Purvis gripped the arms of the chair. "What in blazes were you

doing discussing rents with the DeWitt women? I know they're back
in Town, the oldest daughter swanning about as if her fortune can
overcome the stink of the shop. Whatever they told you, they were
playing on your sympathies, my lord. Ladies all alone in the world,
not a penny to spare when I have generously tripled their allowances
in hopes they can finally get the damned girl launched."

Amaryllis's money was hers, promised to her by her father, held
in trust for her and her alone. That Purvis saw himself doling out
those funds like a weekly coin given to a child in exchange for good
behavior... That he was ever so helpfully trying to assist the DeWitts
in a hopeless cause...

How did I ever trust this pompous, lying old windbag?

Trevor rose and went to the window. "I've inquired of my other
tenants, and if the property is unentailed, then the rents were raised
without my permission, and much of the higher sum went unre-
ported on the tally sheets you gave me. You are embezzling at a great
rate, Purvis, and the tenants will happily testify to that effect. You
will be held accountable for your actions, of that I am certain."

To inform the man of his long-overdue fate brought little satisfaction, merely a sense of a distasteful obligation approaching its
conclusion.

"This matter need not go to the courts," Trevor went on. "You
can simply pay back to the tenants the funds you unlawfully took
from them—I've done the accounting, though I want Jones to have a
look at my figures. From what I've deduced, your larceny dates from
the time Smithers retired, and five years' damage shouldn't be that
hard to undo. I don't expect the whole sum overnight, but you will
pay on a regular schedule."

Trevor watched the street below, a hurly-burly of carts, foot traffic, the occasional elegant conveyance or farm wagon wending along
as well. England in all her noisy variety, which he had not missed, but
ought not to have turned his back on so thoroughly.

"My lord seeks no compensation for himself?" Purvis asked
evenly.

"My trust in you is why the tenants could be fleeced, so no. I want nothing for myself, but to see the tenants made whole and you gone from the practice of law. That you have embezzled funds other than the rents is beyond doubt, but again, I was too trusting and left you unsupervised for too long."

If Purvis begged, Trevor would leave the room. If he pleaded, if he tried any other tactic but contrition and complete reparation, Trevor would—

Purvis chuckled, a sound which struck Trevor as obscene.

"You are so noble, my lord. So commendably selfless. Your father would have been appalled, though I find your devotion to honor equal parts amusing and tiresome. *Sit down.*"

Trevor remained standing by the window, as far from Purvis as he could get. "I do not take orders from criminals."

"Yes," Purvis said, rising. "You do. You shall in the future as well, and that includes courting Miss Hecate Brompton and in due course meeting her at the altar of St. George's."

This again. "Miss Brompton is in every way a lovely and estimable woman, but she and I *will not suit.*"

"You will suit, and you will take long holidays on the Continent, confident in the knowledge that your affairs are secure in my capable hands."

"Are you daft? You've stolen from me and from my tenants, and now you think to expand your thievery with my blessing?"

"Oh, curse me if you like," Purvis said, striking a pose beneath the judicial portrait. "You will nonetheless leave me to deal with your finances as I see fit. I'm not greedy, you must admit that. I didn't bleed your properties dry, as some would. I charge a reasonable rent and leave you a great enough sum to effect repairs and keep yourself in adequate style."

He sounded pleased with himself, proud even. The Marquess of Malfeasance.

"And why, Purvis, would I be complicit in your schemes?"

Purvis rocked back on his heels, his smile beatific. "Because if you aren't complicit, as you put it, then I will let all of polite society know you have a deformed, dim-witted brother for an heir—the fellow is legitimate, lest you get to speculating. Your father thoroughly researched that avenue, but your mother for once put her dainty foot down."

Phillip was neither deformed nor dim-witted. Trevor's mind produced that thought before logic assembled the puzzle pieces for him.

Lark's Nest left off the list of properties.

Lark's Nest paying only nominal rent.

Lark's Nest run by Phillip Heyward however he pleased with no toadying to any landlord.

The name Heyward—assumed, apparently, of all the ironies.

Phillip's unwillingness to venture into the wider world.

The spark of warmth Trevor had felt in Phillip's company.

The truth settled around Trevor's heart, whole and happy, albeit... complicated.

"The poor mite couldn't even crawl properly," Purvis went on. "I'm told he's a Squire Lumpkin with one good arm and a positive obsession for all things agriculture. Not even the village girls will marry him. Your father denied the boy's existence before the lad was a year old. Even the aristocracy suffers the occasional chrisom bereavement."

What response did Purvis expect to this news? What reaction would most thoroughly gratify him and give Trevor time to adjust to this revelation?

Amaryllis had said that London was like one big stage play. Trevor again adopted the disdainful tones he'd heard so often from his father.

"I cannot possibly have a brother, much less one full grown and somehow farming—of all the impossibilities—with one arm. Papa went to extraordinary lengths to ensure the title had both heir and spare, and he would have told me if I had a legitimate younger brother."

Purvis settled behind his desk, no doubt an intentional rudeness when Trevor remained on his feet.

"No, he would not. A child who could not crawl, who was slow to speak, who didn't look much like him? Your mother never forgave the marquess for separating her from the boy, but she did make the occasional journey to Lark's Nest. That was the bargain she struck: Lord Phillip would be raised in obscurity, albeit in reasonable comfort, and he'd be provided for. Your mother had you to dote on and a duty to produce more little lordlings just like you—a duty she failed."

"Do I even own Lark's Nest?" The old marquess could not have put the question more peevishly, for which Trevor silently apologized to Phil—to *his brother.*

"You do, but Lord Phillip has a life estate, provided he keeps to the local surrounds. A codicil to your father's will provides that if Phillip attempts to move in polite society, then he loses his life estate. Wrote that up myself—Smithers was too delicate to come up with the actual wording—and a nice bit of draftsmanship it is too. A very lucky day for me. The luckiest."

Probably an unenforceable bit of draftsmanship. Purvis had banished Phillip from his birthright knowing that all the conniving and chicanery gave Purvis a hold on the marquessate.

"Many aristocratic families fall far short of perfection," Trevor said. "The current Duke of Devonshire is all but deaf, Byron has a club foot, the very king is mad. Do you truly believe I will cede control of my assets to you because of this supposed brother?"

Purvis appeared to consider the question for the first time. "I do, yes. Society takes any hint of bad blood seriously, regardless of titles or fortunes. Your brother is not only physically cursed, he's also said to be eccentric and none too bright. Talks to the birds, wears rags, that sort of thing. Perhaps you should make his acquaintance before you champion the relationship."

"*He is my brother.* No flaw, shortcoming, or human failing will inspire me to overlook the existence of my only living sibling. I hope Lord Phillip shares that sentiment."

Purvis smiled pityingly. "Stubborn, like your father. If you're determined to be difficult, then know that I will take it upon myself to speculate to certain parties about your step-mother. You are fond of her. She is fond of the Dornings. I am *not* fond of the Dornings or their connections. If that argument doesn't convince you, let me assure you, Miss Hecate Brompton's standing in Society hangs by a thread, and her standing is all she has to recommend her besides those settlements. She's not pretty, not charming, and even her fortune hasn't been enough to gain her a husband. Her spinsterhood and ruin will lie at your honorable feet, my lord. Need I go on?"

If Purvis got wind that Trevor intended to court Amaryllis... "You've said enough. What your schemes lack in sophistication, they make up for in simplicity."

"You have much to think about, don't you?"

No honorific, not even a polite *sir* appended to the question. "I'm not out of mourning for my cousin, and you launch this... this assault on my house. Of course I have much to think about."

"Speaking of your cousin, my lord, the bills have started arriving from France. Jerome was living very comfortably indeed."

Purvis's announcement, did he but know it, was a hoped-for ray of sunshine, as if *gaining a brother* wasn't marvelous enough. And such a brother. Faultless memory, voracious intellect, subtle humor, hardworking, a good neighbor.

An all-around estimable fellow, who needed to be acknowledged as such, at the proper time.

For present purposes, Trevor produced a scowl. "I cannot be expected to deal with—what was it?—invoices for beer and boot black when you've just upended my entire existence. If the invoices are legitimate, you will deal with them. To think that my father could be so foolish..."

"He was proud and shrewd, and my hope for you is that you can uphold his legacy in the manner he'd understand."

I will pummel Purvis to death with Blackstone's Commentaries.

In the midst of overwhelming delight at realizing he had a

brother, Trevor was also angry. His ire was on his own behalf and even more so for Phillip. His rage was also on behalf of Miss Brompton, Jeanette, the Dornings, the wretched clerks, and every other current or prospective victim of Purvis's scheming, which included the DeWitt ladies.

"Why do this?" Trevor asked. "The solicitor's profession is honorable, respected, and well compensated. Why break the law you've sworn to uphold?"

"None of your business, my lord, but suffice it to say, your father figured prominently in my own sister's reduced expectations. She was a diamond, the belle of the Town, accomplished in every respect. If she'd made the right match, the Purvises would have risen with her, but your father toyed with her affections, and she had to settle for a damned wool merchant. I am not breaking the law, you see. I am pursuing justice."

Purvis rose from the desk and stood by the door. "You will pursue Hecate Brompton."

No, I shall not. "First, I shall finish proper mourning. Then I will look in on the family seat, the property even you could not bring yourself to pillage. If I'm to court Miss Brompton, she will be told of Lord Phillip's circumstances prior to any settlements being signed, lest she or her family cry foul."

"I give you a week," Purvis said. "One week to pout and sulk in the great Vincent family tradition, and then you will stand up with Miss Brompton, ride out with her, and escort her when she goes shopping for bonnets. If you turn up contrary, you will leave me no choice but to take measures you will regret. Good day."

He opened the door and gestured for Trevor to leave.

What a rubbishing toad. "I'm off to Surrey."

"Godspeed, and see that you are back in London within a week."

By virtue of supreme self-restraint, Trevor left Purvis smirking in his office.

CHAPTER EIGHTEEN

"Mama, Trevor has to be told." Lissa had changed from her riding habit to a modest day dress and was ready to beat a path to her intended's door. "Neither he nor I want Miss Brompton's ruin on our conscience, and the threat to her is all too real."

Lissa left the next part unsaid: If Purvis could ruin Hecate Brompton, who was possessed of both wealth and a spotless reputation, and bring down a young couple in line for an earldom, he'd cheerfully go after Trevor as well.

Perhaps the DeWitts had fallen beneath Purvis's notice as targets for slander—and perhaps not.

Mama collected the latest pile of invitations from the foyer's sideboard, not even glancing at them.

"But you mustn't be seen rapping on his lordship's door, Lissa. His knocker will still be swaddled in black crepe, and a caller who is not family will be remarked. That assumes his staff would even admit you."

"They will admit me." Lissa chose the bonnet with the pink ribbons. "I will make a commotion that would shame the devil if they think—"

Footfalls on the steps that led below stairs silenced her. The housekeeper, escorting none other than Trevor, Lord Tavistock, ascended to the foyer.

"Beg pardon, ma'am, but this gent showed up at the back door." She passed over an embossed card and gave Trevor a skeptical glance.

His lordship looked delectable and deadly serious in subdued mourning attire. His jacket sported a black armband, and his hatband was black as well.

His expression was none too cheerful either. "I apologize for my unorthodox arrival. If I might have a moment of Miss DeWitt's time?"

"Of course." Lissa excused the housekeeper with a nod. "Is something amiss?"

Mama took Lissa's bonnet. "You will stay for tea, young man. If you are thumping on our garden door at this hour and looking so thunderous, you will stay for tea. Lissa, cease gawping long enough to take the man's hat."

Trevor passed over the designated article as Mama bustled off after the housekeeper.

"Mrs. DeWitt is quite on her mettle," Trevor said, handing Lissa his walking stick. A substantial article of gleaming mahogany that would serve well as a cosh. "I cannot say the same for myself."

"You've sacked Purvis?"

"I have not." He took Lissa's cloak from her shoulders and draped it on a peg behind the porter's nook. "I don't know as I can, but I'm determined to try. The situation has grown complicated."

"Because you are to marry Hecate Brompton, else ruin shall befall her, you, her cousins, assorted Dornings, and, if Purvis is feeling rambunctious, likely the DeWitts too."

"How in blazes could you know that?"

"Not here," Lissa said, taking Trevor's hand. "Mama will leave us some privacy." She led him to the family parlor, not the fussy temple to social aspirations reserved for formal callers.

Grandmama's workbasket sat open by the window. Caroline's

latest acquisition from Hatchards lay on a sofa cushion, a green ribbon marking her place. Diana's slippers peeked out from beneath a reading chair, and the household ledger—Lissa's intended project for the morning—waited on the mantel.

"First things first," Trevor said when Lissa had closed the door, but for a few inches. He wrapped his arms around her and hugged her. "I have so much to tell you, but..."

She kissed him, tasting that determination he'd alluded to earlier, and something else. Something fierce and angry and bold.

"Better," Trevor muttered, giving her another squeeze, then stepping back. "Purvis is viler and more ambitious than I'd suspected. How did you come to be so well informed regarding his schemes?"

Lissa took a seat in the middle of the sofa. "I met Hecate Brompton in the park this morning. She felt I was owed a warning that the man she'd seen kissing me yesterday was soon to offer for her."

Trevor took the place beside Lissa. "Miss Brompton is in error, but she is at risk of ruin, as are my Dorning connections. More to the point, if I corner Purvis, and he has the least inkling that we are courting, he'll turn his sights on you. My father earned Purvis's ire by flirting with the man's sister, but Purvis sees ill usage in every passing carriage. He excuses his own criminal actions as an effort to right the scales of justice."

"Are *you* at risk of ruin?"

"Most assuredly. Do you mind?"

Trevor had put the question casually, though Lissa well knew its import. "I've been nearly ruined," she said. "Twice. It's only a problem if you let it be. Otherwise, life goes on pretty much as usual. The trades must be paid, the garden weeded, the mares looked after. I will still love you, probably all the more for the way you nobly endure your exile from polite society, provided you endure that exile with me. I am looking very much forward to—"

Trevor took her hand in both of his. "I cannot ask you to endure exile with me."

"You don't have to ask," Lissa said gently, because clearly, Trevor needed the explanation, and that broke her heart. "If you are with me, it's not exile, Trevor. The exile is here, in Mayfair, where everybody is playing a role, solicitors collect gossip to use against their own clients, and you could not be seen knocking on my front door."

"I don't want Purvis connecting us."

"I want the whole world to know we're connected, but Purvis is a menace, and for the sake of the greater good, he must be stopped."

A rap on the door heralded a footman bearing a tea tray. "Mrs. DeWitt will be along in a moment," he said. "She and Cook are in negotiations over tonight's sauce. Shall I pour, miss?"

Mama was taking a leaf from Jeanette Dorning's book, apparently. "No need. If you could comment at length on the sauces under discussion, that would be appreciated."

The footman, who was a bit long in the tooth for his post, set down the tray. "I have detailed and contrary opinions about sauces, miss. I will give the ladies the benefit of my insights." He bowed and closed the door behind him.

"Leave it closed, please," Trevor said, getting to his feet. "The privacy is warranted."

"Are you about to propose?"

Lissa's attempt at levity earned an odd glance from her beloved.

"Not quite yet. I am about to tell you that I have a sibling, a fellow who was disowned at birth because of insignificant infirmities. Or perhaps at birth, those infirmities were more evident. In any case, he was also a reticent child who could not crawl at the appointed time and did not properly resemble his father—our father—and thus he was banished to obscurity."

"Purvis told you this?"

"Flung the news at me as if..." Trevor gazed out at the garden. "As if I'd be appalled to learn that I share my birthright with another. As if I could be shamed by the knowledge that another man treasures my mother's memory as I do. I *am* ashamed—of my father's unbridled vanity—but if I thwart Purvis, I do so knowing my brother's situation could become public. My brother is shy and *innocent...*"

Lissa rose, because if ever a man needed to know he was not alone, not exiled by what burdened him, it was Trevor.

She slipped an arm around his waist. "You know your sibling?"

"You introduced us." Trevor's arm lay lightly over her shoulders, as if he was ready to let her go.

To whom had Lissa...?

"Phillip," she said, the name igniting joy and wonder in her heart. "You both stir your tea the same way, and you cock your head to the left when you are considering an idea that must be given its due despite your own notions to the contrary. That's why the marchioness's portrait hung in the Lark's Nest family parlor. *Lord Phillip.* Does he know?"

"If he does, he said nothing, and I must respect his silence. I have a week to figure out a way to defeat Purvis, and then I'm to make a spectacle of myself courting Miss Brompton. She could probably weather scandal handily enough, but I gather her family is at risk, and she is loyal to them."

"You and she would make a very impressive couple."

"Oh, right. And Purvis can then loot two fortunes at the same time. I won't have it, Amaryllis, but the measures I've put in place to ensnare Purvis have not yet borne sufficient fruit."

"You have a week?"

"I've told Purvis I'm off to pout and brood at the family seat while I finish mourning and plot a courtship."

Lissa shifted to wrap her arms around him, and so what if the gardener or the neighbors across the alley or God Almighty saw her hugging her intended by the window?

"Trevor, I understand that you feel obligated to protect me, Miss Brompton, her family, Phillip, and probably Jacques, too, but what do you *want?*"

He rested his cheek against her crown. "I want to be honorable. To be your honorable husband. To be Phillip's honorable brother. To not be my father. I have retreated from his example as often and far as I possibly can, until…" He looped his arms around her shoulders and spoke near her ear. "I retreat, Amaryllis. That's what I do."

One did not argue with a man bent on self-castigation, not until he'd finished with his foolishness.

"You retreated to Crosspatch Corners?"

"Verily. That was my attempt to avoid the Season and the match-making. I retreated to the Continent for the same purpose and because nobody should vote his seat when he's not even an adult. I retreated to public school when Papa and his tutors became more than I could stomach—Jeanette argued my case and packed my bags for me, bless her. I retreated to university and then from university when the venery and concerted masculine stupidity were too much. Right now, I want to retreat with you to France."

"A fine notion. I've always wanted to go."

"Be serious. I have no idea what Purvis would do to Phillip or the assorted other potential victims in my absence."

And Trevor did not care that he would be first among those victims. Lissa turned her mind to the conundrum of how a good man could defeat an evil one without resorting to evil himself.

"You labor under a misconception," she said slowly. "You believe that if something is unpleasant, it's your duty to uncomplainingly put up with it until your tolerance is exhausted. Your father's legacy, no doubt, but, Trevor, it's not retreat to search in the direction of what has meaning for you or to abandon that which does not. You are enti-tled to pursue your own dreams. That, too, should rank as a worthy obligation."

Hadn't he told her the same thing, and wasn't it fitting that she should give the words back to him when dreams were crumbling all around them?

"You have meaning for me," he said, "and thus here I am, when I ought to be…" He heaved a sigh and moved away. "I don't know what I ought to be. I needed to tell you what is afoot, and I need more time, and I have only a week."

Lissa brushed his hair back from his brow. "Do you know what I miss most about my brother?"

A guarded look. "Brothers are not my long suit."

He'd soon be an expert, if all went well. "Gavin is not on hand to jolly me past my blue devils. I have nobody to confer with when the steward wants to know whether to put a field in barley or oats. Nobody to make up a fourth when Mama and Grandmama are in the mood for a hand of whist, and Diana cannot be bothered. Gavin was *my friend*, and now he's not there. A brother should be there."

"You sound like Sycamore Dorning."

"I like and respect Mr. Dorning, at least in small doses."

Trevor went to the tray, fixed Lissa a cup of tea, and brought it to her. "As do I. He knows a few things about having and being a brother, whatever his other myriad shortcomings."

Sycamore knew about being family, a challenge Trevor had limited experience navigating.

"Go to Berkshire," Lissa said, sipping a perfect cup of China black. "Consult with Phillip. Discuss, argue, share a pint and a pie at the Arms. Purvis's scheme has arguably affected him most of all. Your father has been gone for years, and Purvis kept you and your brother apart even after the old marquess's death. Phillip might have questions about that. I'll go with you, and Mama can be packed—"

"You cannot come with me. If Purvis learns we've traveled together, he'll wreak no end of mischief. Can you instead convey developments to Sycamore and Jeanette?"

"I can." The equivalent of lighting the Dorning signal tower. "Should I call on Miss Brompton?"

Trevor began to pace. "Good thought. If you could also look up Purvis's sister. He claims she was ruined by my father, and if so, I owe her some sort of acknowledgment, some atonement."

"After all these years?"

"Have you forgotten the ill usage you suffered in your earlier Seasons?"

"I haven't forgotten, but I've certainly put it behind me. I'll do as you ask, though. What else?"

Trevor came to a halt by the unlit hearth. "Call on Kettering and his lady. I have to make a stop there before I can leave for Berkshire, and I will warn him to expect you. He's a powerful ally, has the ear of the Regent, and so forth. Even Purvis would hesitate to twist Worth Kettering's tail."

Purvis did not hesitate to ruin heirs, heiresses, and the occasional blameless marquess. "I will make that call." She took another fortifying sip of tea. "Is there anything more I can do? Mama and Grandmama will want to help as well."

Trevor remained by the hearth, his expression hard to read. "I love you. The words come easily when the moment is passionate, but right now, I am in the biggest muddle of my life, and I could not love you more. I love you, and I will always love you."

Lissa saluted him with her tea cup, feeling exactly the same tide of emotion. "We are equal to this challenge, and we will not be bested. I love you too." The moment did not call for fatuous beaming, but rather, for courage and determination.

Though some luck and hope wouldn't have gone amiss either. A lot of luck and hope.

~

Trevor pushed Jacques to do the entire distance to Berkshire in little over half a day. The hours in the saddle were spent raging, fretting, missing Amaryllis, and pondering what was to come.

All to no avail. When Trevor paused at the foot of Lark's Nest's front steps to remove his spurs, he still had no idea what to say to... his brother.

"You're back." Phillip himself opened the door. He was attired in his usual worn homespun, cuffs turned, an ink stain on his right wrist. "I suppose you'd best come in. How is Lissa?"

"I left the DeWitt ladies well and thriving. You aren't surprised to see me."

Trevor passed over his hat and hung his spurs on a hook next to another worn pair that could have been their twin.

Phillip gave Trevor's greatcoat a thorough swatting and hung it on another hook. "I waited years to see you, and then there you were. I landed in that awkward position of finally having what I'd wished for and having no damned idea what to do about it. Luncheon is on the sideboard, and the kitchen always prepares too much."

Phillip strode off, leaving Trevor torn between amusement and consternation. So that was the great fraternal reunion? *Oh, it's you. Let's eat?*

He was hungry, and Phillip was being hospitable. Trevor followed, feeling every mile spent in the saddle.

"You knew who I was?" Trevor asked as they reached the breakfast parlor. In the early afternoon, no rising sun poured through the mullioned windows, but the view was still restful and the aroma of roast beef positively ambrosial.

"Help yourself," Phillip said, passing Trevor a plate. "I did not know who you were, but I knew *what* you were."

Trevor braced himself for some well-deserved insults. "What was I?"

"My brother. I have few memories of our mother, but I do recall her telling me on one of her last visits that I had an older brother. A lovely fellow, given name Trevor. He looked a lot like me, and someday, my brother would find me. She died, my brother never came. The old marquess died—let there be rejoicing in the land—and then Purvis presented himself and explained the terms of Papa's will. Take more than that if you want to keep up your strength."

Trevor added another slice of beef to his plate. "Purvis told me nothing about you until yesterday morning. He had no idea I'd come to Berkshire. I've been mucking about on the Continent for years, having a grand time, and generally trying to avoid becoming Lord Tavistock."

He could admit that now, though the words still made him uncomfortable.

Phillip took up a plate and piled it high with beef and potatoes. "Purvis is a blight, worse than mildew on a garden crop, but he's not stupid."

Trevor set his plate on the table, which had only the one place setting. That lone assortment of cutlery tore at his heart.

Phillip opened a drawer to the sideboard and passed over knife, fork, spoon, and linen napkin. "Had I known you were coming, I'd have set out the good silver."

The family seat in Surrey had a whole *room* devoted to storing silverware nobody had used in years. Another room stored elaborate sets of porcelain dishes. A third was reserved for elegant table linens.

"Do you have good silver?" Trevor asked.

"Good enough. Will ale do, or should I ring for wine?"

"I sorely missed English ale when I was on the Continent. Ale will do nicely."

Trevor hadn't known what to expect from Phillip. A door slammed in his face, a loud dressing down, simmering fury, demands for money... Those he could have anticipated. That Phillip could be so casual, so blasé about this first encounter as brothers was unnerving.

Then he noticed that Phillip was keeping his right hand from sight, tucking it behind him, using only his left hand to manage the plate, pour the ale, and pass over the cutlery.

"Tell me about your infirmity," Trevor said, taking a seat to the right of Phillip's place at the head of the table. "Purvis made it sound as if you were fit only for Bedlam. Had I not met you, his picture would have been as convincing as it was inaccurate."

Phillip took his place at the head of the table, put his linen on his lap, and sipped his ale. "Granny Jones is my only source for the tale, but I'm told my birth was difficult. The marquess insisted that the midwives be pushed aside in favor of the more fashionable accoucheur. That good fellow got out his forceps and dragged me from the womb literally kicking and screaming. Granny claims the medical expert whom the marquess insisted on employing is the origin of my situation."

"You were injured by the forceps?"

"Granny was present, said the damned fool nearly twisted my little head off, and from birth, my right shoulder hasn't been the match of its twin. I don't pretend to grasp the medical niceties. I only know that the strength in that arm was slow to develop and is still not the equal of my left. The nurses apparently made the situation worse by swaddling me excessively when nature might have been overcoming the problem for me, and that set me back yet further. Then I was mostly kept from sight, and thus other faculties—social abilities, speech—were also slow to develop. Eat your food before it gets cold."

The beef was tender and thinly sliced, such that Phillip could manage with just a fork. How many other compromises and accommodations had he learned to make, all because the marquess's word had been law even in the birthing room?

"I am sorry," Trevor said, taking up his fork. "You have been mistreated as a result of factors well beyond your control."

"I used to see it that way." Phillip poured a thick gravy over his mashed potatoes. "Poor little fellow, no mama, papa disgusted by his own son, a reminder of my failings no closer than my right hand... but perhaps you are the one deserving of compassion."

Of all the things Phillip might have said... "I am a bloody marquess. A dozen properties to my name, more in France and Germany, but don't tell Purvis. I am in roaring good health and soon to be the toast of every hostess in Mayfair."

"Who are your people, my lord?" Phillip posed the question to a forkful of steaming mashed potatoes. "The good folk of Crosspatch know me and would take up for me in a heartbeat, though as far as they are concerned, I have no title, no fortune. I'm simply another squire in thrall to his acres. They know not to expect me often at services and damned be to anybody who remarks that oddity.

"They trust me," Phillip went on, "with their agricultural conundrums, which are legion. They bring me their sick and lame animals because I read pamphlets by the score and have acquired some veterinary expertise. I am valued here, I have a place, and a purpose, and one gorgeous property that is the envy of all who behold it. What do you have?"

"A very self-assured brother prone to lecturing his elders." Trevor surprised himself with that retort, and he'd apparently pleased Phillip, who was grinning hugely.

"My elder, not my better. At least you grasp that much."

Trevor tucked into his meal. "You are happy?"

"Content at least, and happy much of the time. I wish the mares were less coy about foaling, and a good wet spring always brings fears of rain at haying and drought in July."

"You sound like half the vintners I met on the Continent. Doing what God put them on earth to do, but fretting like hens with one chick."

"Lark's Nest isn't really mine," Phillip said, piecing off more roast beef with the side of his fork. "I have a life estate as long as I'm a good boy."

"Meaning as long as you stayed banished?"

"Purvis told you that?" Some of the bravado drained away from Phillip's tone—and it had been bravado.

"Boasted of it. I hate him, Phillip. A gentleman isn't supposed to hate, but that man... He has convinced himself that his crimes are justified by imaginary wrongs done to him or equally imaginary honors due him, and all the unearned coin he's hoarding is simply his just deserts."

"Sounds a bit like the king, doesn't he?"

"Or like our father." Trevor put down his fork because that comment certainly wanted further study. Maybe years of study.

Phillip was also staring at his plate. "When you showed up calling yourself Trevor Dorning, I had no idea what to make of you. You are the old marquess to the life—I have at least three portraits of him in the attic. On my worst days, I'd go stare at them and imagine slicing them all to ribbons.

"I thought perhaps you were a by-blow," Phillip went on. "You did not react to the portraits I hung in the family parlor, and you certainly did not seem to know who I was. I wondered if I had two brothers—a marquess and a by-blow—and I kept my peace."

None of this discussion was resolving the matter with Purvis, but the ground had to be covered, and for the moment, Purvis could wait.

"You are free to come and go anywhere you please, you know. The codicil is likely unenforceable. It's not witnessed, not written in the old marquess's hand, not even signed."

Phillip crossed his knife and fork over his empty plate. "You are saying I have nothing?"

Trevor produced the document that Kettering had prepared for him. "You have Lark's Nest, in fee simple absolute, to bequeath, sell, or lease out as you see fit."

Phillip unfolded the single page. "Witnessed by an earl, no less."

"Kettering's brother is in Town, and they bide together when Grampion comes south."

"Who's the other fellow?"

Would he read every blasted word? "Another earl. Casriel is Kettering's brother-in-law, and he, too, was on hand."

"Casriel is the Dorning titleholder? What is this? About a red silk handkerchief?"

"You gave me Amaryllis's handkerchief, after we timed Roland by the river. Kettering said any item of value would do as consideration, and I value that scrap of silk most highly. Lark's Nest is yours, and I have one less property to worry about. I'm giving Twidboro to Mrs. Dewitt senior. As much excess rent as the DeWitts have paid, they should have it."

Phillip set the deed a few inches from his plate. "Thank you. On behalf of the ladies and myself. I wasn't sure I wanted you to be my brother—you look like *him*—but you are not him, and neither am I."

What an odd, wonderful thing to say. "To quote a fine fellow, let there be rejoicing in the land."

They ate their cobbler on the terrace, the music of the Twid in spring spate accompanying a conversation that ranged from the recent fate of a cousin Phillip had never known, to the possible whereabouts of Gavin DeWitt, to—inevitably—Purvis's schemes.

"He thinks he has you by the cods," Phillip said, sounding oddly like Sycamore Dorning. "Thinks you will dread for Society to find out about me. You are too polite to say that, but we need not be that delicate with each other."

"Purvis has an entire list of wrongs he's prepared to perpetrate in the name of increasing his wealth and influence. Revealing your situation figures on the list, but not at the top."

"He'll go after the DeWitts?"

"If he thinks that would make me more biddable, yes. He's likely been playing fiddlesticks with their investments, though most of their wealth is beyond the reach of even his paws. He also expects me to marry a certain heiress so he can word the settlements to allow him to plunder those coffers too."

"I had rather hoped Lissa would sort you out."

"She has, and if my affairs ever calm down, I will court her within an inch of her dignity, but first I must deal with Purvis."

Phillip was silent for a long moment. The Twid burbled by at the foot of the garden, birds flitted from branch to branch, and a mild breeze stirred dappled shadows on the flagstones. Phillip had found a way to be happy here, a heroic accomplishment, but one that had come at some cost.

"Purvis," Phillip said quietly, "can shout my existence from the roof of Windsor Castle, and I doubt anybody would believe him. Granny Jones can vouch for me, and a few other local antiquities, and I hope I am sufficiently well mannered to put period to the charge of imbecility. I don't see that my relationship to you should alter your plans for Purvis in any degree."

"You are granting me permission to go to battle?"

"Do you need my permission?"

"Yes." Trevor already had Lissa's permission, and her blessing, but Phillip's mattered as well.

"Then you have it. When do you return to London?"

"My horse will disown me if I try to make the journey tomorrow. I don't suppose you can put me up for a day or two?"

Phillip blinked several times, though the breeze had died down. "I've room to spare. Welcome to Lark's Nest, my lord."

He held out his left hand, in his usual fashion. Trevor responded by holding out his right and leaving it extended until Phillip yielded to the gesture and shook firmly with his right hand too.

CHAPTER NINETEEN

Purvis prided himself on never underestimating an opponent, and he had to admit that the present Lord Tavistock was smarter than his father had been.

Though that wasn't saying much.

"A meeting at Gunter's, sir?" Jones asked, striding along a respectful half step behind Purvis. "A legal meeting?" He shifted a few well-chosen files from one arm to the other.

"His lordship doubtless seeks to alert us that we'll soon be drafting marriage settlements. Nobody will think it odd if a peer and his solicitor exchange a few genial words beneath the maples of Berkeley Square."

Purvis thought it odd—a bit odd, anyway—though any element of London's population with pretensions to respectability could patronize Gunter's. Governesses and their charges, toffs and their chums, ladies on the prowl for new bonnets or new flirtations... On a fine spring afternoon, Gunter's would welcome them all.

"His lordship has been out of mourning for only a fortnight," Jones said. "Wouldn't an engagement be precipitous?"

Nobody worshipped at the altar of propriety like a lad from the shires. "Not among the peerage, Jones. They don't walk out together for two years waiting for some auntie to leave the bride a competence. If I can trust the footmen, gardeners, and maids in the Bromptons' employ, Tavistock is maneuvering his courting artillery into place."

In the past two weeks, Tavistock had met the Brompton antidote in the park for a hack, accompanied by a few other ladies, chaperones, grooms, and gawkers.

He'd stood up with her at the Earl of Westerly's do, only the once, but for the good-night waltz.

He'd escorted her and some of her coven to Hatchards.

He was, in short, doing as he was told and with far less sulking and seething than his father would have done. Purvis did not especially care for ices, but he did relish the prospect of a handsome, wealthy, young peer doing the pretty on command like a titled dancing bear.

That the dancing bear had requested a meeting in Mayfair was a tolerable display of resistance, and Purvis quite liked the idea that all of polite society would see the marquess publicly acknowledging his man of business.

"If Tavistock is simply warning us that settlement negotiations are in the offing," Jones said, "why are we hiking halfway across Town to hear the news? He could have dropped a note."

Jones had his strengths, but his imagination was not among them. "He's displaying his influence, tugging at the leash. He has come to heel well enough and deserves this little bit of farce. The workings of the aristocratic mind are not complicated for one who has made a study of its predictable machinations."

"If you say so, sir, but why bring the files? It's not as if we'd discuss his lordship's finances in public."

"To remind Tavistock that we have all the pertinent information and always will." More than that, Jones did not need to know. "Besides, his lordship is particularly concerned with the debts his late cousin amassed, and a peek at the numbers might be in order, particularly if Tavistock had the presence of mind to bring his coach."

The weather had obliged his lordship, at least for the present. Purvis had decided to walk, not because trekking about London on foot had any appeal, but rather, because the carriages lining the square would be the most elegant conveyances in creation. Purvis's town coach, while commodious, did not measure up to such ostentation.

Berkeley Square, with its majestic trees, wide walks, and predictable throng of pedestrians, came into view. Children created a din kicking a ball about, waiters bustled to and from the shop, and ladies held court from within their coaches and gigs.

Tavistock sat in lordly solitude on a bench toward the west side of the square, Gunter's being across the street from the east side. He cleaned up nicely, though he tended more to brutishness than his father had. Even so, the Brompton woman wouldn't have done better no matter how great her fortune.

Purvis was prepared to be tolerant and even a bit flattering, lest the course of his affairs be delayed by lordly tantrums.

"Fetch me an ice," he said to Jones, taking the files. "Barberry... No, vanilla." More exotic, more... worldly. "I have a pouting peer to humor, however temporarily."

～

Purvis came puffing across the street, face flushed, his walking stick apparently serving as more than a fashionable ornament.

Perhaps Lissa should remind him that a steady diet of pastries and cobbler, and days spent mostly napping behind a desk, had consequences.

"Don't look," Mama murmured from the place beside Lissa. "Read to me."

Two benches farther on, Sycamore Dorning and his oldest brother were placidly consuming their ices. Kettering sat on the bench across, and he, too, was demolishing his treats, not a care in the world. Another well-dressed fellow sat buried in his newspaper on the bench to Kettering's left.

Miss Brompton had a ringside seat in one of the coaches lining the west side of the square, and Lissa knew not who else Trevor had recruited for the afternoon's program. She and Mama were both wearing loosely veiled straw hats, while Trevor, without disguises or defenses, prepared to snare a weasel.

Purvis sat on the bench Trevor occupied. Because the breeze blew from the east, Lissa heard every word exchanged.

"Fine weather we're having," Purvis remarked. "Fine weather for a courtship, in fact. One must commend your lordship on getting down to business. I might even be persuaded to write up the settlements without charge if you can get the lady to the altar by special license."

Gracious angels. Purvis was talking business—blackmail business—in broad daylight.

"You've been spying on me?" Trevor asked pleasantly.

"I think of it as keeping an eye on my investments, a concept you are only passingly familiar with, much to my delight."

Trevor consulted a gold watch, then put it away. "You've seen me doing the rounds?"

"My spies have. You aren't galloping for Gretna Green, but you are progressing toward your assigned goal."

Lissa could feel Trevor's temper simmering, but his expression was bland and his posture relaxed.

"You brought the files I requested?"

"Right here, my lord." Purvis patted a trio of folders bound in red ribbon. "I regret to say that your late cousin was something of a profligate. He must have owed half of Bordeaux when he died."

Trevor took the topmost file—black ribbon—and set it aside. "And you are dealing with his creditors in a timely fashion?"

"You may always rely on me to execute my responsibilities in a timely fashion. When can I expect an engagement announcement, my lord? I'm prepared to be patient, but the Season only lasts so long."

"What exactly did your spies tell you about my social activities?"

Purvis steepled his hands on his walking stick. "You stood up with Mis Brompton for the good-night waltz at the Westerly ball. Good-night waltzes are notably romantic, my lord, but next time, the supper waltz would be the better choice. More of Society is on hand to remark the company you're keeping. A dawn hack in Hyde Park among the predictable bevy of spinsters-in-training. A shopping expedition or two, all properly chaperoned, of course."

"Did your spies tell you with whom I enjoyed my supper waltz at Westerly's ball?"

Purvis waved a hand. "You lot don't dance with the same young lady twice. I know that, but next time—"

"I saved my supper waltz for Miss Amaryllis DeWitt," Trevor said. "I accompanied her to Hatchards, while Miss Brompton tagged along. I rode out with Miss DeWitt in Hyde Park, and again, Miss Brompton kept company with us on some of the bridle paths."

"Must you be tedious?" Purvis said with all the long suffering of a nanny on her last nerve. "The DeWitts are gentry, with whom it is my burden to have some acquaintance. You are not to court the DeWitt creature. She's used goods, difficult, and headstrong."

"Is she?" Trevor's smile showed a lot of teeth. "Is she, really? That is no way to speak about my future marchioness, assuming she'll have me. Miss DeWitt?" Trevor rose and extended a hand in Lissa's direction. "Mr. Purvis has a very rude opinion of you."

Purvis had the manners to struggle to his feet. "Miss DeWitt can have no cause to complain about my services, sir, and she will not be marrying you."

"Yes," Lissa said. "I do have cause to complain. You've been embezzling from his lordship's coffers, and that's not the limit of your perfidy."

Purvis glanced about uneasily. "For God's sake, keep your voice down if you must spread such slander. Perhaps you're hysterical,

Miss DeWitt. In need of a repairing lease. I'm sure I could approve the expenses involved."

"Perhaps you are the one on the verge of mental collapse," Lissa shot back. "You have charged his lordship's tenants far more rent than you've deposited in the Tavistock coffers, and speaking as one of those tenants, I will happily testify to what you've done."

Purvis shifted so he stood between Lissa and the busier end of the walkway. "Keep your voice down, you wretched harpy. Tavistock well knows what the consequences will be if so much as a word of—"

Kettering sauntered up and collected the file containing Jerome's expenses. "Forget the rents, Purvis. What I have here is proof positive of embezzlement from the funds of a grieving young peer."

"What is *he* doing here?" Purvis muttered. "And those documents belong to—" He made a swipe for the file, but Kettering— bigger, younger, faster—easily evaded the attempt.

"The file," Trevor said, "belongs to the client. Jerome had no agent or factor in Bordeaux and certainly none with offices on the Rue du Vignoble, because there is no Rue du Vignoble anywhere in the whole city. He finished out his days as the long-term guest of an Austrian household and left no bills behind. The file is a complete fabrication, but the funds you removed from my account to pay those false claims are all too real."

Purvis shifted to stand behind the bench he'd just been occupying. "You can't prove any of that."

"Mama's banker had a word with your banker," Lissa said. "The transactions are all duly documented. I'm told the trail of your thievery balances to the penny."

Mama waved cheerily from her bench.

"So I took a few pounds here and there for services rendered," Purvis retorted. "Do you truly wish to see Miss Brompton ruined? Miss DeWitt's ailing reputation finished for all time? Shall I tell all of Society of your defective relation dwelling in the shires, my lord?"

Purvis was no longer keeping his voice down, and Sycamore and his brother—the Earl of Casriel sort of brother—had left their bench to stand a few yards off. At the busier end of the walkway, heads were turning.

A nattily attired fellow as tall as Trevor came strolling along, his walking stick balanced against his shoulder. His clothing fit him to perfection, and when Trevor gestured for him to join the conversation, Lissa could have been knocked over with a well-aimed hot cross bun.

"*Phillip?*"

"Lord Phillip Vincent." He tipped his hat. "At your service, Miss Dewitt. Rumors of my defectiveness have been vastly exaggerated. Purvis, sorry to disappoint you."

"He's an impostor," Purvis snapped. "The fellow at Lark's Nest has a withered arm and no use of his right hand. Slow of speech. A dull-witted, shambling Lumpkin, and no sort of heir for a marquessate."

"Do tell?" Trevor drawled. "His lordship looks to be quite in the pink to me, and I'm told he has authored at least a dozen pamphlets on Berkshire soils, crop rotation, and how to reap a double crop of peas in one growing season. I'm fairly sure he drafted those treatises with his right hand too."

"Peas?" Had the Earl of Casriel been a hound, he would have gone on point. "A double crop? We really must talk."

"Not now," Lissa said. "Purvis, if you think to wreck Lord Tavistock's prospects by revealing that he has a long-lost handsome and learned brother, please be about it. I'm prepared to inform all of Society that Lord Phillip has been a pillar of the community out in Berkshire. By the time the matchmakers are done fawning over him, and your fraud on Jerome Vincent's estate has been revealed, you will be enjoying the crown's hospitality at Newgate."

She ought not to have said that. Trevor wanted justice, not a public spectacle.

"How dare you address me thus," Purvis spat. "You are little better than a shopkeeper's daughter, and—"

"And that," Trevor said, "means your own sister is no better than a shopkeeper's wife, albeit a wealthy and happy wife. She chose love over ambition, and you turned your back on her."

Mrs. Adelia Winntower had been very articulate regarding her past and the brother she'd all but disowned years ago.

"Perhaps Purvis forgot he had a sister," Phillip mused. "And here I thought disowning innocent family members was one of the stated privileges of the aristocracy. Another gap in my education reveals itself."

Purvis clenched his walking stick before him, as if he were menaced by footpads rather than the truth of his own misdeeds. "I will not stand here and be insulted."

"You were happy to insult me," Lissa said. "You certainly took a few shots at Lord Phillip. You've been none too kind toward Miss Brompton."

"Whom," Trevor said quietly, "you will never bother again, Purvis. She has no use for me as a suitor, but I'm happy to serve as her champion. One word of gossip in the clubs about her or her family, and I will go to the authorities."

Kettering opened the file bearing the record of Jerome's expenses. "Please do. This is precisely the sort of evidence the Old Bailey delights in. Forged invoices, forged records of payment, Purvis's signature on nearly every page. The bank records will dance step-by-step in accord with this file, and every single farthing ended up in Purvis's account." Kettering beamed at the documents. "A public hanging is all but guaranteed."

"Because he,"—Purvis jabbed his walking stick toward Trevor—"lied to me. Fed me a false premise and urged action on me at every turn. When no expenses showed up, I merely sought to... to—"

The fellow who'd been reading his paper folded it down. "Do go on." He rose, leaving the newspaper on the bench. "I thought I was the professional thespian in this crowd, but your performance shows some promise. Such sincere, spluttering outrage, while you clearly battle the urge to run all the way to Dover. Well done."

"Gavin?" Lissa had to lean on Trevor lest her knees buckle. This was not the same Gavin who'd left Crosspatch two years ago. Even his voice was different, more resonant, more cultured. He'd put on muscle and gravitas, and his attire was ever so subtly less staid than that of the other gentlemen.

Mama went hurtling past to wrap her arms around her son. "You are alive. You are alive and well, and oh, I could spank you, Gavin DeWitt. Where have you been?"

"Purvis knew my itinerary," Gavin said, gently hugging Mama back. "I sent it to him town by town, quarter by quarter, along with playbills, programs, and newspaper articles critiquing my performances. He always knew precisely where I was. I labored under the impression—the carefully crafted lie—that all the correspondence I sent to my family, care of my solicitor, was being passed straight on and probably read in the common of the Crosspatch Arms on darts night."

"You were on the stage?" Lissa asked, still not sure this handsome, self-possessed gentleman was her younger brother.

"I have always wanted to act professionally, but at every turn, I was told that Papa had not freed us from the shop just so I could tread the boards. I am respected in my profession, and I have enjoyed every performance—almost every performance—but to have not one letter from home in two years? I suspected that silence was my family's way of shunning me, and Purvis's notes only encouraged my misperception."

"We feared you dead," Mama said, hugging him tightly. "That strutting viper told us nothing and lied about making efforts to find you. All of Crosspatch has missed you, and I daresay you have stories to tell. All that matters—"

Gavin shook his head. "Not all. Purvis led me to believe you ladies were having a fine time, racketing from London to Bath to Crosspatch to Lyme—thus he graciously agreed to serve as my post boy—and buying out the shops wherever you went. Had I known... Had I known that he begrudged you even adequate pin money, I would have come home in a week flat."

The only thing that kept Lissa from whacking Purvis stoutly across the cheek was Trevor's grip on her hand.

"Giles Purvis," she said, wishing she'd thought to bring a parasol, "you wrong everybody foolish enough to trust you. You steal every groat left unguarded in your presence. If Lord Tavistock says you will return the funds you stole from his tenants, then you will make that reparation. You can never repay my family or his lordship's for the harm you've inflicted, but you can at least return the coin you've purloined."

"Or we can," Trevor said, "send you to Newgate. Those are your choices. You will not pollute the Continent with your crooked presence. You will stay on home shores and suffer the brunt of the public opinion you were so eager to turn against people who meant you no harm."

Purvis looked from Trevor to Kettering, who'd rolled up Jerome's file and was slapping it against his palm.

"I will not be hanged," Purvis said.

"A pity," Phillip murmured. "You deserve at least that." He bowed to the company, walked away, and climbed into Miss Brompton's coach, which wheeled away from the square at a dignified pace.

"Purvis," Trevor said, "you will go with Kettering and attend a discreet meeting with the bankers. My funds are being transferred to the Wentworth institution, where you will be forbidden to set foot after today. You will execute bank drafts repaying the tenants before sunset. I've made arrangements for each one to be delivered by express."

Purvis nodded once. Sycamore, Casriel, and Kettering formed an escort on either side and behind him, and he was more or less marched off to another coach.

Mama linked her arm through Gavin's. "You are coming with me, prodigal prodigy. A career on the stage, of all things. I blame those blasted pageants. You always did fancy playing the hero."

"I am not the hero today," Gavin said. "Tavistock tracked me down. My troupe was playing a circuit in East Anglia—scenes from the Scottish play—when his letter found me. I nearly killed my horse getting to Town."

"You nearly killed me with your mad scheme," Mama said. "Come along. Lissa and her marquess will doubtless want to share an ice where all can remark their foolishness."

Mama and Gavin trundled off just as the clerk from Purvis's office marched up, bearing an ice. "Beg pardon, my lord, Miss DeWitt. Have you seen Mr. Purvis?"

"Yes," Lissa said, "and thank the merciful powers and my darling intended, I will never have to see him again."

Jones considered a bowl of melting sweetness. "One applauds your good fortune, Miss DeWitt. Tell me, will I have to encounter Mr. Purvis again?"

"Not likely," Trevor answered. "He's resigning from the practice of law effective today. Kettering will assist with any adjustments the firm needs to make going forward."

"*Worth* Kettering?"

"The very one."

Jones sank onto the bench. "Thank you, sir. Thank you most... most sincerely."

They left him sitting in the spring sunshine, smiling dazedly and nibbling on his ice.

CHAPTER TWENTY

"How did you find Gavin?" Amaryllis posed the question as Trevor led her up the steps to the Tavistock town house.

"You gave me all the relevant clues." He bowed her through the door, nervous to at long last welcome her into a place where they might soon dwell together. "Gavin loved telling stories, loved playing the hero, loved to get the elders yarning on. He decamped for the north, where the provincial theater troupes are more likely to take on new talent. Shrewd of him. Showed patience and planning."

"Those were clues?"

"He also retreated from the very obligations that you, my dearest, took on so courageously. Where better to hide than in plain sight?" Perhaps in plain sight on the Continent?

Amaryllis took Trevor's top hat and set it on the sideboard. She lifted her chin, indicating that Trevor was to have the honor of untying her bonnet ribbons. The courtesies were mundane, but they stirred in Trevor a sense of sweetness and joy.

"Gavin shirked duties, such as swanning about Town?" Amaryllis asked as Trevor carefully removed her millinery. "Doing the genteel bit, trying to ignore all the whispers about the smell of tallow and the reek of trade?"

"Those duties," Trevor said as a surprised butler ascended the steps from below. "Feeney, a tray in my sitting room, if you please, and I am not home to any callers save family."

The butler looked a trifle confused, and too late, Trevor realized what he'd said. "Lord Phillip, assorted Dornings, various DeWitts, Sir Orion and his lot, our dear Miss Brompton if she takes a notion to drop by, Kettering... anybody hailing from Crosspatch Corners. *Family.*"

"Very good, my lord."

"Some sandwiches, too, please," Amaryllis said. "His lordship has just vanquished a nasty old dragon, and that is hungry work."

Feeney bowed and withdrew, looking as pleasantly befuddled as young Jones had.

"The great slayer of dragons is nervous," Trevor muttered when he was certain of privacy. "This house doesn't feel like my home, but it's where I grew up."

Amaryllis glanced around the soaring foyer: white marble flooring, fluted pilasters, a circular skylight allowing beams of sunshine to bathe enormous ferns in copper pots.

Elegant, chilly, intimidating. Jeanette had not been permitted by the old marquess to make changes, and after his passing, she'd limited her influence out of deference to Trevor's prospective bride.

"Lovely ferns," Amaryllis said. "The place could do with some flowers, a padded bench or two for those of us who like to sit when we remove our spurs or change from boots to house slippers."

"Consider it done." Trevor wanted to be away from all the gleaming marble and shining brass, and away from anywhere a curious maid or footman might find him. "The family parlor is this way."

"Don't show me the family parlor just yet," Amaryllis said. "Show me the place you like most in the whole house."

"My study." Trevor wasn't about to sit with her out in the garden, where neighbors, gardeners, and assorted housecats could spy on them. "Jeanette insisted that if I was to be educated at home, a schoolroom would not do. The future marquess needed a quiet place to advance his education, a place worthy of his standing. The tutors agreed—the schoolroom is frigid in winter and stifling in summer— and thus I became the only ten-year-old in Britain with his own study."

"Gavin's bedroom had a sizable dressing closet," Amaryllis said as Trevor escorted her up the curved staircase. "I heard him in there, memorizing the great soliloquies by the hour. I should have known he longed to take to the stage, but even if I had, I lacked the means to search for him."

"I haven't those means either, but I recalled that Kettering has connections to various opera dancers. This way." He led Amaryllis past marble busts of philosophers, kings, and consuls, past Gainsborough landscapes and a pair of Reynolds portraits of scowling ancestors.

A museum of lordly consequence, not a home.

"What sort of opera-dancer connections does Kettering have?"

Woe betide poor Kettering if they were the wrong sort. "He handles their finances, gets ten of them together to buy one share of a promising venture, manages the accounting, finds a replacement investor if somebody needs to sell her portion."

If Amaryllis was overawed by the splendor of the house, she was doing a good job of hiding it.

"Opera dancers," Trevor went on, "know actors and actresses. They have family on the stage and backstage. Theater folk wash about between Paris, Dublin, the shires, Edinburgh, London... Kettering put the word out, and somebody eventually recalled a very attractive male lead playing east of Town. The fellow was down from Derbyshire and had true talent. Styled himself Galahad Twidham, and that was too much of a coincidence."

"Mama will never stand for *Galahad* pursuing a life on stage."

Trevor paused outside the door of his study. He'd peeked in since returning from France, but only that. "Will you stand for it? You know what it feels like to be forced onto a path you dread." *And so do I.*

"You approve of Gavin's aspirations?"

"I approve of allowing people to pursue their dreams. A good play makes us think, laugh, forget our troubles or view them in a different light. Where is the harm in a talented young man pursuing a vocation that does all that?" Amaryllis's answer mattered, and not simply to Gavin's prospects.

She opened the door and preceded Trevor into the only sanctuary he'd had as a boy. "Will you approve of Phillip hiding away in the shires for the rest of his life?"

Phillip had grown very quiet since leaving Lark's Nest and had not ventured from the town house other than to sit in the nearest park by the hour.

"I doubt Phillip sees caring for his estate and assisting his neighbors as hiding away, and yes, if that's what he wants to do, I approve heartily."

Amaryllis picked up a small telescope and peered through it out the window. "You could inspect every corner of the garden with this."

"I took it with me everywhere until I went off to university. Jeanette gave it to me."

Amaryllis went on a slow tour of the room, which was all of twelve feet square. She studied the history books and travel logs, Caesar's Gallic letters, *Robinson Crusoe*, *Gulliver's Travels*. She opened the last of Trevor's botanical journals.

"Are you certain you aren't a Dorning of some sort? These sketches are quite good."

"I got away with drawing flowers in the name of science. Papa would not have stood for it otherwise."

Amaryllis put the journal aside and bent close to the world map framed above the desk. She peered at the leviathan rampant in the southeast corner.

"*Hic habitant monstra*," she murmured. "The real monster was your own father, and you have been trying to leave his realm since boyhood. Are we to dwell in France, Trevor?"

He closed the door, and not only for privacy. "I thought we might dwell in Berkshire, at least some of the time."

Amaryllis began opening and closing the desk drawers. "Berkshire is hardly fashionable."

"Berkshire is beautiful, and it's home to an expert on growing hops—or at least a well-informed source—who happens to be my only living brother and my heir. It's not that far from my step-mother's various in-laws, or from her. My prospective in-laws dwell in Berkshire, and I can purchase good land there at a reasonable price."

Amaryllis ceased inspecting empty drawers. "I am very nervous about becoming a marchioness, Trevor. I am not grand. I have no airs and graces adequate for such a lofty status. I laugh too loudly. I wanted to swat Purvis with my parasol, except that I am not fashionable enough to have remembered to bring a parasol."

She sat on the desk, an informality that would have driven the late marquess to strutting lectures and profanity. Trevor perched beside her—the desk was a sturdy old article—and took her hand.

"I want to make beer, Amaryllis. I want to see to it myself, and if I'm successful, then I'll have managers and whatnot, but I want to build something with my own native wit, experience, and determination. Something good and affordable and English. It's not done for a marquess to be in trade. It's not done for him to turn his back on Town and take up village life. It's not done, but—"

She kissed him. "But it shall be done, if that's the sort of marquess you want to be. I am glad now that you didn't use the title when you first came to Crosspatch. I learned to respect and admire the man rather than scorn the peer. I will marry the man—though you have yet to propose to me, sir—and the marquess will simply have to manage as best he can. My husband's happiness matters to me. His title, other than the responsibility it brings, does not signify."

"You're sure? The gossips can be awful, Amaryllis. They will blame you for turning my head. They will castigate me for disrespecting my birthright."

"Your birthright," Amaryllis said, laying her head on his shoulder, "was a lot of loneliness, posturing, and arrogance. I don't want that for you or for our children. We had best prepare to endure market-day squabbles, trysts by the Twid, and Roland's good digestive health for some years to come—assuming you eventually propose to me."

"I am entitled to court you first. I thought we might discuss the particulars of that undertaking in my bedroom."

Amaryllis hopped off the desk and seized him by the hand. "You thought correctly."

～

"I never thought I'd miss market day in Crosspatch," Gavin DeWitt said, sinking onto a bench on the terrace of the Arms, a pint of Pevinger's finest in his hand. "Did not think it possible to miss Vicar's little homilies or Diana's infernal sonatinas."

"But you did," Phillip replied, taking the place beside him. "I thought a few weeks in Town would part me from my wits." He'd kissed his mares upon returning, foolishness nobody need ever know of, but the sight of them, foals gamboling in the sunshine, the green grass springing up from the good earth...

Somewhere in the vast and stupid lexicon of rules known as proper deportment, an edict had doubtless been inscribed that full-grown courtesy lords were forbidden to cry with relief to be home. The list of inanities required by proper deportment beggared description.

"I missed Pevinger's ale," Gavin went on, taking another sip.

"You missed Pevinger's daughter."

Gavin saluted with his mug. "The fair Tansy did not miss me. Told me to get my handsome arse to London if Crosspatch was a such a penance, try my luck, and quit complaining. She imparted that wisdom with the air of a woman who'd given the speech on previous occasions."

Phillip had nothing to say to that. He understood flirtation in a limited sort of way. He understood procreation as both a man and a farmer. Women as a species, though, were wondrous, confusing, and best left to fellows with an overdeveloped taste for adventure.

"Tavistock is truly putting Miller's Lament into hops and barley?" Gavin asked.

The marquess himself was halfway across the crowded green, in earnest discussion with Granny Jones, who stood about as tall as his elbow. Mrs. Raybourne was getting her oar in as well, and Mrs. Dabney was poised to join the affray.

Talking beer recipes, no doubt.

"Tavistock is also building himself a lovely little distillery," Phillip said. "He negotiates the purchase of barrels with as much verve and determination as a fishwife haggles when her wares are first to market. If you kick him, he starts maundering on about vats and tubing and mash... He is drunk on beer without imbibing a drop."

"Are you jealous?"

Gavin had always been a canny lad, a friend to all, and doubtless the repository of more than a few confidences. Phillip chose to answer the question honestly, rather than prose on about the marquess.

"Amaryllis and I are friends. When she becomes my brother's wife, that won't change." Lissa had been an ally, a good neighbor, and somebody to whom Phillip's weak shoulder and dubious origins had not mattered. Because Amaryllis hadn't made an issue of those oddities, nobody else had. "Yes, I will miss her, but no, I am not jealous. Women baffle me as all the knives, forks, dishes, and glasses at a formal dinner baffle me."

He'd endured one such dinner at some ducal residence, dragged along by Trevor and Amaryllis, who were too besotted to realize they'd landed Phillip in a wilderness where no birds sang and no friendly rays of sunshine beamed down from the heavens.

He'd watched what Hecate Brompton had done—use this fork, sip from that glass—and muddled through, feeling like the bumpkin who had never actually danced the steps he'd studied so carefully in the pamphlets.

"I had to learn all the place-setting whatnot," Gavin said. "Grandmama was a very patient teacher, but then, I had all the time in the world to learn. Crosspatch isn't exactly a hotbed of formal balls and lofty suppers. There they go."

Mr. Pevinger stood a few yards from the vicarage steps, feet spread, arms crossed, chin jutting in the manner of an overbred bull-dog. Mr. Dabney had taken up a comparable stance and was shaking an admonitory finger in Pevinger's face.

"I did not miss the squabbling," Gavin said, "though Dabney and Pevinger make a good study in the postures of ire."

"The postures of ridiculousness."

An argument ensued, about whether cows carrying bull calves took longer to freshen than cows carrying heifer calves.

"And there goes Lissa," Gavin murmured as the lady herself abandoned the soap seller's stall and made straight for the vicarage. "I suppose we ought to practice referring to her as *her ladyship.*"

"She'll sort you out if you do. I have it on best authority that if I call Tavistock by his title when we are private, I'll make the acquaintance of the fraternal left hook."

"I doubt Tavistock has much of a left hook. Schoolyard scrapping can't figure prominently in the education of a marquess."

"Actually, it can. Tavistock apparently had a rough time of it first term at public school, where the higher the title, the worse the bullying. He gave better than he got, and the Dornings tell me he's damned fast on his feet."

"Slow with a courtship, though. Spent the whole Season escorting Lissa about Town, saving his supper waltzes for her and galloping about Hyde Park at her side."

"He was making a point to all the idiots and gossips who'd

slighted his beloved, rubbing their faces in their small-minded meanness."

"Or was he hesitant to finally come home?" Gavin murmured as the marquess excused himself from the Crosspatch Committee for the Betterment of Brewed Beer and joined the melee on the vicarage steps.

When Amaryllis would have interposed herself between Dabney and Pevinger, Tavistock instead led her up the steps.

"That will do, gentlemen," he said in tones that carried across the green. "Cease bickering about bovines, if you please. I hope I have an announcement to make."

"About time!" Tansy Pevinger shouted.

"You're one to talk, Tan!" Lawrence Miller hollered back.

"Let the lad have his say," Granny Jones called.

Pevinger and Dabney stood at the foot of the steps, looking curious and disgruntled. "Say on, lad," Dabney said, "if you must so rudely interrupt your elders."

"He's milord to you," Pevinger retorted.

"I am not milord to Miss DeWitt. I have been a devoted suitor, and these past weeks have been the happiest of my life, but I have yet to put to the love of my life the only question that matters."

"Oh, the Quality," Gavin muttered.

"A man in love answers to a different rule book," Phillip replied. "I do believe we are witnessing the first recorded instance of Amaryllis DeWitt at a loss for words." The sight was sweet, though not without a twinge of heartache.

She and Trevor would be happy. Loud, busy, besotted... and happy. Phillip was losing them both, though he'd never really had either one.

"If you go down on bended knee," Amaryllis said, "I will wish I had a parasol handy, sir."

Trevor took her hand in his and kissed her knuckles. "Miss Amaryllis DeWitt, delight of my heart, light of my soul, harbinger of my every joy—"

"Lord, listen to him," Mrs. Pevinger muttered.

"You listen to him too, George Dabney," Mrs. Dabney said, touching a handkerchief to her eyes. "Man knows how to propose."

Amaryllis glowered at the ladies, who grinned in response.

"Miss DeWitt," Trevor said, stepping closer, "will you make me the most blessed among brewers and the merriest of marquesses, the happiest of husbands, the—"

"Enough with the alliteration," Gavin called.

Trevor bowed in the direction of the Arms, then took both of Amaryllis's hands in his. "Amaryllis, will you marry me?"

The green fell silent, save for the distant tinkling of a cowbell on the breeze.

"Say yes," Tansy bellowed. "You'll break his heart if you don't say yes, Lissa."

"Say yes," Mrs. Dabney and Mrs. Pevinger chorused, and the whole village took up the cry. *Yes, yes, yes...*

Amaryllis shook free of Trevor's grasp and stood very tall as the yeses dwindled to silence. She wrapped her arms around Trevor and yelled so loudly she should have been heard in London.

"Yes!!!"

The reaction was thunderous, lachrymose, and joyous while Trevor lifted Amaryllis from her feet and spun with her on the vicarage terrace. When he withdrew a sealed piece of parchment from a pocket and held it up, the answering cheer reverberated to the heavens.

"Come along," Gavin said, setting aside his ale. "That's a special license, or my name's not Gavin DeWitt. They mean to do the deed in proper Crosspatch fashion."

Phillip rose. "Crosspatch and proper fashion are not even remotely acquainted."

"I have to give away the bride, and you have to stand up with the groom. Tavistock's job is to speak his vows and pay for the ale."

"What's Lissa's job?"

"To enjoy the hell out of a fuss long overdue and to make sure Tavistock gets his part right."

Tavistock, as it happened, got his part right all on his own. Amaryllis managed her vows without faltering or borrowing any parasols, and Phillip and Gavin did their bits with gracious good cheer. The wedding—and the sore heads the following morning—became the stuff of Crosspatch legend, and soon after that, Crown of Crosspatch Ale became the stuff of legend as well!

TO MY DEAR READERS

Oh, that was fun! Now I want to move to Crosspatch Corners, learn to make beer, and find a handsome swain to smooch with beneath the napping oak. Instead, I'll probably write a little tale for Lord Phillip and Miss Hecate Brompton. Somebody needs to put the Town manners on that guy, and somebody needs to show Hecate how to enjoy life's simple pleasures...

Yes, I think that could work. Working title: ***Miss Dashing***, and I've included an excerpt below. The anticipated release date is September 2023, assuming Phillip and Hecate don't give me too much trouble. (And no sass out of you either, Roland.)

Before we get to their happily ever after... I'm also launching a new historical who-done-it series later this year. **The Lord Julian Mysteries** feature Lord Julian Caldicott, who has survived scandal, Waterloo, and captivity while serving his country. All Julian wants is peace and quiet, but life has a series of difficult puzzles and personal challenges in store for him instead.

Excerpt below from the first tale, ***A Gentleman Fallen on Hard Times***, due out in August. Book Two, ***A Gentleman of Dubious Reputation***, is scheduled for a September release.

Following me on **BookBub** is probably the easiest way to stay informed about new releases, pre-orders, and upcoming titles. Or you can sign up for my **newsletter**, which comes out about... monthly-ish. Unsubscribing is easy, and I will never sell, swap, or give away your personal information. You might keep an eye on my **Deals** page, too, which highlights any **web store** exclusives, early releases, discounts, or freebies.

I also post a **blog** most Sundays, and that often includes a give-away or advanced reader copy opportunity.

Happy reading!
Grace Burrowes

Read on for an excerpt from *Miss Dashing, Mischief in Mayfair Book Eight*!

MISS DASHING—EXCERPT

Miss Dashing by Grace Burrowes
Mischief in Mayfair—Book Eight

Lord Phillip Vincent is new to polite society and determined, for the sake of family honor, to make a good first impression on a lot fribbles and matchmakers. The whole undertaking baffles him, but he's the determined sort, so he prevails on the very proper and respected Miss Hecate Brompton to aid his cause. The lady, alas, is less than enthusiastic about the challenge Phillip places before her...

Phillip had put off calling on Miss Hecate Brompton for a week, until it was almost too late, until most of the best families had left the sweltering confines of London for the green and restful shires. He would have decamped for Lark's Nest with them, except that home was Crosspatch Corners, where Trevor, Marquess of Tavistock and his darling Amaryllis, were embarking on their honey month.

"I suppose I should not have served myself," Phillip said. "Is a third cup of tea beyond the pale?" He knew it was, but he liked hearing Hecate Brompton talk. Her words trickled past his ear like a bright, splashing brook. Full of light, purpose, and energy, but never hurried.

"A third cup is occasionally permissible. Appropriating the pot is generally not done. If you are among true friends, rather than mere acquaintances, and nobody has an eye on the clock, the rules are relaxed. The worst sin a guest can commit is overstaying his welcome. Perhaps you'd care for a tea cake?"

He'd like a cold tankard of Pevinger's best ale, served by a smiling Tansy Pevinger in the common of the Crosspatch Arms with a side of steaming cheese toast.

"No, thank you, but neither am I ready to leave. Give me some assignments. Let me embark on a curriculum of manners and I will be less inclined to pace."

The pacing had been about getting free of her scent, which was light, rosy, and brisk. Probably blended specially for her, a failed attempt at convention. The little spicy note—nutmeg and pepper—turned the fragrance intriguing instead.

The severe bun piqued his curiosity as well. How long was that thick, lustrous hair? Did it ripple to her hips, or swing in a soft curtain half-way down her back? When had she adopted the style of governess and why?

"Can you dance?" she asked, eyeing him critically.

"Not well. I've seen the country dances enough times to stumble through them, but the fancier ballroom maneuvers haven't made it to the local assembly in Crosspatch."

"You'll need a dancing master, then. I can recommend several. Can you ride?"

"Passably."

"Do you read the *Times*?"

"The financial pages. The rest is tripe."

She gave him a sharp look. "No, it is not. You will add *La Belle Assemblée* to your reading list, and I will quiz you on the contents. Read the political articles, don't just sneer at the patterns and fashion plates. Can you read French?"

"Competently. My pronunciation is atrocious because I've never heard the language spoken except by our local liveryman. Dabney hails from the Caribbean, and his French is mostly profanity."

"No profanity, my lord, not in the company of the ladies anyway. The gentlemen consider colorful languages something of an art, one I am unqualified to teach."

If so, profanity was the only aspect of polite society's curriculum Miss Hecate Brompton avoided. She prattled on, about tailors (Bond Street), boots (Hoby), handkerchiefs (always carry two, one for show, one for necessity), cravat pins (gold for every day, discreet jewels for evening), gentlemen's clubs (the grand equivalent of the snug at the Arms, having the sanctity of the confessional and the comfort of unlimited libation), and horseflesh (always know the bloodlines before you purchase).

All the while she interrogated and lectured, Phillip pondered his own list of questions. Did Hecate Brompton ever laugh? She had a rare, pretty smile. He'd seen it once, when Miss Brompton had caught him studying her at the only formal dinner he'd so far endured.

The array of cutlery and glasses had baffled him. One did not use any old fork to eat lobster. One used the smallest implement on offer, because that made no sense whatsoever. One did not partake of every dish the footman brought around, lest one be unable to move by the end of the meal. Better by far to waste half the fare, or leave it for the staff to consume cold.

Phillip had survived the ordeal only by closely watching what Miss Brompton did, and at the end of the meal, he'd been assigned to escort her to the parlor. Ladies, for reasons unknown to mortal man, were incapable of navigating a half dozen yards of carpeted corridor without a gent to show them the way.

At the parlor door, Miss Brompton had smiled at him, thanked him, and swanned off. Tavistock had seen the exchange and for once kept his big, handsome, insufferably competent mouth shut.

"And a ladybird," Miss Brompton was saying, "maybe be driven in the park during the carriage parade—you acknowledge only gentlemen when she's at your side—any day except Sundays."

"Because?"

"Because it's the Sabbath."

"And thou shalt not take the air with thy mistress on Sundays? I missed that one."

"It's *not done*, my lord, and if you think to thwart convention in this regard you can find somebody else to explain the mysteries of Mayfair to you."

She wanted to pace. How Phillip knew this, he could not have said, but the martial light in Miss Brompton's lovely eyes told him so.

"Somebody flaunted his mistress before you."

The martial light died, not without a fight. Miss Brompton sipped her tea, which had to be tepid, and topped up her cup with a fresh splash from the pot.

"My lord, I grasp that you are perceptive, astute even, but one does not blurt out one's every insight. One exercises discretion and kindness. If you suspect that I was slighted in the manner you describe, the gentlemanly choice would be to ignore the possibility. Such an occasion would have been an insult to me, had it taken place, and speak poorly of the gentleman."

The tea cup when she replaced it on the saucer, settled without a sound. Her heart had apparently been broken with nobody the wiser either.

"Did some lady snatch the fellow you'd chosen to be your own?" Phillip asked. "You mustn't tell Tavistock, but his marchioness was at one time the object of my fondest fancies." Not particularly erotic fancies, but fond all the same. "Amaryllis DeWitt was the perfect wife for me. Sensible, kind, well bred without being high in the instep. Tall enough that I would not look ridiculous partnering her if I ever did learn the wretched dance steps."

Doubtless a gentleman kept such maunderings to himself, but did Hecate Brompton truly believe she was the only person to stumble on life's dancefloor?

"Does she know?" Miss Brompton asked. "Does Miss DeWitt—does her ladyship—know you harbored a *tendresse* for her?"

"No, and she never will. I've lately concluded that if I was so keen to marry her, I should have proposed. That's how brilliantly astute I am. Our estates march, she was of age and then some, and she needed a husband."

"But you let the moment pass?"

He'd let the years pass, always finding another excuse. Her family was in mourning. Her family had just emerged from mourning. Her family was back in mourning. Her family needed her. She deserved to take her place in London society.

All valid considerations, not a one of them insurmountable to a devoted swain.

"One wants to marry for something more lasting than expedience," he said. "Amaryllis and I would have rubbed along tolerably well. We were and are friends, but that friendship would have been a casualty of matrimony. I have so few friends. It would be a shame to reduce their numbers by even one."

Miss Brompton studied him. "Was that the real reason you did not offer?"

Phillip had given the matter considerable thought, and Miss Brompton could be trusted with the truth—the rest of the truth—perhaps even comforted by it.

"Amaryllis would have married me for good reasons—to ensure her family's wellbeing, to ensure *my* wellbeing, to silence the unkind talk about spinsterhood and antidotes. We aren't fancy in the shires, we understand and respect pragmatism, but if a fellow truly cares for a lady, he wants more for her than practical solutions. He wants her dreams coming true. Tavistock can do that for his marchioness, while I could not. Ergo, all is as it should be, and I am pleased for her."

Miss Brompton's scrutiny became specific. Her gaze drifted from his brow to his features, one by one. He had the sense she was seeing him for the first time, and though he loathed visual inspections of any kind, he bore up without flinching.

"You are a gentleman," she said. "The dancing and cutlery and handkerchiefs are trappings of the role, but the reality is in here." She tapped her sternum with her index finger. "All the deportment instruction and dancing masters Mayfair can't make a true gentleman out of a selfish bore, they can only provide him a handsome and expensive disguise."

"A costume," Phillip said, "and 'the apparel oft proclaims the man.'"

He'd hoped to lighten the moment, but Miss Brompton's gaze narrowed. "You've read Shakespeare?"

"I'm familiar with the plays and sonnets." How else was a country lad to endure English winters? "The Bard was paraphrasing Erasmus, *vestis virum facit*, who was doubtless paraphrasing the ancients. I had an adequate basic education, Miss Brompton, though classical literature never interested me half so much as farming."

"Farming is good," she said. "Gentlemen who take care of their acres are well received, but don't prose on about it."

They were back on safer footing, which disappointed Phillip inordinately, though his call had been, on the whole, successful.

"I should be going, shouldn't I? I've had my polite two cups plus one, and I must not overstay my welcome." He rose rather than put her through the effort of a polite demurral.

"Offer me your hand," she said, gazing up at him. "Assist me to rise."

Phillip stuck out his paw. "You are marvelously vital, fit, lithe, in the very pink and capable of standing without assistance, and yet, I have been remiss..."

She took his hand and stood, and shifted her grip to lace her arm through his. "Some women do need assistance to rise. Their apparel is confining, they are weary, their high-heeled slippers render their balance questionable. A gentleman offers."

"You mean they've been laced too tightly. Foolishness that. Gratuitous torment. If a lady enjoys robust dimensions, then let her dress for her own comfort and to blazes with *La Belle Ass-Whatever*."

He'd barely recognized the French words when Miss Brompton had uttered them earlier, and he'd defaulted to his own pronunciation.

The result had been La Belly Ass Whatever. Close enough.

Miss Brompton dropped his arm. She stared at his boots, which were the work of old George Deevers, not to be confused with his parent, Grandpa Deevers.

Her shoulders twitched, and Phillip feared the tea might have disagreed with her. His worry was relieved in the next moment, when a peal of laughter rang out over the music room, followed by a hoot and more laughter.

"Repeat after me," Miss Brompton said, when her merriment had subsided. "*La Belle Assemblée.* Never that other thing. The whole French language is cowering in terror at your pronunciation."

Phillip composed his features into his best imitation of the marquess on his dignity. "*La Belle Assemblée.*"

"You're a good mimic. That will come in handy." She tried for a return to her usual starch and decorum, but the citadel had been breached, and Phillip had peered over the walls.

Hecate Brompton was beautiful when she was on her dignity, but she was *captivating* when her crown slipped. Phillip resolved to compensate his new finishing governess for the Sisyphean labor of turning him into a lordling by giving that crown the occasion friendly nudge.

Or maybe frequent nudges. The least he could do for her, being a gentleman at heart and all.

Order your copy of **Miss Dashing**, and read on for an excerpt from the first Lord Julian Mystery—**A Gentleman Fallen on Hard Times!**

A GENTLEMAN FALLEN ON HARD TIMES—EXCERPT

Chapter One

Society addresses me as Lord Julian Caldicott, though as that aristocratic curiosity, a legitimate bastard, I bear no blood relation to Claudius, the late Duke of Waltham. Toward the end of His Grace's life, when he and I were both using canes as more than fashionable accessories, we got on tolerably well.

Not so in earlier years, though let it be said both parties as well as my mother had a hand in instigating skirmishes.

I survived those battles and even weathered Waterloo in better shape than many. The worst blows to my body and spirit were dealt long before Wellington's great victory, when I'd been held as a prisoner of war by the French.

The guns have gone silent, the ghosts have not. The best medicine for me of late is solitude and quiet. I was thus starting my day with an ancient Sumerian text involving agrarian metaphors and procreation when Lady Ophelia Oliphant sailed into my study like a seventy-four gunner bearing down on the French line.

"Julian, do instruct your butler that his harrumphing and

stodging are pointless. I call only when you are on the premises, and his posturing will not serve."

"I am at home because you pounce at an indecently early hour, Godmama. Good morning to you." I drew a blank page over my translation—Godmama could read upside down and, I am convinced, with her eyes closed—and came around the desk to kiss her ladyship's proffered cheek. She smelled of bourbon roses and mischief, and in my youth, she'd been one of my favorite people.

Her ladyship had known considerable sorrow, burying two husbands, a son, and a daughter, the latter two in their early child-hoods. She banished life's woes with a determination I envied, except when she aimed her schemes at me. Since I'd returned from the battlefields, she'd left me mostly in peace, though the look in her gimlet blue eyes said my reprieve was at an end.

"How can it be a good morning," she began, "when you look like a death's head on a mop stick and your hair needs a trim? Young men today might as well be die-away schoolgirls for all they primp, lisp, and sigh. Back in my day, men could wear the most elegant fashions and still comport themselves like men. You lot, with your scientific pugilism and Hungary water, make me bilious."

"The only pugilism I engage in of late is verbal, dear lady, and never a drop of Hungary water has touched my manly person. Shall I ring for a tray, or will you swan out the door before my poor, stodging Harris can heed my summons?"

"You wish." She settled onto the sofa, her presence a contrast to the masculine appointments and closed curtains of my study. Godmama had been a beauty, to hear her tell it, and my mother—who would argue with the Almighty over the ideal order of the Command-ments—did not contradict her. The former beauty still indulged in every fashionable whim her heart desired or her modistes suggested.

She donned pale silk when sprigged muslin would have done nicely, and she wore jewels during daylight hours. Her slippers, gloves, and reticules were exquisitely embroidered and usually all of a piece—today's theme was roses and gold. No grand diva ever assembled her stage appearance as carefully as Godmama put herself together simply to disturb my solitude on a Tuesday morning.

My mother muttered about Lady Ophelia's flamboyant style, but I was nobody to begrudge Godmama her crotchets. One coped with grief as best one could, as I, half of England, and much of the Continent had occasion to know.

"Cease pacing about, dear boy." Her ladyship patted the place beside her. "I come to you in my hour of need, and you must not disappoint me."

I settled a good two feet away from her ladyship. I wasn't keen on anybody making free with my person, and Godmama was extravagantly affectionate. I had a valet. Sterling tended to my clothing, and I tended to... me. I was working up to allowing him to trim my hair, but until that day, an old-fashioned queue served well enough.

Though I have yet to obtain the thirtieth year of my age, my hair is snow white, a gift from my French captors. I owe the French army for my weak eyes, as well. My vision is adequate, but strong sunlight, London's relentless coal smoke, or simple fatigue can cause my eyes to sting and water. Tinted spectacles help, though they add to the eccentricity of my appearance.

To my dismay, my looks render me far too appealing to frisky dowagers. Lady Ophelia likely found my situation hilarious.

"I have disappointed you any number of times, my lady. I'm sure you'll weather another blow if need be, stalwart that you are."

Before I'd gone for a soldier, she would have countered with a witty retort about her fortitude being the result of the thankless job of godparenting me, but now she frowned, glanced at the clock, and held her silence.

"What brings you to my door, my lady?"

For all her imperiousness, Godmama could be bashful. On behalf of others, she blew at gale force on the least provocation. When it came to her own needs, she was the veriest zephyr, though I suspected the contrast was calculated.

"The Season is ending."

I refrained from appending a heartfelt *thank God* to her observation. "Will you join Mama for a respite by the sea?"

"Her Grace might find a respite by the sea. I find a lot of aging gossips. I'm off to Betty Longacre's house party. Her darling girl failed to snag a husband, so Betty is compelled to take extraordinary measures. The chit goes on well enough, but she's overshadowed by all those diamonds and heiresses and originals."

Betty Longacre—Viscountess Longacre, in point of fact—was about ten years my senior. That she had a daughter old enough to be presented came as an unpleasant shock.

"What has any of this to do with me?" I asked. "I am firmly indifferent to the concept of matrimony, and even my mother has accepted that I will not be moved from that opinion."

"You are an idiot. Your mother has other children to manage, and thus it falls to me to chide you for the error of your ways."

I rose, a spike of disproportionate annoyance threatening to rob me of my manners. "Chide away, but your efforts will be in vain. We both know that I am not fit for matrimony, much less fatherhood, and there's an end to it."

I expected Lady Ophelia to fly at me, wielding eternal verities, settled law, and scriptural quotation at my preference for bachelorhood. Godmama remained brooding on my favorite napping sofa, confirming that even she conceded my unfitness for family life.

Her relative meekness came as a disappointment and a relief.

"I ask nothing so tedious as matrimony of you," she said.

"Perhaps you ask me to make up the numbers at this house party, to lend whatever cachet a ducal heir has to the gathering. Thank you, no."

I managed to make the refusal diffident rather than rude, and now Lady Ophelia did rise, though she paced before the hearth in a manner calculated to make my heart sink. This, too, was evidence of the damage done to me during the war, and of Lady Ophelia's shrewdness. She'd noted my reluctance to sit near her, and I wished she hadn't.

I was improving in many regards, though the pace of my recuperation was glacial.

"One does not wish to be insulting," she said, "but I assisted Betty with the house-party guest list. The numbers match quite well, thank you, and if we allowed a ducal spare to lurk among the bachelors, the other fellows would all hang back, assuming you had the post position in hand. All I ask is that you escort me down to Makepeace. Maria Cleary will be among the guests, and we were bosom bows once upon a naughty time. I have not seen Maria for eons."

As best I recalled, the Longacre family seat was a reasonable day's travel from Town in the direction of the Kentish coast.

"Since when do you need an escort, Godmama? Any highwayman who accosts your coach would get the worst of the encounter. You'd scold him into submission and demand his horse for your troubles." Or she'd brandish her peashooter at his baubles.

"You don't get out much," Lady Ophelia said, "so I forgive you for ignoring the fact that former soldiers are swarming the countryside. They can't find honest work, many of them have come home to families incapable of supporting them in the shires, and the dratted Corn Laws have driven the cost of bread to the heavens. We all thought we wanted peace, but we didn't plan for the reality. Thanks to the great and greedy men charged with ordering the nation's fate, English highways are unsafe these days."

During the Season, I did not get out socially *at all* if I could manage it, but I read the papers. I corresponded with some of my fellow former officers and a few who still held their commissions. I paid courtesy calls on the widows of my late comrades and the families of fallen subordinates—those who would admit me.

I had a platoon of sisters, cousins, and in-laws who were very active in Society and who made their duty visits to me.

Godmama had a point. The peace following Waterloo was creating violent upheaval in Merry Olde England, for the reasons she'd alluded to. Napoleon had claimed to rule by conquest, and the British economy had thrived on war as well. Without the French threatening our southern coast, the great military appetite for everything—from canvas to cooking pots, wool to weapons, chickens to chaplains—had dried up in the course of a year.

Britain had emerged victorious from two decades of war appended to a century of war, only to find herself fantastically in debt and ruled by a buffoon serving as regent for a mad man. The populace that had made endless sacrifices in the name of patriotism was now deeply discontent for many of the same reasons that had fueled revolution in France.

The rich had grown very rich, while the poor had grown very numerous. The government's response was to counter potential upheaval with real oppression, which, of course, contributed to greater unrest.

The Corsican was doubtless enjoying a good laugh over the whole business, while I... I did not bother my pretty head with national affairs, though I did bear an inconvenient fondness for my godmother.

"I shall see you safely to Makepeace," I said, "then take my leave of you. You can travel back to Town in company with some of the other guests who will doubtless return this direction."

She pushed aside a curtain to let in a shaft of morning sun. Had she taken a knife to my eyes, the result would have been less painful.

"Your staff is remiss, Julian. These windows require a thorough scrubbing. If your windows are this filthy as summer approaches, I shudder to contemplate their condition in winter."

I rooted about in my desk drawer for my blue-tinted spectacles while all manner of profanity begged for expression.

"I shall pass your insult along to my housekeeper. She will delight to know that you, she, Harris, Sterling, and my neighbors on all sides are in agreement."

"The light hurts your eyes," Lady Ophelia said. "That's why you lurk like a prisoner in an oubliette, isn't it? Your mother hasn't said anything about you having vision problems."

Because Mama did not know my eyesight was in any way impaired. Only my older brother knew, and as the ducal heir, Arthur had been consuming discretion before he'd first thrust a spoon into runny porridge. Arthur was the family strategist, also our patriarch, though he was barely six years my senior.

"The physicians assure me the impairment to my eyes is temporary. I see well enough. Bright light is painful, though, hence the tinted spectacles."

She bustled toward me, and I steeled myself to endure a hug, but her ladyship merely patted my cheek with a gloved hand.

"Your secrets have always been safe with me, Julian. That hasn't changed, and it never will. We leave on Thursday, and I will hope for cloudy weather. We can keep the shades down, though you shall not smoke in my traveling coach."

"I don't smoke anywhere."

She collected her reticule, scowled at my window, and scowled at me. "You used to smoke. All young men do."

"I used to do a lot of things. I'll be on your doorstep by eight of the clock."

Thus did I embark on a journey that would involve far more than a jaunt to the Kentish countryside and test much besides my ability to endure bright sunshine.

Order your copy of *A Gentleman Fallen on Hard Times*!